BAILEY HANNAH

LOVE WELLS KEPT

ORION

This edition published in 2026
by Orion Fiction,
an imprint of The Orion Publishing Group Ltd,
Carmelite House, 50 Victoria Embankment
London EC4Y 0DZ

An Hachette UK company

The authorised representative in the EEA is Hachette Ireland,
8 Castlecourt Centre, Dublin 15, D15 XTP3, Ireland (email: info@hbgi.ie)

1 3 5 7 9 10 8 6 4 2

Published by arrangement with Dell. First published
in the United States in 2025

A CIP catalogue record for this book
is available from the British Library.

ISBN (Paperback) 978 1 3987 2846 2
ISBN (eBook) 978 1 3987 2847 9
ISBN (Audio) 978 1 3987 2848 6

Printed and bound in Great Britain by Clays Ltd, Elcograf S.p.A.

www.orionbooks.co.uk

Your favourite authors love Bailey Hannah!

'Relatable, funny, heartwarming, and full of so much heat. A testament to the power of showing up for the ones you love, no matter how messy things get'

Nisha J.Tuli

'Bailey Hannah's writing is beautiful, the characters are nuanced, and the emotions are complex'

Sarah Hawley

'Real, raw, and sweepingly romantic . . . Bailey Hannah tells stories with grit and authenticity that will have you desperately flipping the pages late into the night'

Catherine Cowles

'Angsty, emotional and so damn sexy. Throw in a hardworking hero on horseback and I am sold! Now I just need to go back and meet the other men on the ranch!'

Laurie Gilmore

'Bailey Hannah knows how to deliver the heat! Saddle up, readers – this cowboy romance is about to leave you breathless'

Carlie Walker

'As angsty and emotional as it is swoony and sexy, this romance that will have readers simultaneously wiping their tears and smiling until it hurts'

Lyla Sage

'Bailey Hannah's books are an exhilarating ride. I close each one with my hair blown back and a smile on my face, immediately ready for another'

Tarah DeWitt

Readers are hooked by *Love Wells Kept* . . .

'How do you say goodbye to a world that feels like home? I don't think a book has ever broken me this quickly. If you love emotional, second-chance-at-love vibes with deep, soul-stirring connection . . . this one will *ruin* you (in the best way)'

Nikki, Reader Review

'The ending was absolutely perfect – the best send off for such a perfect series'

Chloe, Reader Review

'I have loved all the books so far in the Wells Ranch series and Bailey saved the best for last'

Sam, Reader Review

'Beautiful, emotional, unforgettable. My heart shattered over and over again . . . and somehow, this story still managed to put it back together'

Anna, Reader Review

'This is one of those rare books that manages to be spicy, heartwarming, and heartbreaking all at once without losing its emotional core'

Donna, Reader Review

'Bailey Hannah, please stand up and take a bow because you have delivered a beautiful, emotional, heart-breaking read that I am so in awe of that I'm ready to go back and read it again less than 24 hours after finishing'

Alanna, Reader Review

'Honestly I'd give this infinity stars if I could. My heart and soul are in Wells Ranch, with the Wells' and their extended family. It's not just a fictional place but people and a town that feels like home, a place that I don't ever want to leave behind'

Lucy, Reader Review

Bailey Hannah is a Canadian romance author with a passion for strong heroines and rugged men who aren't afraid to love their women hard.

Born and raised in small town British Columbia, you can count on a touch of rural Canadian flair (dirt roads, rodeos, and ketchup chips) in her stories. Bailey lives with her husband, daughter, dogs, and chickens. In her spare time, she enjoys reading, enjoying the outdoors, and daydreaming about her characters.

Baileyhannahwrites.com

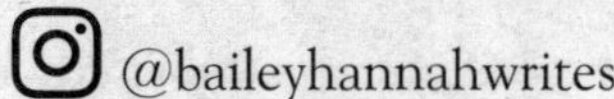

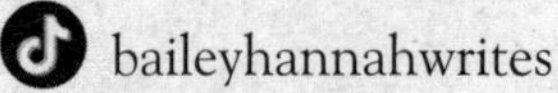

Also by Bailey Hannah

WELLS RANCH SERIES

Alive and Wells
Seeing Red
Change of Hart
At Whit's End

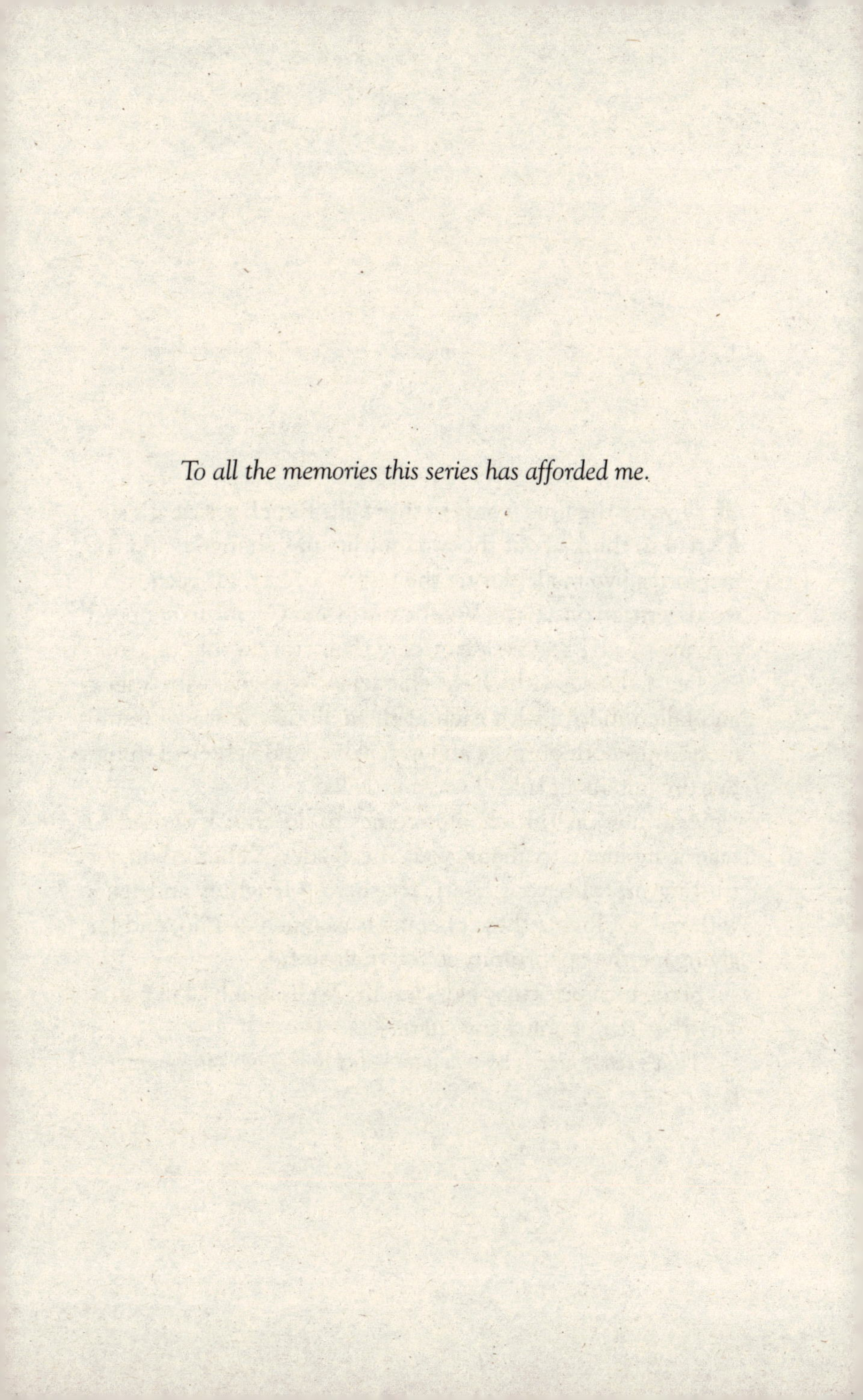

To all the memories this series has afforded me.

As I write the final words in the Wells Ranch series, it's surreal to think about the ways my life has changed, and the memories I've made during the last two years, all because of words written on a page. When Austin and Cecily first popped into my head, I had no idea where their story would take me.

I've laughed with these characters, grieved with them, and fallen in love with each of them along the way. I found friendships both on-page and in real life, and achieved things I've dreamt about since I was a little kid.

And now, as this chapter comes to an end, I wanted to take a moment to thank you, the readers. Thank you for trusting me with your heart, for sharing laughter and tears with me, for loving these characters as much as I do, and for giving me the opportunity to tell their stories.

Some memories may fade, but the Wells family? I'm pretty sure they're not going anywhere.

That's what hearts do when they love someone—they remember.

Content Warnings

- Alcohol consumption (on page)
- Amnesia (on page)
- Blood (on page)
- Castration (discussed, not shown)
- Death of parent (discussed, not shown)
- Depression (discussed, on page)
- Medically induced coma (on page)
- Medical procedures, including brain surgery (discussed, on page)
- Miscarriage (detailed, on page)
- Prescription medication use (on page)
- Pregnancy (on page)
- Runaway child (on page, no harm to child)
- Suicidal ideation (on page)
- Traumatic brain injury (on page)
- Vomit (on page)
- Explicit sex including cockwarming, praise, and public sex

JACKSON

Some mornings make you wish you could stop the clock.

This morning, my daughter's all braids, freckles, and energy, practically floating as she skips toward the barn, and knowing she won't be this small and excited forever, I wish I could hit pause. I watch her closely over the hitch of the truck, trying to burn this moment into my memory forever.

"Don't go far," I call after her. "I'm almost ready to go."

"Okay, Daddy." Odessa beams at me over her shoulder, disappearing through the double doors.

The barn's gilded in morning sun, blurred by dust motes kicked up in Odessa's wake. I run a hand through my hair, racking my brain for anything I might've forgotten. This time tomorrow, Odessa and I will be on our way back home with the horse of her dreams.

Then a scream slices through the crisp morning air.

Odessa.

I run before I think.

She's pressed into the corner of a stall, trembling under the stare of a gelding I've been working with for weeks—his ribs are thin, his eyes wild from the abuse he came from. Fear pulses off him in waves, coiled muscle ready to strike.

Her name is ripped from my lips as I shove the stall door open.

All I have is one step, one second. And whatever comes next.

TWO HOURS EARLIER . . .

No man alive has ever been happier.

Arm wrapped around my wife's waist, I tug the warm pressure of her back tight to my chest. The first hint of daybreak creates shadows and soft edges around the room. The house is still, crisp mountain air spilling in through the slightly open window. It's my favorite time of the day.

A gentle nudge of my nose moves thick brown locks away from her neck. Even while asleep, her head reflexively cants, exposing more of her creamy skin. My lips brush a kiss behind her ear, and I inhale the faint aroma of castor oil still lingering from last night.

I vividly remember the first night she used some new skincare regime with approximately one billion steps. It was right around her twenty-fifth birthday, following a small quarter-life crisis about getting older. She came to bed looking like a glazed donut, and I told her as much, which she didn't appreciate. But with that adorable scowl of hers, I couldn't help but pin her to the sheets and make sure to let her know she *tasted* like a glazed donut, too.

Now, a decade later, I can't get enough of that mild earthy scent. Nothing beats knowing I'm the only one who gets to experience Kate Wells slipping into bed at the end of the day.

The stretched collar of my old T-shirt has slipped off her shoulder, and I let go of my hold on her waist to trace the delicate plane of her bare collarbone. With a twist of my wrist, the backs of my roughened knuckles run the length of her arm. Slipping under the frayed hem, I stretch my hand across the front of her stomach and press a kiss to her shoulder.

Kate exhales slow and long, and her hand spreads over mine.

Confident she's awake, or at least somewhere in that dreamy half-awake state, I softly murmur, "Mornin'."

With the gravel of sleep still in her voice, her whisper matches mine. "Hi, handsome."

Kate rolls onto her back, and I brush away the hair stuck to pillow-creases in her cheek. She looks at me with hooded eyes and a thin smile.

"How are you feeling?" I ask, rubbing our joined hands in slow circles over her stomach.

Her throat clenches with an audible swallow. "So far, so good. Been awake for less than ten seconds, though."

"Good point." I kiss her cheek. Jaw. Neck.

As I shuffle down the bed, kissing every sliver of skin I come across, the comforter pulls with me. I shift the thin T-shirt up to expose her midriff so I can place the softest of kisses just below her belly button, where the stretch marks from our first two babies are thin, white arcs across her skin. They look like glittering sunlight on water. I can't wait for the subtle changes in these scars, and the addition of new ones, in the coming months.

"I love you," I say to my wife. To the baby we found out about yesterday. "Both of you."

"You know you're essentially talking to my intestines right now . . . the baby's nowhere near that high up yet." Kate laughs under her breath.

My thumbs hook under her cotton pajama pants and I let my mouth trail lower, following the slow dip of her pants. Letting my bottom lip drag over the indent from her elastic waistband, I look up at her. "This low enough?"

She gives me a coy shrug, lifting her hips off the mattress so I can tug those pesky bottoms off, then settle myself between her thighs, to make sure she has a *really* good start to her day. God knows she deserves it.

We found out about Kate's pregnancy after she'd been sick all week. Kate doesn't get sick. Honestly, I think germs are too scared of my wife to even consider invading her body.

Blowing a cool breath on her hot skin, I feel the vibration

of anticipation run the length of her thighs. Her back arches like the slow pull of a bowstring, begging me to be the one to let it snap. After sixteen years, I know her every move, every sound, every want better than I know my own.

I kiss her about a quarter of an inch from where she wants my mouth to be. "How's that, Kit?"

She palms the back of my skull, urging me into her at the same time her legs spread impossibly wide. And just as that first savory lick up her wet entrance floods my senses, her fingers knot in my hair to sharply yank my gaze to meet hers. There's a hiss in her tone when she quietly says my name.

"You okay?" I ask.

With a disgruntled sigh, she hooks the thumb of her free hand toward the bedroom door. I prop myself up on my elbows, training my ears.

Sure enough. There's an uneven thud of small feet heading down the stairs. On any other morning, I'm thrilled to have a moment with my wife and at least one of our kids snuggled up in our king-size bed before the chaos of a day on the ranch begins. Before I head out to do ranch work or train horses, and Kate becomes so busy tending to the kids and the ranch hands there's barely time for a brief kiss when we cross paths.

But this morning, the last people I want walking into the room are our children. Love them, but goddamn, we need a lock on the door.

Pressing a firm kiss to my wife's gorgeous pussy, I help her shimmy her pants back up and return to my still-warm spot next to her.

"You tease." She cups my chin and kisses me.

I shift the erection in my boxers, willing it to go away, just as the door swings open and our three-year-old, Rhett, saunters in. At least he's a little bit less hell-on-wheels than our seven-year-old daughter, Odessa, which is a great thing during a moment like this, when my brain's still hazy and sluggish.

Ignoring Rhett for a second, I lock eyes with Kate and say,

"I'll make it up to you tomorrow after Odessa and I get home from the auction. I'll do bedtime and meet you right here afterward."

Then I pop a final kiss on her lips before sitting up and returning my focus to Rhett. "Morning, buddy. How'd you sleep?"

"I had a dream about donuts that fart." He scrambles to pull himself onto the bed, clutching at the thick comforter until Kate offers her hand as a lifeline.

"Wow. Sounds like quite the dream." I plant my bare feet on the worn wooden floorboards, working up the energy to fully remove myself from the bed. A few minutes ago, I had the energy—and virility, apparently—of a twenty-year-old man, but now that I have to get up and do things I'd rather not do, it's taking everything I have. With a stretch overhead, I look at Rhett in my periphery. "Did they poop sprinkles?"

His small, freckled face twists to match the disheveled state of his hair. "*No.*"

Kate snickers.

"Right. Because that would be too weird." My palm scrubs my jaw, and I stand, setting a weary hand down on his head to tousle his short brown hair. "Let's get out of Mommy's hair—let her fully wake up."

Spreading my fingers, I grip the top of his head and gently veer him toward the open doorway. Seems like yesterday I could hold his entire body in one outstretched hand.

I don't loosen my hold on him until we're stepping into the kitchen, because Lord knows he'll head back to the bedroom to talk Kate's ear off about donut farts if I don't keep him on track.

And I'm hoping Kate takes the few minutes of alone time to finish what I started, but even if not, there's a good chance she'll be nauseous when she gets out of bed. Given we haven't told anyone about her pregnancy yet, it's better if the kids don't see her sick.

Slanted sunlight streams through the windows behind our kitchen table, silhouetting an abandoned coffee cup left behind on the wooden tabletop, and pours across the island's white counter. Besides Rhett's rustling through cereal boxes in the walk-in pantry, the only sound is a sharp hiss as the coffeemaker finishes its timed brew. Careful not to let the kitchen cabinets squeak too much, as they're apt to do—particularly when the house is quiet and everyone is sleeping—I grab a clean mug and pad across the cool floors to fill it.

Once Rhett and I have our morning necessities in hand, we settle in at the table. Covered in dents and stains and scuffs, this table has seen multiple generations of Wellses. Rhett and Odessa ate their first meals here, just like me and my father before me.

Mid-sip of strong, black coffee, I look up to see our kitchen manager, Beryl, enter the room. Dressed in dark-wash jeans and a WELLS RANCH T-shirt, she beams at me. "Morning, boys."

"Morning," I say into my coffee mug, watching as she finishes tying off a long gray braid and tosses it over her shoulder on her way to kiss Rhett on top of the head.

He scrunches his freckled nose, but there's no denying the way he relaxes into the feel of her lovingly sifting a hand through his hair.

Beryl came to work for the ranch when Kate was pregnant with Odessa and could no longer keep up with the demands of cleaning bunkhouses, prepping lunches for the ranch hands, and running the house by herself. But she quickly became so much more than an employee to us. It had been a few years since my mom died at that point, and I don't think my brothers and I realized how badly we needed a maternal presence in our lives again until Beryl showed up.

Now my kids call her Gran.

Without a moment to waste, Beryl starts on her morning routine, because within the next fifteen minutes or so, a herd of noisy, clumsy ranch hands will clamber into the spacious kitchen in search of coffee, bagged lunches, and whatever else they can get their hands on.

She tucks a batch of yesterday's blueberry scones into the oven to warm them, leaving one out for Rhett, who prefers them cold, and sinks into the empty chair next to my son.

The sitting isn't long. Never is for her. She swears that's what keeps her feeling young and agile at her age.

"Rhett peed on the toilet seat again." Odessa's attitude enters the room before she does, and when she appears around the corner, her hands are firmly placed on her skinny hips. With wavy, chocolate-brown hair that falls all the way to her lower back and giant doe eyes, she's the spitting image of a young Kate. "It's disgusting."

Rhett turns to me with a guilty expression.

I sigh, pinching the bridge of my nose. "Bud, we've talked about this."

"Sorry," he says. He's not sorry. We'll be having this conversation again tomorrow.

Eyes cutting to where my daughter's filling a bowl with Cheerios, I ask, "How'd you sleep, Princess?"

"Pretty good." Milk splashes into the bowl and a few drops ricochet to land on the counter. Odessa swipes her arm across the mess and continues.

"Good enough you're still up for a drive to the horse auction with me?"

I already know the answer. Odessa's been obsessed with horses since she was a baby, and riding since she learned to sit on her own. She loves horses even more than I did at her age. With her birthday next month and a horse auction that happens to fall in the middle of her spring break, Kate and I agreed this was the perfect time for her first horse.

Her eyes light up. "You were serious? I get to come?"

"Best place to find you a new horse for your birthday, right?"

With an excited shriek, Odessa promptly turns toward the door, abandoning the carton of milk and bowl of Cheerios on the counter. "Let's go!"

"Hold up," I say through a laugh. "I gotta check on the training horses before we hit the road. Eat your breakfast."

Rhett's metal spoon clangs on the table. "I want to go."

I suck my teeth. "Sorry, bud. Just me and sissy this time. You'd get way too bored sitting in the truck that long."

He twists in his chair, gripping the smooth wooden back, to glare at his sister, who sticks her tongue out at him.

When Odessa sits down to eat, she's beaming ear to ear, and over the rim of my coffee mug I give her a discreet wink.

Kate and Beryl have made more than their fair share of comments about Odessa becoming less of a daddy's girl when she gets older. That she won't always want to hang out with me, and I should prepare myself for that, but I'm happier living in blissful ignorance, with a smidge of intense denial. Besides, if she goes through a phase in her teen years where I'm suddenly uncool, I'm going to be grateful as hell for every chance I get to spend time with her now.

And sure, I won't be able to get a word in edgewise with Odessa talking my ear off for the entire ten-hour drive, but I wouldn't trade it for the world.

Besides, I'm used to sitting down and shutting up. I'm married to Kate, after all.

The front door slams then, wafting brisk morning air down through the house, and chaos descends upon the kitchen. Ranch hands tromping through in cowboy boots and winter woolies, grumbling and elbowing each other and grunting their thanks to Beryl as she fills travel mugs with steaming black coffee and reminds the grown men to take a bottled water with them. She's a mother hen tutting after them like they're a group of preschoolers in need of direction.

Somewhere in the madness, Kate slips into the kitchen. She's dressed in a pair of my old blue jeans and a baggy sweatshirt, hair pulled into a messy bun that wobbles on top of her head with every step. My wife typically only wears makeup when we're going out, but I can tell she rouged her cheeks to combat the pallor of morning sickness. Instinctively, I stand and brush past a couple of our long-term ranch hands to get to her.

Stepping in close to her, I quietly ask, "How are you feeling?"

"Like one of those scones is either going to be my saving grace or the death of me." She licks her lips. "And I can't wait to find out."

"Sit." I kiss her temple. "You're in no state to be fighting off these guys to get one."

"I'm always in a state to fight these animals." Her hand shoots up in preparation to swat someone at just the right second to unintentionally threaten my younger brother on his way to the coffee machine.

Denny ducks, cursing under his breath. "Damn it, Kate. What did I do to get this treatment first thing in the morning?"

"Gotta keep you on your toes, Denny," Kate retorts. She gives me a sly grin, then says, "You're right. That took all my energy. Go win me a scone, handsome."

Goods secured, I step in behind where Kate's sitting at the table and quietly place her breakfast down next to the mug of black tea she's cradling in both hands. Mid-conversation with Denny and Odessa, she tips her head to look at me. The wisps of hair sticking out at every angle from her bun flutter through the air, and she squints at the sunlight silhouetting me.

"Come say goodbye before you head out?"

"I'd never go anywhere without saying goodbye first, Kit."

KATE

Between calculated sips of tea and mouse-like nibbles of scone, I stave off the nausea gurgling low in my throat. Though it's bright enough to have everyone at the table squinting slightly, the window frost is so thick I can't feel the warmth of the sunrays despite the way they cloak me.

One by one, ranch hands grab their bagged lunches, fill dented travel mugs with coffee—one of the first things I had an aversion to, hence the tea—and wearily heckle each other in the large kitchen.

In the middle of a strategic slow trickle of tea down my throat, I glance over the rim of my mug in time to watch Rhett pick his nose and wipe it on Odessa's forearm, which is swiftly followed up by an attempted spoon-stabbing in retaliation. If it were a knife, or maybe even a fork, I'd intervene. This morning I'm too exhausted, and the last thing I want to deal with is the two of them arguing, so I pretend not to notice.

"Mom-uh."

I loathe the additional syllable Odessa's started adding to the ends of words when she's annoyed.

So much for me not getting involved.

Odessa whines while wiping her brother's snot off on his shirt. "He's being disgusting."

Rhett's unfazed. He's focused solely on driving a salt grinder around the table like it's a truck.

I set my mug down with an exhale. "Odessa, why don't you go down to the barn and help your dad so you two can get on the road sooner?"

Her lips purse. "Does that earn me more money toward the horse I'm gonna buy?"

"It earns you grace for trying to stab your brother, so you don't have to sit in your room grounded for the rest of spring break."

"But he started—"

I tilt my head, giving her the look. The one that means I'm not fucking around. The one that all of our ranch hands know not to argue with. The one that's landed me in a fight or two with women who didn't understand when to quit running their mouth.

The chair makes a grating nose as Odessa pushes back from the table, rolling her eyes. "Fine-uh."

In socked feet, she tromps across the floor, clearly doing her best to cause a scene. Though nobody notices, since there's still half a dozen cowboys lingering around the island, scarfing down scones and coffee before they start their day. They should consider themselves lucky that Austin, the eldest Wells brother, isn't here yet. He doesn't exactly appreciate dillydallying.

The scone and tea seem to be sitting fine, so I leave Rhett to happily play pretend at the table and begin cleaning up the mess my hurricane-force family left behind.

It's merely the start of a long day around here. Baking homemade bread for sandwiches, driving an hour and a half away to Sheridan—the closest small city with large enough grocery stores to feed our entire crew—then assembling tomorrow's bagged lunches for twenty cowboys. Not to mention, the bunkhouses we have on site for the guys need to be cleaned. And to think I used to do it all myself.

Though the number of "ranch wives" has increased exponentially in the last few years, the work seems never ending.

Maybe it's because of all the extra kids. Though Denny and his wife, Blair, live in the town of Wells Canyon now, she's here with their toddler almost daily. Blair's best friend, Cassidy, married our ranch foreman, Red, and because she runs her own leatherworking business, she has the flexibility to be here as often as she wants. Austin's wife, Cecily, works in the kitchen full time with Beryl . . . at least, she will until she gives birth in a few months.

It's truly a family-run ranch in every sense of the word. Fresh out of my care-aide program in college, I moved here to provide hospice care to the Wells family matriarch, Lucy. And from the moment I stepped foot on this property, I knew it was someplace special. A place I'd never want to leave.

Not only because of the stunning sunsets that cloak the valley in a golden glow, or the crisp mountain air, or even the overwhelming feeling of being away from it all. The Wells family took me in and filled my life with so much joy, even as they were losing the source of theirs.

And it just so happened that Lucy's middle son, Jackson, was my soulmate. We fell in love sitting in this very kitchen, talking for hours over chamomile tea when neither of us could sleep. Somehow it seems fitting that Lucy was my one and only patient, because no other job placement would've felt right after that.

I stare down at the suds gathered in my hands, realizing I apparently zoned out in the middle of washing up. Who knows how long I've been standing here, water at full blast into the farmhouse-style sink, slippery hands wringing together. After a quick rinse, I shut the tap off and head to the pantry.

Bread time.

I could make sandwich loaves with my eyes closed. And on a day like today, that sounds lovely. Get some rest *and* be productive.

"You look a little pale, honey." Beryl wipes a damp cloth over the countertop, collecting stray crumbs the cowboys left in their wake. "Still sick?"

I shake my head, reaching behind me to tie the ivory apron strings in a neat bow at the small of my back. "Just need a couple good nights to get back to one hundred percent."

"Well, good thing it's only you and Rhett tonight. Make sure you get to bed the same time he does."

I suspect she knows the real reason behind my sudden paleness and lack of energy, but I promised Jackson we'd tell everyone together after he gets home tomorrow night. And I'm grateful Beryl doesn't push it further, instead resuming her morning routine.

"Can we listen to music?" Rhett pipes up from the table where he's intently focused on folding a paper napkin into something. A boat? A swan? A pirate's hat?

Without a single second of hesitation, Beryl's tapping the power button on a small black Bluetooth speaker. "Great idea, baby."

Rhett's thrilled when we start with his favorite song by a talking cartoon snowman. He's seated at the kitchen table, looking like a miniature version of his father, with a slight wave in his brown hair, curious almond eyes, and a tall-yet-stocky build. He sings along—loud and off-key—squinting out at the scant traces of snow left on the ground, feet merrily swinging under the table.

After a few moments, Rhett busies himself with stacking wood blocks into a precarious tower on the floor. And Beryl moves with quiet efficiency behind me, checking items off the grocery list and muttering under her breath when she can't remember if we're out of baking powder or baking soda.

It's peaceful, in its own chaotic, domestic way. The rhythm of shaping bread is oddly meditative. Roll, tuck, turn, set aside. The counter's quickly filled with soft, rounded mounds of dough.

"Morning!" Cecily's voice cuts through the music as she steps inside, her hair pulled into a high ponytail, cheeks flushed from the cold, or maybe it's that pregnant glow she wears like it's natural. Of course she looks effortlessly radiant in a stretched-out T-shirt and leggings.

"Morning, honey," Beryl says as she looks up from the multi-page shopping list she's scribbling at the kitchen table. "Need anything from the grocery store?"

I do a double take, eyes cutting from Cecily to Beryl. "Wait—I thought I was going today?"

She gives me a look that dares me to argue. "No, ma'am. Nope, you're going to take a long nap after the bread is done. With this one"—she hooks a thumb toward Cecily, who's tugging the hem of her shirt down to try and cover her exposed stomach—"just about into her third trimester, we need you healthy."

"Okay, well, I'm not a napper. But I appreciate the sentiment." I pick at dried dough around my nail beds. "I'm perfectly healthy. No need to worry about me."

The front door closes with a slam that reverberates through the hundred-year-old farmhouse, vibrating in the old floorboards and echoing through thin walls. It's followed by heavy footsteps, and Austin Wells steps into the room. Hair still damp from the shower, wearing a long-sleeve navy plaid shirt, and with his signature scowl already in place.

He instinctively moves toward his wife, spreading a large hand across her round baby bump and planting a kiss on top of her head. Austin's grumpy, gruff demeanor shifts when she's around. It's not dramatic, but to those of us who have known him for years, it's noticeable. It's good.

"Coffee's fresh," Beryl says.

"Smells like a bakery in here." Grabbing his usual mug from the cabinet, he makes a beeline for the coffeepot.

Beryl shrugs. "With how much your guys eat, that's basically what this place is."

He pours the steaming dark roast into his cup. "Could always buy the cheapest bread they have at the grocery store instead."

Cecily gasps, wide eyes trained on her husband. "How could you suggest that? Kate's bread has ruined me for anything else. I could . . . Wow. I could actually cry thinking about not having fresh bread every day."

I throw my hands up, laughing. "Great, Aus. Now you're gonna make your pregnant wife cry."

"Jesus Christ. It was a suggestion. Ignore me. Just a stupid man here."

"Hey, you said it." I shrug impishly.

Austin starts toward his usual spot at the kitchen table. Even before Cecily came into his life, he spent mornings here with Beryl and me. He takes ranch phone calls, pores over financial paperwork, or reads his cattlemen's magazine. He's never been one to socialize with the ranch hands, so there were many times over the years when Beryl and I were the only people he talked to for days on end.

He trips over Rhett's blocks, fumbling his coffee mug, and miraculously catches himself before he's spilled a single drop. "Seriously, buddy? In the middle of the floor? Come on."

"I'm building a tower."

"Great." Austin exhales, settling into his seat. "But can we not build it in the middle of the highway?"

Rhett grumbles but pushes his blocks a few inches to the left.

The tea and scone did the trick for a while, but nausea is curling in my stomach again, and I need a minute to sit.

At that moment, someone flies through the front door of the big house, and their heavy panting breath is heard throughout the kitchen long before they've reached us.

"Kate," a man shouts from the hallway. Red appears in the

doorway in filthy jeans and a tattered plaid button-up, his face flushed and hair disheveled. "Kate. Austin. You need to come."

"What's going on?" Austin's mug clunks against the tabletop.

There's nothing but the steady stream of the kitchen faucet and the smell of fresh bread and my hands are dripping water across the floor.

"There's been an accident."

KATE

There's been an accident.

I rip the apron from my body, leaving it discarded on the hallway floor, and cram my feet into a pair of old rubber boots on my way out the door. Austin's shoulder brushes mine on our run down the front porch steps.

"Is it Odessa?" Her name slices its way up my throat, begging not to be said.

Over his shoulder, Red replies, "Jackson."

My eyes burn from the combination of frigid air and the overwhelming urge to cry. Gravel crunches underfoot, and even from more than a hundred yards away, we can hear a commotion in the barn.

I know cowboys. They don't panic. *I know my cowboy.* He broke his arm once and it took me two days to convince him to go to the hospital.

This . . . It's different.

A shiver slides the length of my spine, and I reflexively reach for Austin. Hands wrapped around his arm with a bruising grip, I hold him as if a portion of his unwavering strength will somehow transfer to me. And he clasps a steady, warm hand on mine.

"Is he . . ."

"Denny already called for an ambulance."

My next breath is ragged and hollow. I bite my top lip,

digging my teeth in until the pain numbs the rest of my senses, and the tears welling in my eyes don't fall down my cheeks. The last thing he needs is a blubbering wife right now.

"What happened?" Austin asks calmly.

So fucking calm. How can he be so calm when every cell in my body is on the verge of exploding?

"He was in with that new gelding," Red says. "Don't know exactly what happened, but thank God one of the guys was in the tack room—heard Odessa scream and came running."

My grip on Austin tightens like the leather of a cinch, giving me barely enough stability to keep moving. My feet drag through the gravel, weighed down and numb, and a series of tremors racks my body the closer we get to the barn.

"Odessa's okay." A pained smile flickers on Red's lips. "Checked myself. She's okay, Kate."

My tongue presses against my cheek, and I nod slowly, tears welling in my eyes.

We find the barn door wide open and, rather than the chaos I expected to find, everyone is oddly . . . calm.

Unnerving—the calm. It's sterile. Cold. It's heads of hair without cowboy hats. Grown men refusing to look me in the eye when I enter the fucking barn.

"Kate." Red stops so fast Austin and I nearly run into the back of him, and he spins to face me. His hands hold my face, and I don't have enough sense—enough strength—to shove them away. "Do not try to move him. You hear me?"

With the snarl of a frightened wild animal, I push past him. *Does he think I'm an idiot?*

"Somebody tell me what the hell is going on. What happened?" Charging forward toward a far stall, where a couple ranch hands are standing around with their hands in their pockets. "Jackson, can you please tell me what's going—"

Rounding the corner, I step into a dusty stall. No horse.

Only . . .

"Jackson," I sob. My knees hit the ground next to a motionless body, tears falling to the concrete mere seconds later. There's blood—*so much blood*—accumulating on the ground under his head, and I can't catch my breath. "What's—"

The words can't leave. Trapped in the thick, burning bile that I'm drowning in.

Somewhere in the background, a million miles away and through a dense fog, I hear Red's voice. "Seems he was probably kicked, but he's been out cold the entire time so . . ."

I careen forward until my forehead collides with his chest, the soft texture of his shirt against my skin, the scent of laundry soap and his sweat filling my nostrils.

And I pray for a heartbeat. A cough. A movement. The feel of his hand coming up to cup the nape of my neck so he can whisper that I'm being dramatic.

If any of that happens, I don't feel it.

Then there's Denny. He's hugging me from behind, whispering things I can't make out, his breath blowing hot against my neck as his arms wrap tight around me. He takes the panicked blows of my heart against my rib cage and slows them with the even gallop of his pulse on my back. His head rocks side to side against mine. His tears drench my hair.

He's my straitjacket.

"He'll be okay," Denny murmurs. "You'll be okay."

This isn't okay. This is my husband. The love of my life. The father of my children. My person.

Lying in a pool of blood on the cold concrete in the middle of a goddamn barn.

When Denny finally lets up, I lift my head to press a shaky kiss to Jackson's lips. "Please . . . Listen to your brother for once and be okay. I need you to be okay. I love you so much."

Just like so many late nights spent watching him sleep, my hands search his face, reveling in his stubble scraping my palm. I smooth a fingertip over his eyebrows. Sift through blood-soaked hair. Wipe a speck of red from the shell of his ear.

There's a new commotion. Like the beating of a hundred angel wings, the heavy, dense whoosh of helicopter blades echoes through the barn. The guys collectively breathe a sigh of relief. And I clutch the front of Jackson's shirt, digging a button so deep into my palm, it's nearly embedded. Surely they can't separate him and me if we're sewn together.

"Jackson." I lean in so my lips brush his ear, and my breath comes out a tattered death rattle. I lick my lips, holding on to him with a sinking feeling this might be our last moment. "Don't you dare go. Don't you fucking dare. You . . . you promised me. You promised you wouldn't leave without saying goodbye. You can't."

"Kate." Denny's hand rubs a firm line across my shoulder blades. "Kate, the paramedics are here. We gotta let them do their job."

I nod, the side of my face rubbing against the side of my husband's. I need to memorize every piece of him, collect all the different ways he feels. But I have two men sliding hands under my armpits, attempting to forcibly remove me from the last person on Earth I ever want to be away from. The person so ingrained in my soul, I can't fathom existing without him. I couldn't. My heart wouldn't allow it.

"You don't get to leave without saying goodbye," I sob into his wet hair one last time.

Pressing bloodstained hands to the cold, rough surface of concrete, I move from kneeling to crouching to standing. Some part of me keeps waiting for his eyes to flutter open and the gravel of his sleepy voice to tell me he loves me. I can't take my eyes off him for fear of missing it.

Even as my lifeless body is pulled from the barn stall to make room for paramedics and a stretcher, I watch him intently. The fingers on one hand turn white around the edge of the stall door. My other hand's encompassed by the warmth of Denny's palms.

In a series of calculated movements and murmured medical terms, he's loaded onto a board, then brought to the waiting helicopter.

The blades whip through the air like the roll of thunder. Holding my hand over my brow bone to shield my eyes from the sun's glare, I watch the helicopter shrink into the skyline before I turn to Red. "Where's Odessa?"

"Probably back at the house by now. I had Colt take her out of the barn after I'd made sure she was okay."

Fresh air fully inflates my lungs for the first time since the moment Red barged into the kitchen, and I blow a loud exhale through parted lips. I had my moment to be distraught and inconsolable and terrified. Now I need to wipe away the salt that's burned tracks down my cheeks, run a hand through tangled hair, and get my shit together for my kids.

Emotions settle in my chest cavity, weighing down every beat of my heart and cinching around my lungs. Pain radiates through my shoulder blades, tingling down my arms, with every step toward our house.

What do I tell the kids?

Red and Denny follow close behind me, our footsteps falling in sync, crunching over the gravel and pounding on the compact dirt. Trees sway and bend, birds flitting between them fully consumed in early-spring love. Otherwise, the ranch is eerily still, with no distant rumblings of tractor engines or cowboy chatter.

"You okay?" Denny asks softly, stepping in close behind me on the slow drag up the front porch steps.

"No," I answer honestly, voice crack and all. I swallow against the lump wedged in my throat. "Not at all. I can't even think about— Can you help me pretend to be okay? For the kids?"

Both men nod, and when Red steps forward to open the door for me, the cozy scent of wood fire and rising bread envelops me. Home. I swear I can even smell Jackson's body wash lingering in the air.

I stumble forward, flanked by two men who have always been brothers to me, and soon I'm standing in the large kitchen. Rhett's still playing with his blocks, and his singular tower has transformed into a small city. Austin's coffee mug hasn't left its spot on the kitchen table. Someone picked up my flour-coated apron and set it on the island while I was gone. Beryl's nowhere to be seen.

Cecily looks up from where she's shaping a loaf of whole-wheat bread, and runs her hands over the front of her too-small apron. "What's going on?"

Rhett's head whips around to look at us. "Is Daddy okay?"

My eyes shutter, blinking back tears, and I nod slowly. It's so fucking forced. "Yeah, baby. He hurt himself, but the doctors are gonna fix him up."

"At the *hostable*? Is he really super hurt?"

Denny strides across the floor, crouching down next to his nephew. "Your dad is tough, right?" He waits for Rhett to give him an eager nod. "This is nothing he can't handle—tough guy like him. Those hospital doctors will have him fixed up and heading home super fast."

"I want to show him my farm." Rhett points to a dozen green blocks scattered underneath one of the dining chairs.

Giving him an impressed look, Denny says, "That's a badass farm. Why don't you show me?"

I turn my attention back to Cecily. "Did Odessa come back here?"

She nods. "Beryl's up in her room with her."

"I need to talk to her," I announce. "Make sure she's okay before we head to the hospital."

In the midday sun, the short hallway between the front entry and kitchen are cheerful and bright. Sharp lines of golden light cut diagonally across the worn wooden floorboards, and I grip the smooth banister to pull myself upstairs.

When my hand leaves a small streak of muddy-red on the handrail, it dawns on me that I still have Jackson's blood on me, so at the top of the stairs I veer into the bathroom. The faucet squeaks a little when I turn it on. It has since the first time I used it sixteen years ago, the first night I spent in Jackson's childhood bedroom.

Through a thick film of tears, I stare at the crimson blood dried on my hands, wedged under my nails. I swallow down a sob and clutch the edges of the sink to keep myself upright even as the entire world sways and my knees threaten to buckle.

This blood might be the last trace of my husband I ever have on my skin.

All I can think about is how washing this away might mean washing away the last moments of his life. Washing away the last time I get to feel his warm skin on mine.

A droplet falls from my eye, big enough to drown in, and it blurs the red on my palm like watercolor. Shutting my eyes tight, I shove both hands under the streaming faucet.

Lukewarm water rushes over my skin, turning pink and flowing freely down the drain, and I lose myself in remembering that first night together in the room across the hall.

That same room is about to be a nursery.

A nursery for a baby who might never get to meet their dad.

The realization bowls me over, and I grip the curved edges of the pedestal sink to support myself. A choked gasp flees my lungs, and I stumble toward the toilet to unload breakfast in one fell swoop that buckles my knees and forces tears from my eyes. I kneel there for a moment, unsure whether I'm sobbing because I'm not a good puker or because I don't even know if my husband made it to the hospital alive.

I clutch my throat, massaging as if it'll somehow quell the burning and sink to the floor.

Surely I'd feel *if he was gone, right?*

I know the sound of his heartbeat and the way it thrums against my palm better than my own. Sixteen years of intertwining our souls, sharing our DNA. Of promises kept.

He wouldn't leave without saying goodbye.

Even if he couldn't speak—couldn't communicate in whispers or eye movements or the squeeze of a hand—he'd make sure I felt it. I'd feel the loss down to the marrow of my bones and know it was him. I'm more sure of that than anything.

And it's that confidence in my soul that forces me off the floor. I need to get myself together and go to him. After I've splashed cold water across my face, swished children's mouthwash, and scrubbed the last traces of blood from under my nails, I head to Odessa's room.

My knuckles rap on the door once before I push it open to find Odessa half-buried in a pile of stuffed animals on top of her bed, and Beryl sitting cross-legged on the floor. Quiet conversation stops in my presence, and they both look at me.

"Hey, sweetie." I muster up a feeble smile.

Beryl stands and rubs my upper arm before slipping out with the soft close of the bedroom door.

Odessa clutches a small stuffed horse that's wet with her tears. Her eyes are bloodshot, cheeks rouged, and when she opens her mouth, her voice is thick with emotion. "Is Daddy gonna be okay?"

I cross her bedroom, settling onto the small toyless section of her bed, and I grip a small, socked foot sticking out from under a huge pink unicorn Denny won for her at the fair a few years ago. I want to tell her I have no doubt he's going to be okay and, more than anything, I want it to be the truth.

She's so damn smart for a seven-year-old. Intuitive and observant, maybe as a result of spending so much time with adults on the ranch. And though she's never experienced serious pain when it comes to humans, she has a better understanding of animal suffering than non-farm kids do.

"I don't know." I choose to be honest, though every word stabs between my ribs. "But the paramedics got here fast, and they took him to the hospital, so he's in the best place he can be."

Silent tears roll down her cheeks, and the back of her hand wipes her running nose. She opens her mouth to respond, pulling a string of saliva taut between her top and bottom teeth, and the only sound is a hoarse croak.

I hold my arms open, inviting her in and, like she did as a toddler, Odessa crawls out from her stuffed animal nest and curls up in my lap. I wrap around her, pressing my cheek firmly against her head. Unspoken fears hang in the air around us, and despite the endless things I want to say to ease her worries, nothing comes out. No word can be both comforting and true right now.

Once her sobs have slowed, I smooth a hand over her hair and say, "I need to go to the hospital and be with your dad, okay? I wanted to come up here and talk to you before I go."

"I'm coming."

"Not right now, Dess. I promise you'll see him as soon as it's allowed." My lips plant a firm kiss on top of her head. "You know Daddy can't go long without his best buddy, so I'm sure he'll be missing you."

"Can you tell him I love him?" She tilts her head to meet my eyes. "And to get better so we can buy me a horse like we were gonna today."

A silent huff of laughter leaves my nostrils. "I'll tell him."

Thankfully someone other than me was of sound enough mind to get information from the paramedics about which hospital they were taking Jackson to. Of course it wasn't the closest one, which means driving nearly three hours to get to him.

After I've spent a couple hours anxiously sitting in Austin's backseat—fidgeting with every possible thing I could get my hands on to stop me from screaming—the truck lurches into the hospital parking lot, and we weave between rows of vehicles for what feels like a century as I stare out at the looming concrete building.

Austin pulls into a spot at the far side of the parking lot, and my emotionally drained body slips out of the backseat.

I clutch my purse strap, straightening up and tipping my head toward the building. "Jackson's probably waiting in there for me to come and force the doctor to discharge him."

"Like that time you had to rescue him from the woman at the bar?" Austin turns to look at me.

The brief memory of that day eases the nervous knotting in my guts. "I maintain that she was putting the moves on him, and he's too polite to tell her to fuck off . . . but I'm not."

Denny's half-laugh falls flat. "Man, he'd be lost without you."

Fuck. There's the ache and twisting in my stomach again. I blink up at the overcast sky, fighting back the tears suddenly threatening my waterline.

"I'd be so lost without him, too." My fingers jab into the inner corners of my eyes in a last-ditch attempt at stopping the flow.

Denny wraps an arm around my shoulders, tugging me into his side. "Good thing neither of you will need to know what that's like."

"Yeah." I exhale the word out at the same moment a blast of warm air hits us when the automatic front doors glide open.

As per usual, the hospital is dreary and depressing, and every ten feet there seems to be some new, overpowering smell. It's doing awful things to my stomach, and I press a palm against my chest as if I have the magic powers needed to stop my nausea. I swallow it down and do my best not to breathe from my nose, which eventually turns into not breathing at all when we reach the busy emergency department.

"We're here for Jackson Wells," Austin tells a triage nurse.

Sitting on the other side of a desk, she eyes the three of us over her pink-framed glasses. "And you are?"

"Oh, uh . . . his brothers and wife." He gestures wearily at each of us, as if she's unable to tell who are the brothers and who is the wife. "He was airlifted here a little while ago."

"He's in surgery currently, but if you head upstairs to the ICU, that's where he'll be afterward."

The three of us head in search of an elevator in silence, and when we're stepping onto the ICU floor a couple minutes later, I blindly feel through the air for Denny's hand. His palm meets mine, clammy and hot, and his grip tightens with every step toward the large, harrowing double doors leading into the intensive care unit.

Austin—*thank God for Austin*—takes the lead once again, pressing a buzzer on the wall and speaking with a cheery sounding woman on the other end, letting her know we're here for Jackson. And with that, we're instructed to wait. . . .

"For how long?" Denny whispers the question to Austin, encouraging him to relay the question through the intercom.

"How long?" Austin asks gruffly.

"A couple more hours, maybe? You're welcome to wait in the lobby area and I'll come let you know when he can have visitors."

"A couple hours?" My stomach lurches, and I rely solely on Denny to keep me upright.

Denny tips his head back toward the elevator. "Want to go get some food?"

"No." I swallow the dry, hard lump in my throat. "No, I need to wait right here. What if . . . what if something happens, and she comes out here looking for us? I can't leave him. I need to stay."

"Okay . . . yeah." He rolls his lips together and tugs my

soulless body toward a cluster of armchairs next to a window overlooking the city.

Outside, the sky is dreary with an impending storm, and though it's midday, a few random streetlights have accidentally turned on. Sinking into the chair, I let my head fall back into the thick headrest, and I shutter my eyes for a moment. Mere hours ago, the bedroom was dark, my eyes shut just like this, and the love of my life was slipping beneath the sheets to run his tongue across my skin.

How the hell did today end up here?

My legs stretch out in front of me, and I slump deeper into the comfy chair. I wish I could sleep. Wish I could shut my eyes long enough, wake up, and realize this was all a nightmare. What I would give to reach my hand across the soft sheets on our bed and feel him there. Hear the gentle snores and the rasp of his breath. I'd scooch closer, and even in his sleep he'd instinctively pull me into him, curling his body around mine, and lull me back to sleep.

After a long bout of silence, Denny's voice is barely audible, like he's simply thinking aloud and didn't intend for anyone to hear. "Maybe he broke his arm or something, and that's what he's in surgery for."

With a resounding huff, I shoot to my feet, causing both men to nearly leap from their own seats, and I stride toward the intercom speaker. A few seconds after I press the large red button, that same chipper voice crackles through the speaker.

"Yeah, hi, can we get some answers about Jackson Wells? We've been out here for hours." I'm tired and irritated and terrified, and I sound every bit of it.

It's quiet for a moment. Then, "Oh, yes. He's still in surgery. I'll let you know when he's settled in here."

"And what is the surgery for?"

The other end is silent for far too long. *Did this bitch seriously walk away mid-conversation?*

My thumb jabs angrily at the button three times.

"*Hi.* What's the surgery?" I repeat.

"A craniotomy."

Cranio *has to mean head. It's head surgery. Brain surgery?*

"Is that—are you saying he's having brain surgery?" My voice cracks.

"Not exactly. It's a procedure to remove the blood around his brain."

Surely she's not talking about my Jackson. There has to be a mix-up with some other man named Jackson, because my husband can't have more than a mild concussion. Nothing a couple days in bed won't fix.

My voice comes out thick and hoarse. "Sorry, I think you're confused. I was asking about Jackson Wells . . ."

"Yes. He's still in the operating room."

My heart hits every rib on its sudden drop into my stomach.

"Someone will be able to give you more information once the procedure is done."

"Okay . . ." I stumble backward, spinning on my heel and sniffing back the burning sensation. My eyes lock on Denny's. "Not a broken arm."

In the awkward beat of silence that follows, I slump into my chair and stare up at the ceiling. Counting the tiles, running my gaze up and down the strips connecting them like they're roadways for Rhett's toy cars.

The minutes drag slower and slower as they pass. Jackson's been in surgery for *hours*, and there's nothing reassuring about a surgery that takes this long. I've had sixteen years with Jackson, and now I'm counting the minutes.

KATE

The double doors into the ICU swing open automatically, and the three of us immediately straighten in our seats.

"Are you Jackson Wells's family?" The voice I've only heard through the intercom comes in loud and clear, attached to a short woman with black hair pulled into a slicked-back bun.

"Yeah—*yes*. Yes, we are." I quickly scramble to my feet, smoothing my shirt down. The boys are quick to follow, standing at attention in front of seats that likely have permanent butt-imprints in them by now.

"Come on in." She beckons us over and points at a hand sanitizer dispenser on the wall.

Once she confirms we're adequately sanitized, the nurse leads the way down yet another foreboding, fluorescent-lit hallway filled with medical equipment and staff speaking in hushed voices.

"Jackson's right this way."

Bright lights wash everything out in the hall of endless closed-off rooms, and after a few sharp turns, I'm disoriented entirely. Good thing I don't need to know where I'm going, because I'm not leaving Jackson's room until he does.

The petite nurse abruptly stops in front of a door. The floor-to-ceiling windows on either side have white curtains pulled across them. "Has anyone talked to you about his condition yet?"

All of us shake our heads, and Austin's first to open his mouth. "No. We, uh . . . we haven't heard anything since they loaded him into the helicopter."

"I'll send a physician in to speak with you, but I don't want seeing him to be a shock." Her eyes meet mine. "He does have a drain in his skull and a ventilator in place to help him breathe. Right now he's in a medically induced coma, so he won't be responsive, but I still suggest talking to him, holding his hand, and that sort of thing."

I hear the words, but I can't make sense of them.

A drain? Ventilator? Coma?

"You can go in and see him. I'll let the doctor know you're here."

Breath held, pulse racing, I'm first to step into the cool, dark room. The door closes behind us with a soft click, and somewhere under a mess of tubes and wires and bandaging and stiff white hospital blankets, I see him.

My Jackson.

The inside of my cheek has been gnawed raw, and still the tinge of stinging pain does nothing to stop me from grinding my teeth against my flesh. It's the only thing preventing the scream rattling against my sternum from escaping.

I frantically search the small space for a wastebasket or some type of receptacle to off-load bile from my empty stomach. Tears burn at my eyes and every dry heave into the small plastic trash can burns my throat. Gasping for air, I shut my eyes and flatten my palms against the wall to steady myself before I collapse.

"Are you okay?" Denny asks, curling a hand around my bicep to pull me up and into the chair Austin is dragging over. The last thing I want to do is more fucking sitting, but it's either that or collapse to the dirty hospital floor.

"No." What I want to say is, *Are you fucking kidding me? How could I possibly be okay right now? What the hell kind of question is that?*

"I'll find you some water," Austin says quietly before slipping back into the hallway.

Denny pulls up a chair beside me and sinks into it with a heavy sigh. "Fuck."

"Yeah . . ." I swipe my fingers across my lips, squinting to see the slow rise and fall of Jackson's chest. The only movement in a still room.

Denny's phone buzzes violently in his pocket, echoing in the small, cramped room.

"It's Blair," he whispers.

I nod. "Answer it."

For the next minute or so, I listen to him describe the worst moment of my life. His voice low, words stammered as he explains every detail of the sight in front of us. The tubes and pale skin and tufts of wet-looking brown hair sticking up above the bandage they've wrapped around his head. His brother and my husband—barely recognizable and barely alive.

On shaky legs, I stand and drag my chair closer to the bed. The metal scrapes across the floor, and I watch Jackson's face, waiting for a wince at the grating squeal. It doesn't come.

My fingers weave between his on top of the bed, and I'm careful not to touch any of the lifesaving appendages attached to his body when I lean in close to whisper, "Hi, handsome. I love you. . . ." My voice wavers, breathing hot and shaky against his cheek. "Hope you're having a *really* nice sleep right now. You know . . . if you wanted to take a nap, there were easier ways to go about it."

I've never craved a smile from him the way I do right now.

My lips brush the short stubble along his jaw. "And if you were trying to get out of buying Odessa a horse . . . you're not off the hook."

When Austin walks back into the room holding a white Styrofoam cup, I press a soft kiss to Jackson's warm skin and accept the ice water from my brother-in-law with a thin smile. Denny's hushed conversation with Blair is still happening in the corner of the room, and Austin steps in close to me to give Jackson's shoulder a loving squeeze.

"Thank you," I say into the open cup. "For the water and for being here."

His eyes meet mine, glistening in the soft room lighting. "You don't need to thank me for doing the bare minimum. He's my brother. . . . You're my sister. Of course I'm going to be here, doing whatever you need."

"Well, I'm still going to thank you for it."

"God, I hope he's okay," Austin admits under his breath.

The pads of my fingers stroke the length of Jackson's forearm. With light brown hair and freckles scattered across his skin, his arm appears deceivingly tan for this time of year. Golden and warm and full of life, just like he should be. Just like he has to be.

"He has to be okay, Aus. *He has to.*" My index finger takes a wide berth around an IV line, careful not to bump it, then circles a small scar on his bicep.

Austin, Jackson, and Denny suffered so much loss when they were younger, with the deaths of their grandpa and mom, immediately followed by their dad packing up and abandoning the ranch. Somehow, the three of them pulled together and didn't merely keep Wells Ranch afloat; they worked their asses off to ensure that it became more successful than their grandpa had ever dreamed it would be, giving up everything for the sake of their family's legacy. Austin and Denny can't stand to lose Jackson any more than I can.

My touch runs up to his chest, and I lightly graze the old branding scar over his pec. *Speaking of suffering for the ranch.* It's apparently been a long-standing tradition for the men to brand themselves with the Wells Ranch cattle brand—at eighteen, Jackson willingly placed a hot iron meant for thick cow hides on his chest. Now the scar's off-white and barely raised, but the sentiment remains.

I'm so focused on studying the man lying in front of me, I don't notice the doctor step into the room until she speaks. "You must be the family—I'm Doctor Perron."

Startled, I defensively splay my hand wide and look over at her. Denny promptly hangs up the phone and gives her a charismatic smile. If there's one thing you can count on the youngest Wells brother for, it's bringing some light into even the most tense situations, and I'm well aware Austin and I have serious resting bitch faces at the best of times.

"I'm not sure how much you've been told already. . . ." She waits for our collectively confused faces before continuing, "As you know, Jackson suffered some head trauma. That led to a subdural hematoma . . . blood under one of the layers of tissue that protect your brain"—she points to her head, in a spot that I imagine is roughly where Jackson was bleeding—"so we temporarily removed a portion of his skull. . . ."

I hurriedly pull my hand from his chest, losing focus on the doctor's voice as the room spins violently out of control. *A portion of his skull was removed.* My fingers cramp around the metal of my chair's armrests. *His skull.* Black spots blur my vision and the rhythmic hiss of the ventilator floods my brain. *My husband had his skull cut out and he's being kept alive by machines.* Tears roll heavy and hot down my cheeks, and I pitch forward so my head's buried between my knees to fight the urge to vomit again.

Somebody wake me up from this fucking nightmare.

Closed fist held tight to my mouth, and breathing heavily through my nose, I try to think about rainbows, or puppies, or donut farts. *Sprinkle poops.*

Jackson was so taken aback and genuinely hurt by the three-year-old's utter disgust at his suggestion of sprinkle poops. I was a smug asshole, selfishly excited to not be the only uncool parent for once. And I'd take it back in an instant. I want him to be the cool parent. I want him to teach our kids how to drive a pickup truck, how to understand horses, and how to treat the people you love. They need him. They deserve to grow up with their daddy by their side.

And our baby . . .

My stomach clenches and twists. I can't have this baby without him.

"He has kids," I blurt out, looking up at the doctor though my vision's so blurred she's lacking all definition. "Is . . . is he going to be okay?"

Denny's solid hand rests on my shoulder, massaging slowly.

"As I was saying, we were able to clear the hematoma quickly, and that's typically a good sign, in terms of prognosis."

"I need you to tell me he's going to be okay." It sounds vaguely threatening. I shake my head aggressively, swiping the back of my hand across my mouth to remove the excess saliva pooling in the corners and making my words thick. "*Please.*"

"Well . . ." She glances away from me and over to Austin, the pinnacle of calm and rational. "It's too early to say, but we'll have a better idea once we're able to lighten up the coma and see what his level of function is."

The furthest thing from any sort of reassurance.

My teeth locate a small snag in the skin on my bottom lip, and home in on it to keep from saying anything that might get me kicked out. For a moment, the pain of torn skin quiets the pain in my head.

Austin presumably asks some questions that I don't hear past the harsh thump of my heartbeat in my eardrums. Denny's hand falls away from my shoulder. And I spend an indeterminate amount of time watching my husband lie motionless in a hospital bed.

Every muscle in my body aches with the urge to reach for

him, to crawl under the blankets next to him, position his arm around me, and pretend. Make believe we're okay.

The last of the conversation leaves with the doctor. And though time hasn't moved nor mattered since we got here, as far as I'm concerned, Austin must be paying attention. He's the first to gently clap his hands together and speak.

"It's getting late. We should eat . . . get some hotel rooms for the night." He shuffles on his feet, his back brushing against the tiled wall like a bear scratching on a tree. "Get some fresh air."

"You two go ahead," I say without taking my eyes off Jackson.

Denny says, "Kate—"

"I'm not leaving here. I'm not leaving him."

"It'll be a while before they wake him up." Austin's boot scrapes against the floor. "Probably a couple days. You need food and rest."

I ignore him, instead focusing my attention on straightening Jackson's blanket. If I walk away, it might be for the last time. I need to be here touching him, talking to him, confirming the steady beat of his heart on one of the many monitors he's hooked up to.

"We'll come back first thing in the morning," Denny adds.

"Great. I'll see you guys tomorrow." I shoot both of them a placating smile.

"You can't stay here. . . ." Austin's attempt at arguing is half-assed, at best.

"If this was Cecily," I narrow my eyes at Austin, before redirecting to Denny, "or Blair, would either of you leave? *No.* Didn't think so. I can't leave him here alone. I . . ."

I swallow down the sob bargaining its way up from my chest.

Austin nods, a rare touch of softness in his eyes. "Okay."

I maintain eye contact with him while I finish with the scratchy, thin blankets. "If something happened, and I wasn't here, I'd never forgive myself. I can't go. I don't care if I need to sleep right here in this awful chair for weeks on end."

"All right. Then I guess we're staying here." Austin plants his palms against the wall, then propels himself toward the door. "In that case, I'm going to see if I can steal another chair."

"You guys don't have to," I say.

He shakes his head. "But we will . . . just in case."

I settle in for the long haul, scooching my chair right up against the bed rail so I can comfortably rest my hand on Jackson's arm and prop my feet up next to his. It's the closest I can get to climbing in with him. I'll take it.

"You've always been a bed hog." I wiggle my socked feet on top of the bed, letting them collide gently with his through the blankets.

Denny chuckles. "Mom used to make us share a bed when we were out of town for rodeos, and I'd always wake up right on the edge with no blankets while this guy was spread-eagle."

"So nothing's changed, then." I smile over at Jackson's peacefully sleeping expression. "When I . . . well, I'm sure it won't surprise you to know I used to sneak into his room."

Denny smirks. "*Naughty.*"

"Oh, shut up. When I used to sneak into his room, he still only had a double bed. And I told him I wouldn't stay at the ranch and officially be his girlfriend unless we bought a king-size mattress. I got *no sleep* in that double with him."

"Oh, I know, Kate. The walls were thin."

"That goes both ways, *Denny.*"

As if we weren't all sharing the upstairs bedrooms of the main house back when I first showed up at the ranch. There's no privacy in a house that was built over a hundred years ago. Thank God they had enough sense to build the primary bedroom far away from the children's rooms.

"Touché." He shoots finger guns in my direction. "Now look at us all grown up with kids."

"*Shit,* that reminds me—I should call the kids before it gets too late. This is the first time I've been away from Rhett overnight."

I fumble my phone out of my pocket and wince when I realize it's somehow already past eight o'clock. I don't know how so much time managed to slip away when I've been painfully aware of every passing minute all day.

"I'm gonna go out in the hall and order us some food. We're in the city, which means I can download one of those food apps and order *anything.*" Denny stands up with a groan and pats his stomach. "You craving something specific?"

The last thing I care about is eating. Pretty sure any food would instantly come back up, given how unsettled my stomach has been all day. At this point I'm not sure whether it's morning sickness or anxiety.

So I wave him off, tapping Beryl's name, and holding the ringing phone to my ear. My nails lightly scratch Jackson's forearm, connecting freckles and twirling through thin hair, as I wait for Beryl to answer.

"Hi, honey. How's it going?" In the background, there's a familiar squeak of the front door opening then closing. She's likely stepping outside to get out of earshot of the kids.

"It's . . ." My gaze meanders over the man next to me. "It's going. We're in the ICU and he's in an induced coma, but we'll be okay."

"Oh, Kate. I can't even imagine how scared you must be right now."

"I'm trying really hard to be hopeful," I say quietly, knowing Jackson's current state means he probably doesn't hear me, but scared to admit out loud that I'm *terrified*. Terrified he won't live through the night, or he won't wake up from this coma, or he'll never be the man I know and love again.

"I'm hoping with you. And if it feels too hard, I'll hope *for* you."

"Thank you . . . How are the kids?"

"Odessa's worried, but we baked sugar cookies this afternoon and that seemed to help. And Rhett was fine without you. He's sleeping on the couch tonight, I guess, since he's too big for me to carry up the stairs."

"That boy can't make it through a single TV show without passing out." A smile quickly erupts, then fizzles away. "I always make Jackson carry him to bed. . . ."

"He'll be back home and carrying that boy off to bed in no time. And in the meantime, I think tomorrow night we'll set up a bed on the living room floor and have a slumber party."

"They're going to love that idea." I yawn loudly—suddenly overwhelmed with exhaustion from the weight of the day, the darkness of the ICU room, and the comfort of knowing my kids are okay with Beryl. "Is Odessa still awake? I wanted to check in on her before bed."

"Oh, of course." The front door squeals open and clangs shut. "She and I were just having some tea."

After a few moments of rustling and Beryl's muffled voice as she talks to Odessa, a smaller voice picks up the phone.

"You making Gran's life hell?"

I can hear her smirk through the phone. "Always."

"Don't be *too* rough on her, okay? No bringing feral animals into the house."

"What about the barn cats? Sprinkles and Tiny and Gregory are my babies."

"They're *barn* cats. The fact that they're meant to stay in the barn is in the name." I exhale long and hard through my nostrils. "*Please* don't cause too much trouble, okay? I'll be here with Daddy for a while, and I need you to behave. Help with your brother, clean up after yourself, and don't give Gran too much trouble."

"Is Daddy okay?" Her question makes my mouth feel as if it's filled with sand.

"He's . . . yeah. *He's okay.*" I give it a little *oomph* for believability. "He'll be all better in no time."

"Can I talk to him? I want to ask when we can go to a horse sale."

I can't bring myself to tell her the truth. Not like this—over the phone and when I have more questions than answers myself.

My heart bashes my sternum, and despite how tightly closed my eyes are, a rogue tear sneaks out and I hurriedly wipe it away.

"He's sleeping right now . . . but earlier I told him you wouldn't forget about the horse this easily. It's going to be a while before he can take you, Dess. I promise we'll get you the horse, though, okay?"

She's quiet for a moment. Then after a small sigh, she mumbles, "Okay. I wanted one now so I could ride it for the rest of spring break."

"I know you did. . . . For now, though, you can keep riding Daddy's horse like you have been."

"*Fine-uh.*" She groans, and it echoes. Probably off the walls of the mug she's drinking her bedtime tea out of.

Sleepy tea is another tradition Jackson and I started on nights we couldn't sleep while his mom was sick. *Everything* is a tradition he and I started. He's the primary reason for all the good I have. My entire life begins and ends with Jackson Wells.

"Get some sleep. I love you and I'll talk to you tomorrow, okay?"

She mumbles something of a half-hearted agreement and hangs up before passing the phone back to Beryl.

Jackson's cheek is warm and rough against my lips when I give him a goodnight kiss. I linger for a moment, breathing against him and trying my best to inhale his scent around the smell of dried blood and sterile hospital products. When I catch the smallest whiff, I breathe deeper than I have all day, capturing him in my heart, lungs, and soul.

"Remember that night a few weeks after your mom had

died, and I was supposed to move back home the next day?" My lips brush across the shell of his ear as I speak in a hushed tone, hoping against hope that this is the one thing his battered brain picks up on. "I stood in your doorway that night, both heartbroken and madly in love with you. And I told you that you needed to ask me to stay. If you didn't ask, I'd walk away. . . . But you did. You asked. You saved us. So now I'm asking you—*no, I'm begging.* Don't leave me. *Please stay.*"

KATE

The next morning, my eyes itch and burn, and I glance over at where Austin's slouched with his head tilted back and a cowboy hat covering his face. Denny's awake between us, playing a game on his phone. He might've got even less sleep than I did; every time I woke up, I found him sitting there wide awake next to me. He'd give me a gentle smile and a nod to confirm everything was okay, calming my nerves so I could let the rumble of voices down the hall lull me back to sleep.

My chest rises and falls in time with the rhythmic hiss of the ventilator, keeping me sane as it keeps Jackson alive. It doesn't get easier seeing him like this, covered in a blanket of tubes and wires with bandaging wrapped tight around his head.

"Want some coffee?" Denny asks softly once he notices I'm awake. "Was thinking I'd venture downstairs to find some."

I lick my parched lips. Hospital air has a way of sucking the moisture from your skin. "A cup of Earl Grey would be nice, thanks."

"Maybe put a shot of something in it for you?" He chuckles.

"*Now* you're thinking." I smile at him, clasping my fingers around the armrests and pulling myself up to a normal seated position.

"Hey, so, I called Dad last night after you two passed out." Denny glances over at Austin to confirm he's still asleep.

Mere days after their mom died, Bennett Wells decided it was too painful to be on the ranch, so he up and left. At eighteen, twenty, and twenty-five, the three boys had no choice but to take on the multigenerational cattle ranch themselves. It hit extra hard because their grandpa had passed earlier in the year, and not a single one of them really understood what it took to operate a ranch of that magnitude. Dozens of employees, thousands of head of cattle, hundreds of thousands of acres of farmland.

Between the four of us, we managed. We all suffered and sacrificed during those first few years, but we survived. The boys' relationship with their dad, however, has never been quite the same. Denny was the first to let him back in. Jackson held a grudge for a lot longer, but fond memories of growing up with a tight-knit family had him yearning to mend the broken bonds before Odessa was born, for her sake. And since then, Bennett's been around more—not a lot, but more.

But Austin took him leaving the hardest, by far. Honestly, I think we'd all given up on him ever forgiving Bennett, but he surprised us by making his first real effort to form a new relationship with his dad after talking to him at Denny and Blair's wedding.

"Is he coming here?" Austin mumbles under his hat.

"Yeah, he's on his way. Should be here pretty soon, so, uh . . . you gonna be good with that?" Denny tilts his head to get a read on his oldest brother. "Or are you gonna be an awkward motherfucker and make this room even more tense than it already is?"

"I'm fine," Austin replies. "He should be here."

I nod. "Thank you for thinking to call him, Denny."

Leaning forward, I slip my fingers between Jackson's and give a tight squeeze. *We made it through the night.* He's alive, his brain is healing, and one day this entire experience will be nothing but a tiny blip in our story.

"Thanks for staying last night, guys," I say . . . to all three of them, truthfully.

"I'm glad we did. I would've been awake and worried sick in the hotel room all night." Denny slowly pulls himself to stand with a yawn that nearly forces his jaw to unhinge. "I probably would've called you a hundred times to confirm things were all good."

The yawn works its way around the room, with Austin blinking back watery eyes, then I cover my gaping mouth with the back of my free hand.

"Coffee?" Austin asks.

"That's exactly where I was planning on going. God knows I need it." Denny stretches his arms above his head.

"I'll come with you. I should give Red a call—make sure he's got a handle on everything back at the ranch."

I rub at the itchiness of exhaustion behind my eyes. "If you need to go back to the ranch today, I'll be fine here, honest. I know that place doesn't run on its own."

The words barely leave my tongue before Austin's shaking his head, unable to hide how stupid he thinks I am for even suggesting such a thing. "We're here for as long as you are. Or at least I am. I know Blair might need help with the baby so—"

"Nope," Denny interjects. "We're staying here. Blair told me last night that she'll kick my ass for ditching Kate at the hospital." He hooks a thumb toward his brother. "He's checking on Red because he's a control freak. The guys have it handled."

Red's dad started as a Wells Ranch cowboy before any of the boys were even born, and even after town drama drove the Thompsons to move away, Red came back as soon as he'd graduated from high school and has been on the ranch ever since. He might not be a Wells brother by blood, but in this family, that sort of thing has never mattered. He's a brother.

In a gruff, tired-of-Denny's-shit voice, Austin says, "I'm doing my job. My job is to make sure Red is doing *his* job."

"Yeah, yeah, yeah. Same shit, control freak." Denny rolls his eyes and takes a step toward the door. "Kate, you wanna come with us? Get some fresh air?"

My grip on Jackson's hand tightens. "No, thanks. I'll take that Earl Grey tea, though."

I'm not sure I'll be able to stomach it, given the way my stomach's starting to grumble with familiar swells of morning sickness, but I'm so exhausted, I'm willing to try.

Denny smiles. "*Right.* With a shot or two of liquor, coming right up."

"You think they sell *alcohol* at the hospital?" Austin makes a face.

"If there's ever been a place where a lot of people could use a drink, it's here."

The two bicker about it as they exit the room and continue down the hallway. Eventually their voices fade away, and I tuck my chair in directly next to Jackson so my arm follows the path of his on top of the bed, and our shoulders bump into each other.

"If I weren't pregnant right now, your brothers would've already driven me to drink. They bicker like an old married couple."

I pet the bristly five o'clock shadow peppering his cheek, careful not to accidentally nudge the ventilator or anything else as I quietly remind my husband that I'm here, loving him, patiently waiting for him to come back to me.

"If anything, maybe their incessant arguing will make you wake up so you can tell them to knock it off. Or maybe you'll wake up to tell me to shut up. Not that you've ever done that before, even when I probably should shut up." I laugh under my breath. "I'll never forget that first night we sat in the kitchen together, and when I finally let you get a word in edgewise the only thing you had to say was 'You talk a lot, huh?'"

During my second night on the ranch, I'd had trouble sleeping. When I strolled into the kitchen a little after two a.m., the poor guy had been trying to drink some chamomile tea to help with his insomnia. Delirious with my crush on him, a lack of sleep, and an awareness that the old nightgown I was wearing wasn't exactly *sexy*, I resorted to talking his ear off. And after he made that comment—a supposed compliment that wasn't clarified until *much later*—I slid off the countertop I perched on and scurried back to my room. It was weeks before we found our way back into the kitchen in the middle of the night once again and our friendship began.

"This kind of feels like that, since you aren't talking, so I'm left to freewheel. And you know what? I actually *don't* like to talk a lot. I like to talk to *you* a lot. Back then we were strangers, and you're so damn much like your dad and Austin, in that you don't enjoy talking to people you don't know well. Especially back then—you were so shy. But now I love talking *with* you instead of *at* you. . . . I miss your voice. I miss it so much, even though it's only been a day. We've officially turned into that obnoxious couple who can't go a day without each other."

I finally take a breath and notice a stray tear that wiggled its way out to fall down my cheek. I nuzzle into his shoulder, letting his bare skin wipe away the wetness below my eye. And I stay there, relishing his warmth until I drift back to sleep.

The smell of Earl Grey tea wakes me up. I couldn't have been asleep for long, and I feel it. Sandpaper eyelids drag against my eyes, and my vision requires multiple blinks to focus on Austin holding a massive, steaming cup in my face.

"Denny went to meet Dad in the parking lot." He waits

for me to grab the cardboard cup, then cautiously steps backward until he's practically falling back into his usual chair.

"Are you sure you're good with seeing him?"

His face screams ambivalence. "Yeah."

My eyes narrow at him. Swear to God, sometimes I think dealing with the three brothers has been a bigger test for my patience than raising my own children. Denny's voice carries, so Austin and I have time for a long gulp of our drinks and a deep breath before they come in.

Still not enough to prepare for the gut punch of hearing Bennett's voice racked with despair in the same way the three of ours were yesterday. He says nothing but Jackson's name repeatedly. Striding into the room, he all but ignores Austin and me, heading straight for Jackson's bedside. He crouches beside him, placing both hands over Jackson's, and lets out a rattling exhale.

"The doctor said he's doing pretty well . . . they just want to keep him sedated for a few days to let the swelling go down. But last night was the big test, and this guy"—Denny gives Jackson's foot a firm squeeze through the blanket—"passed with flying colors."

Bennett nods, chewing at his bottom lip. Then he looks up at me, and it's my name laced with sadness when it leaves his lips.

He stands, and the next thing I know, Bennett's arms are wrapped tight around me, tugging my head into his chest. He's tall and still coated in ranch-earned muscle despite more than a decade of being away. I breathe out a sob into the cotton of his shirt, and he presses a damp cheek to the top of my head.

If there's anybody here who understands the pain of not knowing whether the love of your life will survive through the night, it's him.

Granted, those circumstances were different. He had time to say goodbye. To prepare.

But is there ever such a thing as fully preparing yourself for the loss of your soulmate? Bennett Wells is living proof there isn't. He barely survived the loss of his wife, and abruptly leaving the only home he'd ever known was his way of saving himself. And of saving the boys, even if it's something they'll never understand. Bennett was leaving that ranch one way or another, and at least this way he didn't orphan his boys.

I get it now.

Without Jackson, I don't know if I could stay at Wells Ranch. I don't know if I could sleep in the bed we shared. Sit at the kitchen table and stare at his empty seat day after day. Walk down the same front porch steps where I leapt into his arms the day I found out I was pregnant with Odessa. Every square inch of that place is a memory, and if those memories were ever to become painful, I'd need to escape, too.

"How are you doing, kid?" Bennett asks as we slowly untangle our embrace.

The pad of my finger presses to the corner of my eye to collect tears. "Been better. But we're going to be okay. He's going to be okay."

"He's going to be okay," Bennett echoes, turning to look over his shoulder at his son in the hospital bed. Then he twists to look at his other sons. "How are you guys holding up?"

Arms crossed tight against his chest, Austin pops a shoulder. "Tired as shit."

"Yeah, I bet. . . ." Bennett blows out a rough exhale.

The room's real quiet. Real tense. To be fair to Austin, it hasn't exactly been chipper in here since we arrived, save for a few funny moments, like when a nurse let out a *loud* fart in the hallway just outside the room and the three of us devolved into a fit of childish giggles.

Finally, Bennett glances around and suggests going on the hunt for another chair and Denny gestures toward his. "I've sat more in the last twenty-four hours than ever before. You can have my chair, old man."

"Might be old, but I can still kick your ass six ways to Sunday," Bennett mumbles but accepts the open seat.

"That's not saying much," Austin chimes in. "I watched Odessa take him out at the knees once."

Denny points at Austin with a correction. "That was a cheap shot. I wasn't expecting it."

"My bad." My hands move to cover my smile. "I told Odessa we don't fight fair when it comes to fighting men."

"I wasn't fighting!" Denny says with a childish, spilling laugh. "She'll have to teach Avery those moves in a couple years though. Apparently it's frowned upon to punch teenage boys for breaking my daughter's heart, so she'll have to do it herself."

Austin clarifies, "Not just frowned upon—*illegal.*"

"You just wait. If you and Cecily end up having a girl, you'll share the same feelings me and Red have about this shit."

Austin shrugs, not denying it.

"I'm glad I didn't have daughters." Bennett sighs. "But I think it's pretty damn fitting you boys have them, given how much hell you raised with girls when you were younger."

"I think it's great. All these badass Wells daughters running the ranch in a couple decades." I take a slow sip of tea, considering it. "Although I'm afraid Odessa will turn it into a barn cat sanctuary."

Austin throws his hands up in the air. "Oh, so basically exactly what she's doing right now."

In the swell of laughter rippling through the room, the next breath of air feels so much lighter than moments ago. I wish Jackson was awake to see this—the slow, thoughtful mending of a fractured relationship between Austin and Bennett—but I have hope that he feels it. Hope that he'll wake up and *know* deep in his soul how much love is around him.

KATE

After the first night, everyone tried to convince me to leave, to get some rest. Assured me it was good for me. But what's good for me is being with my husband, holding his hand, and doing everything in my power to keep him from slipping away for good.

When my stoicism gave way to a tear-filled breakdown, Austin stepped in and demanded everyone leave me be. Since then, no one has dared to comment on my presence.

For the next four days, so many hospital shift changes happened, time lost meaning. I watched doctors and nurses flow in and out of the room throughout the day, pleaded with them for answers, drilled them for information. I watched their movements and read their subtle cues, clinging to anything that seemed hopeful.

Beyond that, I studied every detail of my husband's skin, checked in on the kids—quashing Odessa's worries and listening to Rhett recap all the episodes of *Spider-Man* that Beryl's letting him watch—and reluctantly let Denny teach me how to play poker.

At one point, I became bored enough I got the idea to call my parents, which was an entirely unproductive conversation. I love them—*don't get me wrong*—but they've always been the kind of parents who give you that distant pat on the back when you're sad, instead of pulling your tiny, shaken body into their lap for an all-consuming hug. Not the type to drop everything and drive a few hours to see us. They sent their sympathy, reluctantly told me to call them if I needed anything, as if that wasn't the purpose for my initial phone call.

One of the friendly older nurses slips into the dimly lit room to begin her morning routine. Quickly followed by Dr. Perron, who's told us to call her Tanya. Being on a first-name basis with the ICU doctor doesn't feel like a great sign, if I'm being honest. It gives *take your coat off and stay awhile* energy, as if she wants us to get comfortable in a room that's the farthest damn thing from comfortable.

Austin and Denny no longer immediately straighten up when someone enters the room, but instead wearily lift their heads to acknowledge her. I insisted they could go back to the ranch yesterday, or at the very least spend a night in a decent hotel bed, the way Bennett has been. But the brothers insisted they weren't leaving.

Just in case.

We keep saying those words.

But after four days of watching Jackson lie unresponsive in a hospital bed, covered in wires and tubes, *just in case* has pretty much lost all meaning. At this point, I'm afraid they're here because they're worried about me.

I'm cognizant of the fact that I'm a shell of myself right now. I eat and drink water and walk around Jackson's room only when guilt over the fetus inside my womb weighs too heavy on my heart. I need him or her to be okay, just in case Jackson's okay.

But if he's not . . . how can I raise another baby that looks and acts like him?

I can't.

The nurse scratches her pen across a thick stack of paper attached to a clipboard, dragging me from my intrusive thoughts.

"Good news," Dr. Tanya Perron says nonchalantly, making the boys and me spring to life.

I stare unblinking, on the verge of tears. It's astounding that my body still has the ability to produce tears, given how little sleep, food, or water I'm running on, and how frequently I've cried over the past few days.

"I think we're ready to wean him off the sedation. See if he's ready to wake up."

My breath catches in my throat, and I lean forward to grip Jackson's limp hand. "He's going to wake up?"

Her hand gently raises to stop me. "It's not like waking someone up from a normal sleep—it'll take some time. Could be hours or even days, and it's quite likely he'll be agitated and confused. We don't know anything about his cognitive function yet."

Austin's gruff voice fills the room. "When are you going to do that?"

"The anesthesiologist should be here any time now."

The waiting for days and for hours and for minutes, never leaving this chair for a single second more than necessary, was all for this exact *just in case.* Just in case the doctor came in to wake him up. I don't care much about what happens after that, so long as I get to see his rich, brown eyes, hear his sleepy voice, and feel the hand I'm currently holding tighten around mine.

A few hours later, the gentle clench of his fingers, like the reflexive squeezing movement of a baby, nearly throws me from my chair. The hair on my arm stands on end, leading the way for goosebumps to scatter across my skin.

"Oh my God." I squeeze his hand back, swallowing hard as I search his face for more signs of consciousness. His face remains perfectly relaxed, but surely I didn't imagine the squeeze. "H-he just—he squeezed my hand. Does that mean he's awake?"

The nurse's mouth curves into a slight smile, and she

joins me in watching Jackson for any new motion. "It can take a while for people to become fully alert after such a heavy sedation—especially with a head injury. But he's not receiving any type of sedative anymore, so it's likely he's slowly waking up."

"Jackson . . ."

Chair legs drag across the ground with a grating sound—Austin and Denny sliding in close to the foot of the bed. Opposite me, Bennett's hand repeatedly wrings the plastic bed rail.

"Jackson," I repeat softly. "I'm here. Your dad, Austin, and Denny are, too."

No movement.

I shake my head and glance at the nurse. "I wasn't imagining things. He squeezed my hand before."

"He might be drifting in and out of con—"

An unmistakable squeeze.

I breathe out my husband's name with a relieved, tear-filled sigh and heat travels the length of my spine to settle warmly in my chest when I lean in to kiss the back of his work-worn hand. Somewhere amid the tears, the gentle brush of my lips on his skin, and the full-body ache from days spent in this chair, I feel laughter trying to break through.

I massage his hand. His thumb rubs a slow circle. My insides sing with giddy excitement over the simplest pleasure of having this man hold my hand.

"I love you," I say with a slight waver in my voice.

For the first time since this process started, I take a full breath. Tears form in my eyes.

Denny angles himself, shuffling the metal feet of his chair a few inches to the left, so he can give his brother's shin a reassuring pat through the hospital blankets. "We all love you, bro."

When Jackson's movement stops, so does my heart. I've spent more than enough time staring at his unresponsive body, backlit by the glow of medical equipment responsible for his life. Knowing his body is simply recuperating and tired, slipping in and out of sleep while the effects of his medically induced coma wear off, does nothing to ease the pang of fear deep in my gut when I squeeze his fingers together and receive nothing in return.

Hours pass, the long bouts of deep sleep lessen, and there's a new fluttering of his still-closed eyes. A twitch of his foot. And a rumbling noise from somewhere in his throat when he takes his first full breath with the ventilator switched off.

Jackson may have been the one in a coma, but when his long, dark eyelashes flicker to reveal a sliver of espresso iris, I come back to life.

"Good morning, handsome." I lose my words in a sob. "I'm . . . you don't know how happy I am to see you."

His eyes become slits again. Clearly he's drowsy and struggling to keep them open; they fall shut in a series of long blinks.

Each time Jackson wakes up, his new nurse, Aaron, abandons casual conversation with Denny and Austin so he can focus on the various monitors tracking every aspect of Jackson's health.

And I can't stop staring at my husband. His hooded gaze drifts around the room, never settling in one place for long, and I grip his hand to keep him from floating away. Everything in me wants nothing more than to lock eyes with him.

Funny. Locking eyes with the cute, quiet, middle Wells brother was also my primary goal when I first moved to the ranch so many years ago. A brand-new graduate from the care aide program, I was *thrilled* when Bennett Wells, the boys' father, offered me a job caring for his terminally ill wife. I grew up in the suburbs, with a love for horses and a grandfather who was willing to spend his retirement driving me to and from the stable multiple times per week. A *live-in placement on a ranch?* That was the dream.

Then Jackson sauntered into the big house with wavy, pushed-back hair and a natural uptick in his lips. He was adorably shy—it was weeks before he uttered a single word in my presence—and he averted his eyes the minute they met mine. Slowly we developed a friendship over sipping tea in the middle of the night. And before I'd realized what was happening, my dream became Jackson Wells.

When his eyes fully open, they're awash with confusion and fear. Only a small ring of brown separates his massive pupils from the bloodshot whites of his eyes. In a frantic, uncoordinated movement, Jackson shakes me off and his hands fly upward.

"Jackson," I yelp, frantically catching hold of his forearm.

Even in his weakened, groggy state, he's too strong for me. With concerted effort, he attempts to pull the ventilator tubes away from his face. Thankfully, Aaron seems ready for exactly this, given how quickly he steps in to grab hold of his arms, pinning them to the bed with a huff.

Having the largest nurse on staff in the room for this moment seems intentional. He looks more like a professional rugby player than an ICU nurse. I can't imagine the petite twenty-something we had in here earlier would've been able to stop him with such ease. Jackson's slightly over six feet tall and two hundred pounds, and though he's not strolling into a bodybuilding competition, he's solidly built. Toughened from a life of grueling ranch work.

My teeth dig into the knuckles of my index finger, and I curl my other arm protectively across my stomach, watching as my husband white-knuckles the ventilator tube. His eyes are wild and frightened in a way I've never seen.

Once he's calmly talked Jackson down, Aaron turns to me with a gritted-teeth smile. "*Very* normal. Nobody likes to wake up and feel a tube going down their throat."

On his third bout of panic, it takes all four men in the room to hold him down and pry his fingers from their locked grip around a probe inserted into his skull. I pride myself on being a strong, badass ranch wife—I've pulled calves during tricky births, helped deal with the aftermath of a wolf pack attacking our herd, and slaughtered chickens to feed our family. But seeing him grab hold of that catheter inserted directly into the fluid around his brain has my stomach churning, and I have to shut my eyes, leaning back in my chair with calculated breaths until the moment's over.

"Son, you need to calm down." Bennett's voice is no-nonsense and strict, yet carries no weight. His hands shake as he presses his son's forearm to the mattress.

"Okay . . . Jackson, *my man*. We're gonna have to strap you down for the time being, all right?" Aaron tosses his head back with a long exhale, fighting to catch his breath, then gives me a sympathetic look. "Just until he's not quite so confused. One of us is going to pull a muscle trying to fight this guy."

"My money's on Austin." Denny hooks a thumb in his brother's direction with a shit-eating grin.

"My money's on me," Aaron says through a laugh.

"What are we placing bets on?" Dr. Perron's voice trickles in from the doorway. Her eyes dart from the tight hold Austin has on Jackson's left arm to the display on the intracranial pressure monitor.

"Betting which one of us gets hurt keeping him from hurting himself."

"Oh, my money's on you, too, Aaron." She places a dainty hand on top of Jackson's, and though his eyes have once again fallen shut, she speaks directly to him with a soothing lilt in her voice. "Good news, Jackson. We're going to get this pesky tube out of your throat soon, and I think you'll be a *lot* more comfortable."

The straps that pull taut around his wrists and ankles bring my mind reeling back to the morning in the barn, sobbing inconsolably and watching through a thick film of tears as they loaded him up and carried him away.

My throat burns, bile rising with every slam of my heart bruising my rib cage.

And Denny must notice how uncomfortable I am, because he catches my eye and nods his head toward the open doorway. "Come on, Kate. Let's go grab some dinner and let them do their jobs here."

In four days, I've only left long enough to go to the bathroom. But if I stay here, I might pass out, so I reluctantly rise from my chair and give Jackson's thigh a loving pat before heading into the hallway.

Golden dusk light falls across the hallway in slants, streaming in through slatted window blinds, and it takes a few seconds for my eyes to adjust. Unsurprisingly, I'm still entirely lost in this hospital, but thankfully the guys have spent a lot of time wandering the hallways, and I follow behind them to the elevators.

I thought I'd be an anxious mess the moment I let Jackson out of my sight, but to my surprise, I feel more at ease than I have since the accident. My breathing comes evenly. My shoulders relax. Turns out, my family was right; I needed a break from that room.

"He's finally awake," Austin says aloud and to no one in particular.

Denny leans against the back wall of the elevator with a relieved sigh. "Awake and still strong enough he could kick your ass."

Bennett gives his head a shake, pinching the bridge of his nose but saying nothing.

I raise an eyebrow at the youngest brother. "You basically had your entire body on his legs and were struggling to hold him down. I think he could kick your ass just as easily."

Denny shrugs. "Maybe he gained superhuman strength after the accident."

"Rhett would love to hear that," I rasp.

When we're finally stepping into the fluorescent-lit cafeteria, my stomach rumbles with hunger. The boys have forced me to eat, but between the stress of everything and a constant niggle of nausea, I couldn't fathom more than a few bites. But now, I feel okay. My morning sickness has been entirely nonexistent today. And Jackson's awake-ish. When we go back upstairs he'll be free of the breathing apparatus strapped to his face and hopefully able to talk to us.

Excitement buzzes between us as we eat, and there's genuine laughter, playful banter, and optimistic chatter about how soon he might be able to come home. Surely the facts that he's awake, breathing on his own, and fighting off four grown men at once have to be good signs.

And when we walk back into his room a couple hours later, he already looks so much more like himself, thick facial hair aside. I like it though, and when I sit back down in my usual spot right beside him, I say as much, despite the fact that he appears to be asleep.

Aaron must've seen or heard us enter the ICU wing, because he strides into the room seconds after us. "Good news—he's feeling a lot better without the tube in place. His throat's definitely sore, but he's swallowing and speaking okay. Still some confusion, which is normal and typically doesn't last more than a few days . . . so, uh, don't be alarmed by that."

"So he's talking?" Hope swells inside me.

Aaron drums his fingertips on the back of Denny's chair. "He's talking. I wouldn't expect him to chat your ear off right away—"

Denny snorts a quiet laugh. "He wouldn't chat your ear off *before* he got kicked."

"A man of few words," I add.

"In that case, it sounds like he's on track to be back to his usual self soon. The kind of recovery we love to see around here."

Jackson's eyelashes move across the delicate, freckled skin

above his cheekbones, and when his eyes open, he's finally looking right at me.

My skin tingles in anticipation, and there's a new lightness in my chest.

"Hey," I whisper, blindly feeling for his hand.

I've spent so much time talking to him despite his unresponsive state, and I had planned on giving him a speech better than my last-minute wedding vows once he finally looked at me. But I'm rendered speechless by his searching gaze, so I interlace our fingers on top of his bed and lose myself in the warmth of his palm on mine.

Bennett shifts his weight from side to side, attempting to get comfortable in the world's most uncomfortable chair. "Welcome back."

"About damn time," Denny playfully scolds. "Have a good nap?"

Jackson closes his eyes with the tiniest rock of his head back and forth, and his chapped lips open with a hoarse, barely audible "No."

I dip down to kiss his cheek through an inescapable smile and an ineffable weightlessness. I could float away on the high of hearing his voice.

"I'm so glad you're okay." I nuzzle into him, dragging my nose and lips back and forth across his coarse beard. Tears well in my eyes. "I was so scared I was going to lose you . . . and I don't know what I would've done."

"I . . ." His swallow is audible, and his voice is gravelly and dry. Similar to when he's had strep throat in the past.

I straighten back up, smiling gently down at him and squeezing his hand. The memory of his low voice vibrates through my ribs. "*Shh.* No need to talk if it hurts. I just want you to know I love you so much."

Biting the inside of my cheek, I barely hold myself back from talking his ear off. Telling him about how scared I was, that Odessa's going to be begging him for a horse the second he leaves this place, and that I kept our secret about the baby because I knew how important it was to him that we tell everyone together. There will be time for all of that, now that he's awake. There will be time for *everything.*

Aaron gives him a few tiny sips of water from a Styrofoam cup, and Jackson's exhale has a heavy rasp to it. Eyes flitting from person to person, his mouth tips into the smallest frown. If I hadn't become an expert at reading subtle cues during my time here, I might've missed it.

It must be the confusion Aaron mentioned. I can't begin to fathom what it's like—to be in the barn one moment, the scent of hay in your lungs, the world familiar and grounded—and then to open your eyes to the antiseptic stillness of a hospital room.

"We've missed you." I offer him a smile, tender and hopeful. He doesn't return it, but I press on. I crave his smile like a salve, something to soothe the raw place inside me that's been aching since the moment Red ushered me out of the house. "Odessa's been calling every day, wanting me to remind you that you owe her a horse."

His brows draw together, a crease forming between them.

Okay, he doesn't remember that they were supposed to buy her a horse.

My tongue flicks over my lips, nervous. "Never mind that. I'm just—" My voice catches on the edge of something sharp. "I'm just so happy you're okay."

Jackson's mouth opens tentatively, and I lean in closer to better hear him over the drone of background hospital noise. He squints at me with dark-rimmed, bloodshot eyes. My smile wavers slightly in the space between his lips parting and the ragged sound of his voice.

"Who . . . who are you?"

KATE

For a moment, the words hang between us in the silence, gentle and cruel. A fucking ridiculous smile frozen on my face as I process the fact that he's not joking. All the hope I had shreds into thin paper ribbons with a single sentence.

Who are you?

My world tilts, tipping my smile until it falls from my face. I blink hard, but my vision becomes kaleidoscopic anyway. I pull my hands away and they curl into themselves, nails cutting into my palms, clinging to the echo of his thumb skimming my skin earlier.

Aaron steps in, clearing his throat. "Things are probably a little foggy right now, but Kate's your wife." He gives him a light elbow. "Lucky guy to have a girl like her."

Jackson's eyes sweep over me without a hint of recognition.

"*Wife?*" The hoarseness of a sore throat and the pain evident on his face aren't what makes the word sound foreign—it's the uneasy try-on of a title, a relationship, a life he doesn't remember.

Jackson looks at me in a way that makes my stomach turn inside out. I feel made of glass, and the man who's always held me like the most valuable thing in the world is suddenly haphazard.

"I . . ." He gently clears his throat. "I don't have a wife."

I shatter.

Panic overwhelms my body, and for the first time in days, I need air. I need out of this godforsaken room. Pushing myself out of my chair, I shrug off the feel of Austin's hand on my shoulder on my way to the door.

The door clicks softly behind me and I speedwalk down the hallway, like the pain might catch me if I slow down. I turn a corner, find a quiet alcove near a vending machine, and press my back against the wall.

My hands are shaking. My knees buckle, and I slide down until I'm crouched, elbows on my thighs, head in my hands. The sob hits me without warning—raw and deep, the kind that comes from somewhere beyond words.

Sixteen years. Two children. A whole life. A new baby. And now I'm a stranger.

Tilting my head back, my skull collides with the wall, and it doesn't even hurt. At least, not nearly enough to transpose the agony throughout the rest of my body. Tears slide down past my temples into my hairline.

"Kate." Denny says my name softly. When I open my eyes, he's crouched so close our knees almost bump. "He's just confused right now. This doesn't mean anything."

My breaths come short and shallow. "What—*fuck*. What if—"

"Breathe." He inhales and exhales dramatically to demonstrate.

Eyes locked on his, I force air in and out of my lungs.

Austin saunters down the hall, coming to a stop behind Denny and shoving his hands in the front pockets of his jeans. "Not sure if it helps, but he doesn't recognize us either. He . . . he knows he has brothers but doesn't believe that's us. Dad's the only one he knows . . . he's talking to him."

I sniffle. "At least he knows he has brothers. He doesn't think he has a wife, period."

Denny's lips press together in a thin line. "Aaron said

it'll just take some time. He's gonna remember who you are. Shit's just foggy for him right now . . . give him time."

With a reassuring nod, Austin adds, "You're not the type of person who's easy to forget."

I cradle my stomach, shakily clenching my shirt fabric as a wave of nausea burns deep in my gut. I want to be strong. Want to believe this is temporary, that his memories will come back, that the man I love is still in there somewhere. But right now, it feels like I've lost him.

When it became clear that a few more hours wouldn't be enough to jog Jackson's brain—he wouldn't even look at me when I walked into the room—it didn't take much convincing by Austin and Denny for me to get in the truck and go home. Leaving hurt; staying would've killed me.

Best-case scenario, we get a call from the hospital and I turn right back around because the missing puzzle pieces of his memory magically snapped back into place. Worst case, I'm home with my kids while we wait for him to remember us.

When I stumble through the front door a little after ten p.m., my bones are impossibly heavy. The house is quiet and calm. Too quiet, after nights in a hospital that never fully sleeps. I steal down the hallway, careful not to step on the creaky floorboard, and slip unnoticed into my bedroom.

It feels like him in here. The white duvet's still rumpled from the other morning, his pillows askew because he always sleeps with one tucked under his head and one between his knees, and the musk of his body wash lingers in the air.

I drop my clothes in the middle of the room and shuffle to the shower, where the heavy pelt of water does nothing except remind me of all the times he slipped into the small space with me in spite of my protests that the shower stall wasn't big enough for both of us.

I brush my teeth while staring at his blue toothbrush.

Slather my face in the skincare I haven't used in days—the multi-step toner and serum and cream routine he loves to tease me about. When I comb my hair, I close my eyes and imagine he's brushing it the way he did after I broke my wrist years ago.

Just before I toss my dirty clothes into the laundry hamper, I scoop up the last T-shirt he wore and put it on. At the smell of him, a tear falls from my jaw to splatter on the faded black fabric.

I can't bring myself to sleep in our bed without him. Over the years, he's been on plenty of cattle drives and road trips for the ranch, but this is different. This entire room feels like a shrine to a man who is somehow both here and gone.

This is the undercurrent. Deep sadness held in an innocuous set of cool sheets, waiting to pull me under and never let me up.

So I slip back out of the room without touching anything else, and pad upstairs to Rhett's room. My sweet little boy—the spitting image of his dad—is sprawled across the top of his comforter. I wiggle in next to him and sling an arm around his tiny waist, gently squeezing his hand, and letting the tears flow onto his pillow when he squeezes back in his sleep.

KATE

"Morning, Mama," Rhett whispers directly into my face, waking me up. His small hands are clammy on my cheeks, and his breath blows across my skin.

Without opening my eyes, I exhale deeply and wrap my arms around his body, pulling him into a hug that makes him groan. "Hey, buddy. I missed you."

"Missed you. Did Daddy come home with you?"

My lungs deflate. "He needs a bit more time in the hospital first."

"Is he sick?"

"No, baby. He's not sick. He just . . . needs some time to get stronger."

"Like Spider-Man?"

"*Exactly.*"

"Wait . . ." His hands press hard into my cheeks, making my lips pucker. "Does Daddy have superpowers?"

I fight to lift my head enough that my pursed lips make contact with his forehead, and I let out a loud smacking noise. He giggles and releases my grip while shifting so that he's sitting square on my chest.

"Do *you* think he has superpowers?" I open my eyes as wide as I can in spite of the burning behind them. I need a cool eye compress stat.

Rhett considers my question for a moment. "Yeah. I bet he does."

"I think you're right. We'll have to ask him when he comes home." I grip his waist, hauling him off me and sitting up.

My entire body aches from the combination of days on end with little movement and spending last night sharing a twin bed with a preschooler who kicks a lot in his sleep. I yawn and stretch, listening to Rhett ramble off all the superpower possibilities Jackson might have as he gets dressed for the day.

Wearing Jackson's shirt and a pair of pajama shorts, I follow my son downstairs and into the kitchen. I don't know what time it is, nor do I particularly care, but only a couple ranch hands are still milling about the kitchen. And when they see me walk in—surely looking scarily similar to a zombie—they each grab a croissant from the island and skedaddle out of the room.

Beryl immediately stops what she's doing and slings her striped tea towel over her shoulder. "Are you okay, honey? Tea? Coffee? Food?"

"I could use some water." I plop into my chair at the kitchen table, and it's not long before both Beryl and Cecily are joining me with earnest, sympathetic looks.

"I'm sure it was nice being back in your own bed last night." Beryl reaches across the table to gently rub the back of my free hand with her thin, bronzed fingers.

"I slept with Rhett last night," I murmur into the glass between hearty sips of the cold liquid. "I missed the kids so much. I'm glad they had you guys."

"They always have us," Beryl replies. "You all do."

Cecily runs a hand over her stomach and leans back in her chair. "How are you holding up though? Aus told me about what happened after he woke up. I . . . *God,* I'm so sorry, Kate."

I bite down on the inside of my cheek, still raw from all

the anxious grinding I've done lately. "I hate knowing I'm not there . . . I feel like I should be trying to show him photos and videos, telling him stories, trying to help him remember. But he completely ignored me the entire time I was in the room yesterday . . . so . . ." I blink rapidly and fan my face with my fingers, willing myself not to cry. "So being there seemed like it was doing more harm than good. At least here I'm with the kids . . . and hopefully he comes around soon."

Heavy footfalls end our conversation, and the three of us turn to look at the doorway as Odessa struts in. In the midst of everything, I forgot that spring break has officially ended, and she's back in school. It seems like only yesterday she was Rhett's age, and she spent all her time wreaking havoc on any ranch hands working in the barn or causing Beryl and me to trip over her in the kitchen.

Now she's getting herself ready for school in the morning?

And like me, she's wearing one of Jackson's shirts she must've taken from his dresser while I was gone. Though Odessa's always been tall, so is her dad, and his T-shirt is long enough to be a dress on her.

"Mom," she says in a confused, excited voice, bunching up the hem of the shirt, then letting it go. "Does this mean—"

I interrupt. "Dad isn't home yet. But yesterday the nurse said his recovery so far has been *textbook*—perfect. If he keeps going the way he's going, he'll be home in no time."

I don't know whether that's true, given the memory issues now. He still has his strength and coordination, and his cognitive functions are at or above where they were expected to be, so that's promising.

"Oh." Odessa frowns. "Is he going to be home in time for my birthday?"

In theory, he should be home within the next couple weeks, so long as his recovery continues to go well and he works through the various therapies he needs. Especially since Blair, who's a nurse practitioner, can take over his medical care. In practice, I doubt they'll send him home with a woman he refuses to believe is his wife.

"That's not my call to make, but I hope so."

"Me too. I miss him."

"I know, Dess. *I know.*" Half my lip draws up into a wobbly attempt at a smile. "He misses you, too."

She wraps her arms around my neck and rests her pointy chin on top of my head. "Also . . . I have things to show him."

I hug her tight. "*Things?* Please, that sounds menacing when it comes from you."

"It's not. Promise." I can hear her smirking. It's definitely menacing. "It's barn cat related."

My head tilts and I grip her little wrists to pull them off me so I can look up at her. "Odessa, what did I tell you about the barn—"

Odessa's quick to pull away. "Oh, shoot. The school bus should be here any minute. Gotta go."

"*Wait.*" I beckon her over and grab the hem of her shirt.

With a resolute sigh, her hands meet mine, assuming I'm about to strip the fabric from her body. As if I'm one to judge her for wearing her dad's stuff, while I'm sitting here in his dirty laundry. Not to mention, I steal his jeans on a regular day, because the denim's soft from years of wear, and men's clothing actually has enough pocket depth to be useful.

With a twist, the cotton shirt pulls a bit snug around her hips. And once I convince her to give me a hair tie from her wrist, I have the shirt knotted and tucked against her lower back. It's still comically large on her, but at least it's no longer hanging around her knees.

"Love you, Dess."

I grab either side of Odessa's face and give her a smacking kiss in spite of the disgusted expression on her face. Then she grabs her bagged lunch, and her cowboy boots clunk across the wood planks on her way out the door.

Beryl clasps her hands on top of the table, lowering her voice. "Does he remember *them*?"

I tug at the collar of my shirt, sullenly shaking my head. "From what we gathered yesterday, he remembers some of the basics of who he is: his name, his dad, his brothers—though it took some convincing for him to believe Austin and Denny were who they said they were . . . I think he was imagining them as kids still or something. But he was pretty lethargic, so nobody pressed for much more out of him. I'm going to go back tomorrow. Hopefully by then . . ."

"I'll come with you," Cecily pipes up immediately, cutting off my worried sentence.

"The hospital is hours away, I could never—"

"We're sisters now. It's what I'm here for."

"Honestly . . . I kind of want to go alone. Put on an audiobook and let the drive clear my head a bit."

Her blue eyes narrow at me.

"I'm not saying that because I don't want to be a burden, promise. I think I need to go see him by myself. Yesterday he all but ignored me, and . . ." My tongue skates along the ridges of my bottom teeth. "If he still doesn't remember, I don't want to give him the opportunity to talk to everyone else but me, like he did yesterday. It sounds bad, but I know my husband, and the only way I'm getting through to him is by cornering him."

Beryl snickers. She knows I'm right.

"You can see him by yourself. I'll just tag along for the road trip." Cecily stares me down. In the few years since she showed up here, hiding from her abusive ex-husband, she's come into her own. Found her voice.

I open my mouth, but I don't have an argument, so I press my lips together and stipple my nails over the glass in front of me.

And I'm saved from any verbal agreement that could be held against me when the front door slams shut, and cowboy boots stride heavily down the hall. *Austin.* After so many years, I can tell the boys apart by the sound of their footfalls. Jackson's have always been the quietest, taking up less space than his brothers'.

The moment he enters the space, Cecily's the only thing he sees. Though it surely hasn't been more than an hour since he last saw her, he goes to her before coffee. Planting a rough kiss on top of her head, then holding a hand to her pregnant stomach as he whispers something in her ear.

Under the table, my hand instinctively cradles my stomach and the baby nobody but me knows about. I could tell people now. The secret doesn't need to be kept. Not when the man who asked me to keep it a secret has forgotten.

But if I don't, then it's almost like none of it is real. I can spare myself imagining what life is going to be like to have a baby with a man who doesn't remember me.

I part my lips and force them closed, because an emotionally bankrupt part of me wants this to be unreal. I hate myself for it.

Cecily smiles at Austin, then redirects her sunshine-bright grin at me. "I'm going to the hospital with Kate tomorrow."

"Darlin', you have a doctor's appointment tomorrow."

Her shoulders fall. "Shit. I forgot about that. *Pregnancy brain.* Well . . ." She gives me a stink eye, as if this is somehow my fault. "You got off this time. But next time, I'm coming with you."

I give her the same weak, fake smile I gave Odessa earlier. "I would *love* to have you next time."

"Have you heard anything?" Austin asks me before traipsing across the kitchen to grab a cup of coffee.

"Nothing . . . And I feel like this is one of those rare instances where no news is actually bad news."

Austin sighs with all the disappointment I feel in my bones. "Not bad news. But . . . probably no change yet."

"So, bad news." I toss back the last of my water and look

at Beryl. "I'm gonna clean bunkhouses today. I need some serious manual labor to get out of my head. Do you mind watching Rhett?"

The old woman scoffs. "*Do I mind?* Honey, I would spend every waking hour with that boy, if I could. All my grandbabies.

"As for you? If cleaning bunkhouses and whatever other chores you can find help keep your feet on the ground, go for it. Scrub like hell. Keep those hands busy, but let your brain rest. Don't try to solve this with your thoughts."

I push back from the table, ready to start my day and clean until I'm on the verge of collapse. Then I might stand a chance at sleeping in my own bed.

Cleaning until my nail beds were tattered and every muscle cramped definitely took my mind off Jackson for a little while. Now I'm sprawled across the living room floor, which is golden with the glow of a crackling fire, watching the kids draw pictures for their dad.

The space is a helter-skelter mess of markers, construction paper, and glitter glue. Rhett's sitting cross-legged in nothing but underwear, tongue poking out in concentration as he draws.

I peel myself from the floor, propping my elbows underneath me so I can make out what he's working on. A stick figure with disproportionate arms, a lopsided happy face, and a comically large cowboy hat.

"Is that Daddy?" I ask gently.

"Yes." Tongue swiping across his lower lip, he abandons his brown marker and goes for a cyan one to scribble blobs in place of feet. With pride, he sits up and looks at his masterpiece. "*There.* I gave him super speedy boots so he can run all the way home really fast."

"*Yeah,* so he can get me a horse before my birthday," Odessa mutters to herself.

My throat tightens, and that makes my tone a little higher-pitched. “Speedy boots are a great idea, bud.”

He beams. Struggling to put the cap back on his marker, Rhett stares over at his sister’s lime green construction paper. “Dessie did his hair wrong.”

Lying on her stomach, Odessa has her long legs bent at the knees and her feet swirl around through the air behind her. Without looking up, she snarks, “I didn’t.”

“Yeah, Dad doesn’t have hair that stands up all crazy like that.” He pulls a goofy face, grabbing fistfuls of hair and pulling them out in every direction.

“Because it’s messy from the hospital pillow. *Duh.*” Odessa flicks her ponytail over her shoulder. “Mom, can you tell him that sometimes people get sweaty when they’re lying down for a long time, and it makes it go all weird and fuzzy?”

“No way, man,” I say through a yawn that makes my eyes water. “I’m not getting involved in the hair debate.”

Moving on, Rhett grabs a red marker and gets back to serious business. After a moment of quiet, he speaks up right when I’m on the verge of napping on the floor. “I gave Daddy laser eyes so if the hospital has any bad guys, he can zap them.”

“Very thoughtful of you.” I bite back a drowsy smile, then scooch across the vintage floral rug slightly to get a better look at Odessa’s drawings in the shadows and dancing flicker of firelight. “Great form on that horse.”

Her shoulders roll back, and her marker hovers above the page where she’d been coloring in the mane. “Thanks. It’s going to be an Appaloosa when I’m done.”

“The wording feels a little . . . strong.” I laugh under my breath at where she’s written GET BETTER FOR HORSE SHOPPING in scratchy, little kid font. When she asked for spelling help a few minutes ago, I was admittedly half asleep—a warm fire and plush rug will do that to you—and didn’t care enough about *why* she needed to know how to spell *shopping* for a card to give her dad.

"Dad promised."

"I know he did. And *I* promise that we'll follow through once he's feeling better. . . . I'm sorry you had to miss the auction this time."

"If I wasn't in the way, Dad would've finished his work."

"What do you mean?"

"Nothin'."

I watch her press too hard on the paper, outlining the horse's legs again. She's drawing over what's already there, and the paper's dangerously close to tearing.

I reach over and still her hand, careful not to smudge her work. "Dess, you know none of this—what happened to your dad—that wasn't because of anything you did or didn't do."

She doesn't move for a second. Just keeps staring at the paper like it might rewrite the past if she colors hard enough. "I didn't listen to him and . . . and I didn't mean for him to get hurt."

My heart aches. I keep my voice steady. "None of this is your fault. *None of it.* Okay? Daddy getting hurt was an accident. It's nobody's fault . . . this shit just happens sometimes."

The corner of her mouth quirks upward for a split second, and she whispers, "Swear jar."

I lean into her, softly kissing her on the side of the head. "More money for the horse fund, hey? I love you. Daddy loves you. And he wouldn't want you to be blaming yourself for this."

She nods. I'm not sure she understands or that she'll take my words to heart. And if I could, I'd call Jackson right now so he could tell her himself, but we'll have to settle for me relaying what I know he'd tell her if he was able. If he remembered the accident . . . or his daughter.

Rhett slaps a red balloon sticker in the corner of Odessa's card. She gasps, shooting daggers at him with a single look.

"Rhett," I groan. "That wasn't cool. Keep your stickers on your own card, bud."

"It's so Daddy remembers to come home for Dessie's birthday."

The air thickens around us, weighing heavily on my shoulders. I know both kids, but especially Odessa, are waiting for me to reassure them. To plaster on a smile and elevate my pitch as I squeak out a promise of his return within the next couple weeks.

"He wouldn't forget, dummy," Odessa clips.

Pinching my nose between my index finger and thumb, I say, "Please don't call your brother a dummy."

She ignores me, and I can tell by the tick in her jaw that she's ready to launch herself at her little brother. Granted, he's taunting her with another sticker—consistently moving it toward her paper and pulling away at the last second.

"If you mess with my card again, I'm feeding you to the barn cats."

He sticks his tongue out. "They love me. They won't eat me."

"That big tom cat who bit me the other day would."

This is the first I'm hearing about a cat bite.

And apparently it was a bad enough bite that her threat suddenly means something to Rhett, because he immediately quits messing with her. Though I catch the discreet face he pulls at her after she returns to her drawing.

I let the moment play out. The silliness and chaos. They don't know the full story. They don't understand how bad things are. But I think they feel it—especially her. And she's doing what she always does: hiding it behind attitude and barn cat threats.

When they're all done, the paper and glitter and stickers packed away, Odessa presses her card into my hand.

"Make sure he gets it," she says quietly. "Dad loves my horse drawings."

"I will," I promise. "He's going to love it. Maybe even frame it."

Her chin lifts a little, and I can see that some of the heaviness in her expression has eased.

No amount of deep cleaning could do what this did. What *they* did. For the first time since Jackson woke up and met my eyes with a hauntingly blank stare, I feel like maybe we're going to find our way through this.

KATE

When the warmth of the sun cascading through my bedroom window wakes me up—not that I slept more than an hour or two—I clutch Jackson's pillow and inhale his scent faintly embedded in the soft fabric. Keeping my eyes closed, it's easier to pretend he's next to me. He's here. Life is normal. And in a second, he's going to be laughing with one or both of our kids, hauling them into bed for a snuggle before he starts his day.

Today there are no kids in this bed, either, which feels like both a blessing and a curse. Clearly they've gotten into a routine with Beryl; I can hear their muffled voices echoing from the kitchen. I'd love nothing more than to hold my babies close, but I'm also an emotional wreck, and they don't deserve to deal with that. They need me to be strong and stable, especially when their dad isn't.

My eyes flicker open to confirm what I already know, and I toss his pillow aside with an angry huff. The soreness I've become accustomed to radiates through the marrow of my bones when I pull myself from bed, and this morning it's accompanied by a hollow pang in my gut. Even sixteen years ago, when the simple sight of Jackson in the kitchen each morning set butterflies free in my chest, I wasn't nervous to see him. Knowing I'll see him in mere hours, and he won't truly *see* me, makes me want to vomit.

Hiding out at home instead of being in the hospital to support my husband isn't an option, though, so I wearily trudge to the bathroom.

And then I see something that makes me *actually* vomit.

Blood.

On my thighs.

Infecting the delicate threading of my pajama pants.

On the toilet paper.

In the toilet bowl.

I swallow down the foul taste in my mouth, clutching my heart and my stomach because I don't know which hurts more, and I stumble into the shower fully clothed. The water—cold at first, then scalding—is barely noticeable on my body, numbed by anguish. I crumple to a fetal position, shower water soaking my clothes and washing over my face.

I don't need to be told what this is. My soul knows.

I choke on a silent scream and the burning saliva I can't seem to swallow no matter how often I try. Panic rises like a hot air balloon in my chest, swelling and heating until I can't breathe around it.

Make it stop. Make the pain stop.

The hot water pooled around my body makes my skin itch, and I shakily sit up so I can rake my nails over my torso. The tile's warm and slippery against my back. Wrapped in my own embrace, I tilt my head forward to let water and tears fall in heavy droplets across my lap. My bones are heavy, my head filled with fog, and my heart battered. Pink-hued water swirls around the drain, taking with it what little hope I had for a return to normal. Jackson could regain his memory the second I walked into the room today, and nothing would ever be normal, regardless.

When the water runs cold, the tap unable to be turned any hotter, I force myself to stand and peel the drenched, bloodstained clothes from my wet, shivering, weak body. Clean myself up. Dab concealer over the redness on my nose and ringed around my eyes, swipe waterproof mascara over my lashes, and tousle my hair with enough product to hold a soft wave.

Dressed in Jackson's well-worn jeans and a ranch T-shirt, I dig up the heaviest-duty pad I have. Naturally, it's left over from when Rhett was born. Drunk from exhaustion and the amount of tears shed in the shower, I laugh. The full-body, clutch-my-stomach type. By myself in the bathroom, I giggle uncontrollably about a pad purchased for postpartum being the thing I'm reaching for in this horrific moment.

Life is so fucked up. Fucked up and unfair.

I've never asked for much. All I want is a quiet life with my family. I want to decorate cookies with my kids, wrap myself around my husband at night, enjoy summer days down by the river with my best friends, and spend winters curled up next to the fireplace with a good book. I want us to be happy and healthy and all together. Apparently, that's too much to ask for.

Before I step into the quiet kitchen, I exhale and slap on the final necessity—the fakest smile I've ever worn. A mask for the pain I'm overwhelmed by.

"Morning, honey," Beryl says without looking up from the batter she's making in a giant ceramic mixing bowl.

I head straight for Rhett, who's intently focused on a teetering block tower in the middle of the kitchen floor. Bending over, I cup his head in my hands, breathe in the preschooler wet-dog-esque smell of his messy hair, and place a firm kiss on the very top. He's so perfect. Both of our kids are. Jackson and I have lain awake at night gushing about the incredible humans we made.

This baby . . . would they have been quiet and imaginative like their brother? Or extroverted and fearless like their sister? Would he or she have had Jackson's rich coffee eyes? Or his quick smile?

All the questions I'll never have answers to, and a grief that has to exist quietly, tucked in the crevices around the massive weight of Jackson's accident. Nobody knew this baby existed except Jackson and me. I had my chance to tell everyone, to celebrate, and now it doesn't make sense to drag the entire family farther down.

I opt for coffee for the first time in weeks—I have an uneasy feeling that I won't be averse to the taste anymore. While I pour the steaming dark liquid into a mug, a single tear slips down my cheek. I hurriedly wipe it away before turning around from the coffee machine.

I must look rough, because Beryl drops what she's doing the instant she gets a good look at my face. "Oh, Kate. *Oh.* You should be back in bed."

I shake my head. It'll only make the pain worse.

She lowers her voice, glancing quickly over at Rhett. "Your eyes are bloodshot and you look like you haven't slept in days."

"I *haven't* slept in days. Fitting I look that way. I'll be okay once I properly wake up." To my horror, my mask smiles happily at her.

She tilts her head, seeing through my bullshit. "Kate . . . it's okay not to be okay, especially with everything going on. You can lean on us while you take some time."

"I know." I stir and stir and stir a spoonful of sugar into my cup.

I do know. I could collapse into Beryl, and she'd carry my pain without question. I could ask Cecily to drive to the hospital today, and she'd reschedule her doctor's appointment in a heartbeat. Hell, I could call Denny's wife, Blair, and ask her for a sleeping pill prescription and to confirm that this miscarriage is, in fact, a miscarriage, and she'd have me in her office in less than half an hour.

I have people. And I'm so grateful for them. The way they

love my kids like their own, handle everything in my house so I don't need to stress for a single second, and wait patiently for me to ask them for help.

I have people. But the one person I want to have is in a hospital bed hours away.

"I really need to see Jackson today."

She nods, eyes glassy as she looks me over. "Understood."

Once I've finished my coffee, I refresh my makeup, load my purse with jumbo pads, and sync the filthiest smutty audiobook I can find to my car. By the time I'm leaving, there's a sensation of barbed wire wrapped around my uterus, tugging and twisting deep in my core. Sharp and hot and tight, pain radiates up my back and down my thighs. With enough painkillers, it becomes a dull, grinding ache. Just enough that I can't forget about the loss . . . Not that I could, anyway.

Despite the queasy unrest and all-over tension, I drive the three hours to the hospital alone, because even if I'm a complete stranger to him, Jackson Wells is still my person. Forever. And I need him.

JACKSON

My head fucking hurts. I can feel the slow curve of pain around every fold and crevice of my brain, coiling hot and heavy around where I've been told my skull was cut into.

My shitty Styrofoam cup is about halfway to my lips, trembling and threatening to slosh all over me, when a dark-haired woman breezes into the room and rushes to my side. I think I've seen her here before, but I can't place who she is.

The woman's soft hands tenderly wrap around mine, helping calm the out-of-control shake in my hand and bring the cup to my parched lips. She holds it steady in place with a gentle smile and sad eyes. Glassy and red around the edges, like she's been crying. Something niggles at me, makes me want to ask why she's sad.

After I've guzzled so much I can feel it sloshing in my empty stomach, she pulls the cup away. "Do you want more? I can—I'll refill this for you."

"No, thank you."

"Okay . . ." She steps back, reaching for a chair and pulling it closer to the bed. She sinks into it with an exhale and drops her heavy leather purse to the ground beside her as she gives me a once-over. She points to her own head and grins. "Hey, they took the drain out. . . . That's great."

She smooths a hand across her stomach, pulling at the oversized shirt emblazoned with my family's cattle ranch brand—I recognize it from Austin's shirt and hat—and I realize she doesn't work here.

I think . . . I think this means she might be my wife.

That would explain the sad, defeated expression on her face.

My brain reaches into thin air, feeling around and grasping at nothing while I attempt to remember her name. My nurse, Aaron, reminded me at least a dozen times so I wouldn't look like a total dick when she showed up. And now here I am.

"You're my wife," I state, rather than ask. If I'm right, maybe I'll look less like a prick when I need to ask her what her name is later on.

She bites her lip and nods. "For over a decade now. We've been together for sixteen years."

I grimace. "Shit. I'm *that* old?"

The woman has a honey-sweet laugh. I like the way it echoes through the room and envelopes me, even though it twists the knife that's ever present in my brain.

I grit out, "Sorry, I—"

"Don't apologize to me. You roasted yourself. Don't you dare think about making a comment about how old it makes me." Mid–finger wag, she becomes hazy and distorted by the bright spots in my vision.

I swallow hard, pressing the back of my skull into the pillow and shutting my eyes to focus on calculated deep breaths. The pain's searing, like the voltage of a cattle prod coursing through my skull, singeing brain cells and bringing me to the verge of tears.

"Jackson? Are you okay?" Her voice is distant, each syllable causing another stab of pain.

I groan, squeezing the blankets tight in my grasp. I grip the pillow behind my head, wanting to cover my ears with it, and find the pressure against my skull only intensifies my pain. The woman says my name again, and my hands shake.

She keeps getting louder, and I want to throw up. I want to die.

"Can you shut the fuck up?" My yell is distorted and haggard.

A second, an hour, a fucking lifetime later, the pain subsides, and I notice a hand smoothing over my hair when I return from hell. To my surprise, it's soothing rather than excruciating.

My breathing slows and I slowly open my eyes to discover it's her hand. She's close enough that my next inhale is filled with the soft scent of coconuts. Her fingers comb through my hair, and part of me wants to tell her to stop; a nurse washed it yesterday when they changed my bandaging, but I know my hair's far from *clean* clean. Except her touch feels so good, I selfishly let her continue.

Also, she's gently crying, and I'm guessing that's because of me. So I'm too nervous to say anything that might make her more upset.

"You good, man?" Aaron asks quietly. He must've given me a heavy dose of painkillers direct to my bloodstream via IV.

"What the hell? Told you I didn't want any more drugs." I let my eyes fall shut again.

I hate the drugs. They work, that's for damn sure. But they make my stomach churn, and leave my brain so numb it's like every thought is a mess of fresh ink on wet paper—words and pictures running together. And they make me tired.

I was in a coma for days. I have a wife whose name I don't know. The last two things I want to do more of are sleep and forget.

Aaron side-eyes me, but it's the woman who speaks up first. "Stop trying to be a tough guy. You were literally writhing in pain, and you're covered in sweat—you needed them."

"But I hate—"

"*Jackson.*" She says my name with authority, instantly

shutting me up. Then raises an eyebrow, daring me to argue with her. Keeping one hand gently placed on top of my head, she leans to grab my water and holds it in front of my face. "*Stop*. Have some water and relax."

I take a reluctant sip of the ice-cold liquid. It does feel nice, given how hot I am all over. "You're a bully."

Aaron chuckles under his breath on his way out the door. "Kate might be the most stubborn woman I've ever met. She had some nurses scared to come in here with the way she'd stare them down and hammer them with questions."

Kate.

My wife's name is Kate.

I focus on the forgotten tear moistening her rosy cheek. She's pretty—the nurses who told me so were right. Dark hair, hazel eyes freckled with greens and golds, and a sharp Cupid's bow hung on plump, pink lips.

"I'm sorry for yelling at you." I'm embarrassed to admit I've lost my cool on a couple nurses. I don't mean to. And I don't really know myself, but given how awful my stomach feels each time, I'm guessing it's out of character.

Kate may be stubborn, but she's equally soft. She tuts at me, slowing her caressing touch so she can focus on forcing me to drink more water.

"You know what's funny? I talked your ear off so much while you were unconscious, and I secretly hoped I'd annoy you enough that you'd wake up and tell me to shut up." She holds the water still, letting me take small sips as she keeps talking. "I did some reading about brain injuries while you were in your coma. Outbursts like that are pretty common."

"Do they stop?"

"Sometimes. Some people just get better at managing their anger . . . redirecting that energy in a healthy way."

She continues talking about all the research she's done in the form of reading forums, and watching YouTube videos. I'm sure it's incredibly helpful stuff, but the words blend together into alphabet soup, and I can't manage to scoop them all up into anything coherent.

But I don't mind watching her talk—she has a natural smile, a tiny cleft in her chin pops in and out at random, and her hands move a lot when she speaks. So I take in the rest of her for the first time.

"Are you wearing my clothes?" The question is barely audible. Her hand threading lightly through my hair has my eyelids feeling heavy.

She glances down at her outfit. "Oh . . . yeah. I steal them a lot, but especially when . . ." The muscles in her neck work down a heavy swallow, and she blinks up to the ceiling.

"Especially when what?"

"Especially . . ." Her tongue darts out to wet her lips and her nose crinkles. "Um . . . especially whenever I've been pregnant. Your shirts were the only thing that fit when I was pregnant with Odessa. That's . . . she's our daughter. She'll be eight soon."

My heart twists. "*Daughter.*"

Just like *wife,* the word feels entirely foreign on my tongue.

Kate pulls her hand from my head and digs into her giant purse until she produces a phone. "Let me show you pictures."

"Oh, I . . ." I start to protest, though I don't know why. Maybe because the simple knowledge of a child I didn't know about has me feeling cast out to sea. Seeing a photo of a girl I've known for eight years, but don't know, might just drown me.

Kate, stubborn as she is, won't hear it.

She thrusts the phone at me, and I blink to focus on the screen. A little girl, all freckles and sun-kissed skin, wild hair blowing in the wind, my family's ranch in the background. She looks a lot like Kate, but also a lot like . . .

"She looks kind of like my mom," I muse, shoving the phone back to Kate as I fight for my next breath.

"Yeah . . . Lucy would've loved her. You . . . you know about that, right?"

I nod solemnly, vaguely recalling my dad breaking the news about losing Mom. Maybe it's the medications I've been taking or the brain fog. Maybe I somehow *knew* deep in my bones that she was gone before he'd even told me. But I didn't cry. It didn't cut in the same way finding out I have my own wife and daughter I don't remember does.

"You knew Mom?"

She smiles to herself. "Yeah . . . yeah, I did. I was her care aide for a while. Your dad hired me to help take care of her when she was sick, and that's how I met you."

"We must've been babies."

"We were. *So there.* We aren't as old as you thought." She quietly scrolls on her phone for a couple seconds, then thrusts the phone back at me. "This is Rhett. He's basically your mini-me."

There's a man—*me? I think?*—grinning at a toddler covered in ice cream. It's smeared across the kid's face, and down the front of his denim overalls, and a long vanilla stream is running the length of my forearm.

"We have a son?"

"We do. He's so much like you—quiet, patient, and, like, *crazy smart.*" Her face lights up. "Speaking of which, the kids made you cards last night."

She carefully lifts two folded pieces of brightly colored construction paper from her bag, and I trade her phone for the cards. They're simple paper, covered in crayons and stickers, but they weigh more than anything I've ever held before. I hesitate to open them.

"Kate." *Fuck, even her name feels strange in my mouth.* I think on it for a second, then repeat it with a softer tone. The way I imagine her husband speaks to her. "Kate, I can't look at these. I can't do this."

"You need to look at them, Jackson. We need you to remember your family. We need you to come back."

"No." I slide them onto the bedside cart.

Her jaw tenses and she gives me the same intimidating look she did earlier with the water. She's so goddamn bossy.

I'd get up and get the hell out of here, if I could. I'm stuck with a woman who seems apt to pry my eyelids open and force me to look at these cards, if I try too hard to fight her on it. My mom never took shit from anyone, but I'm a little surprised I married a woman who *literally* wears the pants in the relationship.

The first card must be from the toddler, because it's nothing but scribbles and haphazardly placed stickers. I flip it over, then open it. Granted, I haven't spent any time trying to read or watch television or anything like that since I woke up, but I thought my biggest problems with my brain injury were the memory loss and migraines. Staring at this mess of color, I'm more than a little worried about the state of everything else.

Kate scoots forward in her chair and traces the drawing with a fingertip. "He made you a superhero. You have laser eyes, and giant muscles, and I think this is a cape. You're his superhero."

I quickly set it down and reach for the second.

The sooner we get this over with, the better.

"Odessa wants a horse?" It turns out, I can read. I'm still a little concerned about my ability to comprehend pictures though, because the horse looks more like a giraffe with a drinking problem.

"You were supposed to be taking her to the auction that day. . . . You'd promised her a horse for her birthday."

I scratch at the bandage wrapped around my head and shut the card, then toss it on top of the second. I'm done with this. I want to go back to spending my free time counting the ceiling tiles and watching my own monitors as if they're televisions. It's easier on my heart.

Kate doesn't care about what's easier on my heart. She talks my ear off for an indefinite amount of time, telling me intimate details of our kids. Their likes and dislikes, Odessa's penchant for harassing the barn cats in an attempt to make them love her, Rhett's ability to create incredibly intricate towers out of wooden blocks. She explains that my brothers are both married. There are a ton of kids on the ranch. We have a woman named Beryl, whose job title is hazy to me, but she's apparently like a grandmother to our kids—and this is a good thing, I'm told, because Kate's parents live far away.

She bullies me into drinking sips of water every time the mood strikes, and when food delivery comes in with a particularly heinous-looking plate of lunch, she demands I give each food group a fighting chance. She watches me with an intimidating look as I follow the occupational therapist's direction. When I try to argue with nurses that I don't need or want anything to help with the pain swirling around my head, she shuts me up and insists I don't know what's good for me. She's soft, and tenacious, and unrelenting when it comes to her care for me.

By mid-afternoon, my head tips on the pillow so I'm facing her. Everything feels sluggish and I have a hard time keeping my eyes open.

During a particularly lengthy and confusing explanation of all the friends and family who live on the ranch—her fourth or fifth attempt at helping me understand—my blinks become increasingly long. Yawns frequent. On one of the rare occasions my eyes are fully open, I take a minute to look her over. To really *study* the woman I'm married to. Memorize her and pray I don't forget.

She's pulled her legs up so she's sitting cross-legged in the upholstered chair, dressed in my tattered, baggy jeans and T-shirt. And suddenly a question is niggling at me. "Can I ask—*Never mind*. I can't—Ignore me."

"You can ask whatever you want . . . it's kind of my job to fill in the blanks until you remember everything."

"It's not a question I should be asking. It's too . . . invasive."

"We're husband and wife. You don't know it now, but just last week you knew literally everything about me. There isn't a question on Earth that would be too invasive."

I clear my throat, buying time. "Since you mentioned my clothes earlier . . . and them being the only thing that fit when . . . um, are you pregnant?"

Regret seeps from my pores immediately when the light in her eyes all but disappears in a single blink. It's as if she saw a ghost, and words fly out of my mouth in a stammering, incoherent attempt at backpedaling.

Kate puts her hand up to stop me, eyes shut tight. "No . . . No, I'm not pregnant."

"Shit, see . . . that's why I didn't want to ask."

"It's fine. I told you that you could." She pushes her chair back, and the grating squeal of metal dragged across the floor makes me wince. "You look tired, and I want to get back to the ranch before dark. . . ."

I *am* tired. And for the first time since I woke up, I'm not as scared to go back to sleep. My brain's whirring with stories she's told me, and an image of the smile she has whenever she talks about her kids, and I know I'll be thinking of both while I sleep.

She reluctantly stands, pressing a palm to her abdomen, and rocks on her heels. Purse in hand, she turns to the door, and I wait for her to saunter out.

At the last second, she spins to face me, and I can't explain the sigh of relief that deflates my lungs. I'm counting down the seconds to when my room's silent so I can sleep without her incessant chatter. And yet, I'd love for her to stay.

Kate steps in toward the edge of my bed, then lingers there with her index finger twirling the same loose blanket thread I was messing with earlier.

"Thought you were going," I say.

Movement wary, she bends in close enough the softness of her lips connects with my forehead. And in a low, lulling voice, she says, "I'd never leave you without saying goodbye."

KATE

Before stepping into Jackson's room this morning, I detoured through the walk-in clinic on the lower level of the hospital and all but confirmed what I'd known to be true since I woke up with blood pooled between my legs. Another round of bloodwork in two days will undoubtedly show that there's no pregnancy hormones left. The work my body did for seven weeks is gone, and the heartache is here to stay for the rest of my life.

The physical pain of miscarrying—the cramps that sent fire coursing down my legs and elicited a dull pain in my lower back that was eerily similar to the back labor I endured with both Odessa and Rhett—or even the emotional pain of losing what could've been was nothing compared to the pain of slipping a calm mask over my face and telling Jackson I'm not pregnant. There wasn't a single blip of recognition in his eyes. Nothing to indicate that merely a week prior he was pressing soft kisses to my stomach and talking about how excited he was for another baby. That man would have a dozen kids if it were up to him.

And while I didn't lie to him today, it felt like I did. For the very first time, I sat across from my husband and I didn't tell him the entire truth. That I was pregnant mere hours before. That I was trying my best to keep my composure while actively bleeding. That I fear it's my own doing—the lack of sleep or proper nutrition or the shameful thoughts I sometimes had about things being easier if . . .

Stepping out of his room, I walked in time with my short, shallow breaths to the elevator bank. My eyes shut until I heard the clamorous sound of the elevator stopping. And thank God that tiny space was empty, because I fell apart on the slow descent to the parking lot.

My car door slams shut and I fill my lungs with the aroma of damp earth. The air's cold, but not quite cold enough to turn the drizzle to ice. For a minute, I look out across the ranch I've called home since I was twenty years old. The massive white barn and the staggered cabins and bunkhouses carrying on into the dark. Soft glow filtered through windows painted on the rain-soaked grass. Beyond that, hayfields and mountains and herds of cattle carry on, and though I can't see them right now, I've looked out over this view enough times I can picture it vividly.

When Jackson thinks about the ranch he grew up on, is it a hazy recollection of a ranch that feels fictional, like something he's read in a book, or is it in full Technicolor?

The big house where we live is a gathering place, of sorts. Before I came around, when the boys' grandfather and mother were alive, it was apparently much the same. The ranch was teeming with life—ranch hands, their wives and children, old family friends relaxing on the porch, sipping coffee around the kitchen table, or drinking beer on the riverbank. Then Lucy fell ill, and the entire ranch became crestfallen.

Jackson and I worked hard to revive the energy, and tonight I can hear laughter and the faint echo of music reverberating off the walls. It's warm and cozy and smells like freshly baked brownies. I find Odessa curled up on the couch watching some kids' cartoon with talking dogs. Red and Cassidy's toddler, Hazel, is fast asleep with her head on Odessa's lap, and Rhett's taking up more than his fair share of the couch, sleeping with his mouth hanging wide open.

I creep in, careful not to wake the sleeping littles, and crouch next to Odessa.

She looks at me, wide-eyed, and asks in a hushed voice, "Did you give Daddy my card?"

My whisper matches hers. "He loved it."

"Is he coming home soon?"

"I hope so, Dess. I hope so." I kneel on the antique rug in the middle of the floor and reach for the remote to pause her show. "I need to have a big-girl talk with you, okay?"

Her nose scrunches, collecting the small smattering of brown dots on her skin. During the summer, she'll have more freckles than the sky has stars.

"First of all, I want to make it clear that Dad is healthy, okay? The doctors are amazed by how quickly he's recovering . . . but . . ." A boulder-sized knot wedges low in my throat. "But . . . he doesn't remember anything from before the accident."

"Like that he was gonna buy me a horse?"

"Well, yeah . . . *that* and more. I'm telling you this because I know you listen to the adults when they're in the kitchen, or the guys are talking about stuff down in the barn. I don't want you to hear something and feel confused or scared."

"Does he remember when Santa tracked soot across the floor on his boots last year?"

"No, Dess."

"Does he remember when we hid those barn kittens in my closet?"

I raise an eyebrow. "When you what?"

"Oh, I forgot you didn't know about that." She presses her lips tight together, but a menacing grin plays at the corners of her eyes.

"He doesn't remember. . . ." I mull over my words, trying to choose them carefully.

I sat down with her prepared to spill the truth of the situation because I'd rather her hear it directly from me instead of catching part of an adult conversation elsewhere. But now that I'm here, it's dawning on me that I have to tell her Jackson doesn't remember her. It's not only that he doesn't remember the shenanigans they got up to. He had to be told about her very existence, and he only knows her from the pictures I showed him today.

"Odessa, Daddy's brain was injured, right?" I squeeze her knee. "And the brain has a *lot* of extremely important jobs. One of those jobs is holding on to your memories . . . and his brain's having a hard time doing that right now."

"So he doesn't remember anything at all?"

"Very little."

Her eyes cut to the floor, and the small twitch of her lips tells me she's thinking hard. Making sense of something that doesn't make sense at all.

"Does he remember me being born?"

I exhale heavily through my nose. "No . . . No, Odessa. He doesn't. *Not yet.* We're hoping he just needs time to heal, and he'll remember everything again."

"Oh." Tears brim her eyes and when I lean in to comfort her, she leans away. For a moment she stares at the paused television, silently processing. "S-so am I like . . . am I a stranger?"

"*No,*" I clip. "No, baby. He knows who you are, and he loves you. He just doesn't have all his memories right now."

She mulls that over for a second, then, with a quivering lip, asks, "Does he remember you?"

"Not yet."

Not yet. Two tiny words containing immeasurable hope.

"But . . ." She drags the back of her hand across her wet eyes. "Does his brain need to be all better before he comes home?"

"Nope. He should be allowed to come home soon, and

we'll take care of him here." I hold her small hand in mine, running my thumb along the length of each finger. "I showed him pictures and videos, and told him all kinds of stories today. Talked his ear off. Even if he doesn't remember us yet, he'll feel like he does."

"Good. I want him to be back, even if his brain is still hurt."

I sniff against the sting in my nostrils. "Me too. It's weird not having him here, isn't it?"

She nods. "I miss his bedtime stories. Don't tell her, but Gran doesn't do as good of a job as Dad does."

I chuckle softly. Jackson's imagination runs wild at bedtime, coming up with stories on the spot that tend to incite a lot of laughter, squeals, and even the occasional bed-jumping. And though I roll my eyes and poke my head into the room to remind them all that story time is meant to be *quiet time*, I love the love they have for each other too much to be mad.

"He is *really* good at bedtime stories. . . . Finish your show, then I'll make an attempt at doing story time justice."

"Is Daddy going to be able to tell us stories when he comes back home?"

The wistful shimmer in her eyes cinches something around my heart.

"He might be a bit rusty the first couple times, but I'm sure he's still got some good stories in there." My index finger taps the side of my head, and I wink at Odessa.

After giving Rhett a quick kiss, I slip out into the hallway and head toward the busy kitchen. Everyone's gathered around the table, drinking and snacking and yapping, and when I walk into the room, Denny's wife, Blair, pulls out an empty chair for me.

The ice-cold beer in the fridge is awfully tempting, but somehow a tiny part of me is holding on to hope that the heavy bleeding, excruciating cramps, and empty feeling in my heart are false alarms, so I opt for iced tea.

The first sip hits my lips at the same moment I plunk into the empty chair, and Blair lovingly pats the top of my thigh.

"How was it?" she asks.

All the chatter ends immediately, and attention redirects to me. To that question. I'm sure they're all dying to know whether Jackson's memory is back.

"Intense." I settle into the well-worn wooden seat, looking at the worried faces staring back at me. They might not all be related to Jackson by blood, but he's a brother to each and every one of them. "He . . . he still doesn't remember much, and maybe it'll come back or maybe it won't. The doctors keep saying his brain needs more time to heal, so . . ."

I glance over at Denny, who's cradling his sleeping daughter in his arms, and my heart pinches.

"But he's doing okay, otherwise. He's being stubborn about taking anything for pain . . . but I'm even more stubborn, so he's following doctor's orders now. I wish he was in the Sheridan hospital, so I could go every day, but with the kids . . ."

Denny's beer bottle clunks against the wooden tabletop. "We're gonna go see him tomorrow. I'll bully him for ya, Kate."

"Oh, *please*. You just want an opportunity to win a fight against your brother."

Denny shoots a finger gun in my direction. "Payback for *years* of him picking on me as kids."

"Any word on when he'll come home?" Red asks from the far end of the table.

I shrug. I tried to coerce somebody at the hospital into giving me a definite date this morning but was met with a lot of the usual *we'll see* bullshit. One person said it could be as early as next week, and that's what I'm choosing to cling to. "They removed the drain, and everything's stable, so the plan is to move him to a regular room as soon as there's an available bed. Hopefully home within the next week."

"Good." Blair smiles at that, and her hand squeezes my leg. "That's an amazing recovery."

"Yeah . . ." I nod, hesitating before adding, "Now we just need him to remember his family."

Everyone retreats behind their drinks like they've rehearsed it, all of us collectively avoiding eye contact with the rawest part of the truth. Nobody wants the responsibility of formulating a response. Being the person who has to keep my expectations in check while simultaneously filling me with hope—*fucking hope*. That's all we have, and sometimes it doesn't feel like enough.

So I push past the knot in my throat and clear my voice. "It's fine. If he doesn't remember falling in love with me, I'll start over. Show up at the hospital in tight jeans and a push-up bra. Ask him where a girl can find a hot cowboy around there."

Austin chokes on his drink.

Denny grins, not missing a beat. "Look out, everyone. Kate's entering her buckle bunny era."

I point a finger at him. "You know . . . I think there are bedazzled jeans somewhere at the back of my closet."

Red's wife, Cassidy, drums her fingers against her chin thoughtfully. "You should cut them into short-shorts and show some leg. If you cut 'em right, you'll get the perfect sliver of exposed butt cheek, too. He'll love that."

"Cass, if you own shorts like this, you're putting them on as soon as we get home." Red bumps his shoulder into hers.

"Booty shorts are a great call," I agree. "Bet he falls in love twice as fast if I show up looking like I just got off a shift at Coyote Ugly."

Cecily's hand slaps down on the table, excitement sparkling in her eyes. "I just remembered I have a pair of sparkly cowboy boots. No chance they're fitting on my swollen feet, so you can borrow them. You need a little sparkle when you're spiraling in front of your amnesiac husband."

"Oh, I *definitely* want to look hot while I spiral." I laugh, letting it stretch enough to carry me through the underlying sadness of this conversation.

Austin finally recovers from choking and mutters, "You're all insane."

Denny raises his cup in mock salute. "To Kate's buckle bunny era. May it be short-lived and wildly effective."

JACKSON

Following yet another physical therapy appointment—it feels like I'm constantly being dragged from one type of therapy to another lately—my skull sinks into the plush pillow Kate brought me the other day, and I shut my eyes.

She's been here almost every day over the past week, and on the days she isn't, at least one other family member always is. I've spent enough time with Kate that she's cemented in my mind, and I'm getting pretty good at recognizing which brother is which when they walk into the room. But otherwise the various visitors I've had blend together; they're nameless, faceless blobs in my memory.

And every single day, it feels like I'm letting my family down. Not because of anything I've done, but because of what I can't do. I can't remember most of my life before the accident. Trying to recall moments from my early childhood feels like driving through patchy fog—catching glimpses of moments in time as I pass them by. After that, the haze only becomes more dense, more dark, until it's pitch-black.

It hurts me the most to hurt Kate. Maybe it's because I'm able to comprehend that she's my wife, and I feel like a piece of shit for not being able to magically fix this for her. Maybe it's because she does the worst job of hiding her disappointment when she steps into my hospital room and realizes my head's still fucked up. The smile drops a little. The tone of her voice raises a little. And I think a part of her heart dies a little.

If I could find a way to remember Jackson Wells, I'd do it for Kate.

That's not an option today, but thankfully I have a surprise that should keep the smile held firm on her face.

Kate strolls into the room a little past eleven with an iced coffee in her hand. She's wearing my jeans—I've quickly discovered her comment about wearing them during pregnancy wasn't the whole story because, clearly, she wears them all the time. Today they're paired with a cream-colored button-up shirt that's partially tucked in, and a couple dainty pieces of turquoise jewelry. She has more color in her face, like she finally got a restful sleep.

Kate has a natural beauty that's caught me off guard a few times over the last week, but seeing her cheeks tinged pink and eyes without harsh bags under them, she's a knockout. And I feel a weird sensation that I assume is what the leads in the rom-coms I've been bingeing late at night refer to as butterflies.

"Hey, handsome," she says as she settles into her usual spot on a worn-out upholstered chair with metal armrests and legs.

"Don't make yourself too comfortable." I smile at her as I toss back the bedding and shuffle to the edge of the bed.

She starts to stand, preparing to help me. With what, I'm not sure. I can get myself to the bathroom and even take a short walk around my wing of the hospital without assistance.

I hum quietly to myself as I begin gathering my belongings from my bedside table. Considering I arrived with nothing but the clothes on my back, I've amassed quite a collection of things. It seems my family can't visit without bringing me something they think might be useful. And for a bunch of people constantly asking when I'll be discharged, they've made it seem like I'll be here for the rest of my life with some of the shit they've left here. More than one pair of slippers is entirely unnecessary considering I don't even hit a thousand steps in a day.

My hands pause when I look up at her, temporarily losing myself in the green roaming through her glimmering irises. The anxiety about going home quiets for a second. "Let's get out of here."

With a smile that squints her eyes, Kate scooches forward in her chair to help collect my things. "Finally letting me bust you out of this hellhole?"

"Exactly."

"Are you ready to leave? I mean . . . you feel okay about going to the ranch? Seeing the kids and everyone else?"

The thought of returning to a place I don't remember, with people I barely know, scares the hell out of me. But the alternative is staying here, where I never get a moment's peace between therapies, medical tests, and ceaseless hospital noise. I hate the thought of that so much, I'm willing to deal with the discomfort and fears about leaving. About going *home*.

"Yeah. I'm ready."

"In that case, this is the slowest escape from prison I've ever seen." She stands up and holds her giant purse wide open. "Just sweep all your stuff off the table into my bag and let's blow this popsicle stand."

Our hands brush as together we do exactly that, and warmth floods up to my cheeks.

"You're not gonna question this?" In an effort not to look at her, for fear the blush will spread, I stare at my slippered feet and silently curse my family for not bringing me a pair of outdoor shoes. Who knows what happened to the ones I came in here wearing.

"One thing to know about me, Jackson Wells—I'm ride or

die. If a person I love needs me to do something like stand up to their abusive ex-husband or bust them out of the hospital, I'm doing it without question."

I push myself to stand, holding still for a moment as a stabbing pain in my skull sends shivers down my spine. Then I nod at her, and she gestures for me to lead the way.

Once we're in the hallway, I rely on Kate to show me the way, because I've been walking the halls in my hospital wing during physical therapy, but they haven't exactly shown me the route to escape the building.

She walks slowly without needing to be asked and looks over her shoulder no less than once every thirty seconds. Each step makes my brain feel as if it's about to blow the bone flap they replaced in my skull like the cork on a shaken bottle of champagne. One wrong move and *pop*.

Thankfully the elevator has rails I can support my body weight with and, as if she knew I was getting out today, Kate's illegally parked in a loading zone just beyond where the elevator opens to the parking garage. She hovers over me while I clamber into the passenger seat, likely assuming I don't remember the basic function of a seatbelt. *I do.*

The car smells of a bizarre combination of coconut, Cheerios, and the slightest hint of cow shit. My nose reflexively scrunches at it as I look around the backseat, taking in more clues about my life. The car seat is *definitely* the culprit for the Cheerios smell, based on the amount of sandy crumbs packed into every crevice. Next to it, there's a doll with a botched haircut and streaks of marker across her naked body.

Kate slides into the driver's seat and catches my eye. "The kids are basically a pair of tornados destroying the house, car, flower beds. . . . It's a good thing they're cute."

"Does the house smell like Cheerios, too?" I glance around the front of the car, and I home in on a Polaroid picture wedged against Kate's sun visor.

She laughs softly. "During breakfast, sometimes. But no,

mostly it smells like baking. I bake an *obscene* amount of bread every week to make sandwiches for all the cowboys. And Beryl and Cecily usually make at least one dessert every day."

I reach up and pluck the photo from the visor as she speaks. Me and her. She's in a beautiful floor-length strapless dress. I've got a tight hold on her waist, and her hand's splayed across my stomach. She seems to be mid-laugh, and I have a matching grin—staring directly at her, rather than the camera.

Kate clears her throat. "That's from Austin's wedding a couple years ago."

"We look happy."

"We were." Melancholy lilts in her honey-sweet voice, and she pulls the car out of the loading zone before we can be ticketed.

The sun hits with a fury the second we pull out of the underground parking garage, and I wince like a vampire, instantly drawing my free hand to cover my eyes as I blindly feel with the other to put her Polaroid back. Already the throbbing in my head is more intense. God help me, I hope it's only temporary because I've been cooped up in a hospital, and not because my brain injury means I can't handle the brightness of midday sun.

"Here." Kate nudges my arm. "Wear my sunglasses. See if it helps."

Despite the fact that they're turquoise aviator frames, I slide them up the bridge of my nose and breathe a sigh of relief when they do, in fact, help with the hammering in my skull.

"Thank you."

"They look great." She giggles. "Definitely fits with your hospital escape outfit. A T-shirt, sweatpants, slippers, and women's sunglasses. *Hot.*"

"Don't forget the jewelry." I hold up my left arm, adorned with a white hospital bracelet, and I watch Kate's eyes lock on my hand. Despite all this time without wearing one, the indent of a wedding band remains. "I . . . sorry I don't have a ring."

She shakes her head. "That's a silly thing to be sorry about. They had to cut it off because it was practically embedded in your finger. And even if that weren't the case, I don't expect you to wear a ring to symbolize a marriage you don't remember."

Those words burn and churn in my gut. *Will not remembering ever feel like less of a betrayal?* "Even if I don't remember taking vows, I'd stand by them."

"I know you would. Memory loss or not, you're a good man, Jackson. The best, actually." Her gentle touch grasps my hand and an oddly familiar energy pulses through my veins. "Besides, if there's any type of band that should be in the back of your mind if you're thinking about being unfaithful, it's a castration band. And I think you know me well enough by now to know I wouldn't play about using one."

Sure enough, there's a phantom pain in my groin at those words, and I shudder with a nervous laugh. Kate tips her head to look at me with a smirk. It's cute and wicked, and I wouldn't put it past this woman to castrate any man who messed with her.

Especially after I saw the way she took no shit from anyone in the hospital. Not mean. *Never mean.* Kate simply wasn't going to listen to excuses or be given the runaround when it came to anything I needed.

"I knew you were getting out of there today," she says once the car's been quiet for a moment. "Sorry to burst your bubble. But I figured you'd realize it when we pulled up to the pharmacy in a second, and I happened to have your prescriptions in my purse."

"Honestly, I wouldn't bat an eye. You have everything but the kitchen sink in that thing." I roll the window down a crack to catch the breeze against my face. "Although, you could make up for lying by 'forgetting' to fill my painkiller prescription."

"Fat chance. You need those, and I'll stand there watching you swallow it, if I need to."

Well, it was worth a try. With a huff, I slump deeper into the seat, and when we pull up to the pharmacy a minute later, she slowly pulls her hand from mine. I feel that loss down to the marrow of my bones.

How this woman can have me genuinely fearing castration one minute and missing the warmth of her touch the next is beyond me. But the moment she's dropping back into her seat, I'm reaching for her.

Hours after leaving the hospital, Kate woke me from my routine afternoon nap, announced we were almost home, then watched me with the eye of a hawk as I took my medications while cruising down the bumpy, windy dirt road.

The sky in this valley is overcast, and the afternoon sun is hung low enough in the sky it's filtered through towering, dense treetops. I carefully examine every crooked tree, every bend in the road, every sign, waiting to see if something clicks. If anything on the route to my family's hundred-year-old cattle ranch—a road I've surely driven thousands of times—is memorable enough to send my memories flooding back.

Then we slow to a crawl, turning onto what appears to be a driveway.

"I recognize that sign." Bewildered, I stare up at the carved wooden sign hung high above the driveway. Given that WELLS RANCH is etched into the timber, it's not exactly a monumental moment that I have a gut feeling I know this place.

Kate slams on the brakes, and I lurch forward in my seat. "You do?"

"I do. It was in a dream I had the other night."

A wave of hope washes over us, so deep I could drown in it, until Kate continues down the driveway and I watch the naïve hope dissipate from her big doe eyes the moment it becomes clear this version of myself has never seen the ranch that raised me. In the hospital, I often tried picturing this place, but it felt as if I was looking through chunks of broken glass.

The car comes to a stop in front of a large white house with gable roofs sheeted in metal and a welcoming front porch. Thick greenery, painted with a small smattering of early spring blooms, is nestled at the base of the porch, and the late sun casts overwhelming shadows over the lawn and gravel driveway. Everything is almost familiar, but not at all what I had imagined.

"This is home," Kate says on a sigh. "It feels weird introducing you to the house you grew up in. . . ."

"It feels weird knowing I've lived here my entire life but I don't have that home feeling."

She turns the key to shut the car off, and twists in her seat to look me in the eyes. "Yeah, I can imagine. Want to sit out here for a minute? Or head inside? I told everybody to leave you alone today, so it should only be Beryl and the kids."

Anxiety burrows into the most vulnerable part of my heart. I've been informed I'm a bit of a superhero around these parts, and I'm sure Kate meant it to be a confidence-booster, but it only ups the ante. If these kids were used to an absent father, they wouldn't expect much. They wouldn't be entirely crushed when I inevitably under-deliver and struggle to remember the most basic information about them. Thankfully, Kate almost never stops talking about them, so at least I have their names memorized.

"Odessa knows about my fucked-up head?"

She gives me a look. "It is *not* a fucked-up head. It's a perfect head that went through some serious trauma."

"She knows about my perfect head, then?"

Kate rolls her eyes. "*Yes*. Rhett's too young to understand, so I didn't bother trying to explain. As far as he knows, you were 'big hurt' and had to spend time in the hospital, and now you're coming home but still need some time to recover."

I nod. "Let's go inside. Get the hard part out of the way, I guess. . . ."

Kate insists on helping me to the house, looping her arm around mine for the slow shuffle across thick, dewy grass. The mountain air feels glorious filling my lungs and cooling my skin, and for a peaceful moment, the two of us stand in silence, breathing it in. Clouds drift overhead, temporarily blocking the sun, and I finally take Kate's ridiculous sunglasses off. It's funny how much more I like the view of the ranch when it's not weirdly orange-tinged.

It seems I was too cocky in my physical abilities, because the few steps up into the house are trying. But Kate, God love her, is apparently the most patient person in the world. She doesn't comment on the slow pace or the way I stop to take in my surroundings from every new vantage point on our slow journey to the front door, even though there's a comment to be made about whether I'm simply stalling. The anxiety around meeting my kids is an ever-present beast churning in my guts.

Stepping inside, I'm happy to discover Kate wasn't lying about the house smelling like fresh baked goods. The space is large, yet cozy, with antique furniture and knickknacks and family photos filling every potential empty space. Soft voices giggle from deeper within the house. The phantom sense of nostalgia and familiarity settles the tension bunched up between my neck and shoulders.

Kate grabs my hand, and her thumb draws a slow heart on the back of it. "Ready?"

Ready as I'll ever be to meet my children, I suppose.

After a curt nod, she tugs me down a narrow hallway, and I catch the eye of my mom in a family photo. I want to slam on the brakes and insist we linger here for a moment, looking for something to pull my memories from whatever deep crevice they've become lost in, but I know there will be plenty of time for staring at the photographic evidence of my life on this wall. So I step into the brightly lit kitchen and blink at the faces staring back at me.

"Daddy!" the two kids chime in unison. It's a race to see who can get up from their chairs at the kitchen table first, and they sprint toward me.

"Let's be gentle, please," Kate warns them. Her hand slips from my grasp and a much smaller one is quick to take its place.

A little girl squeezes her tiny hand around my fingers, staring up at me with eyes that match Kate's perfectly. At the same time, a tiny boy is trying tirelessly to climb my leg like it's a tree trunk. I struggle to stay upright until Kate pulls him from me much like one removes a tick.

"Let Dad sit down before you maul him," Kate scolds him.

The girl, Odessa, guides me toward the table, never letting me out of her periphery. And once I've sat, she's quick to claim the empty chair beside me. Her brother, Rhett, is much less understanding of personal space, and he climbs right into my lap. Sticky hands mat down the hair on my bare arms, then he wraps them around my neck to pull me into a suffocating hug.

"I missed you, Daddy," he says softly, pressing his palms to either side of my face so he can lock in on my eyes.

He doesn't know about your fucked-up head, I remind myself.

This is a little boy who hasn't seen his dad in a couple weeks. A little boy who made that superhero card for that man. And I sure as hell don't feel like his dad. Don't even feel like an uncle or cousin or good family friend. Rhett may as well be a random kid I crossed paths with in the hospital.

But he thinks I'm his dad.

"I missed you," I lie through my teeth, justifying it because *Old Jackson* would definitely miss his son, if even half of what Kate told me was true. "Were you, uh . . . were you good while I was gone?"

"Better than Dessie."

Odessa scoffs. "Don't listen to him. He's dumb."

Kate's eyes go wide. "*Odessa.* Come on. You know better."

"As if knowing better has ever stopped her." A feminine voice I don't recognize floods the space, and an elderly woman strolls into the kitchen from the hall.

Her hair's silvery gray all over, and it's tied back in a bun at the nape of her neck. Her rich brown skin wrinkles and creases in a series of lines around her mouth and eyes when she beams at us. She brushes her hands over the fronts of her dark-wash denim and adjusts her simple white T-shirt before heading directly for me.

"I'm Beryl." The old woman crouches in front of me, holding out a hand for a gentle handshake. "Kitchen manager, slash the crazy old lady who spends a lot of time singing in your kitchen—when I'm not doling out unsolicited advice to everyone. And I am *so* happy to see you, honey."

"Beryl," I repeat, willing it to stick. I vaguely recall Kate telling me about her, but the specifics are hazy.

Rhett laughs, his body twisting on my lap. "You guys are silly. Daddy and Gran know each other."

I look at Kate like she's my lifeline.

Beryl stands, playfully smacking the heel of her hand against her forehead. "Oh, *duh.* So silly of me. Hey, Rhett, honey? Want to help me mash the potatoes for dinner? I'll let you lick the masher afterward."

Don't have to ask him twice. He practically leaps from my lap and goes running for the opposite side of the massive kitchen island. There must be a step stool handy, because one second all we can see is his hair above the countertop, and the next his entire upper body is there.

"Was the hospital food yucky?" Odessa finally speaks up. Her feet drag back and forth along the floor under her chair. "Auntie Blair said she's been in a lot of hospitals—she's a nurse pra . . . uh, nurse pratch . . . I don't know, but she said the food is like cat vomit."

"She's a nurse practitioner." Kate moves through the kitchen to grab a glass and fill it with water. "And I feel like that might've been Uncle Denny who compared it to cat vomit."

"Yeah." Odessa nods thoughtfully. "Uncle Denny would know what cat vomit tastes like better than Auntie Blair, I think."

I pull a face that's caught somewhere between amusement and disgust. "I sure as hell hope he doesn't know what it tastes like."

Odessa's mood shifts on a dime from giggly and silly to stone-cold, and she points toward the china cabinet at the far end of the table. "Swear jar."

"Swear jar?" I rack my brain, trying to remember what I'd said that would require money being added to a swear jar.

"I'll give you a free pass, since you don't know about it. Every time an adult swears, they have to give *me* money. I've been saving it for two whole years, and I'm gonna buy hot pink tack for the horse you owe me." She crosses her arms and juts her chin up toward the ceiling. "My birthday is coming up, just so you know."

I bite back a smile. "Noted."

Beryl opens the oven door, wafting the aroma of roasted vegetables and chicken toward us. My stomach rumbles in response. I'm so hungry, I could probably eat every morsel of the feast she's laying out.

"Yeah, the hospital food wasn't great," I admit. "Your

mom made me eat it every single time, though. Said it was good for me or something."

Kate gives me a look. "Because it was *healthy*. We're trying to help your brain recover, and eating nothing but the sugary junk food your younger brother kept bringing you wasn't going to help."

I lean in closer to Odessa and quietly say, "It tasted way better, though."

She giggles, and her eyes sparkle. She's freckled, like me, but with Kate's beautiful eyes and hair. I don't know much about kids, in general, but she seems tall for her age. And the twist of sass she adds to every word that leaves her mouth makes something inside my chest float.

Once Beryl has the early dinner prepared, she and Kate bicker about whether Beryl should stay for dinner with us or not. Eventually, Kate meets her match—which I don't imagine happens often, based on experiences watching her interact with hospital staff—and she irritatedly watches as Beryl loads a plate for herself and heads back to her own home for the rest of the evening.

So it's only Kate, myself, and our kids, for a homey, though weird, dinner. Odessa yaps until my head starts to feel dizzy, and Rhett quietly builds a mashed potato mountain to pour a river of gravy down. When he notices me watching him, he gives me a small thumbs-up, and I awkwardly return the gesture.

By the time it's over, Kate's shoving a handful of pills into my palm and, true to her word, she stands over me until I've swallowed them. I even prove it by opening my mouth wide and wiggling my tongue around, just to make her stop staring at me that way. The kids abandon the table the moment they're done scarfing down their food, and Kate gives me a look that keeps me seated as she clears the table. I feel bad about it, but I also know I'll be no help in my current state.

Once she's finished tidying the kitchen, Kate leads me

down a short hallway I've never stepped foot in . . . rather, *New Jackson* hasn't stepped foot in.

"How are you feeling about all of that?"

I shrug. "The kids are cute . . . but fucking exhausting."

I'm sure Kate was hoping I'd step into this house, see their little freckled faces, and instantly slip back into whatever my role is supposed to be. But they feel an awful lot like kids who belong to a friend or distant relative—I can admit they're cute and funny and generally sweet. I wouldn't want anything bad to happen to them. They just don't feel like they're mine.

She pushes open the door to a spacious primary bedroom, where a pristine white bedspread awaits. Multiple pillows, a thick duvet, and blackout curtains? Compared to the hospital room, this is my personal version of heaven.

"So . . . this is our room." Kate's hand sweeps through the still air, stirring up the faint scent of her coconut perfume.

Yeah, I think I'll sleep pretty good here.

"You can make yourself at home. I'll have to come down here to get dressed in the morning, but otherwise, this is all your space. There's a bathroom, and the tall dresser on the far wall is yours, so . . . yeah. I'm sure you'll figure it out."

Maybe I won't sleep so well, after all.

"Where are you sleeping?" I hesitantly ask.

"Upstairs in the guest room . . . your childhood room."

"You . . . you don't sleep in here?"

"Normally, yes. But I was worried it might be too much for you to jump right into full-on married life immediately after coming home."

"Yeah." My eyes linger on the bed before slicing to her. "This is your bedroom . . . so I'm happy to go upstairs to the guest room. I don't want to be a burden."

She leans against the doorframe, a gentle smile lifting the corners of her mouth. "You're anything but a burden, Jackson. I figured this makes the most sense so you don't have to worry about any stairs. . . . Anyway, it's been a long day, and you need your rest. We can bicker over sleeping arrangements later."

My eyes close for about five times that of a typical blink, reminding me of everything I hate about my pain meds. The nod that follows is in slow motion, and before I've finished telling her to have a good night, she's slipped back into the hallway, and the door shuts with a soft click.

In the bathroom, the shower has men's shampoo next to a bottle of women's. A blue toothbrush sits slanted in a cup next to a purple one. A men's razor is set in a drawer below the sink—a few tiny beard trimmings strewn beside it. It's as if I'm a stranger about to sleep in a married woman's bed, snooping through her drawers and looking at her husband's belongings. When I tug open the top drawer of the dresser she said was mine and grab a pair of gray boxers to sleep in, my stomach flip-flops.

And the bed. *Fuck.* The bed smells like her when she first walks into my hospital room. When she's smiling, hair bouncing around her shoulders, and hopeful that something changed overnight. When my face nuzzles into the soft down of her pillow, I catch an earthy note amid the tropical. I breathe it in, filling my lungs so I can keep her scent there forever, just in case I wake up tomorrow and forget everything all over again.

I've been struggling to sleep—except when the drugs take over and knock me out against my will—because I don't trust my brain. I'm terrified that if I sleep too long, I won't wake up. Or I'll wake up and find the slate's been wiped clean again, and I'll be scared, alone, and confused for the rest of my life.

But tonight, smelling her perfume and feeling the echo of her palm's warmth against mine, the slow hearts her thumb drew on my skin, I'm calm. I don't get angry about the heaviness in my bones or fight to keep my eyelids open even as my eyes burn. I clutch her pillow to my face, balling up in the center of the bed, and drift off with ease.

KATE

The blaring chime of my morning alarm clock comes a little too early for my liking when I couldn't fall asleep until nearly three a.m.

When I returned for my second round of bloodwork at the hospital to confirm I'd miscarried, I hadn't considered that the lab would send those results to my usual healthcare provider. And, as luck would have it, that healthcare provider is also my sister-in-law. Thankfully, when Blair showed up at the house that evening with a worried look and the longest hug I'd had since the accident, she was also able to give me a much-needed prescription for a sleeping aid.

But with it being Jackson's first night at home, I couldn't bring myself to take it. In case he needed me, or the kids woke up and went looking for me—only to find a man who looked a lot like their dad lying in our bed but who wouldn't be able to help them scare away monsters in the way their daddy always can.

Once I've woken up enough to roll out of bed, I slide my feet into plush slippers and amble my way to the kitchen, following the strong aroma of freshly brewed coffee.

I can't help but notice that our bedroom door is still shut, and I consider checking on him, but think better of it right before the ache to reach for him fully consumes me. Before the accident, Jackson was always an early riser, as ranchers tend to be. It was ingrained in his very DNA by his father and grandfather and all those before. Post-accident, he needs his rest, and there's still plenty of time before he needs his morning pills, so I take the fact that he's seemingly asleep as a good sign.

Beryl beams at me from her perch on a counter stool. She already has croissants baking, coffee on, and the sourdough starter fed, and she's casually flipping through a newspaper.

The earlier the sunrise gets, the earlier the cowboys come in to grab their bagged lunches, which we always make the day before. These days, the guys are typically in and out of here around five-thirty a.m., and it doesn't matter how long I've lived here, I can't bring myself to drag my ass into the kitchen that early.

"Morning," I announce wearily to Beryl and to Austin, who's lost in a mountain of paperwork spread across the table.

He grumbles a half-hearted greeting, then promptly sets his pencil down and looks up once he's realized it's me who walked in the room. "How did things go last night?"

"Good, I think?" I sort through the plethora of mugs in the cupboard until I find the biggest one. I think it's technically meant for soup. "I think it was all kind of weird for him . . . being here, seeing the kids."

"It'll be better for him to be home," Beryl says, lifting her own coffee mug to her lips and pausing to finish her thought. "Nothing helps someone recover like having people around who love them. You let us know what he needs from us. What *you* need from us."

Slow and steady, coffee fills my cup almost to the rim, and I top it with a few glugs of creamer and a hearty spoonful of sugar. I lean back against the counter, relishing the warmth of the mug cradled in my hands and savoring the first sip.

"Right now, this is all I need. Coffee and quiet. A peaceful morning."

Beryl taps the empty stool next to her. "Then enjoy it, honey."

With a well-timed yawn, I make my way to sit beside her, settling the heavy ceramic mug onto the speckled white counter. Looking to the ceiling, I gather my hair in one hand and slowly release it. The strands fall across the nape of my neck and fan across my lower back, so thick and heavy I feel it through the threadbare fabric of my pajama shirt.

The quiet doesn't last for long. It never does.

"*Mom-uh.*" Odessa storms into the kitchen with wild, uncombed hair slapping her shoulders with every step. "Rhett licked my toothbrush!"

I stare at the slow swirl of unstirred creamer ribboning through my coffee. "He's your little brother. Rinse it off and you'll be fine."

Her jaw hangs slack with disgust. "No. Ew. He's disgusting."

"Odessa, you put manure in your mouth when you were a toddler. Your brother's germs are the least of your problems."

Austin audibly gags.

"There are new toothbrushes in the hall closet upstairs," I say, not feeling up to fighting with her over a toothbrush.

"*Fine-uh.*" She turns sharply on her heels and strides out like a grass fire, saying something snarky to her little brother that I can't quite make out as they pass at the bottom of the stairs.

My head tilts to the side to watch him stumble into the kitchen, Spider-Man pajamas askew and hair standing on end. "Good morning. Can we not pester your sister before she's had her breakfast? She's extra dramatic on an empty stomach."

He shrugs. "I thought it was my toothbrush."

Yeah, I'm sure he got his Spider-Man one mixed up with her pink unicorn-shaped toothbrush.

Beryl stands and extends an arm toward him, waiting for

his small hand to slip into hers without hesitation. "Come on, honey. Let's make pancakes for breakfast today."

My palms brace the edge of the counter, preparing to push myself to stand so I can help, when Beryl shoots a look at me. "*Sit.* Enjoy your coffee in peace. I think my boy and I can manage some simple pancakes without help."

The creamy coffee goes down smooth, settling in my stomach and warming my entire body from the inside out. Rhett and Beryl waste no time getting started on their pancakes—from scratch, of course—and in a display of questionable judgment, Beryl lets the three-year-old handle the pancake flipping.

"When you see those bubbles there, *that's* when you know it's time to flip them," Beryl instructs, leaning her hip against the counter and brushing flour from the front of her shirt.

Rhett's tongue pokes between his lips, and he awkwardly jams the flipper under the pancake, then sends it cartwheeling from one edge of the pan to the other. When it lands, he gives the air a quick fist pump.

"I'm the pancake boss!" he exclaims, spinning on his stool with wide eyes and a grin. "Mommy, did you see?"

I raise my eyebrows and match his wide smile. "Sure did, bud. Good job, pancake boss."

Filled with confidence, he gets careless in the way he's standing, and Beryl rushes to shift him away from the flame of the natural gas stove before his shirt catches on fire. "Honey, you have to watch the flame under the pan. Can't get too close or you might burn yourself."

At the kitchen table, Austin mumbles into his coffee mug, "I've spent enough hours at the hospital lately to last me a lifetime, and I will *not* be taking anyone there today."

Beryl gives an annoyed cluck of her tongue. "One day this is who's running your ranch, Austin."

With a single breathy laugh, he replies, "I think I might trust Odessa more."

"I'm *very* trust-able." Odessa saunters back in with minimally less attitude than she had earlier. Sidling up next to her little brother, she peers over at the shapes he's creating on the griddle. "What's that one supposed to be?"

"It's a heart," Rhett proudly declares.

Odessa laughs. "It looks like a butt."

"*You* look like a butt."

I sigh. "Guys, can we get through *one* breakfast without any talk of butts?"

Honestly, I doubt it. Butts, farts, poop . . . peak humor around these parts.

"It's a heart," Rhett repeats, rolling his shoulders. "It's for Daddy."

Odessa abandons the pancake-making operation and heads for the fridge to grab a carton of orange juice. "Dad's not even out here yet."

I glance at the wall clock. Somehow forty-five minutes have passed since I woke up, and I don't feel any more awake than I did then.

I throw back the rest of the coffee in my cup, hoping for a jolt of life. "I'm gonna make sure he's awake and hasn't forgotten about his meds. You guys save him a good pancake."

Odessa throws a look at her brother. "Give the cat butt to Uncle and make a fresh one for Dad."

"Great," Austin mutters, shaking his head.

"Oh, you love it, you old grump," I say. "If you didn't, you'd be sitting at your own kitchen table this morning."

Every muscle in my body aches from exhaustion, and I zone out for so long on the stream of cold water coming from the faucet that it overflows the glass, washing over my fingers until they start to prickle with numbness.

"You okay?" Beryl says softly, watching me take a dry tea towel to the sides of the glass to wipe off the excess moisture.

"I'm . . . here."

Here is the best I can be today.

My hands shake with the weight of the half-full glass on my way down the hall, soft sunlight filtered through a vintage window covering falling over the floorboards to light my way. The morning chaos slowly fades into the distance, and my knuckles rap against the door. Once, then twice, before I hear a muffled voice saying my name on the other side.

I cautiously push the door open to find the room's still dark, curtains drawn, and the small nightlight in the bathroom working overtime. The room smells *foul,* which I quickly notice is probably because of the trash can next to the bed. I take a deep breath in through my mouth and gingerly shut the door behind me.

Jackson's curled in the fetal position on top of the blankets. When I step in closer, I see his palms spread around his skull like he's gripping a basketball, and he doesn't look up at me even as I set the glass down on the nightstand. His clothes appear drenched in sweat, and when the nightlight catches his skin just right, it glistens.

"Migraine?" I ask in the softest voice I can.

His jaw's tight, teeth clamped together, and a low groan vibrates up from his chest. I take that to mean yes. I squint at labels on the pill bottles lining the nightstand, finding the concoction he needs to take each morning, and I collect them in my palm.

"Here, love. I have some pills for you."

For the first time, he doesn't fight me on it. Wincing and grinding his teeth with every slow movement, he drags himself into a sitting position and exhales long and slow.

He didn't bother to shave in the hospital, but it seems he attempted to this morning, based on the patchiness of his thick, dark brown facial hair. I press my lips together to stop from inappropriately snickering about it.

He trembles as I pour the assorted tablets and capsules into his clammy hand, and he swallows them along with the entire glass of water. Then he leans back against the pillows, shutting his eyes and surviving in a series of shallow, calculated breaths.

Meanwhile, I get to work cleaning up. Quietly. Quickly. My own exhaustion be damned.

By the time everything's tidy, with the windows open for fresh spring air, he's starting to perk up a bit. He looks at me with his eyelids mere slits in a pale, sad face.

"Feeling any better yet?" I perch on the edge of the bed and place a cool cloth across his forehead.

"Just put me out of my fucking misery," he croaks.

I try to smile at that, but it doesn't come. There's no room for dark humor when the wounds of almost losing him, of feeling my soul slowly detaching from my own body as I watched him lying near-lifeless in a hospital bed, and of losing our baby, are still so fresh.

I fight the urge to tell him all that. And it's damn hard. I'm sitting here, staring at my husband's face, knowing in any other timeline, I wouldn't hesitate to share my deepest, darkest thoughts. Jackson would welcome them.

But the man looking back at me is sick, and hurting, and doesn't know me well enough to shoulder my pain.

I clear my throat. "Let me grab you some breakfast. The kids made pancakes . . . but Odessa should be catching the school bus by now, and Rhett's not going to question it if I grab something else for you. Maybe some toast?"

"Pancakes sound delicious . . . I, uh, heard the kids earlier."

"*Shit*, did they wake you up? I'll remind them to be more quiet tomorrow."

"No, it was nice." He shuts his eyes for a moment. "I woke up confused—I always wake up confused as hell. And it was nice to hear sounds of home. I was gonna come out there but . . ." He gestures weakly around the room.

"Is that what happened here?" Without a second thought,

I reach out to touch his face. The coarseness of his beard scratches my fingers and palm, and he leans into my touch.

"It looks bad, huh?"

Air blows from my nose in a laugh. "It doesn't look *great*. The beard was growing on me, actually. You were always clean-shaven before."

When I pull my hand away, his instantly moves to cover the same spot. "I noticed that in the family photos you've been showing me."

"After breakfast, you can sit on a chair in the bathroom, and I'll shave the rest for you."

"You don't have—"

My eyebrows draw together. "What have you learned about saying no to me?"

"That you're a bully."

"I'm not a *bully*. I just love you, Jackson."

"I know you do. . . ." His words trail off. Stripped of all pretense, the unsaid truth hangs heavily between us. The missing *I love you, too.*

My palms slap the tops of my thighs and I stand. "I'll be back with breakfast."

Thankfully it's only Cecily and Beryl in the kitchen—they inform me Rhett's upstairs coloring more pictures to give to Jackson—and neither of them push me to talk. So I put together a breakfast plate, including a reheated heart pancake, and head back to the bedroom with a gentle reminder not to drop more L-bombs lingering in the back of my mind.

It's hard for me, especially with him back home, to remind myself that new lines exist between us. I can't kiss him. Can't slide under the covers and tuck myself into the crook of his arm. And I can tell him I love him, but I can't expect to hear it back.

I understand why he can't give me that yet, but knowing doesn't make it any less of a letdown.

Handing the plate over, I clarify, "The weird-looking pancake is made with extra love. It's meant to be a heart . . . Rhett's artistry."

Jackson looks down at the plate, and his head lists slightly left. "If you tilt your head and close one eye, it's a heart."

"Spoken like a true dad." I watch him take a slow, cautious bite, and when he lets out a small moan of relief at the taste, I settle in next to him on the bed.

And suddenly he's nudging my arm, muttering my name, pulling me from the waning moments of a dream.

I paw at my face, removing hints of drool from the corners of my mouth. "Oh God, did I fall asleep?"

"Almost immediately. You leaned back and I think you were snoring before your head even hit the headboard."

Once I blink enough to focus, all I see is Jackson on his side, elbow propping up his upper body. He certainly doesn't *look* sickly. Rather, he looks so much like he often does early in the morning, waking me with a kiss and a wandering touch. When he fulfills my every need before I have them, leaving the sheets rumpled and my face flushed.

My breathing stutters, and I swallow down the thought . . . until he looks down at me with a smile that patterns my vision with sunspots.

I blink rapidly until all inappropriate thoughts have dissipated. "Sorry, I guess I was tired."

Understatement of the year.

"Payback for all the times I've nodded off while you were talking."

"Are you feeling better now?"

"I am. Thanks for bullying me into taking meds and eating breakfast."

"Now it's time to bully you into taking care of this mess." I take advantage of the opportunity to stroke the uneven texture of his beard—soft and curly in some spots, short and spiky in others. The warmth of his skin melts my palm, and for a heartbeat, everything feels normal again.

"Suppose you won't let me have a choice."

That sense of normalcy gets the better of me, and I cheekily respond with, "Not if you want to stay happily married to me." Followed by, "Um, I mean . . . sorry, I wasn't thinking straight for a second there."

"I'm guessing that line worked pretty well before my head got fucked?"

I sigh. "Your head isn't *fucked*. And considering we've been married for a decade, and I used that threat no less than once a week, I'd say it worked pretty well."

"Well then, for Old Jackson's sake, I guess I better let you shave my face."

I hate the way he refers to himself as Old or New Jackson. It's as if he's resigned to never regaining his memory, and now things are divided into two very distinct parts of his story without a single string connecting the two.

Before the accident. After the accident.

Maybe he's right. Maybe a random day in March became the moment we'll forever use as a reference point in our lives. Now we'll define every major event by when it happened in relation to our family's worst day.

Having ditched my slippers when I crawled into bed, I pad barefoot across the room, stopping to grab the antique wooden chair that's typically a catchall. A thing to drape clothes over when I don't feel like putting them away.

"Have you done this before?" The chair wobbles under Jackson's weight.

"I've never had to shave your face, no. But I have plenty of experience shaving much more . . . delicate areas. I'll be careful."

His eyes go wide and his cheeks turn a brilliant shade of red. "On *me*?"

My guttural laugh echoes through the small space. "Oh my God, *no.* I've never shaved your balls, Jackson. I would, if you really wanted me to, but maybe we should make sure you're happy with the job I do on your face first."

"I d-don't . . . no," he stammers, blush spreading to redden his ears and create splotchy red marks down his neck.

I pick up the trimmer and smile at his reflection. "I love this. I haven't seen you this flustered since we first started dating. Used to be my favorite hobby—making you blush."

His hand scrubs his cheek. "So you've always been a bully."

Moving to stand directly in front of him, I flick the power switch on the trimmer and it hums to life. Buzzing fills the air. "Bullied the hottest cowboy on the ranch into sleeping with me."

Jackson's quick to avert his gaze. So much like the young, shy boy I met when I first moved here, who couldn't get through a simple interaction with me without turning into a sun-ripe tomato. And I was much more covert with my attempts to make him blush then—certainly no comments about shaving his balls or convincing him to sleep with me.

I move in closer, until Jackson can't decide where is safest to look, so after a tiny glance into my eyes, he opts to close his. Two fans of eyelashes, tipped in gold, flutter slightly when I cup his chin to angle his face to the left.

"Can I say . . . I actually think you look really good with a beard. Not anything that might get you mistaken for a member of ZZ Top, but if you wanted to keep it neatly trimmed instead of clean-shaven, I wouldn't complain."

"Are you going to keep trimming it for me?"

"Anytime." With a soft exhale, like I'm blowing out a candle, I clear the loose hair from his cheek to make sure I didn't miss a patch.

"You're the boss. I'll keep the beard."

It's not long before the searing heat in my lower back is

distracting. I stretch. His eyes open to meet mine, and we quietly study each other. Complexion no longer infused with pink, he's more pale than usual. Even his freckles have faded to a dull tawny color. A lack of long hours in the sun, home-cooked food, and proper sleep will do that, I suppose.

I bow my back in a cat-like stretch, then arch it the other way. "Sorry, this chair is so low, my back feels like it's going to snap in half."

"You don't have to do this."

I raise a brow at his half-shaven face. "You're incredibly handsome, but I don't think you can pull off this look."

"Okay, well . . . will it help if I stand up?"

"And risk you getting dizzy? Absolutely not."

"What if you just . . ." His knees knock together, and he hesitantly pats his lap.

I consider making a risqué comment. It would be so easy to bring some life back into his face. But instead I straddle his thighs and lower myself onto his lap. It's more of a squat, since I don't trust his strength or this rickety old chair to support both of us, but it takes some pressure off my lower back and puts me at the perfect height to finish trimming his overgrown beard.

But here, I'm close to him. Closer than I've been in weeks. The heat of his breath unfurls something deep in my core, and the dark expanses of his eyes melt me. I silently remind myself that I can't treat him like the husband I know and love right now. It takes everything in me to keep from kissing him. Grinding against his lap. Running my hands all over his body and feeling his touch all over mine.

Who knew shaving his face could be this intimate?

I take a deep breath before resuming the beard trim.

Jackson cuts through the silence. "Was this what it was like when you took care of my mom?"

"Yes, I also frequently shaved her face." I laugh, my finger tilting his chin up. "*No.* This isn't the same at all. For one, because by the time I arrived, there wasn't any hope to be found here. My job was ensuring she was comfortable for her last few months. And for two, because that was a job and this is me upholding my end of our wedding vows."

"Mom didn't make it to our wedding, I'm guessing?"

"We eloped, so nobody came, actually." The memory of that day inflates my chest. "But no, we didn't get married until a few years after she'd passed. She knew how I felt about you, though. I didn't have anybody else around here to confide in, and Lucy was such a romantic. She loved hearing every little detail—the first time you and I sat up talking all night, our first kiss, all of it. She ate it up."

I feel the weight of his gaze as I start trimming the hair on his upper lip. At one point I'd tried *hard* to convince him that a mustache would look good, and he argued until he was blue in the face that he'd look like he belonged in a seventies porn movie. This would be the perfect opportunity to run away with the trimmer, but I don't think he'd fight me on it. And oddly enough, that makes the idea of him sporting a mustache so much less exciting to me.

Once I'm confident I haven't missed patches of hair, I tilt back slightly to check that his sideburns are even, and Jackson's large hand instinctively comes up to brace my back. I feel the burn of his splayed fingers through my shirt. The protective grip of his fingertips firmly pressing into my flesh. Heat prickles from my core down the fronts of my thighs.

"You good?" he asks.

Honestly? No . . . yes . . . I don't know.

I want things to be normal, so I can kiss my husband and drag him into the shower to wash off the small whiskers scattered over us like itchy glitter.

"Y-yeah. Had to check my handiwork." With a sexually frustrated exhale, I peel myself from his lap before I do something crazy like kiss him. "More handsome than ever."

I step aside so he can see himself in the large bathroom

mirror. He beams at the reflection, twisting his head side to side for the full view, then his eyes meet mine. "Looks good."

I brush a couple stray hairs from his chest. "Should we do your balls now?"

He bites back a smile, lips rolling together. Like I'm twenty again, I'm addicted to seeing this man get flustered around me. Might follow through with the push-up bra, short shorts, and sparkly boots, after all.

"How about my head?" It lists sideways so the shaved patch is visible in the mirror. The surgery site is healing nicely and looks significantly less scary since they removed the staples a few days ago. His fingers gingerly stroke the thick, red scar. "Might make this mess back here less noticeable if my entire head's shaved to match."

"I love this scar." I reach out and place my hand on his. "This is the reason you're still alive, and that's the only thing I care about."

Our hands fall away from the stubble of brown hair surrounding the scar running across his head. And Jackson slowly stands to brush loose beard hair from his shirt, littering the bathroom counter and sink.

"Shit. Sorry." He grimaces, frantically splashing water around, trying his best to clean up after himself.

"Damn, like you never left. All this facial hair on the counter." I shake my head in annoyance, but it's hard to be irritated with something so small when I consider how close we came to not having him here at all.

"Trying to fake it 'til I make it with this husband thing."

"Oh, yeah?" I chuckle. "What are your plans for today?"

Maybe we could sit out on the porch swing, or he could play blocks with Rhett, or he could come to the kitchen and visit with his family, or . . .

"Honestly . . . I'm so tired, I could fall asleep standing up. The damn painkillers tire me out."

"*Oh* . . ." I try my best to hide my disappointment. "Well, we don't need you doing that. I have a ton of work to catch up on, anyway. I'll refill your water, then leave you be."

I help him finish cleaning the counter with a damp cloth, then urge him toward the dark bedroom.

"Thank you for all of this, Kate."

"Napping while you ate pancakes, then sitting on your lap and shaving your beard. I'm *so* hard done by." I watch him flop down on the bed. "Get some rest, handsome."

When the bedroom door shuts and I'm alone in the hallway, I clutch his empty water glass to my chest and curl in on myself with a silent sob.

JACKSON

I'm not entirely sure how long I've been home, but it's been at least two weeks. And in that time, I've rarely left bed. Not because I'm not physically capable. Staying here, wallowing, rather than inserting myself into a life and family that don't feel quite right is just . . . easier somehow.

Being here feels a lot more like a five-star hospital stay than being *home*. The bed's better. The food is incredible. But in the hospital I had a steady flow of people coming to visit and therapy appointments to go to, and as exhausting as that was, now my days are filled with nothing but watching TV and staring out the window. And without any recollection of my life before a few weeks ago, I'm left with a lot of bleak thoughts.

Life is carrying on outside of this bedroom, and I'm not part of it.

It's fucking depressing.

Shortly after breakfast, Kate strolls into the room and pulls the curtains open, to my chagrin. Morning sun streams through, filtered by the thick leaves of a maple tree outside the bedroom, and something about the way it falls over the white duvet feels oddly familiar. Though I can't pinpoint why, melancholia weighs on my heart.

I watch her pick an outfit for the day. I don't understand

why we have two separate dressers when she typically wears jeans taken from my drawers.

A pair of light-wash blue jeans draped over her forearm, she steps into the walk-in closet and shuts the door. A moment later, she reappears fully dressed for the day, tucking the front of her drapey beige shirt into the jeans. It's adorable how my jeans fit her hips but need to be rolled up multiple times at the bottom to keep them from dragging on the ground.

"The kids and I are heading to town. Want to come?"

I huff. "No."

She frowns, obviously frustrated despite my answer being the same every time she asks if I want to get out of the house, but she's quick to swipe the look away with a lick of her lips. "I figured as much, but thought I should ask . . . just in case."

Just in case today's the day I decide to start being Old Jackson again.

I expect more of a pushback, given how quick she is to bully me when it comes to everything else, but instead she quietly steps into the bathroom. Presumably to put on makeup and do her hair, not that she needs to do either. I like her when she's in my jeans and an old T-shirt, her hair falling out of a messy bun, and her complexion colored by the brisk spring air.

Unsurprisingly, when she turns back up minutes later, she's stunning. Kate heads for the extensive jewelry collection spread across the top of her dresser, reaching for a pair of beaded earrings and a simple necklace. The last step of her routine, as it is anytime she's leaving the ranch, is to slide her simple diamond engagement ring onto her left hand. She wiggles it around next to the gold band, then turns to face me.

"You look pretty," I blurt out.

"You think?" She looks down at her outfit. "Hot enough you want to stay married to me? Or do I need to grab my push-up bra?"

This woman really does love to make me blush.

She laughs and runs a hand through her silky hair, letting it slowly fall over her shoulders and down her back. "Sorry, I made a joke a while back that if you didn't remember me, I'd put on my hottest outfit and make you fall in love all over again."

She looks as far from sorry as a person can get.

"You think a push-up bra will be enough to do the trick?"

It will be. It absolutely will be.

"It worked pretty damn well for me the first time." She moves in to kiss me gently, *platonically,* on the cheek. "We'll be back in a bit. Take advantage of the quiet, kid-free house, and get some rest before the occupational therapist comes this afternoon."

"What are you doing in town?" I ask, mostly to get my mind off the thought of Kate in a push-up bra. I suppose there's nothing wrong with trying to picture that, since she's my wife, but it feels perverse.

"We need supplies for Odessa's birthday party. Her uncles got the bright idea to do something extra special since . . . *you know.*" Her wrists limply gesture to a whole lot of nothing, but she's clearly talking about me. "So, yeah . . . I have to pick up princess tiaras and dresses, the whole shebang."

"Forgot her birthday is coming up. *Eight* . . . right?"

"Yep." Kate inhales the word. "Somehow. The years went by scary fast. Feels like yesterday she was small enough you could hold her entire body in your hands. You used to sit in bed like you are now, and she'd nuzzle right into your chest to sleep."

Unable to contribute anything to the conversation, I take to clenching my fists around balled-up sheets, lean back against a tower of propped-up pillows and shut my eyes. Waiting impatiently for Kate to take the hint that this isn't something I want to hear about.

When she leaves, I spend an indeterminate amount of

time begging and bargaining with my brain to remember Odessa on the day she was born. Reaching into thin air and turning up with nothing time after time.

I can't hear her first cry, can't picture the room, can't remember holding her in my hands the way Kate described. That should've been the best day of my life. And it's just . . . gone.

An uttered curse leaves my lips, and I slam a fist down.

A creaky floorboard outside the bedroom announces the arrival of someone.

"Kate?" I croak.

Maybe she came back because she forgot something, then I can apologize for being a dick and ask her to tell me everything about that day.

The door slowly opens. It's Denny. "Sorry to disappoint."

"Go away."

"*Rude.*" He sighs, but doesn't leave. "I brought peanut butter cookies and this is how you treat me? They're your favorite. Well . . . *probably*. Do you think maybe your tastes in things have changed since you don't know what your favorites are anymore?"

"Denny, I swear to God—"

"Yeah, yeah, yeah. *Go away.* You're too sad and tragic for visitors. Beryl warned me." He walks across the room to plop a handful of cookies onto the bedside table, then shoves my legs toward the middle of the bed so he has room to sit. The mattress dips under his weight. "Thought you might like some cookies and company while you sulk."

"I'm not sulking." My voice wavers on the edge of breaking. "I'm trying to remember the day Odessa was born."

His face falls.

The room's silent except for the droning buzz in my ears that's been unrelenting since I woke up in the hospital.

"I've been trying, but it's not there. I don't remember holding her. I don't know what Kate looked like, or what we said to each other after Odessa was born—and did we always know she'd be named Odessa, or were there other names on the list? Did I cry when I saw her?"

I squeeze the bridge of my nose between my finger and thumb.

"You caught her," Denny says. "The doctor asked if you wanted to step in and help catch your baby, and you were all about it, apparently. For months, you wouldn't stop talking about how that was the greatest thing you'd ever done."

I squeeze my eyes shut again, trying to force an image. I need to see that moment. Feel it. I want the thought of catching my newborn daughter to *matter* to me the way it's supposed to.

Yet nothing comes.

It's like I know the lyrics to the song but can't hear the music.

"Fuck." My fist strikes the mattress beside me.

My brother's hand quickly grabs mine midair as I go for a second strike. "Bud, the memories will come when they come. You can't force this shit."

"I can't even remember meeting Kate," I admit. "I look at her and the kids, and they feel like . . . like someone else's life I got dropped into. And everybody keeps acting like I'm going to wake up one day and be the man I was. What if that doesn't happen?"

Denny doesn't hesitate. "Then you'll make new memories because the people matter more than the stories, and we're all still here."

"You're all out there, and I'm in here." I suck cool air through my teeth, grappling with the pressure building behind my eyeballs. "Everything fucking hurts, and the drugs make me feel so hopeless and despondent, I want to die. Consider yourself really goddamn lucky you don't know what this is like and leave me alone."

I roll to my side, facing the window and the big maple tree. A distant mountain range leaves only a sliver of sky in my field of view, snowcapped and blanketed by the same sun that warms my bed. The brightness exacerbates the throbbing in my skull. I should get up and close the curtains, but I can't be bothered.

"Leave, Denny."

The mattress shifts, and a second later the door hinges gently whine.

"You don't have to be okay, but don't shut us out while you aren't," Denny says before leaving.

The pain climbs until my vision blurs. Unable to make out the leaves or the curtains bracketing the window, I roll to my other side and pray for sleep or death, whichever comes first. Press my face to a pillow and breathe through the searing pain and accompanying nausea. Let the day pass without me, just like all the others.

KATE

I watch Odessa with bittersweet nostalgia hung in my throat. Seems like it was yesterday when she was tucked safely in a baby carrier strapped to my chest while Jackson and I rode. Today she's riding one of Jackson's geldings with the seat and technique of someone who's been working with horses for years, plaited hair bouncing on her back with each step down the narrow, rocky trail back to the ranch.

"You're a natural," I say.

She grins over her shoulder. "That's what Daddy always says."

"Well, he's right. And that's a big compliment coming from someone with as much talent as he has." I fidget with the reins, staring past her at the house in the distance. There's no telling whether Jackson will ever get back to being one of the best horse trainers around. People from all over the province sought him out. And now . . .

"One day I'm gonna train horses just like him," Odessa says.

"That's a great pl—"

"Or I'll be a cat rescue person."

I laugh, remembering Austin's exasperation over the thought of Odessa turning the ranch into a cat sanctuary. "You can always be both."

With a thoughtful nod, she pinches her lips together. "Is Daddy still gonna get me a horse?"

All the emotion in my throat binds together in a hard-to-swallow mass. "Oh . . . well . . . yeah. Yeah, we'll make sure you get a horse, baby. Right now, he just . . ."

Doesn't want to leave bed. Barely wants to interact with the kids.

It's been a month since his accident, and though I know recovery from a traumatic brain injury is a slow process, it's hard not to feel frustrated watching him refuse to leave the bedroom for days on end. I can't bear to think this might be our new normal.

Her shoulder lifts half-heartedly. "I guess it's okay if I get my horse after my birthday."

We round the corner of an outbuilding, and the main barn comes into view. It's a large white building, desperately in need of a good cleaning and some fresh paint after a long winter. In the distance, smoke from the wood-burning fireplace in our house curls up through the spring air, obscuring the gently swaying treetops and the mountain range beyond that.

"Thank you for being patient about the horse thing," I say to Odessa as I climb out of the saddle. I haven't been horseback riding in a while, and I feel it in every muscle. "In the meantime, we could get some more riding in with these two. I had a lot of fun today."

"Maybe next time you'll beat me in the race across the field. . . ." Her boots hit the ground with a heavy *thunk*, and she ducks under the gelding's neck to smirk at me. "Probably not though."

"Oh, *it's on*, little miss."

Saddle tucked against my side, I stroll past her, stopping briefly to smooth my free hand over the choppy bits of hair sticking out of her braid. My heart pounds when I step into the barn, the smell of hay and horsehair and dust lodging in my throat. I don't dare glance toward the far stall. Not sure I'll ever be able to without reliving every second of that day.

"How was the ride?" Red's voice yanks me away from the edge of spiraling.

"Good." I sigh, tossing my saddle onto the rack.

"Bet getting some time away felt good."

With a breathy laugh, I say, "Yeah, the fresh air was nice."

Riding with Odessa, just the two of us, had felt good—better than I wanted to admit. She yammered on about school and plans for her birthday party, taking up space and not giving my brain the chance to wander. For the first time since the accident, my mind rested—*actually rested.*

And yet, guilt gnaws at me, knowing Jackson's ensconced himself in our bedroom, lying sick and heavy and alone in our bed. It feels wrong to be in the sunlight, laughing and chatting with Odessa, acting like everything is fine. What kind of wife takes off riding while her husband battles demons a few hundred yards away?

Red follows me back outside and grabs the saddle that Odessa's struggling to pull off her horse.

"Mom tried to race me and *lost,*" Odessa says proudly.

"Did you cheat like you did that time me and you raced?" Red raises a brow.

She huffs, indignant. "Going through the creek instead of taking the bridge isn't cheating."

"It is when we agreed the bridge was part of the racecourse." He laughs, shaking his head, then turns to me and gestures to the gelding I was riding. "I was going to trim this one's hooves, so I'll put them away for you guys."

He doesn't mention that it's Jackson's horse, and Jackson should be the one taking care of it, since Red has about ten of his own to deal with. But I thank him with a soft smile I hope expresses all the gratitude I can't speak yet.

Odessa utters a hurried thanks over her shoulder before taking off down the gravel driveway, skipping and humming to herself. She needed the break, too, and that helps ease my guilty conscience.

I saunter behind Odessa, eyes set on the house and the way it seems to be tugging at me, drawing me back in. It's not that I don't want to be there, or be with Jackson, because I do. My entire body physically aches when I'm away from him, but a small, selfish part of me wants more of the carefree bubble Odessa and I were in on the mountain.

"Hey," I call ahead to get her attention. "Want to make beaded bracelets when we go inside? We haven't done that in a long time."

She beams back at me. "Okay!"

I'm careful with the front door, gingerly closing it with a soft click rather than letting it swing shut. Using the side of my foot, I hold down the heel of my other boot and wiggle my foot out of it, watching in my periphery as Odessa does the same. We're both silent, walking on eggshells, knowing Jackson is likely in bed. If this is our new normal, I'm not sure how we'll survive it, to be honest.

The kitchen greets us with the scent of freshly baked cookies, and the mess around Rhett's mouth when he grins at us over a large glass of milk tells me they're chocolate chip. Odessa roots around in the bottom cupboard of the china cabinet for her bracelet-making kit, then flops down into her chair at the table as if she's come in from a long day of working cattle.

Beryl's quick to sidle up to her, cookies and milk in hand.

I steal a bite from one of Rhett's cookies—no preschooler needs a stack of *five* cookies all to himself—and tousle his hair. "Hey, bud, we're going to make bracelets, if you want to join us."

He mumbles something incoherent around the cookie crammed in his mouth, but quickly slides off his seat to move closer to his sister. And it's evident that horseback ride did good things for Odessa, because she doesn't make a single snarky comment about his grubby fingers reaching into her bucket of multicolored beads.

Once I have a fresh cup of coffee in hand, I sit across from them at the table and cut a piece of elastic cord for his tiny wrist.

"I'm making one for Daddy," Odessa says, eyeballing the length of elastic held between the sharp points of her scissors. "Do you think this is long enough?"

I reach for the clear strand, looping it and trying to imagine his wrist. The way it felt with my hand wrapped around it when I held on to him for dear life in the hospital. With a gulp, I nod and hand it back.

Without missing a beat, she begins recounting our race to Beryl and Rhett, adding her fair share of embellishments. Her laughter fills the air, and though I know there's a good chance it's bothering Jackson, I don't stop her or ask her to tone it down. This all feels too good to stop.

Rhett dumps beads across the table, sending them scattering across the wooden top. "I'm making a Spider-Man bracelet."

"Okay, so you need red and blue?" I confirm because, honestly, who knows with him. He could suddenly decide he needs purple and green because he's going for Green Goblin instead.

"*Lots* of red." His chubby fingers pick out all the reds within his arm's reach.

"That's going to be a cool bracelet." I give him an impressed nod. "Maybe I should make one, too."

"Mommy, you should make a rainbow one." With his free hand, he shoves all but the red beads in my direction.

"A rainbow missing red." Beryl chuckles.

My sweet, gentle boy, who is so much like his dad it makes my heart ache, slides three reds across to me.

I work on my bracelet, listening to Rhett talk about Spider-Man, while keeping a close eye on Odessa in my periphery. For a kid who almost never stops talking, she's uncharacteristically quiet and intensely focused on the pink bracelet she's making for Jackson.

Once she's satisfied, she fidgets with the loose ends, tying knots that keep coming loose.

"Here, Dess." I hold a hand out. "Let me show you a trick."

Her small hand slips the bracelet into mine, and I pinch the elastic between my fingers, looping it carefully and tying it with the same knot my mom once showed me when I was a little girl. Odessa leans in close, quietly observing and learning.

"There." I tug the ends to prove the knot will hold. "Now it won't come apart."

Odessa's whole face lights up. "Can we give it to Daddy now?"

Her excitement is contagious. I feel it too, thrumming under my ribs. But it's woven tight with nerves. I sip my coffee, stalling, before finally nodding.

"I want to come," Rhett says, immediately abandoning his own bracelet.

"No. Just me and Mom."

"Stay here, bud. Finish making your bracelet with Gran," I reassure him. "We'll be right back."

We leave behind the laughter and lightness of the kitchen, but I watch the bounce in Odessa's step and the way she's cradling the pink bracelet in her hands like it's made of glass, and I'm determined not to let the heaviness of our circumstances fully settle over me. Not today.

Where I usually hesitate, Odessa throws open the bedroom door. Despite it being mid-afternoon, the room is nearly black, and Odessa doesn't think twice before flicking the light switch.

Jackson's arm flops across his face, shielding his eyes.

Odessa climbs onto the bed next to him. "Hi, Daddy."

His voice is rough when he answers, but there's warmth in it. "Hey."

He lifts his arm, blinking against the harsh overhead light, and his eyes meet mine as he shuffles to a seated position.

"How are you feeling? Need anything?" I ask as I settle in next to Odessa, and my hand falls to rest on the blankets covering his legs.

"No, thanks." He gestures to the bedside table, where the water and food I left him before we went out riding is still sitting untouched.

"Jackson, you need to eat something."

"You're a bully," he says with an exasperated exhale. But he plucks a couple green grapes from the plate and pops them into his mouth. After spending an hour on the back of a horse with my girl by my side, I'm feeling more than ready to sit here and force him to eat every piece of food on that plate, if that's what I need to do.

Odessa waits for him to finish chewing, then holds out the bracelet. "I made this for you."

Jackson's hand trembles slightly as he takes it, turning the string of pink beads over in his palm. Slowly, he slips it onto his wrist. The elastic stretches, then settles snug against his skin. "It's really pretty. Thanks."

Odessa beams, satisfied, and moves to curl against his side. "Now you'll think of me all the time," she says simply.

Jackson tilts his head to look at her, then glances at me, and for a heartbeat I see something there—a flicker of the man I fell in love with. He whispers, "I always do."

JACKSON

A month out of the hospital and there's still no escaping the pain—not in sleep, not with warm showers or gentle head massages, not with dark rooms and plenty of water. The prescribed drugs knock it down, but those same medications make my brain feel soupy. I fall asleep hard and fast, then wake up groggy and scared. I don't sleep well. And when I sleep with a drug-addled brain, I don't dream.

And I *want* to dream. Because my dreams feel like memories. Whether they're true memories or stories pieced together from the things people have told me, I'm unsure. It doesn't matter, though. They feel real enough to me, and they're the only thing I have.

So despite Blair's willingness to give me a different prescription to try, I've taken to primarily using over-the-counter medication, which turns the scorching halo into a slow smolder. I can deal with the throb of a regular headache. After so long, it's a lot like being permanently submerged in cold water. You get used to the pain. Acclimated.

Kate forces me to take the heavier drugs when my poker face falls through, and she can tell how badly I'm hurting. She forces me to do all kinds of things she swears are good for my health, and I put up with it because she's trying so damn hard to love me even though I'm broken.

Even though I don't love her back.

Not for lack of wanting. I *want* to love her.

I want to be the husband she had before, because everyone tells me stories about how fucking great he was, and now she's stuck with me. A guy who can barely get out of bed most days. Who winces like a fucking vampire when he steps into a brightly lit room—and God knows my skin's starting to resemble that of a vampire from the lack of sun.

And it's not just Kate. It's the kids.

They're always screaming, shrieking, running, and stomping. From the moment they wake up until the moment they go to bed, it's constant noise. Yesterday, in a bout of overstimulation because my head was throbbing, Rhett and Odessa were bickering, and the microwave kept beeping, I yelled at my family. I cursed and slammed my hand against the top of the dining table, which made pain ring through my skull like I'd whacked my head rather than my fist. Rhett cried. Odessa stared at me like I'd grown a second head.

I don't think Old Jackson ever raised his voice around them, judging by their reactions.

I hate that New Jackson does.

So even though today's Odessa's birthday, I'm hiding out in bed with the curtains drawn, because my family deserves so much more than the shell of a human I've devolved into. And I pray to fall asleep and find the safe, unaching peace that comes only in my dreams, when I'm breathing in the sweetness of Kate's shampoo and we're sitting on the porch watching our children play together on the lawn. Sometimes the rest of the family's there, too. And sometimes the kids aren't around, and Kate's on my lap like she was when she trimmed my beard.

My eyes squeeze tighter, as if that'll help sleep come.

There's a series of knocks on the door. Gentle at first, but quickly growing louder.

"Yeah?" My voice is muffled by the thick white duvet.

"Daddy?"

I'm not sure I'll ever get used to being called that.

The door creaks open, then shuts softly.

"Are you coming to the party?" Odessa nervously asks.

Fuck. The decision to stay in bed was so much easier before I heard her tear-filled voice wavering through the dark room.

"My head really hurts right now," I grit out. I shift and the pillow crunches under my head, loud and jagged as gravel.

"But . . ." The weight of her small body dips the mattress right next to where I'm lying. "But it's my birthday and . . . and I-I want you there."

"Odess—"

"You have to come." She gets more whiny with each word and slams an indignant fist into the mattress next to my leg. "It's my birthday. You. Have. To. Come."

Gripping my skull in a vise-like hold, I accidentally say, "I don't give a shit about going to a party right now."

Silence should be blissful, but in the aftermath of my admittedly harsh words, it's fettered with heartache.

"Sorry, I didn't mean . . ."

"*Please.*" The word sounds wet, and she sniffles loudly. "I made an early birthday wish that you wouldn't have to miss my birthday 'cause of the hospital. . . ."

The tears welling along my lash line burn. Clenching my jaw in preparation for excruciating pain, I slowly wiggle my hands along the mattress and push myself up to sit.

In a poofy purple princess dress, Odessa sits on the bed, fighting with a loose sequin. Her tiara's a little lopsided, the French braid in her hair coming undone in a few spots, and the tears seem to have streaked the bright purple makeup around her eyes.

"Please don't cry." Not sure who that's for—her or me.

"I promise the party is gonna be fun. We have a purple cake . . . and Mommy got me this dress." She smooths her hands down the front of it.

"It's a pretty dress."

"I know you don't remember me. And I know your head hurts all the time. Mommy told me not to come in here and bother you, but I miss you." Doe eyes rimmed with long, dark lashes stare up at me. "*Please.* All I wanted for my birthday was for you to be okay."

I fidget with the pink beads around my wrist for a moment, trying not to let the pain in my head influence any more of my words.

"Okay, birthday girl. You're a tiny bully—like a miniature version of Kate. Let's go," I say, because how can I possibly say anything else?

Looking incredibly similar to her mother, Odessa sits on the edge of the bed with an expression of mingled worry and care, waiting as I run a comb through my hair and brush my teeth. For the first time, I put on a pair of jeans that require a *lot* of trust in a belt to hold them up. Evidently I don't only seem sickly because I'm pale, I've also lost a shocking amount of weight . . . assuming these pants fit Old Jackson.

"Ready?" She starts toward the door. "I saved you a pretty tiara to wear. It's outside next to the chair Mommy set up in the shade for you."

With a deep breath, I nod. Grabbing my darkest sunglasses from the top of my dresser, I follow closely behind her, and seconds later we're stepping outside. Fuzzy white spots flicker across my vision, and I blink rapidly to clear them and refocus.

The massive lawn space in front of the house is littered with people—children running amok and parents circled up in collapsible lawn chairs. Two white tent-like structures sit amid the chaos with an intense roof glare from the late April sun. The air's a lot less brisk than it was the last time I was outside. . . . *When was that? A week ago? Two?*

Odessa's small hand slips into mine and she leads the way. Careful not to walk too fast. Periodically looking over her shoulder at me with a wide grin.

A few strangers say hi, pat me on the back, tell me how great I look, ask how I'm doing. Not a single introduction, and I can't be bothered to double back and ask for names, because there's a princess yammering away next to me. She's talking about princess cowboys and Denny having fairy wings and other nonsense.

Except it's either *not* nonsense or my migraine is making me hallucinate, because my younger brother is donning a blue knee-length dress and a pair of wings are slung over his shoulders. It's hard to tell from this distance, but the sun reflecting off his skin makes it seem like he has glitter on his face.

Confusion twists my entire face, and when I see Austin dressed somewhat similarly, I cut Odessa off mid-conversation. "Are they dressed like princesses?"

Her eyes grow twice their normal size, and she nods her head eagerly. "*Yes.* All the boys dressed up like princesses and fairies because they said they wanted to make my birthday extra special. Uncle Denny, Uncle Austin, Uncle Red . . . a bunch of the ranch hands, too."

I look around at the sea of people and discover she's right. There are a *lot* of men in ill-fitting dresses and bedazzled crowns.

Kate's honeyed tone floods my senses, and seconds later her arm is looping around mine. Her brown hair falls around her shoulders, and she's wearing a dainty gold crown that emphasizes the caramel highlights woven between darker strands. She's so beautiful, her complexion infused with a golden hue from the sun. Her smile makes my heart beat a little faster. Damn. I have a crush on my wife.

"You made it. And in jeans, too." She gives me an impressed look. "How are you feeling?"

"Okay. I might've been coerced by a princess."

"You and everyone else here," Kate says out of the corner of her mouth.

Odessa chimes in, "I told him we had a special chair for him."

"We do." Kate's hand slides down the length of my forearm, and her fingers hook around mine in a way that feels so comfortable and natural, I have to assume this is the way we've held hands for the last sixteen years.

Her own burnt-orange dress swishes around her thighs with every step, rustling up the scent of her coconut body wash. I've never seen her in anything but my jeans, and it's hard to catch my breath when she looks this good.

"Can't wait to see this chair," I say, entirely genuinely. Then to Kate, "You look . . . *wow.*"

Actually, *wow* doesn't cut it. Words escape me, and I chalk it up to my brain not running on all cylinders.

The simple compliment seems to do the trick, though, because a light pink hue brushes across her cheeks. I should compliment her more. Maybe one day I'll be able to form the words to hit her with something better than *wow*.

"Better in a dress than your brothers?" She swishes the material around her knees.

"That's an understatement."

"You look pretty handsome yourself." Her grip tightens around my hand. "Come on, your chair's right over here. Front row for the show."

"For the show?" *I thought this was a kids' birthday party.*

"You'll see." She tugs me across the grass. "I'll bring you to your chair, then I have a few things left to set up."

They weren't kidding about a special chair. While everyone else has flimsy camping chairs, I'm parking my ass in a well-padded, oversized lounger underneath one of the tents.

It's bright outside, but tolerable, and within seconds of sitting down, Rhett's wriggling his way into the space between my legs so he can snack on chips loaded on a paper plate, as if nothing has changed and I haven't spent weeks mostly confined to a bed. It takes a minute before I've found a way to be comfortable despite his intrusive presence, but eventually I settle in.

"Daddy, I have your tiara," Odessa announces.

With a deep breath, I turn to meet her eyes. I can handle Rhett relaxing in my chair because, for the most part, he's quiet and calm and just wants a comfy place to rest while he snacks. But Odessa is a *lot* of person in one small package, and on the days when my skull feels like it's been set on fire, she always seems to stroll in with a jerry can full of gasoline.

"It's your birthday—shouldn't you be the only one in a tiara?" I ask.

"Duh, I have one, too. It matches yours." She rolls her eyes, as if I asked the dumbest question ever. Then pulls a crown from behind her back with an excited wiggle.

It looks like it's from a discount store, with most of the blue gemstones slightly off-kilter. And I think I can see a few thin wisps of hot glue remnants like spider silk between them.

"Wow, it's a great crown." My attempt to be believably excited falls flat, but Odessa doesn't seem to notice as she delicately places it on top of my head.

"It's perfect. But don't move, because the little pokey pieces that are meant to grip your hair might stab you in your brain, since there's no hair there."

"Well, they won't go right into my brain." They did put my bone flap back in place, after all.

Just when Odessa's mouth opens to argue, she becomes distracted. "Grandpa!"

My dad. The one person around here I didn't struggle to recognize after I woke up, because aside from more gray hair and a few extra lines around his eyes, he looks the same as he does in the patchy childhood memories that somehow survived my accident.

He strolls over, wrapping his arms around Odessa and lifting her into a bear hug. The old man's wearing a crown, too. Once he sets the tiny princess back down, he strolls toward me and pulls up a chair next to mine.

"I like your bracelet," Dad says with a wink. "Very cute."

Immediately defensive, I reply, "Odessa made it for me."

"Reminds me of the time I came to visit and you'd let her paint your nails lime green. That daughter of yours has always had you wrapped around her finger . . . all of you boys, really. That's why her uncles are all wearing dresses." He laughs.

I look down at my wrist. At the gift *my daughter* made because she's scared I'll forget about her without some sort of physical reminder attached to my body. How could I not put it on and refuse to take it off after hearing something like that?

"Anyway, I'm glad to see you outside." His palm smooths over the curve of my shoulder. "It's good for you to get some sun, fresh air, and family time. You'll never get any better if you hide out in that dark room all the damn time."

"Yeah . . . I guess."

"I'm right on this one." He leans back in his chair and crosses his legs. Rhett offers him a chip, and Dad takes it with a smile. "Even when it hurts, you have to buck up and deal with it. That's part of being a dad."

I give him a look.

"Doesn't matter that you don't remember making the decision to become a dad in the first place," he adds, snagging another chip from Rhett. "I can confirm it was a decision you made and were *very* excited about."

I'm a father.

I don't feel like I am, but denial doesn't make it less true.

Eventually, Odessa finds a spot on my lounge chair that requires my feet to be *off* the chair for her comfort. So I sit awkwardly, with my feet hanging off either side, and lie back against the thick seat cushion to relieve some of the heavy pressure on my skull. I want to ask her to find somewhere else to go, but with my dad's words playing on repeat, I buck up and deal with the minor discomfort.

"You guys all good?" Kate hovers over her chair, waiting for confirmation that nobody needs anything before sitting the rest of the way down.

For a second, if I pretend my head isn't throbbing and my entire body doesn't feel weak, it's like I'm in one of those dreams I keep having. Where we're all sitting together in the sunshine, and everyone is happy, and I'm not an overwhelming burden on my family.

Denny strolls by in his dress and blows a handful of glitter in our direction, much to the delight of the kids, before he disappears behind a long line of fencing.

My eyes shift to where Austin's propped up against a fence rail wearing a flowy pink dress that skims the ground. He looks ridiculous. And he looks like he knows it—hates it, too.

"Mom, look." Odessa points. "There's a horse in that chute. Is Uncle Denny going to ride a bronc in a princess dress?"

Kate visors her eyes with a flattened hand. "I think he might."

Odessa's hands clap together. "I hope he gets bucked off."

"Princess dresses are like kilts, right? So that means this PG show might turn R in a hurry," one of the ranch hands I've briefly met since coming home says with a laugh.

His name slips past me, teasing the tip of my tongue before drifting away. He's been hanging around in the kitchen a few times when I've shuffled in there for tea or toast when it's too much to ask Kate or Beryl for some, and it pisses me off that I can't remember something as simple as a name.

"Colt, please tell me you're not saying what I think you're

saying," Kate replies. *Colt.* Fuck. Now I'm even more annoyed I couldn't remember his name, given it's a simple horse term. "You do have underwear underneath that dress, right? I have to take it back to the costume store."

"You think they'll be able to tell if somebody was wearing underwear?" Colt jabs his entire arm toward the fenced riding arena where Denny's climbing on the back of a horse in the chute. "Meanwhile he's doing some ranch bronc shit out there."

Austin whistles to get the crowd's attention, and Odessa shrieks and excitedly jumps off my chair, running to stand on the metal fence rails to watch. Within seconds, Denny and a wild bronc are soaring through the arena. His plastic crown immediately goes flying, and the fairy wand held tight in his free hand follows suit. The sun glimmers across the glitter I'm now certain he's covered in, making his bare arms shimmer. With every buck, Denny's dress whooshes all around him, floating up through the air, then falling around his knees. He looks absolutely ridiculous.

Bubbles of laughter fizz inside my stomach, becoming more intense the harder I try to tamp them down, until the urge to laugh overcomes my need for self-preservation. Typically, laughing, sneezing, or anything more than calmly speaking makes the pain in my head unbearable. But aside from some uncomfortable pressure, everything feels okay. Maybe I'll pay for it later, but right now I'm laughing.

Denny falls from the horse sometime before the unofficial buzzer, but he stands up so triumphantly, it feels like a win. He pumps his fist in the air as Red runs across the thick arena sand to slap the crown back on Denny's head, and everyone cheers—myself included.

"That was great," I say through the waning bouts of laughter. "Like that time he dressed up in one of those inflatable dinosaur costumes for the Halloween charity rodeo in town."

Kate's hand smacks against my arm, and only then do I realize what I've just said. I look at her, wide-eyed. *Fearful? Hopeful? I have no idea.*

My dad leans forward in his chair. His voice thickens. "Y-you remember that?"

"I . . . I guess I do." I desperately try to recall specifics of that day, but they're foggy. *Present,* but foggy. And the harder I try to remember them, the more it feels like they're slipping away. It's as if I stumbled upon a memory, rather than holding one of my own.

"Jackson, this is *so good,*" Kate says with nervous excitement. "What else do you remember?"

"Um . . . *shit.* I don't know. I don't know how I made that pop up in my brain the way it did." I focus my gaze on the grass, letting my brain wander in the hopes I'll pick up another straggler memory, but it's all a dark void. When I think about something specific—something I *should* remember, like my wedding day—there's simply nothing. It's black. As if it never happened at all. "I wish I could remember everything else."

"It's okay. The doctor said it'll come with time. This is a great first step," she reassures me.

Dad nods. "Earlier I said sun, fresh air, and family time is good for you. *Told you so.*"

"I don't want to get anybody's hopes up," I say.

Kate's thumb finds the back of my hand, drawing those small hearts she always does, pulling my eyes to meet hers. When I say I don't want anybody to get their hopes up, I mean her. Because she's holding on to hope like she's lost at sea and hanging on to an overturned boat, and I don't want this little glitch in my fucked-up brain to be the ship she sees in the distance. The thing she recklessly swims toward only to find out it's a mirage.

I do my best to ignore her soothing touch. "Maybe it's not

a real memory. . . . Denny might've told me about that when he came to visit in the hospital one time."

Dad's instantly skeptical. "You think Denny brought up a random bronc ride from when you boys were in high school? Doubt it."

"He could've." I shrug. "He loves to relive his glory days any chance he gets."

Kate's hopefulness falters. "I guess we'll have to wait and see if you remember anything else."

Odessa bounds toward us with a smile spread wide across her face, thrilled about Denny's bronc ride and her uncles wearing princess dresses. And probably more than anything, she's thrilled about me being here. Even though I'm still a shell of the person she knows and loves, she throws her scrawny arms around my neck and squeezes tight.

I'm glad I came outside for this. If anything, maybe Denny was right the other day when he told me there's an opportunity to make new memories with these people. Though I don't remember these kids, and don't know if I ever will, they need more than a dad who can't bring himself to leave his bed. Neither of them deserve to grow up in a home where they feel anything less than loved, even if I have to fake it for now. And if a time comes when I wake up and know everything about my marriage, I'm sure I'll be unable to forgive myself if Kate resents me for the way I've been acting.

"I love you, Daddy. Thank you for coming to the party," Odessa whisper-yells directly into my ear. It hurts in more than one sense of the word.

KATE

He remembered something.

Maybe it wasn't much, and he entirely shut down when he was pressed for details, but for a moment I saw hope color his face. And I've been floating on that high ever since.

Grabbing a cold can of beer from the cooler, I crack it open and lick the spattering of liquid that splashed onto my hand. The party's winding down, with Odessa's school friends gone home and her uncles finally taking off the gowns they wore all day. Naturally, Austin was the first one to look for an excuse to change back into jeans and a T-shirt—not that I blame him. The fact that he donned a dress to begin with shows the lengths these guys will go to for their niece.

Little did they know, all she needed for an extra special birthday was her dad to leave the house. I don't know what she said to convince him to come, but I'm glad he did. And leaning against the arena fence rail, sipping my ice cold beer, I watch him talking to his dad and brothers, and I think he's glad he came, too.

Blair strolls across through freshly cut grass with her daughter, Avery, on her hip. I'm afraid no matter how much time passes, seeing a baby will make something in my heart twist a little bit.

"Pretty great party," Blair says on her approach, then nods her head toward the boys. "I'm happy to see Jackson here."

"Me too." I let out a sigh of relief.

"How are you holding up? Sleeping better now?"

"I've been trying not to take the pills you gave me unless I *really* need them, because it scares me to think about potentially sleeping through an emergency with the kids."

Blair gives me a look. "*Kate.* It scares me that you're trying to take care of everything when you aren't taking care of yourself. You have a lot of people you can lean on here."

"I know."

Looking around at the party full of people who showed up for my daughter, I know they'd do the same for me, if I wanted a break. The problem is that taking a break means being alone with my thoughts for a prolonged period of time, and that's the last place I've wanted to be since the day of Jackson's accident. The only respite I need is exactly what I have now, a cold beer while leaning against the fence before I jump back into being a hands-on mom and doting wife.

"Our entire story is just . . . gone. I'm the only one who remembers being in love. Do you know how hard that is?"

"Not exactly, but having a mom with Alzheimer's, I know what it's like to be on this side of unrequited memories. To carry those stories—and the weight of some of them—all by yourself." Blair exhales and meets my gaze with watery eyes. "You don't need to carry all this weight yourself."

I look across the field at my husband, and sniff back the tears threatening to spill. "I never wanted to. That's why I had him."

"Well . . . for the time being, use us." Blair shifts Avery's position on her hip and carefully pries her chubby fingers away from the gold chain around Blair's neck. "This family can be a crutch of sorts, and you know you can always call me."

"Between running the clinic practically by yourself and taking care of this little cutie, you have your hands full. Everybody does—the number of babies around here right now, it's . . . I didn't think my kids would ever end up with so many cousins. I can't wait until they're all running around together. But I can't ask you all for more than you're already doing."

"Speaking of your kids, how are you doing?" She's the only person who knows anything about the miscarriage, and despite her suggestion that I talk to the other women in the family about it, I haven't. The last thing I want to do is add to the heartache and stress this family's been dealing with in the month and a half since Jackson's accident.

"No signs of getting my period back yet. Is that—"

"That's not abnormal, especially given how much stress you're dealing with." Her smile's downturned. "I'm saying this as both your medical provider and your sister-in-law, *please* take care of yourself."

"I will. *Promise.*"

Just as soon as I don't feel like I'm single-handedly keeping my husband alive.

Blair's free arm wraps around me, pulling me into a tight side-hug. "Love you, Kate. You guys are going to get through this."

"We have to. There's no other choice."

The rest of the party goes off without a hitch, and aside from the need to reintroduce Jackson to people he's known his entire life, it feels completely and utterly *normal.* There's laughter and children running amok and friends that feel more like family.

I check in on Jackson from time to time, making sure he's hydrated and—to his delight—letting him get away without taking his heavy-duty pain medication. I know he hates the way they make him feel, but I can't stand seeing him in so much pain he can barely move without getting sick. Today, though, he seems okay. Maybe Bennett was right, and some fresh air and family time was the cure.

Once things wind down, I plunk my weary body into an empty lawn chair next to where Jackson is showing Rhett how to bite the ends off a Twizzler to make a straw for his juice. "Seems the party's over—you boys ready to head inside?"

Rhett whines for a moment, but when he hears Jackson agree, he sticks the piece of red licorice between his teeth and scurries off the chair.

My arm weaves around Jackson's, and we take one slow step at a time back toward the house. Rhett's sprinting, arms waving wildly, ahead of us, and Odessa's quickly gaining on him even though she's cartwheeling across the lawn, rather than running. The air's cooling off rapidly, now that the setting sun is obscured by the mountain range on the other side of Wells Canyon, and I shiver slightly.

Jackson shakes off my grip and slips his arm around my shoulders instead, so I'm tucked against the warmth of his body. His palm slides up and down my arm, rubbing warmth into it. I'm pleasantly surprised he stuck around long after the party ended, even when I could tell he was getting tired and the pain in his head was becoming unbearable.

"What time of day was Odessa born?" he asks out of the blue.

I tilt my head slightly to look at him, his question catching me off-guard. Typically when I bring up memories of the kids, he shuts down. "Four a.m. on the dot."

"What did she look like?"

I watch our now eight-year-old attempt a handstand, fondly remembering where we were eight years ago. "She was so tiny—less than seven pounds—and all legs. Just this little wrinkled, leggy, alien-looking thing with a head full of thick brown hair."

He's quiet for a moment. "Denny said I caught her. . . . Did I cry?"

"Even more than I did." I squeeze my arms around his torso. "I thought you didn't want to hear any of this stuff."

His voice is softer than usual. "I thought I didn't . . . but I think not knowing is going to end up killing me."

The grass is pillowy under our feet, and the kids bound up the front porch steps like a herd of cattle. Odessa lets the screen door slam shut behind them, and it's only Jackson and me out here. The golden hour glow illuminates treetops across the ranch, and our massive farmhouse casts a harsh shadow on the earth.

I take a deep breath and dive into all the things my husband ought to know. "Odessa came a week before her due date and after an excruciatingly long forty hours of labor. Denny was right about you catching her, and I've never seen you look prouder than you did in that moment. . . . You were sobbing, and you kept kissing me, holding her between us. It was so magical."

His mouth twitches, and his swallow is audible. "What about with Rhett?"

"Rhett showed up *on* his due date and, besides a ton of back labor, it was over pretty quickly. You convinced me to catch him myself, and I immediately understood the look you had with Odessa. It was so special. You cried again. Honestly, when both the kids were babies you cried a lot, in general. Some nights we'd watch them sleep and tear up over how cute they were."

His fingertips practically gouge out his eyes as he works hard to prevent inevitable tears. "Thank you for telling me that."

"Jackson, this is *your* history as much as it's mine. I'll tell you anything and everything you want to know."

He stops walking at the bottom of the steps, and stares toward the explosion of greenery in the garden beds.

"Were we happy?" he asks bluntly. "Before the accident?"

"*Unbelievably so.* We're best friends—or . . . we *were* best friends." My words are unpolished and ragged, as if something is stuck in my throat and I can't quite get it out. "If we had nothing else, we had each other and that was enough.

And whoever has said couples lose the 'spark' after years together has *clearly* never seen the things you and I got up to."

That brings a healthy dose of pink to the planes of his cheeks.

Jackson clears his throat on the gradual ascent up the steps. "I'm . . . I'm sorry about the way I've been acting lately. I realized today that spending the rest of my life hidden away in bed isn't fair to anyone in my life . . . least of all you. You deserve the world."

"The whole world?" I tease.

"Mine, at least."

Through it all, he's still a romantic. My shy cowboy with beautiful words is still there, still stealing my heart.

"I'd really like to get back to being your best friend, Kate."

"Well, that was a title you were never going to lose, regardless. But I'd love to be your best friend again."

"I have a feeling you're going to bully me into it."

KATE

Nothing's new about my inability to sleep in the middle of the night. Insomnia's plagued me for most of my life. In fact, my mom still laments about all the sleepless nights when I was a child.

What is new, however, is the clunking noise coming from downstairs at two o'clock in the morning. This house was built a hundred years ago—floorboards that creak under the slightest weight, windows that whistle during storms, and pipes that rattle are part of the charm. So I'm used to hearing things while I lie awake, staring up at the white ceiling, but I'm not used to hearing *this*.

With a groan, I throw back the thick homemade quilt—a wedding gift from one of Jackson's great-aunts—and roll out of bed. The wood planks are well-worn, full of divots and dents that my feet conform to with every step across the dark room. I slip into the hallway expecting to find that one of the kids has gotten out of bed, but their bedroom doors are closed.

Skipping the second, fifth, and seventh steps, I gingerly make my way downstairs, fingertips skimming the rounded wood banister. Light pours out from the kitchen, illuminating the hallway and casting shadows at harsh angles. I lick my lips, curling my sweaty palm around the newel post at the base of the stairs.

Once we had a raccoon find its way into the kitchen after

one of the kids didn't properly shut the back door, but as crafty as they are, raccoons don't need the help of warm overhead lighting to wreak havoc on a trash can.

I blink down the adjoining hallway, struggling to confirm whether the primary bedroom door is open or shut. For how seldom Jackson leaves the bedroom, I can't imagine he's rummaging through the kitchen at two o'clock in the morning.

Under normal circumstances, he'd be the one dealing with a potential intruder. Here I am without a weapon or even a plan, creeping into the kitchen and praying I'm about to come face-to-face with a bear, rather than a strange man. With a gulp, I press a hand to the wall to steady myself and decide I can probably run fast enough to get to the knife block, if needed. Assuming the home invader hasn't thought of that and taken the knives for himself. *Fuck.*

And I left my phone upstairs, so calling the police is out of the question. *Double fuck.*

Typically I handle pressure with ease. Years ago when Cecily first came to the ranch, her abusive ex showed up here while the boys were out on the range, and I didn't so much as flinch at the danger.

The hallway floor planks are smooth on the balls of my feet as I tiptoe out of the shadows and into the kitchen to find Jackson seated on one of the counter-height stools. He's in a baggy, dark gray shirt and his hair is messy, likely from tossing and turning in bed. Two mugs are set out in front of him. Relief courses through my veins like the slow flow of warm whiskey.

"Jackson?" I whisper-yell.

He startles, and his arms flail in front of him, searching for purchase on the smooth counter to keep him from toppling backward.

"I heard noises and thought somebody had broken in."

"Sorry." His nose scrunches and he slips off the stool, preparing to leave. "I . . . I needed to get out for a minute."

"You don't have to go. This is your house, too. You're allowed to be in the kitchen—*or anywhere*—whenever you want." I meet him across the island, watching him settle into his seat again, and my eyes fixate on the second cup, filled to the brim with a creamy liquid. Tea, perhaps. "Who's that for?"

Jackson's focus flits between the two matching off-white ceramic mugs. "Oh, uh . . . I don't know, to be honest. For some reason, I was craving a cup of tea, and then I must've been confused and made two. . . . You can have it, if you want. It's—"

"Sleepy tea." I finish his sentence, reaching for the mug and cradling it with all the care in the world.

He's coming back.

He thinks it's random. He was confused and accidentally made two cups of herbal tea because he couldn't sleep. But that first summer, when I was nothing more than his mom's aide, neither of us were sleeping well. Lucy Wells loved her chamomile tea, so that's what Jackson poured for me that first time we found ourselves alone in a kitchen cloaked in moonlight. The sicker his mom became, the more often he and I ended up here. Until eventually, I knew that if I tiptoed into the kitchen in the middle of the night, he'd be waiting with two mugs.

We fell in love over cups of tea in the middle of the night, whispering our deepest secrets and fears, laughing silently about silly, delirious jokes, until laughter led to kissing with my lower back pressed to the counter edge and our tea growing cold.

If I'm going to get my husband back, this is the place.

My elbows knock against the quartzite counter, and I prop my heavy head in my hands. Steam gently billows in the space between him and me, and I watch him with adoration as his shaky hands lift the mug to his mouth.

"Did I wake you up?" he asks, licking a stray droplet of tea from the corner of his lip.

"No, I couldn't sleep and heard a ruckus down here. Thought I better make sure a wild animal hadn't gotten in."

"I couldn't remember where anything was . . . practically had to open and close every single cupboard to find what I needed."

I smile. "I'm not sure you knew your way around this kitchen before, if that makes you feel any better." Hot liquid trickles into my stomach, the warmth spidering out through my veins until my entire body feels flushed. "But you remember how to make a good cup of tea, so who cares if you don't know where the mugs belong."

I nearly spit out the blend of chamomile, spearmint, lemongrass, and whatever else when Jackson quietly says, "I think I remember my mom dying."

"Sorry . . ." I cough and sputter, setting my mug down and wiping my mouth with the back of my hand. "You do?"

He nods, and I watch the muscles of his throat move with a large gulp of tea. "My brothers and dad don't want to talk about it, so if I'm right, then that's gotta mean it came from my own brain, right?"

Playing it cool, I respond, "I guess so."

"You were here then. . . . Can you tell me if I'm right?"

I was here, all right. Sobbing as I kept myself busy making tiny triangle sandwiches that no one would ever eat. There was nothing else to do that day. The ranch was eerily quiet, as if the entire world was taking a beat of silence, and I couldn't possibly take up space at Lucy's bedside. I heard the sobs. I felt the rush of cool air pass through the entire house when she took that last breath and stole the color from some of my favorite people.

One by one, her boys stumbled out of the room forever changed. Austin retreated to his room, and when he came back out days later, he was a mere shell of the guy I'd met months prior. Denver sobbed so hard he threw up. Jackson punched a hole in the wall just outside the room, which Bennett meticulously patched in the middle of the night—his own form of working through the pain, I suppose.

I nod hesitantly. "I can tell you."

Slow and steady, with breaks to compose himself, Jackson relives the day his mom died. Some details are missing—he remembers music but not which song—while others, like the slow thump of the rocking chair in the corner of the room, are clear as a bell. I love that some hazy memories are returning, but I hate this for him. Of all the moments to remember, his brain chose the one he's probably spent years wishing he could forget.

"I'm so sorry, Jackson."

"I'm right . . . aren't I?"

Instinctively, I move around the end of the island, and I envelop him in a hug like I did that day. Wrapping my arms tight around his torso and letting him give me his weight. Jackson pulls me closer, sweeping the heat of his palms down to my lower back and pressing my cheek to his chest. Our heartbeats fall in sync as if no time at all has passed since I was last in his arms, and I can't help the tears that fall in meandering rivulets down my cheeks.

He has no idea how something as simple as a hug has every fiber in my being yearning for more. I didn't know if I'd ever have this again, and now that I do, I'm so scared to let go. I'm right back in the hospital, clinging to him for fear that letting go would make him slip away. He's been home for weeks, and while he should be getting better each day, Jackson's only become more detached. Odessa's birthday party felt like the first positive change, and now I'm terrified a single bad memory will carry him deeper into depression.

"You're right. I'm so sorry," I mumble against the soft fabric of his T-shirt. "I didn't want you to get your memory back like this. Did something trigger it?"

I'm instantly racking my brain for ideas of what might need to change in our bedroom. It was all renovated before we took it over, because the last thing either of us wanted as we started our own family in this home was the constant reminder of Lucy's final moments in the room that should be our sanctuary.

Jackson's hot breath cascades from the top of my skull down to my shoulders, and I relax into it. "I've been having these dreams lately, and they feel . . . I can't quite tell if they're memories or stories my brain is making up. That one felt too raw to be made up."

"Have you been having good dreams, too? Maybe they're all real."

I feel his nod move my hair around. "Yeah, not any big moments. Just us outside—me and you on a porch swing. Sometimes the kids are playing in the grass."

Closing my eyes, I envision it. That dream could be from any number of evenings, when we sit outside after dinner and sway on the old wooden swing hung on the back porch. I don't think he's been out there since he came home from the hospital, so I pull back from our tight embrace enough to grab his hand and give it a firm tug.

"Let's go sit on the porch swing." I grab my tea and start toward the door.

"Isn't it too cold outside?"

"We'll only be a minute. I want to see if it sparks anything." I tug him again. He's sturdy as a damn tree. "Besides, the fresh air will be good for you. Come on."

He shakes his head but follows, muttering under his breath, "Bully."

Okay, so it's a little colder out than I anticipated. The air's damp, bordering on frosty despite it being late April, and our breath is clearly visible in puffs of vapor as we shuffle across the dark porch. On second thought, the tea was a poor choice, because I'm immediately shivering so hard, it's hard to maintain a steady grasp on the ceramic mug. Scared I'll slosh hot liquid everywhere, I abandon the mug on a windowsill before slowly lowering onto the wooden swing. The boards are cold, permeating through my thin pajama pants and straight into the marrow of my bones.

Jackson hisses as he sits next to me. "This is crazy. It's so cold out here."

"Sit for a second. Tell me if it feels familiar." The patter of hope in my chest is the only thing keeping me from aborting this mission and heading back into the warmth.

My knees tuck up to meet my chest, and I wrap my arms around myself. Feet firmly planted on the deck, Jackson straightens then bends his knees, and the swing begins to move. The frigid metal chains holding us in place creak and squeak with each pendulum motion.

I tip into him, and his hand falls to my side. He's warm and comfortable, and honestly, if it were a few degrees warmer, I could fall asleep right here. The cadence of his heart is soothing against my head, and I wiggle to get the tiniest bit closer. I'm taking everything I can get today . . . just in case.

"I don't know if this is working, Kate. I'm too cold to think."

"What are we doing in your dreams? Just talking?"

"Sometimes . . ." His hand dips lower, so it's covering my hip bone. And it feels the strangest kind of wrong and right to feel heat spread through my thighs before uncoiling low in my stomach. "Mostly you talk."

A burst of air blows from my nose. "Now I know this is fake. I do *not* talk as much as you like to believe I do."

"You do. You didn't shut up the whole time I was in the hospital." His fingers toy with the hem of my shirt, seemingly mindlessly. Brushing my goosebump-speckled skin so briefly, I start to wonder if I'm the one making things up in my head.

"In the hospital you wouldn't talk back. If I didn't say anything, we'd sit there staring at each other in silence the whole time."

"I let you do all the talking because I like listening to you."

Is he . . . flirting?

I'd assumed after years of marriage to this man that I'd be able to tell when he was flirting with me. But now he has me questioning it, and the whole thing makes my heart stumble a beat.

"What would you like me to talk about?" I debate what to divulge, whether to keep it reasonably light like I did in the hospital or dive into the thick of it the way I would've before he erased his version of our history.

"Anything. Everything."

He shifts in place, getting comfortable, tucking me closer into him, and dragging his fingers from my hip to my lower stomach. The swing rocks a little quicker. My heart beats a little faster. The air between us is whirring with electricity, and I'm afraid to tilt my head for a view of his face, scared I'll find he's entirely unaffected by the feel of my skin on his. His big rough hand splayed across my stomach—it's so much like that last morning when he still loved me.

"Your voice is like honey, the way it oozes around my brain, coating the sharp angles so they hurt a little less and muffling the incessant ringing in my ears. It's calming, and I like hearing it. It doesn't matter what you're saying."

My heart keens, overwhelmed with want. I could tell him anything and everything. That I'm desperate to feel the familiarity of his kiss. That I thought he was going to die. That there's a mounting ache between my legs. That I miscarried our baby.

I can't bring myself to risk ruining this moment with all

the things I could say, so I push them aside for now and stay here in the moment.

"Well, damn . . . when you put it like that, I can't exactly say no, can I?"

"You and Odessa aren't the only ones around here who know how to get what they want." His smirk is audible. The bastard. I love him.

With a small shift, I'm looking right at him, mere inches from our lips touching. His grip on my shirt fabric tightens, sending a rush of heat through my groin, and his eyes flicker to my lips.

"What else do you want?" I whisper.

I lean in expectantly and lift a hand to stroke his cheek. The way I'm staring at him in desperation would be embarrassing if he wasn't my husband. My bottom lip catches on his in an almost-kiss, a tiny whimper rises in my throat, and Jackson pulls back, putting the smallest amount of space between us. I can still feel the sweep of his breath across my mouth, but his reticence is impossible to ignore. It's heartbreaking and infuriating and *mortifying.*

Jackson sighs. Part of me hopes he's annoyed with himself for fucking up the kiss.

"I want to fix things," he says quietly. "I've done a shitty job of showing my appreciation for you, but today . . . well, I realized how badly I've been fucking up."

"You haven't—"

"I have. No need to deny it. I'm just so lost . . . and I want to be the Old Jackson because I know you loved him. And the kids loved him. But maybe these blips of memory are flukes and I'll never remember anything else, so you're stuck with this depressed asshole version of Jackson who yells at his kids when he's overwhelmed and has contemplated so many fucking times whether dying would've been easier on everyone—how much easier things might be for you, if you didn't have to take care of me every day. Not having to deal with this"—he smacks his free hand against his head—"would definitely be easier for me. . . ."

I sit upright, wrenching his grasp away from my body. My eyes and throat burn. "*Easier?* How . . . how can you say it would be easier if you were—that *dying* would be easier than sitting here with me right now? I know you're in constant pain. I know you're struggling." I'm shaking now, and not from the cold or the lingering humiliation from my attempt to kiss him. There's fear and rage and sadness broiling under my skin. "When you were in the coma, I was fucking terrified. The *only thing* I cared about was having you back. Is it devastating to think about you never remembering the way we fell in love, or the excitement of finding out I was pregnant, or the births of our children? Absolutely. But nothing in my life would be easier without you, Jackson.

"If you died, I would find a way to carry on for our kids' sake. The sun would continue to rise and fall. The world would keep turning. And our lives would always be hard. Your mom died over sixteen years ago and not a damn person in this family has gone a single day without feeling that loss. We can handle the days where you need to stay in bed, or when the kids have to be extra quiet. We can't handle losing you."

My words drown in emotion, and I clutch a hand over where the warmth from his palm remains as if I'm holding pressure to a stab wound. Honestly, there's a possibility blood's weeping from my skin with the way his words continue slicing through me long after he's finished saying them.

He frowns. "I wouldn't . . . I'm not. You don't need to worry."

"Unfortunately, all I do is worry, so . . ." I find my way onto my feet, knees trembling. I blink down at him through the tears, taking in lungful after lungful of crisp night air to suppress the rising panic. "Please don't do what you think is easier."

"Can . . . can you sleep with me?" His voice quivers. "In the hospital, I always slept better when you were sitting next to me."

This is *not* the way I thought we'd find ourselves sharing a bed again. But just like in the hospital, I'll know he's still breathing if I'm next to him, so I gently nod and reach for his hand. My ribs constrict at the feel of his fingers interlacing mine, and in silence—in darkness—we wind our way through the house to our bedroom. And I don't sleep for a single second, just in case.

JACKSON

Everything's foggy in the way it always is when I first wake up, but this morning my senses are overwhelmed by the aroma of coconuts and soft fabric folded in the tight clutch of my hand and a shaft of sunlight pouring in through disheveled curtains.

We didn't fall asleep cuddling. We each lay flat on our backs, staring as moonbeams reflected onto the ceiling and danced across the painted wood planks. My hand crept across the sheets until my pinky was nudging hers, begging for the intimacy of her touch. Everything calmed inside me the moment her little finger looped around mine.

My lungs inflate with her scent, and when my eyes slowly focus, there's a mess of brown hair inches from my face. Inhaling slow and deep, I loosen my grip on Kate's shirt and, careful not to wake her, relax my hand across her hip.

Is this what mornings were like before?

Quiet and soft—the type of morning that, despite the twinges of sharp pain in my head, makes me feel like all of this is doable. I feel normal. I'm not a burden being woken up with a fistful of pills thrust in my face by a wife who only ever looks at me with adoration I don't deserve.

Kate's chest rises and falls in a steady cadence. My index finger smooths across bare skin, following the gathered waistband of her pajama bottoms. For once, I welcome the way my pulse hammers through my skull so hard I can hear it.

My tongue darts out to lick my lips, and my hand settles over the soft skin of her lower stomach. I pop my head up to get a better look at her as she sleeps, and I'm met with a softness in her expression that I don't recognize. Because when Kate walked into my hospital room with a smile or when she laughed alongside me during Odessa's party, there was always something severe about her expression. Something uncomfortable, like a mask that doesn't quite fit.

And last night . . . the pain in her eyes was unlike anything I'd ever seen.

I'm not going to kill myself.

Not that I haven't thought about it. I have. I've eyeballed the amber plastic bottles filled with prescription medication and questioned what the right dosage would be to put us all out of our misery. But then Kate—*fucking Kate*—walks in and calls me handsome, and all I can think about is how quickly that smile of hers would fall to ruin; she'd probably never walk into a room without an anxious feeling again.

Like she's done to me many times, I drag the pad of my thumb back and forth across her skin. She's warm and my blood's hot, wanting more. I want to touch her everywhere, glide my hand up her shirt and between her thighs. And I want to squeeze her hip bone, trace the curve of her spine, and cup her face in my hands.

Her eyelashes flutter, then her body rolls into my touch, forcing my fingers to nudge the waistband of her pants. I'm so damn close to a place I haven't let myself think about touching before now. I freeze—caught between my head telling me to stop and my heart screaming at me to continue. Her hips twitch before widening slightly in invitation.

Fuck, I should've kissed her last night.

I stare at her soft, strawberry pink lips. Her bottom lip has a natural pout in need of a gentle tug between my teeth. Lips like that deserve to be kissed well and often. The tendons in my groin pull tight at the thought, and I reluctantly withdraw my hand before I do anything stupid.

She wanted me to kiss her, but I couldn't do it. Of all the things I'm interested in learning about my old life, the feel of Kate's lips and the weight of her body on mine are both high on the list. But she wants to be touched by her husband. According to a piece of paper, and a warped indent in my ring finger, that's who I am. But until I feel like him, I can't.

Fuck me, I desperately want to be the lucky bastard who's married to—*in love with*—Kate Wells.

Kate sleepily murmurs, "Mornin', handsome."

"Morning." Unable to stop myself from feeling her soft skin on mine, in whatever way I can get it, I cuff her wrist gently. That's a safe place to touch. Doesn't give either of us the wrong idea, but I still get the overwhelming pleasure of keeping her close.

She squints at me with glossy eyes. "How do you feel this morning?"

"Honestly?"

Kate lifts her head just enough to run a hand under it, flaring her hair across the pillow above her. "Always be honest with me."

"This is the closest to normal I've felt."

She gives me a sleepy smile. "Your head doesn't hurt?"

"Oh, no. Feels like somebody's digging at my brain like it's a bucket of too-hard ice cream. I mean I only remember a few weeks of my thirty-some years on this Earth, and this is the first time I haven't been a patient. A brain injury survivor. That poor sap who forgot everything. I'm simply a guy waking up next to the most jaw-droppingly beautiful woman he's ever seen." *A guy running his hands all over her and picturing doing so much more, to be specific.* "Instead of waking up to you reminding me to take my pills, asking if I need help getting out of bed to go to the bathroom, and sitting in that awful wooden chair staring at me while I eat breakfast."

Her jaw ticks. I can see her turning my words over. Trying to make sense of what I'm getting at.

"I do those things because . . ." She trails off, brushing a stray curl of cocoa hair away from her temple.

"At this juncture, I'd be worried if you stopped bullying me into taking care of myself," I say while watching her mouth, taking pride in the way it tilts and lifts. The sun would be jealous to know how much warmth and light Kate's smile brings to my day. She makes being alive easier. "But . . . can we wake up like this first, with a moment of normalcy before you start fretting over me? Will you move back into our room?"

Her swallow messes up the delicate lines of her throat. "That might not be a good idea. . . ."

"Why not? We're married, so it's not breaking any rules. I know it's got to be a nuisance that all your clothes are here and you're staying upstairs. We both slept better together than apart. . . . I-I want to take the harder route and try like hell to get better." With a shaky touch, I tug at a set of non-functional strings on the front of her pajama pants. "Stay here with me, Kate. Please."

I must have said something right because Kate agreed without argument. We stayed there together, sharing space and holding each other's gaze for a long beat, and those plump, bitten-pink lips taunted me. I considered a kiss. A soft one to see how it felt. Maybe it would be like a scene out of a movie, where all my memories come rushing back as sparks zap between our joined mouths and romantic music randomly begins playing all around us. But before I worked up the nerve to try, Kate slipped from the bed and went about her normal routine.

Now she's gone—off to get Odessa ready for school, presumably. The smell of Kate's hair is finally back on her pillow, and I fold it around my face to breathe her in while reliving the silkiness of her skin under my callused fingertips.

God, I can't wait to fall asleep touching her tonight. Wake up touching her. Dip my hand a little farther below her waistband. A little farther up her stomach. Explore every inch of her bare skin, until I know her as a husband should. I want to locate the spot that makes her back bow off the mattress and find what makes her lips part with a sated moan.

The thought of that has my heartbeat pounding heavily in my skull, heavier in my groin. I can't spend all morning lying in bed thinking about Kate. It's only going to make it that much harder to maintain boundaries when she's back here with me tonight. So despite the brief wave of nausea when I sit up, I force myself to the bathroom for a cool shower.

Today's the day I'm going to start getting my life back. I made a promise to Kate while half-asleep last night that I'd finally make an appointment to video chat with the therapist my doctor recommended. And if there's one thing that'll keep me from imagining Kate naked, it's the dread of having to talk about all my problems with a stranger.

Or so I thought.

The cold water raining down on my scalp does nothing but ease my nausea and free up space in my brain for daydreams. Kate's full breasts held in my hands. The softness of her lips on mine. My tongue dragging across the spot on her hip where my hand rested this morning.

By the time I'm stepping out of the shower, my dick's rock hard and tenting the plush white towel I wrap around my waist, and I'm bargaining with myself for the slow shuffle to my dresser. Surely it's not inappropriate to have these thoughts about my wife, or to act on them. Certainly more appropriate than imagining any other woman. And maybe this is a good test for how well my brain's functioning. Despite everything, I'm still a man—I'm able to picture a woman naked and get a raging hard-on as a result. I may as well jerk it to determine if I'm able to orgasm . . . *y'know, for science.*

But also, if I masturbate while thinking about Kate, there's no way my dick won't immediately get hard when I feel her next to me in bed tonight.

Who am I kidding? I'm already well past that. I'm getting hard the moment she slips under the covers beside me regardless.

A valiant soldier for no good reason, I do my best to ignore the way my cock twitches and aches between my legs. The way my hips subconsciously thrust against the softness of the towel, desperate for relief. Finally reaching my dresser, I tug at the gathered corner of the towel responsible for keeping it tight around my hips, and a rush of cold air as terry cloth puddles around my feet almost makes my dick go soft. *Almost.*

It juts out from my body, proud and throbbing. A bead of clear liquid sits nestled in the slit. And I give it one quick stroke. That's all. Just something to take the edge off.

Okay, maybe two strokes.

Now I'm fully fisting my cock, dragging a hand from root to tip, collecting slippery pre-cum on my palm and starting over with a low, rumbling moan. In a last-ditch effort to stop myself, my free hand yanks open the top drawer of my oak dresser, as if a pair of boxers is going to magically prevent me from fucking my hand.

I blindly feel through the drawer, fingers closing around something extraordinarily soft and untangling it from the mess of underwear and socks. Soft, thin, and light pink—I'm clutching a pair of Kate's underwear. My breath stutters before turning to small, frantic pants. I stare at the fabric held between my fingers, tightening my grip on my cock until my vision becomes hazy.

Surely they got mixed up with mine while Kate was doing laundry, and she didn't notice. She wouldn't have slipped this pair of pretty pink panties into my drawer in the hopes I'd find them, not when her dresser is mere feet away, and I've had unlimited access to her underwear for weeks.

But then again . . . didn't the pink stand out in a drawer of black and dark gray?

I stumble backward toward the bed, rolling the thin cotton between my finger and thumb. What I'd give to see Kate wearing these and nothing else. I prop myself up against the headboard, and the grip on my cock stills at the thought of Kate walking into the room and catching me masturbating with her panties. I watch the door, ears perked for the unmistakable floorboard creak of her footsteps, cock pulsing and dripping down the back of my hand. Without second thought, I use her panties to wipe the mess, then slowly brush them down my shaft.

I thrust upward into the fabric, pretending it's the softness of her pussy enveloping my thick cock, and an unbidden moan escapes my lips. I immediately pause, eyes trained on the door handle, waiting to see if she heard the sounds of my agony and is coming to check on me.

For some reason, I think I want her to see this.

Feral, I fuck her underwear, sliding them up and down the length of my shaft. Silky and smooth on my skin. I shut my eyes and press my cheek to her pillow to help my fantasy.

I imagine Kate opening the door to see me with my legs spread wide in invitation. With a lustful smile, she'd shut the door and drop her clothes, showing off the body she's been hiding from me. I'd make her crawl up the bed, and she'd do it because I know—based on the way her knees fell apart for my touch this morning—Kate's hungry and impatient for my cock. She'd take its thickness in her soft hands, plump lips parting to welcome me into her mouth, tongue flicking across the tip.

I shift the pink panties, smoothing them over the head, moaning into Kate's pillow. Picturing the way her pussy might feel as she straddles me in the middle of the bed and impales herself, soaking wet cunt gripping and squeezing the life out of my cock. My hand squeezes around my shaft like I'm trying to pull the thing clean off my body. Like I'm angry at it.

I *am* angry. At myself for the fact that I'm secretly fucking my wife's underwear, and for the fact that I'm not charging out into the kitchen and dragging her back here so I can shove these panties in her mouth and thrust my cock so deep into her she feels it in her throat.

My teeth clench together. I know she'd sound unbearably sweet as she fell apart, her moans bringing life to the room, rough and smooth all at once. The daydream has my balls tightening with an all-over ache, my stomach and legs tensing and flexing as a familiar throbbing sensation overwhelms my senses.

I roll my wrist, squeezing the sensitive head. Kate's panties are coated in my pre-cum, catching on the deep ridge and forcing yet another primitive grunt that has me burying my face into her pillow. Heat unfurls from my groin with the hard, fast fuck of my hand, until my muffled cry bounces around inside my skull and I spill hot ropes of cum across my bare stomach.

Entire body trembling, I loosen my hold on my cock and roll away from the pillow to catch my breath. Kate's underwear swipes up my stomach, half-assedly cleaning the cum threaded through the thick trail of hair running from my belly button down to my dick, which is still twitching and bobbing.

I don't remember losing my virginity, or being intimate with Kate, or even how many women I've slept with, period. It's all foreign and yet I can picture her so fucking clearly I'm left wondering if the vision of Kate riding me, eyes clouded with lust and moans giving life to an empty room, is a memory I've somehow recollected.

I'm still clutching Kate's pair of now-dirty underwear and honestly considering snooping through her drawer to see if she has more pairs like these. Something to aid in my future jerk-off sessions, because now that I've thought about her this way, I'm not sure it's an image I'll ever shake.

The air smells salty and sweaty, and I'm in need of a second shower to properly clean the sticky mess from my stomach. I slowly shuffle to the edge of the bed and toss Kate's underwear into the nearby laundry hamper. Fingers rake through still-damp hair, and I take concentrated breaths until my heart beats steady and slow. My head hurts, but it's a good kind of ache, like I've worked a muscle for the first time in a long time.

Also, *good news:* my dick works fine.

KATE

Outside, a spring storm whistles across the dead grass and pelts the house's metal roof with thick curtains of rain. Naturally, the men are working regardless of the storm, because ranch work doesn't stop even when Mother Nature is doing everything in her power to kibosh it.

I stare out the large kitchen windows at the porch swing twisting and rocking with sporadic wind gusts that swirl around in the covered porch, pattering delicate raindrops on the glass panes. So many things changed after Odessa's birthday last week—good and bad. Good: I'm going to curl up beside my husband and sleep tonight, then hopefully wake up with his hands on me like I have every morning since he asked me to move back into the bedroom. Bad: I'm not entirely convinced by his insistence that talking about how much easier things would be if he was gone was nothing more than talk.

But right now, down the hall and behind the closed door of our bedroom, he has my laptop propped up on two stacks of books at the foot of the bed. He's meeting with a therapist for the third time this week and, just as during his other appointments, there's a thrum at the base of my brain when I think about it. Not panic. Not dread. More like . . . a heightened awareness, as if I'm waiting to hear a tree fall somewhere deep in the woods.

Which is why I'm aimlessly stirring a giant soup pot filled with chili, dragging my wooden spoon along the bottom of the pot, and staring at the jittery wood swing. The chili doesn't need to be stirred, per se, because it's been at a low simmer for the better part of the day, with Beryl watching it like a hawk. She knows I need a distraction, but when I nearly chopped my finger off after she tasked me with dicing onions, she decided this was a safer activity.

It's for the best, anyway. If I started crying over onions, I'm afraid the tears would quickly become about something else, and they might never stop.

So Beryl's seated on a counter stool, casually chopping onions on a chunk of butcher block. The best part about the men being gone overnight is that the wives get to enjoy some much-needed girl time. Apparently when the boys were young, the ranch housed a couple families—including Red's—but by the time I came into the picture, this entire place was overrun with masculine energy. Sure, the occasional woman would come around until they realized dating a man who's as committed to the ranch as these guys are wasn't all they thought it would be.

But now we have a *girl gang* of sorts. Outside of Jackson and our kids, these girls are the best thing to ever happen to me.

Cecily leans back in her chair, pregnant belly rounded out under a tight-fitting T-shirt, flipping casually through a seed catalogue. She glances up at the window and her entire face scrunches. "I can't wait for some nicer weather."

"Trust me when I say the cool weather is a blessing during pregnancy. You don't want to be massively pregnant in the middle of summer." Blair tops up her coffee and leans against the counter, taking a long swig while simultaneously checking the video baby monitor set up in Rhett's room, where her daughter's taking a nap.

Her words pinch my heart. I'm not sure I'll ever be able to

think about pregnancy or babies without feeling a touch of grief over everything I lost. I should be spending the summer pregnant and complaining about the heat while I sit with my swollen ankles in the cool river.

"I want to get the garden planted before I'm too pregnant to bend over," Cecily says. "Was hoping the weather would cooperate so I could get things in the ground sometime in May."

"There are a lot of kids around here who never pass up an opportunity to dig in the dirt," Cassidy chimes in from her end of the dining table. She's making a futile effort to keep Rhett and her toddler, Hazel, from mixing all the Play-Doh colors together—the sort of thing you give up on altogether after enough time as a parent.

Rhett's head pops up. "Can we use *exabators?*"

"Toy ones," I clarify.

Rhett shakes his head. "No, the big one. I know how to drive it."

The other day, Red took him in the ranch's mini excavator to help get him out of the house, and that's all he's been talking about ever since.

Cecily laughs. "You know, I've been asking Uncle Austin to make me a couple new garden plots. I'll get you the keys now. Aus won't mind at all, I'm sure."

Rhett promptly drops his Play-Doh and swipes his hands across the front of his jeans as he hops off the chair.

My spoon clunks against the side of the pot. "She's joking, buddy. No excavators for you until you're older."

"How old? Five?"

Blair juts her thumb upward, indicating he needs to pick a bigger number.

"*Seben?*" Rhett squints at his aunt. "Daddy lets Dessie drive it."

"Lord help us all," Beryl mutters with a snort. "That girl should *not* be permitted to operate heavy machinery."

"We'll talk about it when you're seven," I say. "Until then, go back to your Play-Doh."

He rolls a ball of blue and red around on the tabletop for a second before looking at Hazel and asking if she wants to play with toy excavators in the living room.

"Be quiet—Daddy's talking to somebody on the phone," I remind Rhett.

The two take off at a run, bare feet slapping against the hardwood floors, while Cass gets to work meticulously trying to separate the Play-Doh. Again—*futile*.

A rare moment of silence in a kitchen that's typically bustling with laughter and music and the whir of kitchen gadgets for the majority of the day. And I can hear Jackson's sonorous voice stretching the length of the hallway, the rise and fall of his deep timbre. I can't make out the words, even when I strain to hear them.

"I'm glad he's talking to someone." Beryl scrapes tiny onion pieces from the cutting board into a mixing bowl.

"Me too." I give up on the chili stirring, setting my spoon down and popping the lid back onto the pot. I need to move farther from the kitchen entry. Farther from where I might catch part of his conversation, because I promised myself I wouldn't eavesdrop. He's been sharing a lot from his therapy sessions, and that's trust I refuse to break, regardless of how desperate I am to know everything he's feeling.

So I slip past Blair's long, lean body and fill a cup with coffee. I'm tempted to go for something stronger, given the circumstances, but with half the women in here either pregnant or breastfeeding, I'll stick with nonalcoholic options in solidarity.

Odessa charges in, pink cheeks and flyaway hair, holding her school water bottle with something suspiciously dark—*and chunky*—sloshing inside. She tosses her backpack to the ground with a lightened sigh.

The smooth roll of my wrist stirs cream through the dark

liquid in my cup. "Hey, Dess. How was school? And what's in the bottle?"

It's definitely not the water she left here with this morning.

"Mom," she says, urgent and serious. "The rain made a pond under the cattle guard at the end of the driveway. I found a tadpole and I want to grow it into a frog."

She holds the pink water bottle up and squints at the cloudy liquid, twisting and turning the plastic bottle around in her hands, looking for the tadpole. Blair sets her mug down and strides toward her, then crouches to get a look at Odessa's science experiment.

My brows pull together. "I don't think you can grow a tadpole in a water bottle. . . ."

"Especially when the 'pond' you pulled it from is probably mostly cow pee." Blair laughs.

Odessa glances at her hands and quickly wipes them on her pants. "Well . . . Rainbow Sparkles needs a place to live. *Oh,* I'll put her in the bathtub with clean water."

"You will *not.*" I make a mental note to double-check all tubs and sinks before bed tonight. "How about an old ice cream pail? We have a couple clean ones in the pantry."

She thrusts the water bottle into Blair's hand and heads straight for the pantry.

"Girls in STEM." Blair jostles the water bottle, holding it directly in front of her face to track down the elusive tadpole somewhere in the mingling rainwater, cow urine—probably shit, too, if we're being honest—and mud. "I love it. Maybe one day she'll be in the clinic with me."

I chuckle. "Whether she'll be there as a patient or a doctor remains to be seen."

"Probably both." Cecily shrugs, reaching across the table with a groan to grab a box of crackers the kids opened earlier. "At least that'll be convenient."

There's a kerfuffle inside the large walk-in, with the metal twang of crashing pots and pans, followed by the faint sound of Odessa assuring us she's okay.

"*Definitely* both," Cecily corrects herself.

Laughter hums through the kitchen, warming my bones. Moments later, Odessa saunters out from the pantry with a white pail tucked under her arm. She lets out a giant exhale that makes the hair fallen loose from her ponytail flutter against her forehead.

The plastic rings hollow when she plunks it onto the kitchen table and makes a grabby hand in the general direction of Blair. "Lady Rainbow Sparkles, *please*."

Cassidy makes an impressed face. "Oh, now she has an official title."

"Princess Lady Rainbow Penelope Sparkles," Odessa deadpans. "The third."

"Oh, good. She brought home two tadpoles none of us knew about before this one." Beryl snickers, slowly rising from her seat and giving Odessa's hair a loving pet on her way to check on the simmering chili. Evidently she doesn't trust my stirring abilities today.

Blair hands over the water bottle, peering into the bucket as Odessa slowly dumps the questionable liquid into it.

"You're sure there was a tadpole in here?" Blair leans in closer, pulling a face at the smell emanating from the water.

"*Yes.*" Odessa reaches in and stirs the muck around with her hand, much to the utter disgust and objection of her aunts. "I *know* she was in here. I saw her."

Sipping my coffee, I pad across the kitchen and peek into Odessa's science experiment. "Dess, I think you have an escaped tadpole. All I see floating in that water are bits of mud and dead grass."

"I need to go rescue her from the puddle."

"Not in this rain—you'll catch a cold," Beryl says.

I brush Odessa's rain-dampened hair behind her ear. "Sorry, baby. Take this as a sign that she was happy in the puddle and wanted to stay there."

Her small shoulders fall, but she quickly recovers. "I'm gonna find Clementine and see if she wants to have a tea party."

With that, she abandons her concoction of mud and cow shit, skipping out of the kitchen. After a lot of ups and downs since Jackson's accident, I'm glad to see she's back to her normal self, causing chaos across the ranch and fretting over all the animals nobody else around here pays any mind to.

I grab the white pail and head for the back door to toss the sludge off the porch. Based on the stench of the water, that water bottle of hers can go straight in the trash.

When I reenter the kitchen, Jackson's there. For the second time in recent weeks, he's wearing jeans and a fitted T-shirt. He's standing at the island with a glass of water, looking at me in a way he hasn't since before his brain injury. Even with other people in the room, the air between us crackles with attraction.

His eyes flick to my lips, holding there while I slowly lick them. Butterflies pilfer my chest and heat washes over my cheek.

"Hey," I say softly, stepping closer.

My hands shake, tightening around the handle of the pail to keep from dropping it. Once it's in the oversized kitchen sink, I press my palm flat to the counter to steady myself. Not because I'm panicking over his therapy session or any of the things that have been commandeering my every thought all day. The intensity of his gaze, and the light-wash denim paired with a thin cotton shirt pulled across his upper body, has me feeling like I'm twenty again and secretly crushing on Jackson Wells.

My hip presses into the counter next to where he's standing. "How did it go?"

"Good." An affectionate smile curves his full lips. "I'm . . . good. Want to, uh . . ." He glances at the other women in the room, who are doing a great job of pretending to mind their business, sitting around the kitchen table and talking quietly among themselves. "Want to sit on the swing?"

"I'd love to."

The damp, cool outside air prickles against my bare arms, and as we settle onto the wooden swing I skate my hands up the goosebump-covered skin.

"I didn't realize how cold it is," Jackson says with a whole-body shiver. "Should we go back in? Are you too cold?"

"I'll be okay. It's refreshing." I tuck my knees up to my chest, reveling in the pitter-patter of rain hitting the metal porch roof. His breath. Mine. "So . . ."

"So . . . I fucking hate the lead-up to every therapy session. I'd rather do damn near anything else. But I think this is helping, Kate. I honestly do. A big part of why I've been struggling is because I'm beating myself up over everything. Not being a good father, or husband, or that I'm a burden . . . and today we talked a lot about how those are thoughts, not facts."

I hug my knees tighter. "Those are *definitely* not facts."

"She gave me some tips to remind myself of that." His fingers scrape on his neatly trimmed beard. "We also talked a bit about what happens if my memory never comes back."

I swallow the emotion amassing in the back of my throat, but refrain from saying anything about holding on to hope. The brain's intricate and fickle, and I know that means there's a chance some degree of memory loss could last months, or years, or the rest of his life. I can't blame him for wanting to prepare for the worst, even if I refuse to believe things won't get better.

"And did she have any suggestions?" I stare out through sheets of rain at the dark clouds hung low over the tree line.

"She suggested small steps. Finding ways to . . . I guess,

uh, get to know you—*and everyone*—again without pressure to feel a certain way about it. If you think of something that maybe I can do, let me know."

His hand rests on his shaky knee, and I'm inexplicably pulled to touch him. The rain around us heightens all my senses, until *everything* is him. I hesitate, secretly loving the magnetic pull between me and him. And when I finally stretch my fingertips across the space between us, he opens his palm to me, and our fingers interlock naturally.

I turn to face him, giving our fingers a squeeze. "The only thing I want you to do is exactly what you're doing now. Being here. Trying."

And he has been trying. In the last week, there's been a marked change in his attitude. Of course, there are still some days when it takes hours before he can leave bed because of excruciating migraines and nausea, but he's making the most of the days he's in less pain.

"I want to do *more*. Family movie nights and taking you on a date and . . . whatever it is the kids like to do."

"Careful what you offer them. Odessa's going to take full advantage. But honestly, they've been impatiently waiting for you to be healthy enough to do story time before bed. They'd love having you do that." It might be asking too much of him, but even if story time now looks nothing like story time then, it's better than nothing. "Beryl and I have nothing on you, apparently."

He's quiet for a second before, "What if I'm awful at it now?"

"Then it's a good thing they love story time because it's you, not because of the quality of your stories." I lean into him. Everything's cool and sticky from humidity, and Jackson tucks me into the space under his arm. The sound of falling rain and the warmth of his body are lulling me into a euphoric state, and the heaviness of our reality is noticeably absent.

"And what about taking you on a date? Any suggestions for that?"

I scoff and my fingers playfully rap against his forearm. "*Jackson Wells.* You don't ask a woman on a date then expect her to plan it."

"I want to make sure it's something you'll like." I feel his chin press to the top of my head, and an unsteady exhale blows through my hair.

"Our early 'dates' were the two of us drinking tea in the kitchen at two o'clock in the morning, and that was enough for me to fall in love with you, so you'll be hard-pressed to find something I won't like."

"Well, in that case," he says, voice slow and a little more sure than before, "maybe I'll make you tea and we'll sit at the kitchen table again. Two in the morning, if you're up for it."

I blow a laugh through my nose. "I'm always up for that—*literally*—unless I take the sleeping pills Blair gave me."

"It's a little weirdly reassuring to know it's not just me and my fucked-up brain who can't sleep."

I hate when he talks about himself as if he's beyond repair, as if even glass shattered into a million pieces can't be pieced together to make exquisite art.

"*Kintsugi,*" I say hesitantly, trying to remember the word from an elective art course I took in university years ago. "It's Japanese art. They repair broken pottery using gold, embracing the breakage and imperfections, and it's even more beautiful of a piece after."

"So you're gonna put me back together with gold?"

"No. *You are.*" Warmth travels through the tight hold of our hands, through the thin gold band of my wedding ring pinched between our interlaced fingers, and flows through my veins.

His brain. Our story. Both felt a little bit irreparable in the beginning. But I swear I can *feel* the gold filling in our cracks and smoothing out the rough edges. One day we'll look back and realize how much more beautiful everything became after the fracture.

"I didn't know you're an artist," Jackson says.

"No, no. I only took the class because of a girl I had a crush on at the time, but at least it's finally serving a purpose. I don't have a single artistic bone in my body."

He pulls back to get a good look at my face, and when his eyebrows bunch tightly together in confusion, it dawns on me that I momentarily forgot he no longer knows everything about me. I have to re-share all the parts of myself I was nervous he wouldn't like back when we were kids—*what if he doesn't like them now?*

What if he doesn't like me *now?*

Amid the trauma of his accident, and the fear he wouldn't survive, then the intense caretaking role I stepped into with hesitation, it didn't occur to me that after all this, he might not like me. For years, I've made teasing comments about whether or not he wants to stay married to me, and for the first time, I'm afraid of what his response would be.

I speak back up before he has the chance. "Yes, I said a *girl* I had a crush on. I . . . uh . . . forgot you don't know that about me. I like both men and women, I've been with both, and I married a man but that doesn't mean I don't still find women attractive—I would *never* cheat on you or anything, though . . . *God,* now I'm rambling."

The rain's slowed to a spit, and I'm tempted to go stand in it with my flushed face held toward the sky. Very few people know I'm bisexual—not because I'm ashamed, but because when you're a woman who's been married to a man for over a decade, it doesn't come up in casual conversation often. And this is the first time I've had to share this part of myself with anyone in a long time.

After a few too many heartbeats of silence, Jackson clears his throat. "You've been with both?"

"I have, yeah. A *long* time ago, obviously. I'm not a cheater. You're the only person I've been with since I moved to the ranch when I was twenty."

"I didn't ever cheat or do anything fucked up like that, right?"

"You still have a dick, don't you?" I know him well enough to know the thought of looking at another woman that way has never even crossed his mind over the last sixteen years. "You didn't cheat. You weren't with anyone before me, either."

"Damn." His gaze flicks over my face, nostrils flaring. "My wife's been with more women than I have."

The laughter that bubbles up in my chest surprises both of us. He has no idea how much weight he lifted with a simple touch, a look, and zero judgmental undertone in his words. Every cell in my body aches to wrap my arms around Jackson's neck, let him pull me into his lap, and kiss my husband like it's our first time all over again.

My free hand holds his jaw, the sharp bristle of facial hair a delicious scratch on my palm, and I search his expansive brown eyes. They're the warmth of black tea in the middle of the night.

Just kiss him. Do it.

I've been fighting the urge since our almost-kiss. If I'm being honest, I've been fighting the urge since he woke up from the coma. I'm tired of being patient, waiting out a miraculous recovery that—according to Jackson and his therapist—might never happen. I want my husband back, in every sense of the word. Maybe a kiss would do exactly that.

I'm so close to finally giving in, silently begging for him to close the space between us, when Odessa's voice radiates from deep within the house. The raucous yelling of *Mom!* pulls me from the moment. I gather my hair in my hand, then let it fall with an exhausted sigh.

"I should go see what all the screaming is about. Rhett's

probably being a minor inconvenience and Odessa's being a touch dramatic about it."

Our kids are miniature versions of Jackson and me, I swear.

"Date night—tonight at two o'clock?" If I was the one needing to fall back in love with him, I'd already be a goner thanks to the arrogant smile curved on his lips, crinkling his eyes. "I'd offer to come pick you up, but you'll already be sleeping in my bed, so . . ."

JACKSON

Though I've been home for well over a month, I haven't stepped foot upstairs before tonight. Granted, until recently, I wasn't leaving the bedroom unless necessary. My hand wraps around the smooth light wood of the stair banister, and I head up the long, wide staircase to read the kids a story before bed.

I didn't admit to Kate exactly how disconnected I feel when it comes to the kids. It feels easier to find that footing with Kate again—maybe it's that the feelings never stopped on her end. But there's also something about her that makes me feel comfortable opening up to her. Even if there was nothing else, the wanton look in her eyes and the way her touch sends heat through my entire body would catch my interest. The chemistry between us is pretty damn undeniable.

While they're mostly sweet and cute, Odessa and Rhett still feel a lot like random kids in the house, and the guilt over my detachment—whether not immediately having that bond with them makes me the world's shittiest father or will screw them both up permanently—only makes me less likely to engage with them. Almost like pretending it's not a problem will make those fears disappear.

But my therapist told me to make room for the guilt, sadness, anger, all of it. Sit with the kids while they're doing things, even if I feel detached. Take it slow. Don't expect that paternal bond to happen overnight.

Rhett's waiting impatiently at the top of the stairs while I take my time, being cautious to not get dizzy on the ascent. His hair's still wet from the bath, and there's a bit of toothpaste dribbled on the front of his Spider-Man pajamas. Once he's confirmed I'm nearly to the top of the stairs, he darts into one of the bedrooms, and the sound of the kids bickering soon follows.

The moment I walk into the room, I'm hit with, "*Dad-uh,* Rhett jumped onto my bed and hurt my ankle."

Odessa's sitting in the middle of her hot-pink bed, hands tenderly wrapped around her injured ankle.

"I said sorry," Rhett protests. He's sitting cross-legged at the end of her bed with a sheepish look on his face.

"You *aren't* sorry." She thrusts her foot toward his face. "Kiss it better."

"Gross." He chops at her ankle with the narrow edge of his flattened hand.

I blink between the two of them, watching the argument turn into full-fledged fisticuffs over . . . *an accident?!* Odessa's kicking her foot at him, clearly not in as much pain as she made it seem. And Rhett's doing his damnedest to avoid the strike of her heel, but he's smaller and slower, and his sister's whupping his ass.

"Um, hey . . . okay, let's stop." I half-assedly attempt to prevent any major injuries. I've witnessed Kate disciplining them a few times, but I swear it only takes a simple look from her to make them smarten up. I don't have that look, as far as I know.

Worth a shot anyway.

My eyebrows knit together, and I scowl, struggling to stop the irritation from boiling over. I've yelled at them before, and I hate it. I don't want to do that again. My hands curl into fists, squeezing hard enough my knuckles hurt and my fingernails are cutting into my palm, wounding myself to keep from losing my cool with them. With a deep edge to my tone, I say, "Knock it off."

Odessa briefly stops to stare at me.

"I'm here for story time," I announce. "So let's do that."

Thank God, that does the trick. Odessa kicks at least a dozen stuffed animals from her bed to make room for me to sit, and before I'm settled into my place between them, the two kids are practically crawling into my lap. Odessa's bare legs sprawl across my thighs, and Rhett shoves his way under my arm so he's pressed tight to my side. Damp from the bath, his hair soaks through my thin T-shirt, and he stares up at me with giant brown eyes and a face covered in tiny freckles.

"Okay, what story am I reading?"

"You don't read us a story. That's boring—it's what Mom and Gran do." Odessa giggles. "You always tell us a real-life funny story or you make one up."

Anxiousness swells in my chest. Aside from a couple funny moments in the hospital, I have nothing kid-appropriate to share from my stingy memory bank.

Making something up seems equally as impossible, at this moment, since the pressure of their doe-eyed stares has my brain quickly turning into a mashed potato consistency.

"I can't think of any good stories right now. Maybe we'll start with reading one tonight and I'll come up with something better soon."

I'm scouring the internet for a children's book they don't own and trying like hell to memorize it.

"That's stupid." Rhett pouts.

Odessa reaches to poke her brother. "Swear jar."

There's rapid escalation in his pitch. "I don't even have any dollar bucks to give you."

"Then you have to clean Clementine's litter box for one whole week," she sasses back.

"Can we stop fighting and read a story?" I'm barely audible over their incoherent squabbling.

I'm not cut out for this. That's clear as day.

Then I notice Kate in the doorway, my jeans slung low on her hips so that the sharp angle of her hip bone is visible in the minuscule gap between her pants and a fitted blue tank top. Too beautiful for words. She runs a hand through long brown hair, letting it fall tousled down, then ties the thick locks in a bun on top of her head. And when her eyes meet mine, the skin around them crinkles ever so slightly with a delicate smile.

"Odessarhett." Their names blur together into one stern word that demands their attention. "If you want story time at all, you better knock it off. Dess, why don't you tell a story? I bet your dad would like that."

Kate leans against the doorframe, sliding a hand into the back pocket of her jeans in a way that has me wanting to abandon this futile attempt at establishing a relationship with our kids so I can spend time with her.

But for the sake of every one of us, I stay put.

Odessa nods, and both kids practically swarm me again, pressing their small bodies so tightly to mine I can hardly breathe. I don't know how to sit with them—whether to tuck my arms around their shoulders or if it's weird to rest my arms on Odessa's legs laid across my lap. I opt for leaning back on my hands, though it's not necessarily the most comfortable with the additional weight of Rhett pressing against my side.

Taking her new role *very* seriously, Odessa leans to grab the water glass from her nightstand and takes a long drink.

Her bedroom is simple and girly, with pink accents throughout and enough princess paraphernalia to supply an entire castle. Her bed has so many stuffed animals we may never find Rhett again if he accidentally falls into the plush pile. And between the brightly colored makeup strewn across a small vanity and the Barbie dolls in the corner, it's a strange juxtaposition; she's caught in the middle of being a little kid and a teenager.

I swallow the harsh reality that this girl—*my daughter*—is

halfway to being an adult, and I don't remember any of those crucial younger years. The therapist said to sit with that emotion, but *fuck me,* it's painful.

"Okay, do you want a real story or a made-up one?" Odessa asks me, once she's certain her voice is the best quality possible.

"A real one, definitely."

It never gets less strange hearing people tell stories about things I said or did that I don't remember whatsoever, but maybe this is the kickstart I need. I want to remember all the things that made them love me as much as they do. Odessa and Rhett look at me like I hung the moon, and I want to look at them like they painted the stars.

"Okay, I'll tell you my *favorite* one. I was six or . . . seven? Mom, how old was I?" She glances toward the door.

"I don't know what story you're telling." Kate shakes her head, straightening her spine and rapping her fingers across the doorway. "Anyway, your age doesn't matter. I have to go swap the laundry, then I'll be back to tuck you in."

"Okay, whatever, my age doesn't matter. But I know I wasn't eight when this happened." *Makes sense, given I remember the days since she turned eight.* "It was a hot summer day, and I fell in love down by the stables. It was love at first sight."

She sighs dreamily, and I exchange a confused look with Rhett.

"Her name was Banana, because she was a black cat with a white patch shaped like a Banana."

This story is heading nowhere fast. I can feel it. "You fell in love with a cat . . . got it. . . ."

"So Banana and I wanted to get married. It was perfect because for our year-end fun day at school, we had a competition to make dresses with toilet paper and I was *pretty good.* Mom wouldn't let me take enough T.P. to make a dress for me—but that's okay because I have a lot of princess dresses—*but* I made a dress for Banana.

"But then I remembered from Uncle Austin's wedding that we needed somebody to tell us we were married. Rhett couldn't talk yet, so you did it."

I snort. "I officiated a wedding between you and your cat?"

"Banana isn't *my* cat. Clementine is. Banana lives in the barn because she's an independent woman."

Every muscle and tendon aches as I hold back the urge to laugh. And the more I restrain myself, the harder it is to fight that bubbly feeling rising in my body. When it finally bursts free, the kids join in with me, and all the awkward tension finally leaves my limbs.

"You gave us a piece of paper for getting married and played fancy-sounding music on your phone so we could dance." She sighs fondly at the memory. "And we had ice cream after the wedding except you said cats can't have ice cream, so Banana had tuna."

Rhett proudly beams at me. "I was a ring bear."

"Bearer," I quietly correct. "That all sounds . . . *fun*. Are you and Banana still married?"

"Yes, but I haven't seen her lately." Tiny brows furrow with a frown that consumes her face and instantly brings down the energy in the room.

Here I thought I was playing along with the story. Engaging. Connecting. And I fucked up by asking what is evidently a triggering question.

I cautiously press on. "Why not?"

"Because . . ." Her lips rock side to side as she mulls over a response. "Because she always hangs out in the rafters above one of the stalls in the barn, and I don't like going there anymore, so"—her hands clap together and, as if she broke herself out of a trance, her eyes light up again—"I'm pretending she's away on a long work trip and I'm writing her letters, but cats can't read, so I'll read them to her when I see her again."

"That's a great idea. I'm sure she'll love the letters."

Odessa gives a single nod. "She will."

"That was a great story time, O—Dess. . . ." My voice stumbles as I try out the nickname I hear Kate use for her.

"Can I tell a story?" Rhett asks right as Kate reappears in the doorway.

"Tomorrow you can have a turn. It's time for bed." She hooks a thumb toward the doorway, indicating he needs to get to his own room.

But first, he wraps tiny arms around my neck, letting his entire body weight hang limply. And I hug him back, though it feels weird, mostly to keep his tiny hands from wrenching on my neck and hurting me.

"Night," I say, slowly peeling him off me and steering his small body in Kate's direction.

Before I can grab Odessa's ankles to move them so I can stand, she wraps her arms around my neck. Similar to her brother, but less aggressive. She smiles thinly—*sympathetically*—at me, then hugs me so tight a groan slips out.

"You don't ever call me Dess," she whispers in my ear mid-hug. "You always call me Princess."

In their wake, her words leave scars on my heart.

I force myself to swallow. It hurts.

I *think* I don't deserve this family. I *think* I'm a horrible fucking father for forgetting her nickname. I *think* my kids would be better off without me.

They're thoughts, not facts. Thoughts. Not facts.

Like the slow spread of water up a sheet of paper, thoughts have a way of saturating my brain until they feel factual.

"Goodnight, Princess," I rasp.

"Night, Daddy. Love you." After one last hug, her arms fall away and she shuffles across the bed to tuck herself under the thick comforter amid her hoard of stuffed animals.

And thank God, when I stumble out of the bedroom, Kate's there. Holding a palm outstretched, waiting for me to grab hold.

In our bedroom, pale moonlight streams through the window, and I wait until Kate's disappeared into the bathroom before stripping to boxers and climbing into the bed. Nerves whirl around in my stomach, waiting for her to reappear as if she hasn't been sleeping next to me every night for over a week. As if she hasn't slept beside me in this bed for more than a decade. Knowing we'll be having our first official date makes tonight feel different.

The bathroom door sits open a crack, allowing for a sliver of Kate's reflection in the white framed mirror. I watch her with intent, memorizing the way her fingers stipple moisturizer across her skin and how the light catches her hair as it tumbles out of the messy bun. The sight of her during this private moment sends a few bits and pieces of memory swimming through my brain, beyond where I can reach them. I've lived through this moment before. I reach blindly for something to pull me back into that night, and I turn up with nothing.

But I have her now.

"The kids were a bit wild tonight, but I think they were just thrilled to have you there." Kate's voice is soothing, lulling as it echoes from the bathroom. "How did it go?"

"Apparently I officiated a wedding between Odessa and a cat once." A smile tags along with my words. The story sounded too insane to be true.

I roll the string of pink beads around on my wrist, trying like hell to picture the wedding Odessa described.

She laughs. "Last summer. You said—*and I quote*—'Better she marry a cat than decide to marry some stinky little boy on the playground.' You both took it very seriously, too."

"Sounds like I was a good dad. . . ."

"You *are* a good dad."

Flipping off the bathroom light, Kate steps into the darkness wearing a matching satiny set—a thin-strapped flowy tank top and a pair of shorts that cut high on her milky thighs. The front of her top dips low between her full breasts, and something stirs in my groin at the sight. As she gets closer to the bed, the pale blue glow of the moon makes the fabric shimmer.

Still wringing her hands together to evenly distribute moisturizer across them, she adds, "Nobody's expecting you to immediately jump back into things like nothing's changed. You're trying, Jackson. That's all it takes to be a good dad."

She tosses back the covers on her side of the bed and slides in next to me. She smells so fucking good, my hands itch to drag across the sheets and touch her.

Propping herself up on her side, she tucks a hand under her hair to hold her head up. She smiles over at me, waiting for me to match her posture so we're lying face to face in the dark room. Her face is glassy and wet-looking somehow, and I'm tempted to touch her cheek to see if it *is* wet.

"You look like a glazed donut." I accidentally say the quiet thought out loud.

Kate howls a laugh, tossing her head back and nearly falling off the edge of the bed in the process. "*Holy shit.* If there was ever a doubt in my mind that you're still the same man deep down, it's that comment. You said the same damn thing when I first started playing around with skincare stuff. I do this skin flooding thing and then mix castor oil with my moisturizer before bed to hydrate my skin. *Years ago,* you told me I looked like a glazed donut, and asked if I tasted as good as I look. . . ."

Suddenly I have that same question. In a lustful timbre, it spills out. "Do you?"

Her laughter's replaced by shallow breaths. "You've never complained."

"I can't imagine any man in his right mind would." I reach under the blankets to adjust my hardening dick.

I told myself I'd wait until I feel like her husband again, but how am I supposed to stop myself from touching her when eye contact and a single flirty sentence makes my cock stiff?

"We should get some sleep." Her eyes drag over my bare chest, and I can't help but wonder if sharing a bed is as torturous for her as it is for me. "That two a.m. wake-up is going to come sooner than you think."

She flops down onto her back, hair splayed all over her pillow. Reluctantly, I do the same, and take to my usual night routine of watching shadows from the tree outside dance across the far wall and ceiling. I took my medications before story time, but thanks to the chaos of that and the tension in my jaw now, the near-constant headache I'm always suffering through is becoming sharper by the minute.

The room's quiet and still for no more than a couple minutes before the soft sounds of Kate's sleeping breath and adorable snores fill the space. I roll to face her, taking in the sight of the beautiful woman sharing my bed. And there, imagining kissing the softness of her parted lips—tasting all the sweetness I'm sure I'll have no complaints about—is where I fall asleep against my will.

KATE

The vile sound of an alarm clock clangs around inside my brain and pulls me from the best sleep I've had in weeks. I groan, cocooning my head under my pillow and simultaneously reaching out to smack Jackson on the arm, praying for quiet.

He takes so long to turn it off I'm contemplating getting up and smashing the stupid device. If only I weren't so tired.

"Kate." His voice is muffled by the pillow. He gives my shoulder a gentle shake and my limp-wristed slap against his hand makes him hiss.

Still, the relentless bastard tries again, muttering my name a couple more times.

I drag the pillow from my head. Pieces of my hair stick to the still-tacky moisturizer on my face, and I paw at it with an exasperated grunt. Suddenly there's the rough feel of Jackson's callused fingers delicately plucking each individual strand from my cheek.

"Thank you," I whisper, blinking to make out his face in the inky night. "Why are we awake?"

"Date night."

The words don't immediately compute.

Giving me a curious look, he adds context. "In the kitchen . . . with tea."

I yawn. "You were serious about that?"

"Yes."

His thumb scrapes along his jaw as he seems to consider whether this was a bad idea. It wasn't a bad idea. It's just that sharing a bed with him was working better than the sleeping pills, and I'm woefully overtired these days.

He's trying to connect, and anyway, it was my comment about bonding over our insomnia that led him to this date suggestion, so woozy as I am, I let him take my hand. Pull me from the bed. Lead me down the dark hallway to the kitchen.

I find a spot in the middle of the kitchen island, sitting with my legs crisscrossed on the cool quartzite countertop, lit only by the small light above the stove. The unrelenting yawns make my eyes wet. And the sight of him wearing only a pair of boxers, meticulously crafting two cups of chamomile tea, sends a wave of heat cresting and crashing in my core.

"Do you usually sit on the island?" He leans against the counter opposite me, waiting for the kettle to boil.

"I usually come strolling in after the tea has already been made and you're sitting at the kitchen table." I rest my elbows on my thighs. "Thought I'd try this new vantage point out."

I wanted to sit but couldn't stand the thought of the entire island—*or more*—between us. My insides are giddy, and I feel like a damn teenager, nervous and excited and desperate to be close to him. I watch the flexion of his back muscles when he turns to reach for two mugs, and the two perfectly round dimples in his lower back. The slope of his Adonis belt dipping below the waistband. I know what's underneath, too, and that's not helping the deep-seated want low in my belly.

"And how is it?"

"The view is ten out of ten, but I think that would be the case regardless of where I sat." I gesture at him. "I basically have a male model in front of me."

A splash of red colors his cheeks, highlighting the myriad freckles splashed across his face and down onto his kissable chest and shoulders.

"I love making you blush," I admit.

"You certainly have a knack for it."

"I have a *lot* of practice, and it got so much harder over the years. I'm sure if you scrolled far enough back in our text message history, you'd find some incredibly raunchy texts from me." I smirk. "Maybe even some titty pictures."

Jackson's quick to avert his eyes then, and he's so red he looks as though he might spontaneously combust. The kettle whistles in a *saved by the bell* type moment, and Jackson hurries to shut it off. Water gurgles into each cup with his slow steady pour, and by the time he's delivering my tea to me, his complexion is almost back to its normal shade.

I relish the mug's radiant heat in my hands. Jackson takes a careful sip, then sets his own mug down and hops onto the counter next to me, awkwardly crossing his long legs so our knees bump. With a deep breath, his stomach tightens, defining the curves of his toned musculature.

"So, uh, what do I usually call you?" Jackson asks. "Like . . . a nickname. I was informed that I call Odessa 'Princess'—though maybe she was pulling my leg."

"You've always called her Princess," I confirm. "It's done wonders for her ego. Not that I'm sure she needs any help believing she's the most important person on this entire ranch."

"She has everybody wrapped around her finger, doesn't she?"

I nod, taking a swig of tea that singes the tip of my tongue. "Guess that's what happens when you're the first baby in the family . . . and she was the only one for a long time. A lot of uncles and honorary uncles who have never been able to say no to her."

"I think it has more to do with what type of person you are than you're admitting to." He gives me a look. "You had almost everyone in that hospital unable to say no to you. Hell, I can't say no to you. *Bully.*"

"I told you, it's *love.* Not bullying."

"To-may-to, to-mah-to," he says over the rim of his charcoal WELLS RANCH CATTLE COMPANY mug. "So, if Odessa is princess, do I call you queen?"

"You've cycled through a lot of nicknames for me and somehow never landed on queen before now . . . and I'm going to hold a grudge about that for the foreseeable future."

"Great. Hate to see how mean you'll be now," he says under his breath, flirtatiousness laced in every word.

"You called me Kit . . . it started as Kate—*naturally*—then Katie, Katie Kat, Kat, KitKat, then Kit." My thumb taps a finger with each nickname. "I don't know where you'd go from there, but I'm sure if I gave you a few years it would evolve again somehow."

"Kitten?" he suggests.

I make a dry heaving noise. "Please, no. Do I look like a kitten?"

"Want my honest opinion?"

My fingers rap against his calf with a playful scolding, then stay there. He's so warm, the hair on his leg the perfect combination of rough and smooth. I mindlessly loop small hearts on his shin with my thumb.

"Kit," he whispers. Beckoning me closer or testing the way my nickname feels on his tongue, I can't quite be sure, but it feels intimate. And it sounds so much like the way he quietly moans my name into the crook of my neck, the weight of his body pressing on me from pelvis to breast, trying and failing to be quiet so the kids don't hear.

My core clenches around nothing with a familiar ache.

In the quiet dark, Jackson's hand finds its way to where I know the scar is still raised and bumpy on his scalp, making me wonder if it's bothering him. "What do you miss most about before?"

"I miss . . . the little moments. These two a.m. tea dates,

but then also the way I'd stroll into the kitchen in the morning, and you'd have a coffee poured for me. I miss sitting together watching our kids do silly things like dance to old country songs in the kitchen or create mashed potato volcanoes on their plates. I miss the quick hand squeezes or kisses or taps on the butt whenever we passed each other as we went about our day—sometimes without even saying anything because we were too busy to chat. I know . . . or, I guess, I *hope* we'll get back there one day. But I do miss it. . . ."

"We'll get back there." He sets his tea down and his extra-warm palm rests on top of my hand. His eyes flick to my lips. "There is nothing I want more than to kiss and touch you every time the mood strikes."

Then do it now, I want to scream. *Do it. Just touch me and kiss me and haul me off to bed.*

"You can . . . I mean, if you want to. No pressure though."

But also . . . *Please,* I silently beg. *Kiss me.*

Yes, we're married. Yes, when we were dating I kissed him first. But this is different. I have sixteen years of history on my side, and he's known me for a couple months. I remember our firsts; I want his new memories to happen on his terms.

A veil of hesitation hangs between us in the thick air. That's all I need to know this is another no. Or maybe, if I choose to remain hopeful, it's a *not right now*. Silence is rejection in one form or another.

Pulling my hand from his leg like it's red hot, I twist and slide from the counter in one smooth motion. When my bare feet hit the planked wood flooring, I lean against the kitchen island and will myself not to cry.

I want normal.

I miss normal.

I miss my husband the most when he's standing right in front of me, entirely out of reach.

It feels so fucking selfish when I pleaded with higher powers for him to live. I wanted nothing more than to hear his voice and look into his eyes. And now it feels like maybe my prayers fell a little short.

Jackson gets off the counter and moves to stand in front of me. I look up to find his eyes locked on mine, deep and dark and all-consuming, pupils staining the colors in his irises. My breath catches as he steps in to bracket me between his thick arms, gripping the edge of the counter on either side of me. He bends his head, so close to kissing me I can smell the chamomile lingering on his breath and feel the coarseness of his beard on my skin.

He draws his lips in, wetting them, before quietly asking, "Was I a good kisser before?"

My whisper matches his. "The best."

JACKSON

My lips brush hers, and I tighten my hold on the counter to hide the fact that I'm shaking. I giggle—and it really is a giggle, like I'm drunk on the possibility of her kiss. That barely-there touch is all I need to know that once I start kissing her, I'll never want to stop.

Her hands cradle my face, ever so gentle, with a smile begging to be licked away.

At long last, I kiss her. Delicate and tender. Her hands plunging into my hair. My tongue gliding across her lips, tasting the way they part with a gentle sigh.

For the first time, I'm kissing Kate.

For the hundred thousandth time, she's kissing me.

I'll relive this in every dream, and finally, I'll know for certain it's a memory. Her kiss is sweet and hot and demanding. Her wrists link behind my neck, pulling me deeper until my cock's tugging at the fabric of my boxers and I'm pressing myself into her with a moan vibrating deep in my chest.

By the time I trust my knees not to buckle, there are deep grooves in my palms from the square counter edge, and I wipe them on the soft fabric of my boxers before running a hand down Kate's spine. Her back bows, arching her into me, filling my lungs with her breath. Memories of kissing my wife before may be gone, but my body's quick to remember.

Our kiss is unhurried and deep, with passionate strokes of

our tongues and the occasional suck or nibble on a bottom lip. I hold Kate tight to the counter, running a hand through her hair the way she's done to me countless times.

Kate's hands coast over my naked upper body, knowing every curve and dip better than I do. Meanwhile, I explore her, traveling the length of her torso, the satiny fabric catching on my rough skin. Desperate to familiarize myself down to the most minute details, I'm undecided where to touch. Selfishly, I want it all. She feels better than any dream—and I've done my fair share of dreaming about this moment.

The thin fabric of her tank top catches on an upward stroke, and my palm flattens to span her rib cage. Kate moves into the touch with a soft sound that sears my nerve endings and makes my dick throb. My thumb strokes small circles and hearts against the side of her breast, caressing her the way she deserves.

We kiss and kiss until my lips feel bruised and her chin's reddened from the scrape of my beard. Kate's mouth pulls away from mine, our foreheads connecting with panting breaths heating the gap between us.

"You're still the best," she says, a little huskily.

"No, you are." I chase her lips, tasting every bit of Kate.

She toys with the elastic waistband on my boxers, slipping a finger underneath to nurture my insatiable need for more. Kate kisses me again, teasing and playful, clearly wanting more with the way she's fidgeting with my underwear. She nuzzles into the space between my collarbone and jaw, and her front teeth nip at the hollow of my neck.

There's no way she doesn't feel my hard dick pressed to her thigh.

I wonder if feeling me rock against her is making her wet?

My heart tips and spills into my stomach at that thought. I want her so bad it hurts. But I care about her so much, I can't have her. And that hurts, too.

"God, I missed this." Her voice wavers. "I missed feeling your hands all over me. I missed you making me feel good."

Fuck.

The trust and desire in her gold-flecked hazel eyes destroys me. Kate deserves rose petals on the bed and gentle lovemaking with her sweet, attentive husband. She doesn't want to be fucked against the counter by a man who isn't in love with her—*yet.* Three little letters carrying the weight of those three little words.

I want to love her the way I loved her before, and maybe better. Once I'm a man worthy of her, I will love Kate Wells the way she deserves.

I take her hand, raising it to my lips, and dust soft kisses along the sharp ridges and valleys of her knuckles. Then I take a step back. Put some space between us before my dick makes decisions my heart can't pay for.

Bleary-eyed, with kiss-swollen lips, she blinks at me in confusion.

"I, uh . . ." I nervously lick my lips. They taste like her. "What's your middle name? I just realized I've never asked."

She holds my gaze, glassy eyes reflecting the soft glow of the stove light behind me. "You stopped kissing me because you wanted to know my middle name?"

"I asked you on this date so I can get to know you. I want . . . I want to feel like you're my wife again. And what kind of husband doesn't know his wife's middle name? Or . . . *hell,* any number of things I don't know about you."

The way you feel and taste and sound when you come, for starters.

"Renee." She bends at the waist to reach out and catch my wrist, pulling my arm across the empty space. "Kate Renee Wells. Before you, I was a Dumont. So . . . there. Now you know."

I take a single step in her direction. Pebbled nipples poke

through the thin fabric of her top, begging to be toyed with, and I silently negotiate the terms of what *might* be allowable. If I learn enough about Kate first, fondling one of her full, rounded breasts should be fine.

"What did you want to be when you grew up?"

Her free hand cups the back of her neck, tilting her face toward the ceiling. "When I was a kid, I wanted to compete in dressage in the Olympics."

My eyes widen. "Wow, you were that good of a rider?"

Laugh dolloped in wistfulness, she shakes her head. "No, definitely not. But that didn't mean I didn't want some sort of natural talent to appear out of nowhere."

"And then you became . . . a nurse? Is that what your job was when you took care of my mom? I know you told me once before, but . . ."

"A care aide," she softly corrects me. "When I was a teenager, I spent a lot of time with my grandpa while he was in hospice. He had some of the best people helping him every day—making sure he was comfortable and felt loved in his final days. I wanted to do that for people."

"Being a world-famous equestrian would be cool, but I think the path you took was more important." Another small shuffle toward her.

"And it gave me everything I didn't even know I wanted. This ranch, your family, our kids, *you*. This life is so damn good, and I wouldn't have any of it if I hadn't become your mom's care aide."

How fucking good of a guy was Old Jackson that this perfect woman wanted to marry him?

"What did you want to be?" she asks, then quickly scrunches her face with a regret-filled wince. "Sorry, I forgot for a second. . . . *Shit, sorry.* Disregard. I'm an idiot."

I bark a laugh. "Wait, this is fun. I can make up anything, and nobody can prove it's not true. I wanted to be an Olympic swimmer—*wait.* Can I swim?"

She smiles only with her eyes. "Yes, you can swim. One time I watched you do a backflip off the rope swing down at the river. Maybe you could've been an Olympic diver."

I snap my fingers. "That's it. That's what I wanted to do. Then I would've met you at the Olympics in some far-off country."

"So your imaginary career goal is simply a means to meeting me?" Her whisper is hoarse. "That's a gross misuse of kismet."

"A childhood dream that brought me anywhere but this moment would've been a waste of time," I confess.

The joy in her eyes makes my heart skip a beat, and I step in to feel her warm palm against my chest, her fingers threading through the fine hair.

And suddenly—*fuck, so much for me keeping my distance*—we're kissing again and my hands curve to fill the valley along her spine. She whimpers into my mouth, hands cupping my ass and pulling me to her.

"Kate."

Her pelvis rolls to drag against my crotch. I'm aching to feel her. Hands, mouth, pussy. Any and all of it.

"Kate," I weakly protest. "We should go to bed."

She bites my lower lip. "You think?"

"And *sleep*."

Kate's touch immediately drops. I watch the haze of lust leave her eyes, replaced with disappointment. "Oh, sorry, I . . . I shouldn't have—"

"It's not you. You're perfect, Kate. You're you and I'm . . . not me. Or, *shit,* it sounds stupid saying this out loud." I gnaw at the inside of my lip. I expressed this thought to the therapist and now I'm lost for the right words to say.

She doesn't say anything, but nods, barely. Takes the stupid, unintelligible bullshit I'm spewing with a straight face. Her muscles tense, a slow twitch in her arm. A slow, careful motion. But one that indicates she's preparing to run.

"I just . . ." I swallow. "I don't feel like your husband right now. And I'm scared if I cross that line too early, I'll only feel *further* from him."

If words had the power to inflict physical pain, I think mine just stabbed her right in the chest.

"It's fine. I thought—it doesn't matter what I thought. . . . I shouldn't have pushed you to do something you clearly don't want to do."

"I want to touch you, Kate. *Kit.* So fucking bad. It's like my body remembers you and my brain's still trying to catch up. And fuck, I want to know you the way you know me. That's the hardest part of all this. You haven't changed. You still look at me like I'm yours . . . like nothing's broken. I want to know what it's like to love you again. I don't want to take something that was built on love and reduce it to muscle memory. . . ." I fight to catch her gaze and hold it, whispering my darkest truth: "And if I . . . if I never remember what it felt like to love you, I don't want what we do now to seem like I was only using you . . . *pretending*."

Watching the hope in her eyes crash and burn, and the subtle flinch like something inside her folded in on itself, I hate that I was honest. Everything would be easier if I ignored the niggling guilt in my gut and gave in to the sparks of chemistry between us for tonight. I told myself—told her—that I wanted to do things the hard way, but not like this. Not in a way that hurts her.

Kate blinks hard, but she doesn't cry. The tiny muscles below her eyes spasm for a moment. When her voice finally comes, it's quiet and controlled. "Okay . . . thank you for being honest."

"Kate," I start, already regretting everything I said. "I didn't mean to hurt—"

"No, truly. I mean it. Thank you for telling me. I'd rather you be honest than fake it—that would've been so much worse." With a stifled exhale, she wraps her arms tight around herself. "I'll, um . . . give you some space tonight. Go back to the guest room."

"I don't want that."

"I know," she says, already stepping away. "But I think maybe I do."

I watch her calmly leave, her hand brushing against the kitchen archway on her way out. Quiet footsteps disappear quickly in the night, and the stairs creak gently under her weight as she heads back to the guest room.

A balled-up fist slams down hard on the counter. Once, twice, then three times.

You fucking idiot. Your wife wanted you to touch her, and you pushed her away.

It feels as if my heart's been torn from my body and run through a shredder. I hate this. This isn't the hard way, it's the excruciating way. And just when I think it can't get worse, I return to a bedroom that feels like her, sheets that smell like her. My heart and head pound.

I don't sleep.

KATE

At five a.m., the kitchen's abuzz with cowboys grabbing paper lunch bags and fighting over Beryl's strawberry Danishes sitting on the speckled white island counter. Right where I kissed Jackson and inflated my lungs with his breath, felt the familiarity of his taste on my tongue. Right where he said sleeping with me would be *pretending* and knocked the wind from my chest without warning.

Trying is enough. That's what I told him. The truth is, I was still hoping if I waited long enough, loved hard enough, he'd come back to me. I was hoping so hard, I didn't notice when it turned to begging.

Bleary-eyed, I make my way through the throng of ranch hands and reach for some caffeinated elixir to bring me back from the dead.

Beryl flicks the end of a dish towel at Colt's arm, scolding him for taking two Danishes when there aren't enough for everybody to even have one. He yips, dropping the gluttonous second pastry on the counter, and the other guys heckle him.

"Get out of here, you animals." I groan through the headache. I feel hungover from the lack of sleep and excessive crying. "You're going to wake up the kids and Jackson, and then you'll have a *serious* problem."

"Too late." Jackson saunters into the room before nine

a.m. for the first time since he's come home. His fingertips press so hard to his temple, I feel the stabbing sensation in my own skull.

Everything in the kitchen is normal except me. I may as well be trapped inside a glass box. Seen, but not felt or heard.

"Well, good morning, honey," Beryl says. She's the only person I've known who's genuinely cheerful so early in the morning. Even Austin, who I don't think has *ever* slept later than five o'clock, is sitting in his usual spot at the table and scowling at his cattle ranching magazine as if it's personally wronged him.

Shoving a Danish into his mouth, Denny raises his hands high above his head to shoot finger guns at Jackson from across the room. He chews frantically, leaning forward so stray flakes of pastry crust land on the counter. At least he's a *tiny bit* more respectful since getting married and having a kid.

"I'm taking him fishing today." Denny looks directly at me as he says it.

"Oh, um . . ." I perceive Jackson in my periphery. Things have shifted since last night—he doesn't feel like he's my husband, doesn't know whether he'll ever love me again, and I don't know where that leaves us.

Yesterday, hearing that he's leaving the ranch for some quality time with his brothers would have me jumping for joy. Today it feels like an awfully convenient excuse to avoid being anywhere near me because I'm hanging on to a marriage he's not sure he wants to be in.

"I'll be fine." Jackson addresses my hesitation. "It's sitting in a camping chair on the pier."

Denny nods. "The fresh air will do him good. Dad's gonna tag along too—the old man's been working himself to the bone around here. He needs a day off. Poor guy's not even awake yet."

"Okay." I give the both of them a thin, tight-lipped smile over the rim of my coffee mug.

"I need some coffee before we go," Jackson says. His eyes cut to mine, and he starts toward me. Well . . . toward the coffee machine next to me. Coffee usually gives him a headache, so he must be *exhausted* if he's willing to risk it. "Couldn't sleep at all last night. Was just lying in bed, tossing and turning."

Whose fault is that?

His pained expression meets mine, and I hope my eyes convey that I didn't sleep either. I'm sure the under eyes that appear bruised and my sallow complexion give it away.

"Don't worry, I'll have him back before dinner," Denny says, popping the last bite of Danish into his mouth. "Probably in one piece. Except . . . can you drink beer with all your meds?"

"No, he can't," I answer for him.

"Designated driver?"

"Hasn't been cleared to drive yet," I reply.

Denny scoffs. "Shit, what *can* you do?"

Break my heart.

Jackson takes a sip of coffee, catching my eye again.

Colt rocks back and forth on the wooden stool tucked in tight against the counter, frantically gripping the edge seconds before he careens backward. Beryl scolds him, because of course she does. And Denny lunges in his general direction, as if he's going to push him the rest of the way over.

"Damn, wish I was going fishing today." Colt shoots a pointed look at his boss, Austin. "Nothing I love more than relaxing with a rod in my hands."

Denny winks. "That's what she said."

"That's what who said?" Beryl lifts a brow. "Is Blair going fishing with you?"

Austin breaks first with a bark of a laugh that catches him by surprise, and the rest of the room follows suit. Even me. I'm laughing, though it quivers in my throat and threatens to become sobs.

"No . . ." Denny chokes on his coffee, coughing and smacking the side of his fist against his sternum. "No, Blair's not going fishing. I was . . . God, I don't want to have to explain this to you."

I look at Beryl. "It's a joke. An inappropriate one . . . about *rod holding*."

"*Oh.*" Realization dawns on her deeply tanned face. "You perverts."

The guys are still giggling like a group of preteens when Jackson's hand skates across the counter edge to bump my arm. "Can we talk before I go?"

I nod, letting his fingers slip between mine, and follow him quietly into the still-dark hallway until the voices and kitchen noise have dissipated and I'm standing in the middle of our bedroom, staring at his tired, pale face.

I'm sad. Frustrated. And, quite frankly, so fucking tired of being the one who has to single-handedly keep this family afloat.

Even though living with a husband you can't kiss or touch or really talk to is a special kind of hell, I was happy to do it because I love him. And even though I knew it in my heart, I didn't need to hear him say that he doesn't love me.

Before Jackson can begin fumbling an apology I'm not sure I'm cut out to hear, I tell him, "I want to say something. Last night . . . I know you weren't trying to hurt me. You were being honest, and I appreciate that."

He opens his mouth and I hold up a hand, insisting he let me finish.

"But I need you to understand that it *did* hurt me. All the memories you don't have anymore . . . they're all I have. That's my *entire life*. And the thought of losing all that, and you never loving me again, absolutely fucking guts me. You're my husband and . . ." My heart beats violently and a solitary tear wiggles free from my tear duct. I sniff. "And I'll always make sure you get the medical care you need, but . . . I can't keep doing this"—my index finger draws circles to signify *us*—"if there's no light at the end of the tunnel."

He rubs his fingers across his lips, staring at where my hand's still suspended in the empty space between us.

"That said, I won't beg you to love me, Jackson. If it comes back, it can't be because I coerced you into it."

I'm not the kind of girl who begs to be loved. Lord knows I did enough of that with my own parents growing up. Even when I showed up in his doorway the night before I was supposed to leave the ranch all those years ago, it wasn't to beg or plead or convince him I should stay. I simply gave him the option to let me go, knowing if he loved me half as much as he said he did, he'd force me to stay.

I suppose the difference is back then my actions were bolstered by my confidence in his love for me. Now all I have is foolish hope. Hope is a bit of a plea, in and of itself, isn't it?

A burst of air blows from his nose. "That doesn't sound like something a bully would say."

"Told you I'm not a bully. Just a girl who takes caring for the people she loves extremely seriously . . . even if that love is unrequited."

Never thought I'd find myself in a marriage with someone who doesn't love me back.

Jackson sinks onto the edge of the bed, making it dip, and gently pats the space next to him. For a moment, I hesitate—the simple act of accepting an invitation to sit down feels like letting him win. Then he looks up at me, and I realize there's no fight to be had here. He's as lost as I am.

So I sit.

"I'm sorry." Jackson breathes out the words like they've been weighing on him this whole time. "Everything I said last night came out wrong, and I'm . . . I'm scared, Kate." Seemingly absentmindedly, he strokes the craniotomy scar. "I'm scared I'll never be able to live up to what everybody expects out of Jackson Wells, and you'll end up disappointed when you look at me one day and see a man who's nothing like the person I was before. And if I let myself be selfish—enjoy you now—I'll risk hurting you."

I spin the thin gold wedding band on my finger. "You think you're the same person you were when I met you sixteen years ago? I can handle you changing. You might spook easy. *I don't.* But if you're saying all this because you're scared to admit you don't want to kiss me or touch me or . . . don't want to be married to me . . ." The hot prickle of unshed tears presses against the backs of my eyes, and the thunderous heartbeat in my ears drowns out all other sound. "Don't bullshit me. Tell me there's no light at the end of the damn tunnel."

A tiny head shake sends bile creeping up my throat, and I will myself not to completely break down. Jackson takes hold of my hand and the calluses padding his thumb rub over my knuckles. Our joined hands tuck into his lap, and he frowns at me, eyes scanning my face.

"I'm not giving up on us. When I was in the hospital, you were the only good part of my day. I kept thinking to myself—and talking my nurses' ears off—about how damn lucky I am to have a wife like you. I'm the problem here. I don't know if I'll ever deserve you, Kit."

"You do, and you always have."

JACKSON

This early in the morning, there's a nip in the air as we unload tackle boxes and fishing rods from the back of Denny's truck. Plunking my stuff down onto the solid wood pier, I grasp the corduroy collar of my lined denim coat, tugging it tight around my neck to cut the biting chill from the cold lake. Apparently the last of the ice melted away only days ago, and none of the other fishermen in town seem to have gotten that memo because we have the place to ourselves.

Arms loaded with fishing gear and a cooler Beryl insisted on packing full of food for us, Denny and Dad head down the narrow, overgrown trail toward the lake. The heavy thud of the plastic cooler hitting the dock makes the entire thing vibrate, and I struggle to steady myself on my feet to keep from falling in. A dip in this lake would probably be nice mid-August, but not so much right now.

Water ripples out from around the dock as the wavy, boat-like motion slows right as Austin steps onto the long, narrow pier. With an expert whip of his elbow, the black collapsible camping chair in his right hand opens in one smooth motion, and he sets it down close to where I'm standing. Then repeats the same with the other chair he had tucked under his arm.

At the last minute, Cecily talked Austin into joining us, and though he was silent for the entire drive to the lake, he looks happy to be here. There's a marked decrease in the tension he usually carries in his shoulders, and his facial features seem more relaxed than normal.

The four of us arrange our chairs into a sloppy line, sinking into them with a collective sigh of relief. Denny was right—the fresh air is good. It's crisp enough to squash the inklings of a headache I had after the emotional talk with Kate this morning, and refreshing enough to wake me up after a night with little sleep. Haunted by the reminders of her in our bed, I spent the entire night slumped over on the same uncomfortable chair I sat in while she shaved my face.

"This reminds me of when I'd take you boys fishing when you were kids." Dad sits forward, lean body curved over his knees as his gaze bounces between my brothers and me.

Austin sifts through the small tackle box on his lap. "Except Denny's a bit less annoying now than he was then."

"A rare compliment from my brother. I'll take it. Thanks, Aus," Denny says. I'm not even sure he's here to fish—at least, he's certainly not in a hurry—with the way he's slumped back in his chair, hands in his pockets, feet propped up on the wooden lip running the edge of the pier. With the dark shade of his sunglasses, I can't tell from here whether his eyes are open or closed, but unless I'm missing something *really* interesting on the opposite side of the lake, I can't imagine he's staring that intently at anything.

Dad looks Denny up and down. "Didn't get much sleep last night?"

"Avery's teething, so nobody in our house is sleeping." Denny shifts in his seat, shoving his hands deeper into his coat pockets.

"When you guys were babies, Grandpa kept insisting we rub a bit of liquor on your gums, even though your mom told him that wasn't appropriate anymore. One night, Jackson wouldn't stop wailing, and I swear he snuck in and did it anyway. But hey"—Dad shrugs—"Jackson slept through the night. Didn't make a peep."

Denny half-laughs, lolling his head against the back of his chair to face in my direction. "How much liquor did he give him? Jackson barely made a peep his entire life."

"Hard to get any words in edgewise with you," Austin mumbles around the green fishing lure held between his teeth.

I watch Austin intently, copying his motions as he ties a lure to the fishing line on his rod. Embarrassed heat creeps up my neck, and I consider giving up—pulling a Denny and leaning back in my chair to try and get a nap in. I can live without most of my memories; it's hard to miss what you don't remember. But it's the moments like this, or like story time, when I feel deficient.

Austin ties a knot before I've had the opportunity to figure out *how* he's tying it. I tuck my tongue into my cheek. Seconds before I throw the entire bloody contraption in the water, Austin takes the fishing rod from my hand without a word. His big, work-hardened hands tie a delicate knot in the thin line, slowly and in my line of vision so I can watch how he does it. And when he hands the rod back to me, I mouth a *thank you* that earns only a tiny nod in return.

I shakily stand and copy Dad's casting motion. Thankfully, that one's a bit easier to fake than setting up the rod. And when the small blue-green lure, designed to look like a minnow, hits the calm lake with a *kerplunk,* something goes *kerplunk* in my brain. A brief memory ripples across the surface, and I fight like hell to reel it in.

"I remember that time we went fishing and Denny lost *two* rods in a single day," I say. Not because I'm looking for a reaction out of them. Repeating things out loud helps them stick. "Grandpa looked like he wanted to kill him."

Dad's eyes meet mine, and he gives the same soft smile I recall getting from him on rare occasions as a kid. The thin skin around his eyes crinkles. A glint of love twinkles in his coffee-colored irises. He used to be tougher, from what I remember. Gruff and quiet and hard to please. I wonder if it was losing Mom or getting older that softened him, or maybe it's being back here with us. From what I understand, this is the first time the four of us have spent time like this together since my brothers and I were kids.

"Grandpa shouldn't have trusted a twelve-year-old with his expensive rods," Denny mutters. "That was his first mistake."

Dad makes a face that says Denny has a point. "Definitely shouldn't have trusted you with anything after the first rod fell off the boat."

Details of that day pebble into place. "We were at this lake, weren't we?"

I glance around at the familiar setting that shouldn't feel any different than the hundreds of lakes I'm sure I've visited in my lifetime. Dense trees line the small lake, a loon dips and dives beneath the gray-blue water, and morning sun slants through the treetops to glisten over small waves lapping against the rocky shoreline.

"This was Grandpa's favorite lake to fish," Dad says. "Swore he caught a sturgeon here once and refused to listen to logic that the creeks running in and out of this lake aren't big enough for sturgeon to end up here."

Austin snorts. "A man of few words, *except* when it came to fishing and rodeo stories."

Denny chimes in, "If you heard him talk about his younger years, you'd think Grandpa was the best roper there ever was. Not a single piece of evidence, but don't you dare question it."

"Nah, we all know Austin and I were the best team ropers back when we were both in our prime." Fishing rod held between his cowboy boots, Dad bends to grab his travel mug with a small groan.

Austin's face twists. "Speak for yourself, I'm still in my prime."

Denny livens up a bit, though there's still a tired grit in his voice. "Oh, I think we need some friendly competition between you two."

"Wouldn't be fair. Dad hasn't been working cattle for more than a decade." Austin's verbal jab is meant to be lighthearted, I think, but coming from a place of deep hurt, it's no wonder it doesn't land that way.

Dad tips his face toward the sky and blows out a breath before speaking. "I want all three of you to know I'm sorry. I never should have left the way I did. . . . It's a shitty excuse, but I guess I didn't know how else to deal with . . ." His lips press firmly together and his hands gesture something that says everything he can't. Even after all this time, he can't find the strength to talk about his wife dying.

Denny clears his throat. "I get it, Dad. Losing the person you love does fucked-up things to your head."

Our dad sniffs, burying the emotion deep enough his tears never crest and fall. "It's a pain I hope none of you have to face until after you've lived long, happy lives."

My mind wanders to Kate. The raw, honest pain in her voice and the way my words hurt her time and time again. If I had died, would she be sitting here years from now, still unable to talk about me? I think so.

The silence that follows is deafening. I imagine my brothers are thinking about their wives, too. What it might feel like to lose them. I lost mine . . . in a roundabout way. She's still here, the only one holding on to our shared history, doing everything she can to ensure we get those long, happy lives we vowed to have. And I've been playing fast and loose with her heart.

Denny lets out a sigh and tips his head back toward the sky. "Man, it is way too peaceful out here. What the hell are we doing working our lives away on the ranch?"

"Paying our bills, feeding our families, putting roofs over our heads, that sort of thing," Austin mutters.

Denny huffs. "Maybe I could become a fisherman instead. Sit here every day, sell what I catch . . ."

"You gotta be able to catch something first," Dad points out.

"Hey, that's not fair," I say with a smirk. "He caught some pretty good Z's earlier."

That gets Dad and Austin laughing under their breath. Denny shakes his head, hooking a thumb in my direction. "Big talk coming from a guy who was asleep for almost a full week straight."

I shake my head. "That was medical hibernation, not sleep."

Denny cackles. "Having a baby means my sleep's medically required, too. I'll get Blair to write me a doctor's note that says so."

We lapse into quiet again, fishing lines dragging lazy paths across the lake's surface. The silence isn't so awkward or tense or sad this time.

Then Denny breaks it like he always does. "Hey . . . not to get all serious or anything, but it's good to have you back, man."

I squint at a dragonfly flitting an inch above the water. "It's good to be back."

Dad glances over. "You doing okay with everything?"

"Yeah . . . kind of . . . getting there," I say. "Kate and I are . . . well, I'm trying to figure it out. She's holding everything together, which is more than I deserve. I keep waiting for her to get tired of being patient with me."

"She won't." Austin stares out at the water. His typically deep voice somehow finds an even lower pitch. "She's always the one holding it together. The ranch would've been fucked after Mom died if Kate wasn't there."

"If she loved you enough to stick around during that, she's not leaving now." Denny's toe repeatedly taps the edge of the dock.

"Yeah . . . I said some stuff last night that I shouldn't have, so I don't know if that's true anymore."

"That was a stupid choice." Dad calls it like it is. I can't disagree. He's right. So damn right. "But marriage is a lot of messing up, saying you're sorry, and showing up the next day anyway. Sounds like you got some apologizing to do now."

The red bobber attached to my lure spins and dips below a small wave created by a family of ducks swimming past. My guts twist. *Dad's right.* I need to make this up to Kate.

"If I wanted to take Kate somewhere, do you guys have any suggestions?"

"Like for the night?" Austin asks.

"Not necessarily, just . . . somewhere that's more than a quick dinner date, y'know?"

Denny taps the soles of his boots against the boards underneath him. "You're probably not cleared to go riding yet, hey? I'd say the weather's only getting warmer, you could pack a picnic and go out for the day."

I shake my head. "Horseback riding is out."

I don't tell them I doubt I'll remember how to ride, if and when I climb into the saddle again. Given what a burden I feel like while still in recovery, I've been actively avoiding thinking about what my life will look like once my head has fully healed. My role on the ranch has long been training horses, and I don't imagine I'll relearn decades of horsemanship quick enough to be useful to the ranch in the way I was.

"Cecily and I spent a few days at some hot springs a few hours from here for our honeymoon," Austin says. "They have these fancy-ass rental cabins. I tried telling her we could sleep in one of the cabins at the ranch instead, but she wasn't having it."

"You cheap bastard." Denny shakes his head.

"Hot springs would be good," I agree.

My bobber bobs once more, barely tugging the line. I don't

move. Instead I watch it float steady again on a lake surface the sun's stitched in gold.

I want to fall in love with my wife again.

And a single weekend might not be enough, but maybe finding our footing again starts with a cabin, some quiet relaxation, an opportunity to forge the connection we're both longing for, and a view of her in a bikini—

Shit. I'm definitely not going to be able to keep my hands off my wife if I see her in a bikini.

Dad casts his line out again, then shifts his attention to me. "I can stay in the house with the kids. It's, uh, getting a bit less hard to spend time there, and Beryl stayed with them the entire time you were in the hospital. She deserves a break, too."

In my excitement over seeing Kate in a bathing suit, I momentarily forgot about Odessa and Rhett, and the fact that they'd need a babysitter.

"Thanks, Dad. That would be great."

He nods. *No problem.*

Austin shifts in his seat to slowly bring his line in, keeping the rod held tight between his knees so he can spin the reel with one hand and sip coffee from a beat-up old travel mug with the other. Such a big guy looks goofy in a tiny little folding chair, even goofier all hunched over the way he is now.

The air's quiet, save for the gentle whir of Austin's reel and the zipping sound of a plastic baggy filled with beef jerky. Denny shoves a chunk of thin, brown jerky into his mouth and awkwardly crouches—not wanting to fully lift his ass from the chair—to offer it around.

The final stretch to give a piece to Austin is the straw that broke the camel's back. The wood dock's a little slippery with morning dew and lake condensation, and the feet of Denny's chair slip out from underneath him. In a kerfuffle that surely scares away what few fish were anywhere close by, my brother goes down, nearly taking out Dad in the process.

The sight of Denny and every last one of his belongings spread across the dock is impossible not to laugh at. And boy, do Austin, Dad, and I laugh. Our howls carry clear across the lake, bouncing off trees and echoing far up the valley.

Groaning about the pain in his knees—and making a *that's what she said* joke at his own expense—Denny crawls across the slick wood surface to fish his now-empty plastic bag from the lake.

He pouts, staring longingly at the beef jerky sinking to the lake bottom. "That was the good kind."

"Hopefully the fish agree," Dad says, reaching to wipe tears away with the back of his hand. "Should've held on tighter."

"Should've kept it all for myself instead of offering it around. No good deed goes unpunished."

The dock creaks as Denny collects his stuff, then ensures his chair is perfectly stable before sitting back down. A loon calls somewhere along the far shore of the lake, and I relax into my chair, face tilted toward the sun.

Here with them, I like this life. I'm more Jackson Wells than ever before.

KATE

You'd think by now I'd have a method for making sandwich loaves that doesn't involve destroying the kitchen, but unfortunately there's flour dusting every surface and a mountain of dishes whispering rude things to me as I sit down and enjoy my coffee. I'll get to the dishes shortly, but first I want to take advantage of this rare moment of silence.

Rhett's outside helping Beryl in the garden—under Cecily's supervision, of course. And Odessa's softly humming to herself as she focuses on her homework at the kitchen table.

The coffee warms its way down my throat before settling like a blanket in my stomach, and an exhale from my nostrils blows small ripples across the milky surface.

Then the front door hinges squeal, raucous laughter warbles through the quiet home, and heavy cowboy boots tread down the hallway. Austin briefly stops in the entryway, narrowed eyes sweeping the kitchen before spotting his wife in the garden—Odessa and I don't even get as much as a grunt in greeting on his hastened walk outside.

Denny strolls in hot on his eldest brother's heels, adjusting the fit on his backwards hat and immediately pulling up a chair right next to Odessa so he can pester her. His chair scrapes against the floor as he shuffles it to get even closer, peering over her shoulder and pointing out a mistake in her math.

"You smell like fish." Odessa turns up her nose, pushing her uncle away.

"I smell like a *winner*. I caught the biggest fish today." He picks up a colored pencil and fills in an empty space on her multiplication table.

"Dad caught three times as many as you, though." The low pitch of Jackson's voice fills the room, and I shift my gaze to the archway connecting the hall to the kitchen. His broad shoulder leans against it, his hands tucked into the front pockets of his jeans. A day spent outside has left him rumpled, loose-limbed, and sun soaked. His complexion is infused with vibrant color from the spring air. Locks of dark brown, wavy hair are disheveled, practically begging to be played with.

He looks more like my husband than I'm used to seeing since the accident. It takes my breath away.

Odessa gives Denny a firm shove on the upper arm, and he scoffs. "*Geez*. I'm trying to help you with your homework. You know, I used to be the smartest kid in my grade."

"Really?" Odessa lifts her eyebrow. "*What happened?* Get knocked off a bronc one too many times?"

Jackson hides a snort behind a closed fist.

Denny's jaw falls slack as he spins in his chair to look at me. "Damn, when did she get so *mean*?"

"Go home and snuggle that sweet baby of yours. This is what you have to look forward to in a few years," I say with a laugh, eyes bouncing between Denny and Odessa.

He has a point—how did time go by so fast? I remember walking circles around this kitchen island trying to get her to fall asleep as a newborn.

After another small push from Odessa, Denny rolls his eyes and stands up. "All right, all right. I know when I'm not wanted. I should go give Red a hand with fixing the old tractor, anyway. Poor guy's been busting his ass lately."

"You should've invited him fishing," I say.

Red's picked up all the slack around here since Jackson's accident, ensuring it's business as usual at the ranch, even when Austin and Denny were in the hospital with me.

Denny heads for the fridge, grabbing a cold can of root beer. It cracks open with a loud hiss. "Tried. He said he pulled the engine apart yesterday and couldn't leave it."

Once he's clomped his way back out of the house, everything's quiet and calm again. Jackson crosses the kitchen slowly, fingers grazing the counter, until he's sitting down next to me and the bump of our knees ignites a million sparks under my skin.

"How was it today?" I ask under my breath, mindful of Odessa eavesdropping.

"It was nice . . . *normal.* It was good to get out of the house for a bit."

I smile at the red hue of a sunburn across his nose and cheeks. It highlights his freckles, which is always something I've loved about him. Without a second thought, I brush my thumb across his rosy skin. "You should've worn sunscreen."

With an impish shrug, he grins. "Forgot where we keep it."

"Same place it's always been."

"I figured." He catches my hand when it falls away and gives my wedding band a slow spin. "Since I'm feeling pretty good today, I was thinking of heading down to the barn. . . ."

In my periphery, I clock the way Odessa perks up at that.

Jackson must, too, because he continues, "Rumor has it, there's a cat named Banana that I need to reintroduce myself to."

"Can I show you Sprinkles and Tiny and Gregory?" Odessa bounces in her seat. Any hope of her finishing her homework before dinner is gone.

"Are they cats, or . . ."

"Yes." She stands. "Let's go."

"Hold your horses," I interrupt. "Dad didn't say he wanted to go right this second. He just got home. Maybe give him a minute to relax."

Odessa's bottom lip quivers, and Jackson falls for it immediately. To be fair, he fell for that constantly before the accident, too.

"We can go now." Jackson's big eyes search mine. "Do you want to come?"

"I could use a few minutes outside of this house, too." I chug the last of my coffee, then send Odessa outside to ask Rhett if he wants to join us. The door rattles when it slams shut behind her, and I wearily pull myself from the chair, having only had a few moments' worth of sitting all day.

"So, hey . . ." Jackson follows me to the sink, getting so close it reminds me of the way he'd pinned me against the counter and kissed me last night. How good things were before I pushed it too far—pushed *him* too far. "Going fishing today made me realize maybe the kitchen date wasn't my best idea. You deserve better than that. Maybe that's all I could offer when I was twenty, but that doesn't mean it's what you should've had. Austin told me about some hot springs he and Cecily went to. Apparently we can rent a cabin . . . Dad offered to stay with the kids."

Cecily told me about the hot springs after they went for their honeymoon, but trying to get a weekend away when you're married to a rancher is like pulling teeth. And it never happened. . . .

"I think a weekend away, just the two of us, could be exactly what we need. Plus, you deserve the relaxation. Think about how good it'll feel to be kid-free, soaking in the hot spring, eating at a nice restaurant. . . ."

"I *have* always wanted to go there," I quietly admit.

"Let me call them and see when there's availability."

My fingers press hard into the tension in my trap muscles,

and I roll my neck. "I think I'm having a bit of whiplash, Jackson. Last night you wanted to put more distance between us until you figure out what you want and now . . ."

Odessa and Rhett come barreling into the kitchen with mud on their hands and smiles on their faces. Their cheeks are pinkened from running around, and Odessa's hair is noticeably less smooth than it was before she went outside. Only our kids can find a way to go from clean and presentable to looking like feral farm kids in less than a minute.

"Uncle Aus was trying to spray me with the garden hose." Odessa explains her bedraggled appearance before I even have the chance to ask. "I had to run *super* fast to get away from him."

Rhett, on the other hand, clearly couldn't move as fast. His T-shirt's drenched and his hair's plastered to his forehead. His waterlogged shoes make a squishy sound when he walks.

"He sprayed me like he was a firefighter," Rhett proudly says. *Okay, so he didn't run away, period.* "Now I don't need a bath tonight."

I laugh. "Nope, definitely still need a bath. Come on, let's go down to the barn."

The kids take off at a run. They have two speeds: dragging their feet and sprinting.

Jackson catches my arm when I try to brush past, pads of his fingers pressing into my bicep. "I know what I want, Kate. Knowing what I want has never been a problem. . . . I'm *scared* of what I want, because I'm not sure I'll ever be able to have it."

"You have it." I give him a reassuring smile. "You just need to be willing to reach out and grab it."

At one point when Jackson's great-grandparents and grandparents ran this ranch, the large whitewashed building not far from the big house was the only barn. With a herd the size of the one the guys run now and a remuda to support the cowboys working only on horseback, we have a few barns and outbuildings spread across the ranch nowadays. But that original barn is where the family still keeps our personal horses.

My stomach clenches at the thought of walking into the barn, and I shove my hands in my pockets to hide the uncontrollable shaking. I can smell the copper aroma of blood in the air, the sound of my own scream rattling through the rafters of the barn, the helicopter's blades vibrating through every cell in my body.

Rhett grabs hold of my pant leg, tugging the loose denim and leading me down the gravel driveway. A clucking noise out of the side of his mouth pierces through the fog. "C'mon, horsey. Let's go to the barn."

With a concentrated effort on breathing, I smile weakly at him. I can't fall apart and panic in front of my kids. Rhett leads me right into the scene of my nightmares and, in spite of the twisting in my guts, I let out a quiet *neigh*.

A couple ranch hands are shoeing their horses when we step through the large opening of the main barn. The kids race ahead of us, and Odessa wastes no time locating one of her favorite barn cats, Gregory. I'm pretty certain the massive tabby cat is a girl . . . but I guess she's a girl named Gregory. I don't know where Odessa gets her names from, but this is one I support. The cat looks like a Gregory, somehow.

Horses watch us from their stalls, my boots scuff over the concrete floor, and the smell of drying hay overwhelms my nostrils. Rhett's using an overturned feed bucket as a table for an imaginary feast of hay shrapnel and bits of gravel.

Odessa packs Gregory the cat around like it's a stuffed animal, swinging loose below Odessa's arms yet somehow also squeezed unbearably tight against her chest. She introduces it to Jackson, followed by wildly theatrical introductions to her other barn cats—at least, the ones she can catch.

But when Jackson mentions Banana again, there's a noticeable shift in Odessa.

"It's okay. She's usually way up in the rafters, so it's going to be too much work." Odessa shrugs, turning on her heel to leave.

"Well now, hold up. That was the entire purpose of coming down here. Shouldn't we at least see if she's around?" Jackson peers around the barn, presumably looking for this elusive cat. "Where does she normally hang out?"

Odessa quietly points to the far side of the barn, and I understand exactly why she doesn't want to find Banana. Without hesitation, Jackson starts down the alley, dodging a wheelbarrow.

"Dad, don't," she pleads, tears welling.

Jackson ignores her, strolling down the alley. Odessa looks to me.

"He's okay, Dess. It's safe. *Promise.*" I grab her hand and put on a brave face.

She shakes her head. "No, I don't want to go down there."

Tears swell and fall down her cheeks, and she blubbers something incomprehensible. Crouching to her level, I pull her into my arms, feeling the weight of her head on my shoulder. Tears soak through the thick fabric of my shirt, and I quietly remind her to breathe.

She's been seeing a children's therapist an hour away in Sheridan every other week since Jackson came home, where she apparently spends most of her time yapping about everything *but* the accident. Regardless, with the way snot and tears are pouring out of her at the thought of stepping into that horse stall, I think we need to make therapy a weekly thing.

Jackson pauses, and turns to look at us, stoic yet curious. "Is she okay?"

At the sound of his sister crying, Rhett comes wandering

down the barn alley. He doesn't know exactly what's going on but, given the heightened emotions and tension thick in the air, naturally he wants to be in my arms too.

I hold both kids, squeezing tight, before offering Jackson some explanation. "This is where the accident happened. It was just you and Odessa here."

God help me, I hope knowing that doesn't trigger anything for him. I can't possibly be expected to hold all three of them as they fall apart. Not when I'm struggling to keep it together myself.

His chin juts toward the farthest stall, voice lowered. "In here?"

"Yeah," I whisper, then to Odessa, "Take a deep breath, baby. It's all going to be okay."

Metal clangs together as he opens the door to the empty stall. The blood has long since been cleaned, so there's no sign that anything bad ever happened here. After no more than a few seconds of standing in the empty space, Jackson comes back and kneels on the cement floor in front of me. And rather than falling apart himself, he wraps his arms around me and the kids, holding on to us as we do.

JACKSON

The late morning sun casts long shadows across the ground, glinting off the metal fence rails and drying the dewy grass. Though it's been over two months, and Kate no longer needs to dote on me all day, I haven't been cleared to do much of anything, and Denny's wife is my nurse practitioner, so I don't dare risk it. Thankfully my brothers are willing to let me tag along when I've overstayed my welcome with the women in the kitchen.

The overturned bucket Denny offered me isn't the most comfortable place I've ever sat, but it feels so good to be outside, in the fresh air, watching the boys work, I'll put up with some mild discomfort for the time being.

From the back of his horse, Colt tosses his rope with casual precision, looping it perfectly around the cow's head and cinching. "Damn, somebody sign me up for the Calgary Stampede this summer."

Denny chuckles. "He ropes *one* heifer—which was barely moving, I'd like to add—and suddenly thinks he's a pro. You gonna actually sort them like you're supposed to, or just keep roping them for the hell of it?"

My younger brother's leaning against the gate, waiting for Colt and his dog to sort the right heifers and cut them from the herd. He's got one hand on the gate lever, ready to usher them into the chute. But mostly he's hanging around with his hat pulled low, free hand shoved in the front pocket of his dirty jeans.

"Speak for yourself." Colt loosens off the rope, setting the heifer free. "You could help me instead of standing around looking like a Carhartt model."

Denny pops a hip. "Sorry, all I heard was that I look like a model right now."

From my perch, I laugh quietly.

They move together without thinking, years of shared work turning what seems like it should be chaos—sorting a handful of cows from an entire herd—into choreographed routine. There's comfort in the rhythm of watching them work, or maybe it's comfort in knowing ranch life goes on even when my part in it is momentarily paused.

Perhaps one day I'll be able to stand out here long enough to work a gate for the guys. But the idea that one day I'll be able to move cattle while on horseback feels unattainable, and the thought of what my future role on this ranch might be—rather, the lack of any role I could fit into—sits heavily on my chest.

"You doing okay?" Denny calls over to me.

I shake off the inadequacy niggling at me, knowing I can't do anything about it yet anyway.

"Yeah. Watching you guys is better than the reality TV shows I'd watch in the hospital sometimes."

"Just wanted to make sure Colt wasn't giving you as bad of a headache as he's giving me," Denny replies.

Colt lazily swings his rope around. "When my girlfriend, Whit, has headaches, she rubs peppermint oil on her temples."

I chuckle. "I'd need to dunk my entire head in peppermint oil."

"Well, my girlfriend buys pretty big bottles of it. We could probably set that up."

"You know you don't need to constantly refer to her as

your girlfriend," Red says, riding up alongside Denny and motioning at his metal water bottle sitting on the ground, silently asking him to hand it over. "We all know who Whit is."

"Jackson doesn't," Colt replies.

After a long chug of water, Red swipes the back of his hand across his mouth. "He might not remember meeting her, but he could use context clues to figure it out."

Red picks a black heifer from the herd, expertly separating it, and alongside Colt's dog, they move it down the chute. Denny kicks the dirt, hopping onto the metal gate and riding it until it's shut. The lever locks with a reverberating bang.

"Colt's just excited to have a girlfriend. Poor guy spent all of his twenties thinking he never would," Denny says. "Let him have this one."

Colt's horse sidesteps, inadvertently helping Red, and when Red thanks him, Colt pats himself on the shoulder. "Well, that's enough productivity for today."

Red snorts. "You're unbelievable."

"I'm charming." Colt grins. "And moderately helpful."

"Does your *girlfriend* tell you that?" I quip, earning laughter from all three of them.

I shift a little in my seat. The sun's a little higher than it was when I sat down, blanketing me in warmth. The ache in my skull is present—it always is—but it's dulled some, like even the pain knows better than to interrupt a good moment like this.

JACKSON

I stroll into the kitchen shortly after seven a.m., eager to see Kate. Seeing her smile is like feeling the warmth of the sun on your face. More energizing than a cup of coffee, and without the migraine caffeine tends to give me.

Despite the progress we've been making since Odessa's birthday last month—movie nights with the kids, family dinners every night, and talking on the porch swing until the night air has us both shivering so hard we can't form sentences—she's been back in the guest room since the night of our kitchen date, and I fucking hate every second of it. Two whole weeks of sleepless nights. An insatiable urge to defile every pair of underwear in her drawer. An almost empty bottle of her shampoo because I've taken to using it instead of my own.

The one thing getting me through this is knowing we'll be on a road trip to the hot springs in a matter of days and somehow, someway, I'm going to fix things.

I look around the kitchen, confused. She's not here. Kate is *always* here before me—getting breakfast for the kids, sipping coffee as she talks to Cecily or Beryl, meeting my eyes with an adorable smirk. But not today.

One hand cradling her pregnancy bump, Cecily loads the coffee machine with spoonfuls of coffee grounds. The aroma pleasantly mingles with Beryl's morning scones—the fact that this woman sets out fresh baked goods daily and we aren't all seven hundred pounds is astonishing. One thing's for certain, my jeans aren't hanging off my hips the way they were when I first came home from the hospital. Soon I'll be punching a new hole in my belt.

At the long antique table, the kids are both deep in bowls of cereal, Austin's glaring at papers spread in front of him, and Dad's sipping coffee while flipping through a newspaper.

Rhett's the first one who notices my presence. With a mouthful of Rice Krispies, he grins at me. A small dribble of milk escapes the corner of his lips and trickles down his chin, but he's quick to wipe it away with the sleeve of his favorite Spider-Man pajamas—I know they're his favorite because he wears them damn near every night.

"Morning," I say, so I'm not the weird guy standing quietly in the doorway.

Cecily punches a few buttons on the machine and looks up at me. "Morning. We'll have fresh coffee in a couple minutes."

"I'm all good, thanks. Where's Kate?" I ask nobody in particular.

And because I ask nobody in particular, I get nothing in return. To be fair to them, I don't expect Dad or Austin to know, but I'd love it if *somebody* could at least give me a shrug to confirm they heard me.

"Nobody knows then?" I grab a blueberry scone and hover above the sink to take a bite. It's flaky and buttery and I'm *so glad* I'm not feeling nauseous today so I can fully enjoy it.

"Oh." Odessa spins in her chair, running a hand over the plaits in her chocolate-brown hair. "She's sick. Auntie Cecily braided my hair for me today."

"Your hair looks beautiful, Princess."

"Thanks," she says, fingers fanning out the hair at the end of her braid. My words glow on her freckled face, and I make a mental note to compliment her more often.

I've been attentive and rapt during story time each night, receiving secondhand memories from the kids that I later piece together with Kate so I have the full picture. I feel closer to them now than I did weeks ago. Not quite there, but trying. Learning little things about my children that other people might never notice—despite spending all her free time playing in the dirt, Odessa loves anything that makes her feel pretty, and whenever Rhett's bored for even the slightest moment, he whips his wrist forward to check if he has Spider-Man powers yet.

I look to Cecily, who offers, "I didn't know she was sick. Odessa asked me to braid her hair, and I assumed Kate was helping you with something . . . I'll go check on her."

I shake my head, setting my half-eaten scone on the counter. "I'll go."

Glass of water for Kate in hand, I head upstairs and, through process of elimination—I know which one is Odessa's room, the bathroom door's wide open, and a third door has the letter *R* on it—I find the guest room. My knock's gentle at first, then a little louder, and when Kate's weary voice beckons me in, I slip into the darkened room.

"Hey." I keep my voice soft. I know all too well what it's like to have people barging into your space, causing a ruckus, when your head feels on the verge of explosion. "Odessa told me you aren't feeling well."

"Oh . . . hey." She sniffs. "I'm okay."

Her voice sounds like she's been crying.

My eyes slowly adjust to the dark, and I head for her bedside, setting the water down on a small table. She shuffles away from the edge of the mattress, making room for me to sit beside her.

"You sure?" The details of her face are too obscure to pick out, but I sweep a tendril of hair from in front of her eyes, tucking it behind her ear, as if it'll help me see her clearer. "This is the first time I've been out of bed before you."

"I needed my beauty sleep," she says with the faintest laugh.

"I'm using that excuse the next time you barge in demanding I take my medications at a specific time. In fact . . ." I reach for the glass of water and wobble it in front of her face until she reluctantly sits up. "It's now *my* turn to bully *you* into staying hydrated and taking meds and whatever else."

She mutters "How the tables have turned" into the cup before gulping half the water in one go.

"What can I get you? Is it a headache? Stomachache?" I take the glass back from her.

"I have my period." She cozies back down in the bed so the pillows nearly envelop her head entirely and the comforter's pulled to her chin. "I already have tampons, enough drugs to knock out a horse, and a heating pad. I'm all set."

Well . . . surely there's something I could do—*should do*—as her husband.

"Beryl made some really good scones." I'm immediately embarrassed by my offer. A scone made by somebody else? *That* is the best I can do? "I mean . . . shit. What did I do for you before?"

"Cuddled, usually . . . But you don't have—"

Her sentence hangs incomplete. I have a fistful of blankets in my hand, and I'm shoving my way into the bed with her. Kate doesn't fight it. She simply rolls onto her side to make room for me.

It takes a minute to figure out how I should lie—more accurately, where the hell to put my right arm so it's not interfering with either of our comfort.

I breathe heavily against her hair, reveling in the way her body naturally molds around mine. She's small in all the places I'm big. Neither of us has to work to make things fit. She's slipping into a space she belongs in, and a contented warmth melts over me. We shared a bed for a few nights before, but we didn't cuddle quite like this. Now I'm even more pissed off at myself for letting her move out of our room.

Kate seems to be wearing nothing but underwear and an oversized T-shirt, and I try not to think too hard about that. Even as her ass presses to my lap, and I can feel the heat radiating from her back against my chest. She takes hold of my hand, drawing it around her waist, and my fingers spread wide over the heating pad on her lower stomach.

After a minute or two with only her and I and the whir of the ceiling fan, she's been so quiet and still I wonder if she's fallen asleep. Until a silent sob racks Kate, making the entire bed shake slightly, and she fights to catch her breath. Unsure how to handle this, I stay quiet and weather the blunt force of her heaving breath against my ribs. I didn't know someone could cry so hard without making a noise.

With both my hands incapacitated, I smooth my lips over her shoulder and make gentle shushing sounds. "You gotta stop crying, Kit. Stop and tell me what you need. More drugs? I got some of the *good* painkillers downstairs."

Her laugh is wet and half-hearted, driving a sharp edge between my ribs. I've never seen her cry like this before, and I hope I never do again.

"Ice cream? Chocolate? I don't know if we have either of those things, but I'll learn how to make ice cream, if it'll make you stop crying."

"No . . . just hold me. That's all I want."

My hand moves with the gentle rise and fall of her stomach, and her breathing slowly returns to near normal. Kate momentarily releases her hold on me to aggressively rub away the tears, even though I can tell by her constant sniffling that more are falling faster than she can wipe them away.

Outside the room, Odessa yells something about heading to school, and Kate musters up the energy to fake a cheerful, "Have a good day!"

Inside the room, it's still dark with the curtains drawn shut, and she's falling apart in my arms.

"I'm such a wreck for no good reason," she mumbles. "I swear I'm not usually like this when I get my period."

"Bleeding, in pain, hormonal. Feels like good reasons to cry, to me. I wish I could be of more use to you."

"It's only—back when it was happening, I thought . . . I was alone—" Another silent sob cuts her off, and she presses our joined hands hard into her abdomen. "*Goddamn it.*" A forceful exhalation makes her stomach quickly press inward. "Life is really nothing more than a bunch of fucked-up moments one after another. Hurt and hurt and hurt, forever and ever."

I don't have the faintest clue what she's on about, and I say as much. "Can you tell me what we're crying about?"

I say *we,* because my eyes are burning from the simple act of holding her in the dark as she weeps, without any idea how to fix it. Déjà vu pokes and prods at my brain, making me think we've held each other this way and cried before. I blink up at the ceiling, eyes tracing a narrow beam of light from a tiny gap in the curtains, trying to tease specifics from my tangled, matted mess of a brain.

"Please don't be mad that I didn't tell you about this sooner. I wanted to—I would have, if things were different. I just . . . it didn't make sense to. Probably still doesn't. It's not like you know any different, so . . ."

My mouth presses to her shoulder. I hope she feels the brazen heat, the care, through her shirt fabric.

"Right before the accident, I was pregnant." Her words are soft and steady, yet thunderous in this dark room and in the depths of my soul. "Nobody knew . . . just me and you. It was our special little secret. I w-wasn't far along. . . ."

My throat goes instantly dry.

I'm scared to ask, "W-what happened?"

I suspect the answer before she says it, but my heart stops in wait anyway.

"I miscarried."

Hand held tight to her stomach, I start to roll her toward me. I need to look at her face. I need to search her eyes and hold her close and, fuck, I need to kiss her. Tell her I'm sorry, because I know this is my fault. Kate has suffered so much because of me, and I'm not sure anything I ever do will make up for the pain I've caused.

She vigorously fights my attempt. "No, Jackson. I can't—if I look at you, I won't be able to talk. I can't tell you this while you're there watching me."

"Okay. Keep talking." I nuzzle against her soft, thick hair.

"I miscarried," she repeats, inflicting even more pain the second time. "It was after you woke up. I don't . . . the doctor and Blair both said it had nothing to do with . . . but I know it was me. I should've—"

"No." My voice is surprisingly firm. "Don't you fucking dare blame yourself."

"I was a wreck in that hospital. I didn't sleep, barely ate . . . sometimes I wonder if somehow I did it on purpose because the thought of having a baby without you was too much to bear. Subconsciously sabotaged myself, or like . . . wished the baby away." She's sobbing again, and I can't take another second of it.

Shaking away her hold on my hand, I lift up and prop myself above her on the bed. Kate rolls to her back, cheeks noticeably blotchy and puffy even in the dim light. My forearms sink into the pillows on either side of her face to cage her in, and I lean in so close our lips almost brush. My heart pounds against my ribs, threatening to seize with every shiny tear I watch roll down past her temples.

"Kate, you did *nothing* wrong."

"You don't—"

"*Kate Renee Wells.*"

Her hand creeps up between us to wipe the dampness around her nose. And when she doesn't immediately move to clear the tears from her skin, I gently kiss the brackish rivers away from her temples, with my nose nuzzled deep in her hair. My lips wick away her sadness, working my way up to the outer corners of her big, beautiful eyes.

She quietly giggles in spite of herself when my lips press a barely-there kiss to her closed eyelid.

"There she is." I blow out a laugh against her cheek. "I'm so sorry. I should've been there for you then."

The thought of her losing a baby that was mine pinches something in my heart, and I'm sure I'd be as gutted as she is if I remembered those early days in her pregnancy. I can handle the blip of heartache when I consider that she should be pregnant right now, but the agony of knowing she was in pain all by herself is almost unbearable.

"You were . . . sort of. I woke up to so much blood. . . ." She gulps. "And I knew. I could sense it. I visited you that day and . . . I don't know. Knowing you were alive, even if you didn't know me from one of the hot nurses on staff, kept me going."

I definitely knew her from the nurses. I think if they woke me up from the coma, told me I had a wife, and asked me to pick her out of the lineup, I'd find Kate. Something about the steady gallop of my heart and the tingle under my skin when she's near tells me that my body never forgot her, even though my brain did.

"I wish I could remember the before. I bet it was great," I say.

A small smile curves her lips. "You were so happy. If I could bottle the joy we shared in secret for the one day we had it, I'd carry it with me forever."

"We'll have more days like that," I quietly promise, brushing the backs of my knuckles across her flushed cheek.

"You think?"

I catch myself leaning into her, until her shallow breath fans across my face. I open my mouth to say something, but my bottom lip catches hers, and I forget everything but the way her kiss tasted in the kitchen that night.

Our mouths touch softly, lightly at first. Tasting, hesitating, slowly deepening. I'm kissing her not because I want to make her happy—or even slow her tears—but because a surge of emotions I don't recognize are flooding my brain. It's wanting her to feel safe, protected, cared for, *loved*. And I jump headfirst into the feeling.

The way my body's hovering over hers, the weight of my pelvis on her, the feel of her pillowy lips pressed to mine, wakes every nerve ending. My hand weaves through her hair. I kiss her lips, her nose, her tears. Kiss her like she's my sole source of oxygen.

When I can't possibly remain in the plank position for another second without my muscles seizing from overexertion, I press my lips to her forehead and flop back onto the bed, satiated from the simple pleasure of kissing her.

Kate rolls to her side, backing her rounded ass up to me. My dick's hard from kissing her, and only gets harder when I slip in behind, pulling her tight to me. My palm rubs up and down her thigh, and she lets out a contented exhale. I'll spend the entire day being her big spoon, if that's what she needs from me.

She murmurs, "It's really hard to remind myself that touching you is off-limits when you kiss like that, then press your thick cock against my ass."

"It's really hard not to be . . . *hard,* when you kiss like that and your ass is rubbing all over me." I brush dark tendrils of hair from the nape of her neck, and her skin there looks so delicious I can't help but drag my bottom lip across it.

Her head tips, exposing even more of her neck to me, in a quiet act of persuasion. I'm but a man so, naturally, I give in and kiss her there. My hand slides to grip her waist. Her shirt shifted during our make-out session, and my callused palm on her bare skin sets a million butterflies free in my chest.

Honestly, thank God we're spooning, because I can feel the heat in my cheeks, and I know Kate would have a lot to say about that. I'm a married man who's painfully turned on and blushing like a teenager from touching his wife's *torso*.

My pinky finds the seam of her underwear and runs along the top of it. We both know she's on her period, so this is nothing more than a tender, caring touch. Her hips cant and, in a move we're mutually responsible for, my fingers slip under the elastic. My heartbeat floods behind my ears.

I want this. Want her. And my hesitation before did nothing but hurt both of us. So what if . . .

I drag my fingers across the skin right above her pubic bone, letting the barely noticeable movement of her hips guide my touch. If she wants it, I'll give her anything. If she doesn't, I'll wait patiently. Continue biding my time with jacking off in her underwear, with her body wash, to a Polaroid of us I found in her nightstand—lately I've had the sexual drive of a man in his early twenties, instead of late thirties.

Her neck twists so that she's looking at me in her periphery. "My period."

"I know," I softly reply. "If you don't want me to touch you, that's okay."

"What happened to waiting until you love me?" Her breath stops as the last word slips from her lips.

I'm falling for my wife so hard and fast, it's breathtaking.

I kiss the goosebumps along the back of her neck. "No need to wait anymore, Kit."

She shifts the tiniest amount, no more than an inch or so toward her back, so she can kiss me. The move also forces my fingers even lower. A nervous inkling that I won't know how to make her happy in this way anymore, since I don't remember anything about what she likes, dissipates the second Kate's fingers interlace mine.

"You're sure?" There's clear nervousness in her voice.

The blood racing through my veins is hot. Invigorated.

"So fucking sure. I'm dying to touch you."

"You . . . you used to do this for me when I had bad cramps. An orgasm usually helps."

The thought of taking some of her pain away is all the motivation I need. I shut my eyes, nuzzling into her hair and pretending this is one of the many daydreams I've had that lead to me coming in a stolen pair of her panties. I'm such a damn Casanova in my imagination, versus the ball of nerves I am now.

"Show me how I used to make you come, Kit."

Kate trails my fingertips over the neatly trimmed hair and presses my middle finger to her clit. The silky creases of her pussy hug my fingertip, and if it weren't for the fact that I jerked off in the shower less than an hour ago, merely touching her would make me come.

Moving our fingers in slow, meandering loops, she teaches me how she likes to be touched. Light pressure, small eights. Her hips lift to meet our hands, and I groan into her hair. It's a fucking sin that I can't see what she looks like, yet I can feel her. And she feels So. Fucking. Good.

Kate pulls our hands from her underwear, letting the elastic snap back into place. I gulp, wondering if I've *already* done something wrong. But Kate glides my hand up between her breasts, and suddenly she's taking my middle and index fingers into her mouth. Her cheeks hollow out with a hard suck that would bring me to my damn knees, if I wasn't lying down.

I'm throbbing. Burning up. My cock's stiff as a board, rubbing raw against the zipper of my jeans.

After my fingers are thoroughly soaked with her spit, she licks her lips. "Make me come, handsome." Her voice is breathy and sexy as hell.

No fucking pressure.

Left to my own devices, I take my time. I stroke the velvet hair there, trace the edges of her pussy lips, stipple my fingers along the crease of her thighs. I explore the gorgeous woman in front of me, imagining how beautiful her pussy looks, considering it *feels* this damn good.

Once she's writhing with need and whining small pleas to be touched, I find her clit again, circling with a featherlight pressure. After all, my only concern today is making sure she feels good. I'll make damn sure we have time for everything else once she's feeling better.

"Next time, I'm doing this with my tongue," I murmur against the curve of her ear.

Fingers drifting across her pussy, I squint to make out her facial expressions in the dark. Switching up my technique, relying on the muscle memory I'd previously condemned, until she's squirming and panting and squeezing her eyes shut. She whimpers, hands fisting the sheets on either side of her.

"Oh my fucking God." Kate's entire body tenses all at once, back bowing off the bed.

That's the spot.

"You like that?" I ask with an arrogant smile and a self-satisfied lilt to my voice. "Let me hear you come. I need to know if the way I've been picturing you is a memory or my imagination."

Kate kisses me—*no,* she *devours* me. Her teeth clash against my bottom lip, and she sucks it into her mouth. Our tongues frantically explore one another in time with the steady rhythm of my fingers on her swollen, wet clit. I lick the moan from Kate's hot mouth, feeling it travel down to pulse in my cock.

Pressing her head into the pillows, Kate's nails practically embed into the flesh on my forearm, and she bites down on her lip as an orgasm makes her twist in my arms. Every muscle contracting and relaxing in one fell swoop. And as my fingers slow to a gentle pet, she exhales through a sated smile.

Only a few memories have pebbled back into place since the accident, and I'm so fucking glad the honeyed sound of her coming undone hasn't been a figment of my imagination.

My nose presses to her hair, and I kiss the skin behind her ear as she comes down. I run my wet finger along the seams of her panties to fix the crooked fabric, then settle my hand back over her lower stomach. "That's a good girl. Feel better now?"

Kate's head lists to the side, and her orgasm-glossed eyes meet mine. "So much better. Thank you."

"Just doing my husbandly duties." I'm floating somewhere above us, feeling a whole lot like I'm the one who came.

A small crease forms between her eyebrows. "Jackson, I hope you didn't do that because you felt obligated."

I was worried before that touching her would feel like touching somebody else's wife. But Kate Wells is all mine. I might never remember proposing, or marrying her, or what the honeymoon sex was like, but I remember every moment of the last couple months. The soft words and softer touches, the love in her eyes when she looks at me, the way making her smile feels a lot like winning the best game at the carnival.

"God, no. That was purely selfish. I've wanted to touch you since the first time I saw you." I gently knead her soft stomach until her eyes close. "I want to be a husband—*your* husband. You're my wife. I want to cuddle you while you cry and make you come so hard you forget why you were crying in the first place."

"I love you." She exhales the words out like a pent-up breath.

And I consider saying it back to see if they feel as good coming off my tongue as the words *husband* and *wife* do.

"Don't." Kate cuts me off, clearly sensing the spiral. "Don't say it until you really feel it. It's okay. I don't need to hear it, Jackson. I need you to stay with me."

"I can do that." I pull her closer. "I can do anything for you."

KATE

It's been days since Jackson held and touched me in the guest bed, and we've yet to take things further than that. Not for lack of wanting. I want to feel him the way I used to—in fact, it's all I can think about when I'm tossing and turning in bed every night. But his words in the kitchen hold more weight in my heart than everything he said in bed that morning, and I'm so damn afraid of being rejected again.

With cruise control on, old-school country music quietly playing, and the midday sun on my face, we start down the highway away from Wells Canyon.

I blindly rummage through the mess of receipts and granola bar wrappers and pens without lids in the door of my car before producing a pair of purple sunglasses. The lenses are smudged, and the one arm doesn't sit perfectly straight, but they'll get the job done.

I jokingly offer them to Jackson first. "You looked cute in my sunglasses last time."

"I think I'll risk the migraine and squint instead."

I slip the glasses on. "You say that until you're laid up in bed and I'm in the hot springs alone later."

Sunshine paints the rigid angles of his face in gold when he turns to me with a scoff. "You wouldn't ditch me for a hot spring if I had a headache, would you?"

"Don't worry, I'll set you up with a glass of water and a

cool cloth before I go." I give him a quick smirk before returning my attention to the winding highway. "I deserve an uninterrupted soak, and if you want to stay happily married to me, you'll let me have it."

"You do," he says. "Sorry we never put in that big soaker tub you wanted."

My eyes dart rapidly between his face and the road. He doesn't even realize that he remembered something just now, and while it's not huge, it's *everything*. Granted, I'd love it if the thing he remembered about our marriage was something that cast me in a better light than my hissy fits over wishing I had a soaker tub in the bathroom.

"This is so much better than a soaker tub." I place my hand on the center console, palm facing up, and he takes the hint.

For a few minutes, neither one of us says anything. We simply hold hands, listening to the faint reverberations of Odessa's favorite country singer, Andie Wilson.

"I have a suggestion," Jackson says in a quiet beat between songs, "if you're up for it."

"Yes, I'll shave your balls before we go skinny dipping."

He coughs, choking on his own spit. "Oh my God, *no*. My brain's already fucked up. The last thing I need is to be accidentally neutered."

"Your brain is *not* fucked up," I sternly reply, then smile over at him. The speed at which his skin took on a rosy hue is astonishing. What I would give to feel the heat of his cheeks on my lips. "Those capillaries in your face, on the other hand."

He shakes his head, pressing his free hand to his blush. "Now my suggestion is going to be lame in comparison to whatever you're planning for this weekend."

"I'm honestly not planning anything except spending time in the hot pools." *And hopefully continuing what we started in the bedroom the other day.* "Sorry for hijacking that—tell me what you're suggesting."

"After therapy yesterday, I looked up some questions we could ask each other . . . like a get-to-know-you game. But, well—it's mostly going to be me getting to know you." He pulls at his pant leg, loosening the denim around his thigh. His nervous excitement is so pure and honest, it wouldn't matter what the suggestion was, I'd go along with it. I'd go anywhere, do anything, with him.

"I'm an open book. Ask away, handsome."

With a nod, he fishes his cell phone out of his hoodie pocket. After a handful of light thumb taps, and a few more twists and bends in the sun-drenched highway, he turns sideways in his seat to face me.

"Want to start easy, or go for an intense one?"

"Um . . ." My head rocks side to side on the upholstered headrest. "Toss me an easy one so I can get warmed up."

"Okay." His thumb moving across the screen makes something coil low in my stomach. "What's your favorite time of day and why?"

"Does it make me an awful mother to say right after the kids go to bed for the night?"

He snorts a laugh. "You're the furthest thing from an awful mother. Those kids are *a lot*. If you didn't want a break at the end of the day, I'd be concerned."

"Specifically, it's the moment when I crack a cold beer or pour a cup of tea—depending on how the day went—and finally catch my breath. Then some nights I torture myself by looking at their baby pictures on my phone. It feels like it was only yesterday we were bringing them home . . . and they were so little. Perfect," I say with a sigh.

So lost in memories that seem both yesterday and forever ago, I don't notice right away that Jackson's observing me with a look of adoration.

"You're an incredible mom, Kate. If there's one thing I did right in my old life, it was convincing you to be the mother to my children."

"It took very little convincing." No convincing, in fact.

Some people spend their entire life in pursuit of a dream. My dream has always been one thing that so few people achieve, and yet it came to me in a rushing wave that summer sixteen years ago.

I want to be happy.

And with him, I am. Always will be.

He looks back down at his phone, knuckles creating a scratchy grating sound as they run over his coarse facial hair. My fingers tap the steering wheel, drumming along to the low bass in a song I can't quite make out. The radio station cuts in and out with the cadenced curves of a mostly-empty highway etched into the side of a sky-high mountain.

"Aren't you going to answer?" I ask, when it becomes obvious he's looking for a new question to ask. "Your favorite time of day . . ."

"You probably know the answer."

I shake my head. A few months ago, I knew everything about my husband. And I've struggled to shake the notion that this man beside me is exactly the same person he was before.

"In the morning, when I wake up and remember that you exist."

The car rolls to a stop in the parking lot of a small-town shopping complex. Another twenty minutes up a dirt road, and we'll be at the hot springs, but the incessant growling in my stomach is starting to interfere with both my ability to answer Jackson's road trip questions *and* my ability to remain calm and collected with so many terrible drivers on the scenic highway route. I squint at the assortment of businesses laid out in front of us. Between the post office, liquor store, pizza place, and hair salon, this really is a one-stop shop.

"Divide and conquer?" Jackson drums his hands on the black metal hood of my SUV. "You grab us dinner and maybe find something to drink by the fire tonight"—he gestures toward the hole-in-the-wall liquor store squished between a laundromat and bookkeeping service—"and I'll stock up on snacks from the grocery store."

"Look at us working as a team."

He scratches the back of his head and looks over his shoulder briefly. "Should, uh . . . should I buy *condoms*?" He whispers *condoms* as if he's suggesting something illegal.

"A little presumptuous, don't you think?" I tease, arching a brow and watching his cheeks turn pink.

With a bashful smile, he shrugs.

"If it'll make you feel more comfortable. Even when we've wanted to get pregnant, it's taken months of careful planning, plus I'm not ovulating . . . but if you don't want to risk it, that's fine with me."

"Stupid question, probably, but we didn't use them before, did we?"

"Not since we were in our early twenties, no. I'm okay with whatever you're okay with, Jackson. I don't want to pressure you to do anything."

"Okay . . ." He nods thoughtfully. "Okay. I'll buy some, just in case."

It's a short walk to the only dinner place here that isn't a chain restaurant: Poppy's Pizza. Whether it's named after a girl named Poppy or the nickname somebody has for their sweet old grandfather, I immediately trust a food establishment with a name like Poppy's Pizza.

The wafting aroma of pizza dough reminds me of home, and of the other night when we had *make your own pizza night*. Rhett smothered his in so much sauce the sourdough crust I'd made became soggy, and topped it with enough cheese

Jackson warned him he wouldn't be able to poop for a week. Then the kids devolved into a fit of giggles over pepperoni looking like poop, their conversation turning gross enough Jackson peeled the pepperoni off his own pizza with a disgusted grimace. And while the kids picked a movie, and the pizza toppings bubbled in the oven, Jackson leaned back against the messy counter and gripped my waist in his firm, steady hands. Tugged me into him like the moon pulls the tide. Kissed me until my insides were more melty and gooey than the cheese on our pizzas.

Once my pizza and sparkling wine—I'm typically a beer girl, but this weekend deserves something fancy—have been acquired, I traipse back to my car, where Jackson's waiting with a bundle of flowers and a bag near bursting with snack foods. When I proudly hold up the bottle of wine as I wait for a car to pass, he gives me a lopsided grin that makes my heart squeeze. Too handsome for words, that man.

"What are the flowers for?" I ask on my approach.

"Saw them in the store and thought of you." He plucks the hot pizza box and wine bottle from my hand.

"They're lilies."

"If you don't like them, we—"

I cross the narrow space between us, barely giving him enough time to plop the pizza box on the hood of my SUV before I capture his mouth with mine, kissing him breathlessly. Flowers pressed between our heaving chests, we break apart for a sharp intake of breath before crashing into each other again. His tongue sweeping between my lips, and his hand cupping my face. My core aches at the feel of his callused fingers smoothing up my jawline, knotting in my loose hair.

"So you like the flowers?" he murmurs against my mouth when we finally come up for more air.

I attempt to spiff up the smushed white petals and bent stems. Tears pinprick and tingle in my eyes, nose, cheeks. I breathe in the sweet floral scent and blink up at him through tearstained vision.

"They're perfect, Jackson. They're . . ." I roll my lips together, blinking up at wisps of cotton-candy clouds in a light blue sky. This moment is so perfect, I can't believe it's real. "These were our wedding flowers. Did you know that?"

His eyes widen. "No. I saw . . ." Jackson's tone is guttural, full of emotion. The column of his throat moves up and down with a thick swallow. "I saw them and felt like you should have them because you deserve nice things like flowers. You deserve an uninterrupted soak in the hot springs, for me to make you coffee in the mornings, and to be kissed as many times as I can fit into a day. So . . . so I bought them because my wife deserves pretty flowers."

"And to be kissed as many times as you can fit into a day?" I tease, reaching past him to carefully set the bouquet on the hood next to our pizza and snacks. "That's a lot of kisses."

"I have sixteen years' worth of practice I need to make up for." He taps a finger against my lips, a wicked smile playing at the corner of his, and I can't help but assume he's thinking about making up for much more than simple kissing practice.

Jackson's hand glides into my hair, tugs my mouth to meet him in a kiss. Swept up in the moment, he slowly grinds his pelvis on mine. His hands move to grab at my ass. It's anything but small-town parking lot appropriate. Twenty minutes of driving to get to the hot springs suddenly sounds unbearable.

A car slows next to us, and an older woman shouts at us to get a room.

Kisses transform into uncontrollable giggles, with my head resting on his shoulder and his hand sweeping across my back. Then we're racing to grab all our belongings off the hood and hop into the car before the woman and her black sedan make their second loop of the parking lot.

The woman slows right down as she passes by, and I flip her the bird out of my window.

"Now this *really* feels like when we eloped. The random small-town pit stop, grocery store bouquet, sparkling wine for our hotel room . . . I don't remember anybody yelling at us, but I'm sure some people wanted to with the amount of PDA we had going on."

Turning the key, I look over at Jackson and take in the features of his face as if I haven't seen them a thousand times. A thousand times or a million, I'll never tire of it. Strong jaw, kissable lips, gently sloped nose, and eyes staring back at mine with so much love in them, my heart skips a beat.

"I can't believe of all the bouquets they had in there, I grabbed these." Jackson looks down at the flowers—still a little worse for the wear, but somehow better in their damaged state. It feels like a metaphor for our life.

"I can." Reaching to slip the shifter knob into reverse, I stop for a quick squeeze of his hand. "A lot of the memories are out of reach, but you're still you. It's not Old versus New Jackson, like you always refer to yourself. You're the same observant, thoughtful, loving man I've known for sixteen years. Maybe you can't see it because you don't remember, but everyone around you can."

"You think?"

"I know."

He tips his head back, eyes drifting to look out the passenger window, and his left hand falls onto my lap. I feel the drag of his thumb drawing circles through my jeans. "Why did we elope?"

"Um . . ." I turn the radio dial all the way down. "A few reasons. After your mom died, the ranch changed—the way you see it now, with people always around, laughter throughout the house, kids running around? It wasn't like that for a *long* time after she died. Would've made for a bummer of a wedding.

"And because we were all busting our asses to keep the ranch going in those first few years, we didn't exactly have disposable cash to spend on a party. My parents would've paid, but . . . you'll meet them when they visit at Christmas and see why I wasn't having a big wedding to appease them. They're . . . I love them. *I do.* But they're so different from the family, and the home, we've created. I grew up riding English because they saw it as a classy sport—one where I'd surely meet some well-off man to sweep me off my feet."

He snorts. "And instead you ended up with a cowboy."

"Oh, they *hated* it. Not that they'd ever say as much to your face, because *appearances.* They've come around to you over the years, thankfully. But I think the sight of Odessa covered head to toe in mud, barn cat tucked under her arm, would send my mother into a coma—*oh my God,* that was a fucked-up thing to say to you."

Jackson's booming laughter fills the car, vibrating through my chest and tingling the skin from my scalp to my toes. It's the best sound in the entire world. Better yet because I wasn't sure I'd hear it again.

"The next time they come over, I'm paying Odessa to do exactly that," he says.

"I'm afraid you wouldn't even need to pay her. That's just a typical day in our house."

He shakes his head. "That's what I love so much about it."

JACKSON

Kate's infectious laughter fills the one-room cabin, a wash of color warms her fair skin—whether from the heat of the crackling fire in the stone fireplace, the sparkling wine she's been sipping straight from the bottle, or the question I just asked her, it's hard to know. Flickers of firelight play across the bedspread, illuminating the wine bottle, the pizza.

"No, no. *Skip.*"

"Don't be a poor sport." I've only had a couple minuscule sips of her wine for fear that I'll get a headache later and not be able to take my painkillers, but I feel a buzz tingling the length of my spine. I bypassed all the platonic or emotional questions and went right to the bottom of the list—the explicit section I almost didn't note down because I was positive I'd never have the balls to ask Kate such deeply personal things. Funny how liquid courage works. "We've come so far. You can't start skipping questions now."

"Says who? You failed to mention there were rules." She untucks her knees from under her and extends her willowy legs across the bed, then picks a piece of pineapple from the pizza between us and pops it onto her tongue. "But *fine*. I guess my favorite sex position is the butter churner."

My eyes go wide. *The what?!* I'm aware I'm a solid sixteen years behind where I used to be when it comes to sexual knowledge—my body seems to know what to do, but my brain's playing catch-up—but how freaky were we before the accident?

"The . . . like . . . the old-timey thing?" I do a butter-churning motion with my hands.

A goofy, lopsided smile overtakes her face.

I groan-laugh. "You're fucking with me, aren't you?"

"Guess you'll have to wait and see. Your turn to answer the question." She's been making me answer, not accepting my argument that I don't *know* a lot of the answers. I make them up. She tells me my ability to come up with a story on the fly is the reason the kids love my story time better than hers.

"The, uh . . ." I glance around the impromptu picnic we have strewn across the bed, seeking inspiration so I don't hit her with something lame like *missionary*. Though, to be fair, I'd happily have sex with my wife in any position. "The Double-Hawaiian Pretzel."

"Oh yeah?" She lifts the bottle of wine to her lips. "How does that one work again?"

"Well, it's kind of—" I twist my hands, mangling my fingers into what could be a depiction of tangled limbs or the mess of fishing line that ultimately made me give up early when I went fishing with my dad and brothers.

She smiles up at me. Big hazel eyes, fluttering eyelashes, rosy cheeks. And I feel achy not only in my chest, but all over.

I reach for the wine, take a pull and let the heady, fizzy liquid sit on my tongue for a few seconds before swallowing. I take in my surroundings, taking pleasure in the bubbly feeling in my stomach. The cabin's rustic, decorated with antiques that remind me of home, and the firelight casts our shadows on the wall behind Kate. Anywhere with her is my favorite place in the world, but here tonight might be my favorite of favorites.

"Okay, but *where* is your favorite place to have sex?" I ask.

"Here's the thing . . . you've always been a bit . . . *vanilla,*" she says, then quickly adds, "That's not a bad thing. It's always been good—best I've ever had, genuinely. So I didn't push for you to be more adventurous."

She says it's not a bad thing, but there's no way it's a good thing, either.

"Let me change the question then . . . where would you like to have sex?" My heart beats a hundred miles per hour as I wait for her answer.

"Jackson, it's not a big deal," she insists. "I'm more than happy with our sex life."

"If you could pick anywhere." My voice wobbles. "Doesn't mean we'll necessarily do it."

We will.

Kate studies me. Her elbows dip into the thick bedding to support her upper body, and her tongue skates between her lips.

"I guess . . ." She thinks another moment.

I reach to brush the hair off her shoulder. Touching her feels second nature to me now, and a slight brush of skin on skin is enough to tame my darkest demons. Kate's smile, the look of adoration she always has for me. I'm not sure she knows she does it, but her presence is inherently calming. Funny, given she's also my biggest bully.

"I guess I'd say in the hot springs."

"*In* the hot springs?"

Her hackles raise. "You said anywhere and it doesn't mean we'll do it."

"You're right, I did." *We will.* I don't know how, but we will. "I think I'd pick . . . on an airplane."

"You've never even been on a plane."

"Then it would be the perfect way to ease my nerves about flying for the first time."

She giggles, flopping back onto the bed and blowing a breath up to the ceiling. I join her. Our heads nearly collide at the foot of the bed, and I snake my hand through the food mess to pinch the fabric of her shirt between my finger and thumb. I slip underneath it to stroke her lower stomach, circling around her hip bone and tickling up the side of her torso.

"Can I ask you a question?" Kate's eyes meet mine. Molten. Warm. She slings an arm overhead, and her fingers wrap around the brass bed frame. "Do you want to have sex with me this weekend?"

Oh, God. Do I.

"Kate." Her name leaves my lips in a breathless, wanton rasp. "If the only time we leave this bed is to go have sex in the hot springs, I'll be perfectly happy with that."

"No, no. I'm still getting my soak. I will *not* be missing that." She jabs an index finger through the air at me. "I only asked because I want to make sure we're on the same page."

"We are."

I don't know how to transition from *talking* about sex to doing it. In my dreams, we're always mid–sex scene. And in the kitchen, it was a heat-of-the-moment situation, versus this well-thought-out sex-having weekend. Now we're here and we both know we want to be having sex, but surely I can't just jump on top of her and get to it.

"I guess we better clean up this mess—don't need pizza crumbs getting into unsavory places." Kate takes the initiative I apparently can't. "Let's do that, then take a hot shower since we spent all afternoon sitting in a car, and we'll go from there. No pressure."

No pressure. It plays on repeat while I close up the pizza box, pass by her on the way to the tiny fridge, give her perfect ass a soft love tap that she reciprocates. It plays on repeat as I toss another chunk of timber into the fire. And it's reverberating through my skull as I follow her into the bathroom.

There's so much damn pressure my heart *thrashes* to fight against suffocating under the weight of it. *I've lost my virginity before,* I remind myself. Lost my virginity and made love to this beautiful woman at least three times in my life—got the kids to prove it. Doesn't mean I'm any less nervous now than I imagine I was all those years ago.

Kate tucks her hair behind her ears and rummages through her toiletry bag for that body wash I love so damn much.

"Remember when—" She freezes, deer-in-the-headlights style.

Through a throaty laugh, I press, "No, no. Keep going. You have about a ten percent chance here."

"I was going to bring up the time you tried to go down on me in the shower years ago, but you slipped trying to kneel and took out the shower curtain."

"Shoot, that fell into the ninety percent. But maybe that explains why I haven't been too adventurous? Less chance of an embarrassing sex injury if we stay in bed."

"Maybe. You've always been surprisingly risk-averse for a cowboy and horse trainer." She shrugs, plunking the nearly empty bottle onto the shower shelf. I'm sure she's noticed how much faster she's going through it since I came home, but she hasn't said anything.

Kate turns the shower on. It's plenty big enough for the two of us, but after hearing the story about my near-death shower sex experience, I'm a little worried about the glass door—not that my natural risk aversion is going to keep me from being under that hot water with her. Then Kate grabs my hands and slips them around her waist. I've never known desire the way I do with my hands on her waist.

She twists in my arms. Back pressed to my chest, her reflection finds mine in the small mirror above the sink. Kate grasps the hem of her shirt, pulling it up and overhead, tossing it to the bathroom floor. I drink in the sight of her in a pair of my old jeans and a thin black bra. I want to touch her. Lick every inch of her skin. But I remain paralyzed in place, hands trembling against her hips.

"It's okay to want it, Jackson . . . it's already yours. I'm yours."

She tucks her hair in her hands, sweeping it over to one side, exposing the creamy skin on the back of her neck. Keeping my eyes locked on hers in the mirror, I gently kiss her there.

My heart stops so abruptly at the slow unbuttoning of her jeans I'm afraid it'll never start again. And when they fall to the floor, so does my jaw. Muscular, lithe legs stretch all the way to squeezable hips. Thin white scars glitter across her stomach, and with fingertips light as a whisper, I trace each one. It's unlocking a secret code; I'm overwhelmed with the feeling that I've done exactly this before. . . . The scars were a dark purple then, and Kate was poking and prodding at them, lamenting the changes in the mirror.

"Kit." *I love you,* I say in my head. Aloud, it's, "You're the most beautiful woman I've ever seen."

She lifts a brow. "You only remember the past couple months. How many other women do you have to compare me to?"

"None," I say, leaning to kiss the tendon pulled taut along the side of her neck. "There's no comparison."

In a fleeting moment of confidence, I nudge her bra strap from her shoulder, pulling the thin fabric down to expose her. I palm her full breast, budded nipple pressing into my skin, and Kate arches into my touch, silently begging for more.

Her nipple glides between my fingers, and a gentle pinch has Kate frantically reaching behind her back to unclasp the bra. She spins around in my arms, and her mouth clashes with mine. It's desperate and heated, and within seconds, she's stripping me. Fumbling with the button on my jeans at the same time I'm grabbing the back of my shirt and pulling it off.

Hot anticipation churns in my belly, nixing the nervous tingles. Standing together in nothing but our underwear, her naked breasts pressed to my chest, I slide a hand between us and touch the soft fabric of her panties. They're so delicate the slightest pressure has my fingertip slipping between her pussy lips.

"Is this okay?" I ask tentatively. The fabric pulled taut against her pussy is wet, growing wetter with every gentle brush of my finger over the area.

Fuck, she's not just wet; she's soaked.

"It's okay. *I'm yours.*"

My breath comes staggered and panting, and Kate stares up at me, hazel eyes swirling with wonder. The bathroom's humid, a thick cloud of condensation hanging in the air and making our skin damp.

"Let's get in the shower, handsome." Kate's hands run through my hair. "We have all night."

With a lick of my lips, I nod and let her pull my boxers down my thighs. My cock springs free and bobs in the narrow space between us. Kate takes an audible breath. Then without hesitation, she wraps her fingers around my shaft and gives one slow, anguishing stroke. I nearly come.

"Fuck, Kate. *Fuck.*" My stomach clenches, pulling me in on myself. I fold in her arms. She's my sun, my world, my everything. And right now, she's my undoing.

Letting go of her hold on my dick, she hooks both thumbs in the waistband of her panties. Then they're sliding down her ivory thighs, and the sight of my wife's pussy . . . *no words.* Just more "*Fuck, Kate.*"

She turns to open the shower door, showing off the delicious curves of her ass, and I waste no time getting into the scalding stream with her. Water rolls down her body, narrowing into two steady streams from her peaked nipples.

She gathers her mess of brown hair in one hand, holding it on top of her head. "I don't want to go to bed with wet hair."

"Then relax and enjoy the hot water." I grab the coconut

body wash and pool the milky substance in my hand. Typically, this is where I'd spread it down my shaft, lean against the shower wall with my eyes shut, and pretend it's her getting me off. Tonight, I spread it across her luscious breasts, and her soft whimpers aren't imaginary.

I continue over her shoulders, down her midsection, and when I slip a hand between her legs, we both draw in a sharp breath. The water runs down her body, washing the soap away. Floating somewhere outside of my body, I watch the way my wet hand strokes her pussy. She's so pink and soft and beautiful.

"Watch." My voice is stretched thin, teeth gritted.

Kate's head tips so she's no longer staring up at the ceiling, and her eyes briefly bounce over mine before continuing south to where I'm touching her. Biting her lip, she moans at the sight of my finger circling her clit.

"Oh, God. Don't stop." Her whine is so sexy I want to hear it again and again. While I touch her, eat her, fuck her.

"Your pussy is so fucking hot and"—I glide my index finger between her pussy lips, collecting the sticky wetness on my skin—"slick. Oh, God. It's . . . it's better than anything I've dreamed of." One finger slips inside her, I discover heaven, and she moans my name. *Old Jackson, New Jackson,* the only version of my name I care about is the one slipping from her wanton lips. "Can . . . can I use my mouth, Kit? Can I taste you?"

I'm already bending at the knee when she gives a frantic nod of approval.

Then, "Careful you don't slip."

"I don't give a shit if I do," I respond honestly.

I kneel in front of my wife. Cock strung out and throbbing between my thighs, I part her with my fingers, trailing slow, firm circles around her clit, then skimming lightly over it. Sliding my rough fingers inside her core.

"So fucking hot. Your pussy's so beautiful, Kate. I don't

know what I did to deserve this," I murmur up at her, getting so close the mingling of coconut and her natural musk makes my dick twitch. I feel her muscles squeeze at the sound of my voice, and a small whimper gets lost in the sound of falling water.

"You like hearing me talk about how gorgeous I find your pussy?" With a small gasp, she tightens around my fingers. Oh, she likes it, all right. I swallow down the last of my nerves, focusing on all the things I've imagined saying to her in my filthiest daydreams. "My fingers are fucking soaked, Kit. Bet you wish it was my tongue—I do, too. God, I'd love to know if you taste as good as I imagine."

I kiss her pubic bone and then her inner thigh, driving her wild with desire. Her hips buck against my touch as I move to repeat my teasing kisses on the other side. Her needy whine crowds the shower, sending shivers skating down my spine. I rub my beard against her thighs, relishing the view of my knuckles dragging in and out of her entrance.

The gentle spread of her glistening pussy with my fingers makes me salivate. "Tell me you want me to fuck your pussy with my tongue."

Her legs spread a little wider. "I do."

"*Tell me.*"

The muscles in Kate's neck bob with a hard swallow. "Use your tongue and make me feel good."

Arching my neck to bring my lips to her slick, heated skin, I replace my fingers with my tongue. Water cascades down her legs on either side of my face, and I lap her up with a slow ice-cream lick. Broad strokes, savoring every part of her. Sweet and salty, the intoxicating flavor of her pussy lingers on my tongue and tingles something deep in my mind. Specks of reminiscence like drops of water pattering against my brain.

"Could you—" Kate grips my skull, guiding my tongue exactly where she needs it, and her back arches.

"Like this?" The tip of my tongue gives her tender bud a barely-there flick.

"*Yeah.*" She groans. "*That.*"

Shower water drips on my head, falling from her tits as she tosses her head back with a needy plea to come.

Left to my own devices, I loop the letters of the alphabet—a technique I read about online yesterday—while paying close attention to every tremor in her thighs, every rake of her nails across my scalp, every rasping moan. I move in consonants and vowels around the silken contours of her. And I learn my wife, one muttered cuss word and near-buckle of her knees at a time.

Until she's gripping the back of my skull and riding my face with a hoarse, "Oh, fuck. God, don't stop."

I pull her swollen clit into my mouth, glancing up through waterlogged eyebrows to watch her tits jiggle with stilted breaths and her mouth fall into an O shape that I'd love to do so many things with. I give my cock a quick stroke, careful not to touch the sensitive head for fear I'll blow my load all over the shower floor, instead of filling my wife with it the way I want to.

Two fingers plunge inside her tight pussy, and she clamps down around them. "Fuck, fuck, fuck. I'm gonna . . ."

Her muscles squeeze my knuckles together as her thighs tremble and tense with the force of her orgasm. A moan vibrates off the shower walls, and I keep licking and sucking even as a zap of electricity tingles my spine. She comes in waves of unending whines and hips rocking against my mouth and hands knotted around my hair.

"Jackson . . . I . . ." She shakes her head, all the hair she'd previously insisted on keeping dry now hanging loose, with soaked tips plastered against her breasts. "Holy shit. I wasn't sure if you could still do that."

I press the most gentle of kisses to her sweet pussy, pulling my fingers from her powerful grip and sucking them clean. Then I rock back on my heels, and with shaky legs and a cock that's one light brush away from painting her in cum, I find my footing.

"That was good?" I nervously ask, brushing the pad of my thumb over her flushed cheek.

Kate kisses me. Really kisses me. Then smiles against my lips, letting out a satiated giggle between the sweet kisses that taste like all the best parts of her. Her tongue drags my bottom lip, then she's pressing her mouth to my chin, my jaw.

"So good," she finally says, voice vibrating my Adam's apple.

"I've dreamed about that so many times and . . ." I tilt my jaw up, letting her tongue continue its journey to my naked, damp chest. "Tasting you—it was, sweet God. Best thing I've ever eaten."

Her nails drag down my front, leaving raised, red claw marks in their wake. And she swirls her tongue around my—*holy fuck*—nipple. I moan and fist her hair, pulling her mouth to mine, and she responds by grinding against me. Nails dug into my ass, she forces my cock to glide against her slick pussy. A hungry growl catches in my throat at the feel of my hard cock pressed between us. She's managed to unleash something feral.

"Kate," I groan into her wet mouth. "I need to be inside you. I need to be inside my wife."

It's like in the movies where everything is in slow motion. She's grabbing my hand and dragging me out of the shower. The fire-dried air is warm, but not warm enough to prevent the goosebumps scattered over our skin. And the bed is too far to go. So I snare her wrist and tug her in for a fervid kiss. In the middle of a firelit room, floorboards creaking under our weight, her naked body pressed to mine, I've never felt more like husband and wife.

Her smile against my lips warms my entire body.

"I've never been this happy," I admit quietly, cupping one of her breasts and running a thumb over the stiffened peak.

A little sob of anticipation leaves her. "You were right when you said we'd have more happy days."

I nuzzle her neck. Feel her quiver at the brush of my beard against her tender skin.

"Fuck me," she whispers against my ear, "and let me make you *really* happy."

Passion-drowsed, eyes half closed, we kiss and shuffle toward the bed. Stumbling and giggling as if we both drank twice as much of the sparkling wine as we actually did. Kate falls back on the bed first, arms and hair splayed above her head, with an audible exhale of contentment.

I use the opportunity to stare at my sexy wife—she's the most stunning creature to ever exist. My eyes dance over the curves of her body, reacquainting myself with every beautiful piece of the woman spread in front of me. The damp spots on her skin she missed during her speedy toweling off, and the shimmer between her thighs that I want another taste of.

She looks up at me through long lashes. "Did you buy the condoms?"

Fuck the condoms.

"I did . . . but I don't want to use them."

She lifts up onto her elbows and cocks her head. "You're sure? It's okay if you do, Jackson."

"I'm so fucking sure."

She bites her lip, running a hand over the mess of partially wet hair sitting like an intricate crown above her head, then playfully patting the bed. "Then what are you waiting for?"

"Taking a minute to appreciate my gorgeous wife."

"Appreciate your wife from on top of her." Her hand snakes between her breasts, skipping over her stomach and settling at the apex of her thighs. She squirms a little, thighs clamping shut around her hand, as if the way she's touching herself surprised even her.

"Fuck, I plan to." I glide toward her, kneeling on the bed and forcefully spreading her knees wide.

If she's going to play with herself, I *need* to see it. My cock leaks pre-cum, cold as it runs down my head before dripping. I rub my thumb over the steadily beading liquid and stroke it down my shaft.

"I'm going to slide my bare cock deep inside you—appreciate every square inch of your beautiful cunt."

She moans, fingers picking up the pace. She's spread open, so wet it's pooling on the white sheets. God, she's beautiful.

"Look at how wet you are. You love the dirty talk, don't you, Kit?" My thumbs dig into her fleshy thighs, sending them impossibly wide.

She sighs a "yes" while slipping her fingers down her slit. It sounds so wet and messy, I can't help but briefly let go of my firm hold on her legs to give my cock one quick pump. Pre-cum leaks and drops to the bed, seeping into the spot she's already made damp.

"Want me to tell you all the filthy things I think about when I'm stroking myself at home?"

"With my underwear?" Kate asks, curious, not judgmental.

I blink at her. *Of course she noticed.* How could she not? Suddenly she's going through twice as many pairs in her laundry every week.

"That okay with you?" I draw a heart on her knee to distract myself from the overwhelming shame boiling under my skin.

She nods. "It's really hot to think about."

"For weeks I've been rubbing those silky panties of yours over my cock, imagining it's your pussy squeezing me. Fuck,

Kate—I can't wait to feel the real thing. I want that wet, tight pussy stretched around me, want to bury myself deep inside you."

Kate's eyes widen, but her fingers are sticky, glossing over her clit so quickly her legs shake. Her thighs press hard against my palms, threatening to close, and her ass hovers just above the bed. I can feel the heat creeping across my cheeks, her unwavering stare like a magnifying glass held over an ant. Whether I spontaneously combust or I lose control and fuck her into the mattress, only time will tell.

"You want me to fuck you bare?" I quietly ask, fighting like hell to muster up some more false confidence.

"Mhm," she hums.

I *tsk*. "Use your words, gorgeous."

"Please."

"Please what?" I lift a brow, massaging her inner thigh.

Her lips roll together, the hand working her pussy slows. "Jackson . . . I-I . . ." She stumbles over the words. For a woman who's teased me about shaving my balls and sending me photos of her tits—I scoured my phone and found no naked photos—she's so shy in this moment.

I don't push her. With a gentle humming sound, I move between her legs, placing my hand over hers. Together, we press her sensitive clit, and she bows off the bed with a guttural moan.

"Fuck me." Her whisper is the last straw.

My cock drags along her inner thigh, taunting and teasing the both of us. Breath held, we hold each other's stare for an unreasonably long time. I want her. *I love her.* And the way she's looking at me, I'm not a mirage on the ocean the way I thought. I'm the boat; she's my lighthouse.

The tip grazes her entrance, catching on her clit with a rush of pleasure that floods down my thighs. Electrical currents arc out from my taut balls, and I careen forward to kiss her with a groan tinged with both relief and pain.

I watch my wife with rapt admiration as she uses her wet fingers to coat my cock in her arousal. And my entire being spirals into a euphoric haze as she kisses me deeper, reaching between us to guide the head of my cock inside.

I pitch forward with a gravelly moan. "Holy fucking God, that feels so good."

God is a woman named Kate Wells.

Then I'm stroking into her, slow but deep, pinning her to the bed like a flower pressed in a book. I'm delicate and deliberate in my movements, wanting to commit every inch of her to my memory. Kate's entire body clenches around me, her pussy squeezing my sensitive cock, arms looped around my neck, the arch of her foot rubbing up and down my calf.

I thrust with more intention, filling her to the hilt and feeling the slap of my balls on her tight ass, *oh fuck*. She's so fucking tight, I break out in a sweat. Impossible it's this good. I can't think straight. My vision's shattered—a kaleidoscope of color and light, and Kate writhing, arching, begging underneath me.

With a frayed moan, I drag my cock nearly all the way out, then slam back in, and an orgasm barrels into me. Pulse after pulse of heated pleasure courses through my veins, a wildfire under my skin.

"Fucking—" I grit my teeth. Quit moving my hips. Try to stop it. "Goddamn it."

My balls tingle and throb, everything tightening as the most intense pleasure I've ever felt engulfs me. I could fucking scream, both in utter euphoria and furious embarrassment. My cock pulses inside her tight walls, filling her with cum and draining all the achy feelings from my chest.

It takes a second for her to process what just happened, then, "Jackson, it's okay—"

"No." I shake my head, pressing a cool hand to my burning cheek. *Fuck*. "No, I refuse. I'm staying here with my cock inside you until I can go again. This is *not* what I want for our first time together."

Her hands cup my face, and she smiles softly at me. Lowering to my elbows, I relish the repeated collision of our chests as we both fight to catch our breath. I kiss her forehead, lingering with my lips pressed to her warm skin so I can breathe her in. I brush away a strand of dark hair stuck to her temple, and kindle the fire between us with gentle, loving kisses.

KATE

Planting a forearm on either side of my head, Jackson cages me in, places his forehead on mine, and lets out a shuddering breath. I reach overhead to catch his fingers with mine, squeezing them to let him know this is okay.

It's nothing I haven't experienced before, given the lack of experience he had when we first started dating. We took our time, I taught him how to make me come, and in the sixteen years we've been together, there have been times when one or both of us come incredibly quickly . . . and times when we don't come at all. It's par for the course. It's marriage.

"I love you." I squeeze our hands once more.

"Just . . . give me a minute," he insists. "I'm sorry."

"*Hey,*" I say softly. Hopefully reassuringly. "Do you know how sexy it is to know it felt *so good* you couldn't make it last?"

"I wanted you so fucking bad it hurt, Kate."

"Speaking of hurt." I wiggle slightly to relieve some of the pressure of his hip bones grinding into mine. "Should we change position so you're more comfortable while we wait? Maybe that Hawaiian Pretzel move or whatever it was you said was your favorite?"

A laugh blows from his nose. I'm happy to have relieved a bit of the stress and shame evident in his serious features.

"No, definitely not a more comfortable choice for either of us."

I nod, smiling up at his handsome face. "Should've guessed with the word *pretzel* in the name. I'm afraid the butter churner is out, too. My boobs would be all up in my face and I'd suffocate."

Cupping my breasts, I push them upward to demonstrate that, with the help—or hindrance—of gravity, they'd be consuming my face. It's not even that they're *that* big. They're decent. More than a handful. And they've also fed two human beings, so . . . *yeah.*

Jackson snorts, and a smile sweeps my face, turning into a giggle as I carefully try to put my boobs back into a place that looks sexy. It feels good—the laughing, the sex, the laughing during sex.

"You're sexy as hell." He does his best to be reassuring. "If anyone is suffocating in your tits tonight, it's me."

"Please, don't. I just got you back." I don't mean for it to come out so heavy, but it does. And it presses against my throat with even more suffocating weight than my boobs. I blink away the prickle in my eyes and press a chaste kiss to his lips.

His forehead knocks against mine, and his hips inch forward just enough that I feel a distinct tightening in my core.

"Fuck, Kate. Do that and I'll blow my load too fast again." His pained moan hums under my skin.

For a long while we lie there, joined together, eyes locked, my heartbeat chasing the steady thump of his.

"Want to know something? We used to sleep like this." I stroke his muscular arm. "With you . . . inside me."

"We *slept* like this?" His hips move in one smooth, unbroken circle to hit every spot inside me.

"It started sometime after your mom died. We were running off our feet at the ranch just trying to keep everything going without your grandpa or dad around. We both fell asleep mid-sex, and it was so intimate. I loved it, so it became our thing." I hook a leg around his waist, pressing our pelvises together and eliciting a gentle moan from my husband. "It's been a long time, though."

The threat of kids crawling into the bed at all hours of the night put a stop to things like that real fast.

"No way I'd get any sleep inside you."

"The half-asleep sex in the middle of the night is part of the fun. Seeing how far you can push it before the other person wakes up." I tilt my hips to draw him deeper.

He lifts a brow. "I like the sound of that."

"It's the best way to get woken up."

Jackson slowly grinds his cock into me. "We're doing exactly that tonight, Kit. I want to wake up feeling this tight pussy squeezing me."

He's definitely hard again—every inch pressing against my walls—and the extra lubrication from his cum has him slipping in and out with ease. Inch by goddamn inch, he feeds his cock to me. My need for him borders on desperation, and each leisurely thrust only heightens the tension crackling between us.

My hips roll of their own volition, and I breathe out an "Okay."

"But first, I'm fucking my wife the way she deserves."

"How's that?"

He grips my thighs, cinching them tight around his waist. The lust-filled gaze and blown-out pupils of his, the delicious stretch, the languid stroke of him inside me—all of it coalesces into something I recognize yet can't form words for right now.

He presses into me, folding to nudge my hair with his nose. "Like she's loved."

Love. That's what it is.

The kiss that follows isn't a loving peck. It's desperate,

ravenous, as if he needs the oxygen from my lungs to keep him alive. When we finally break apart, it's with a frantic, gasping breath and hearts that beat in sync. Time stretches on outside us, and with his eyes locked on mine, Jackson says so much without uttering a single word. He's my husband again.

Every slow grind of his cock forces his cum out of me, leaking down my ass and pooling on the sheets. He ruts into me, shoving his face into my neck. His bristly beard rasps my skin, followed by hot gusts of shallow, soothing breath like a balm over the sensitive spot. Curling my fingers, I drag my short nails down his back, then up to tangle in his damp hair.

I tilt my pelvis, taking him as deep as I possibly can, and he hisses against my skin. "*Shit,* Kate. You feel so good."

Jackson lifts to his knees, dragging my hips to meet him with a firm grasp, bordering on painful. He drives into me, and my vision blurs. The room's filled with crackling fire and the sloppy, wet sounds of our bodies meeting over and over and over. He fills me to the hilt, shoving my body across the sheets, then his bruising grip pulls me back to him, forcing his cock impossibly deep inside me. I want him this way. So embedded in me, I never need to worry about losing him again.

The muscles in my butt and the backs of my thighs strain, and I feel blindly overhead for the brass rungs on the headboard to grab hold of. I moan, loudly and often. When his thumb presses to my clit, a throbbing heat blooms in my clit, pussy . . . all over, really. I'm not sure I know what's what anymore. I'm a fucking goner.

"That's it—fuck, my wife is going to look so gorgeous coming on my cock."

The dirty talk tightens my core. He could make me come with his words alone. But it's the gravelly, undone way he calls me his wife that sends a rush of pleasure from head to toe. His words do as much as the friction of his fervid thrusts.

An uneven hum wriggles free from my clenched jaw, and I twist in his lap, hand cramped around the bars of the headboard.

Sweat glistens on his forehead, his breath fast and broken. "That's my girl. Keep squeezing my cock like that."

As if I have any control over my body right now. My mind's whirling like a runaway Ferris wheel, crashing into his hips and scratching at his taut arms. A sob rattles in my chest as pleasure overwhelms me, a flush of heat up through my belly and down my trembling legs.

A solitary tear trickles down past my temple. I can feel it, but holding on to his arm and pressing the other hand to the headboard to ground myself in all the intense pressure takes priority over wiping it away. With his eyes trained on my face, Jackson notices it too. I can tell by the slight twist in his features.

"So good." An explanation for the crying. It's so overwhelming mentally, physically, emotionally, that this is the best my brain and mouth can agree on.

After securing my legs around his waist, he leans in close, and the pump of his hips slows. The soft warmth of his tongue skims over my skin, wiping away the brackish tears, which have become a meandering rivulet since the initial one fell. His cock pulses inside me, coiling more pleasure in the spot behind my belly button.

"Please," I whimper.

Jackson softly cradles my cheek in his hard, callused hand. His shaken voice blowing hot against my mouth. "Again? I wish I'd known before just how fucking horny my wife is for my cock."

He pushes forward, and I writhe under him.

Breathless and wanton, I ask, "Would you have touched me in the kitchen then?"

"In the kitchen, the day you trimmed my beard . . ." His

thumb traces my Cupid's bow. Voice low and rough. "Hell, I would've put this mouth to good use when you wouldn't stop talking in the hospital."

That knocks the wind from me. I glance away, cheeks growing hot. Before the accident, Jackson always knew how to make me come—*hard, fast, often*—and he stuck with what he knew. But now there's a new hunger, a new desire to learn me, and this dirty talk is certainly *new*. In a way, it feels like I'm fucking my husband while also fucking somebody new for the first time in over sixteen years, and it's so hot it makes my head spin.

"Look at me, Kit." Jackson tips my chin up with a hook of his finger. He's still grinding against my pelvis in a way that's so slow it's excruciating. "I want to see the look in your eyes when we come together."

He grabs hold of my hips, pulling me into him again, again, again, until we're a pair of whimpering, moaning messes and our bellies and thighs are slick with our combined arousal. My body takes every inch, clenching desperately on the withdrawal as if trying to keep him inside.

His breathing falters, stomach clenching, and I can feel the throb of his cock inside me. Firelight picks up the gold flecks in his dark eyes, and he pins me with a hungry stare. He's close. Knowing how easily this man is going to come for the second time tonight catapults me into an unrelenting, tumultuous wave of pleasure. I'm tumbling through the surf, unable to catch my breath. More intense than anything I've experienced.

The orgasm radiates out from my core, turning my entire body into a shaking mess. Even my nails lack the bite into his skin they had earlier—turning soft and sensual as they glide down his arm.

I wilt like the petals of a flower, coming down from the euphoria as the last few jagged pumps of his cock in my pussy send him hurtling forward with a choked gasp. And I swear to God, I hear him whisper that he loves me.

Flicking off the bathroom light, I saunter across the tiny luxury cabin, relishing the way he's staring at me with heated interest.

Stark naked, save for a thin white sheet covering him from his navel down, he could be a male model. It's incredibly rude of whatever higher power exists to make men finer as they age, while I'm slathering myself in toners, serums, essences, *snail mucin*, to prevent me from looking old for my age.

Jackson shakes his head with a lopsided, arrogant smile. "Your face looks like it's still wet."

"That's the point. It's hydrated and youthful."

"Come get into bed, my glazed-donut wife," he murmurs sleepily. "Can confirm you taste sweet like one, too."

"No complaints?" I tease.

"Oh, God. *Never.*" He reaches behind his head to fluff up the pillows, then slings his arm across my empty side of the bed, waiting patiently for me to crawl in next to him. I tuck into the crook of his arm, slinging my leg across his, and breathe a sigh of relief.

"We should take more vacations." Jackson's chin rests on top of my head. "Did we take them before?"

With a yawny laugh, I answer, "We went to Calgary to see my parents a few times . . . took Odessa to the zoo there when she was a toddler. But you and I haven't had too many opportunities to get away like this."

"Well, we should. Maybe go to a beach, a big road trip, take the kids to Disneyland . . . all of it." He's so matter-of-fact. As if this decision isn't affected by the difficulties of traveling with kids, or finances, or *life* in general.

I lift a brow, calling him out in silence because, as much as

I doubt any of that will happen, I have to admit it's nice to dream of it. My fingertips skitter across his bare chest. The hair there's light brown, a gradual ombré into dark, coarse hair over his pubic bone.

"Denny reminded me a while back that I get a second shot at creating memories with you," he says. "Trying to make it worthwhile."

"It's all worthwhile, Jackson. Most of my favorite memories were simple moments. Every year we go out on horseback to find a Christmas tree—even when the kids were babies, you'd put them in the wearable carrier and away we went." I draw loopy interconnected hearts across his solid pec.

How different memories feel now that I'm not obsessed with needing him to remember. What I truly needed was this—our bodies and hearts reconnecting. There's a softness to him now, a slowness, like he's choosing me deliberately, one moment at a time. I'll remember the beginning of our story enough for the both of us, and we can focus on writing the rest together.

Between the comfort of the cozy fire and Jackson's strong arms around me, my eyelids struggle to stay open. I yawn, eyes watering, and snuggle in closer to feel Jackson's heavy heartbeat on the side of my face. It's a low, lulling echo that has put our kids—*and me*—to sleep many times.

"Roll over, Kit." His husky voice drags me from my half-asleep state.

"Huh?" I mumble.

"You wanted to sleep with me inside you, right? Roll onto your side."

I blink up at him, eyes burning. I must've been more than half-asleep, because I missed him reaching to turn off his bedside lamp, and the room's shrouded in darkness, save for the amber glow from the fireplace.

With a groan, I roll to my side and back my ass into his lap. His arm falls across my torso like a weighted blanket, and a few seconds later his hand's sliding between my legs. Delicate, gentle touches tease until I feel myself becoming wet, prepped to take him.

His fingertips pressed into the meaty flesh of my thigh, I part my legs, sleepily humming at the feel of his smooth head pressed to my entrance. I faintly hear him spit in his hand, and a few seconds later he's rocking into me.

The pillow captures my drowsy whimpering. It's been so long since we've slept this way, and for a moment, I wonder how I'll ever fall asleep with the tempting intrusion rooted in me. But Jackson cuddles up to my back, scoops my hair in his hand to pull it away from my neck, and lovingly kisses me there.

With his hand holding one of my breasts like a comfort item, he breathes heavy and slow over my skin. The dull thud of his heartbeat on my back soothes the lust zipping under my skin. And I fall asleep thinking about how madly in love with my husband I am.

JACKSON

I wake to the air being punched from my lungs. I'm hot all over and frenetic with the need to come.

Bleary-eyed, I stare off into the dark and panic washes over me. Everything except my racing heart is paralyzed.

Where the fuck am I?

In the pitch-black room, I smell my wife before I see her. The overwhelming scent of coconut fills my nostrils, and the entire evening comes crashing back.

We're in the cabin I rented. Kate and I ate pizza, made out, and fucked in this bed. And now—*I press my mouth to my arm to muffle my panting.* Instinctively, my hips drive forward, and I remember my cock's currently swathed in Kate's tight pussy.

Based on how difficult it is to keep my eyes open, we can't have been asleep for more than an hour or two.

The comforter's askew, sheets twisted around our ankles, exposing her creamy skin and endless curves. I stifle a moan, trying to keep my hips from bucking out of control, despite the way my dick's twitching against her ridged walls.

Her muscles flutter around me, and Kate lets out the softest, sweetest moan. Her hips roll until my cock's halfway out of her pussy, then another shift has me gliding with ease into her wet heat. My wife's practically dripping. I'm sure there's a wet spot somewhere between us on the sheets.

She moans a little louder, and my hips move a little of their own accord. My dick's aching for relief.

"Kate." I mutter her name, delirious.

Her tight pussy squeezes around my cock again, and my head lists forward to rest on her shoulder. She wasn't wrong about this being incredibly intimate. It's also cozy, soothing. It feels like the ultimate way to reconnect with my wife—she's trusting me to keep her safe, make her feel loved and protected. And the brute caveman part of me likes that it's my dick shoved inside her, claiming her. She's *my* wife. *Mine*.

Then I hear her yawn, and that's when my eyes perk up like I've received a direct shot of caffeine to my bloodstream. People don't yawn in their sleep.

"Kate," I try again. "You awake, gorgeous?"

I know she said half the fun is seeing how far you can get without waking the other person, but all I want is to hear her voice, raspy from sleep, saying my name as she gets herself off.

Barely audible, she strings together something entirely incoherent. The way she starts grinding my cock into her is a damn good indication she's awake, though.

A moan hums low in my throat. Languid heat melts over me. "Oh, Kit. You're making a mess of my cock right now. Too horny to wait until morning, hrm?"

My arm wraps around her waist, fingers tingling with the need to touch her. There's a smear of wetness in her soft hair down there, which tells me she's been awake and touching herself for a while. The pleasure racing through me when I awoke likely has something to do with that.

She was right. This is the best way to be woken up.

"Couldn't sleep with my thick cock inside you?"

"It was"—she exhales hard through her nose—"too much. I thought I'd . . . I—"

"Oh, Kate, *baby* . . . You thought you'd get yourself off on me while I slept?" I smile against her bare shoulder. "Thought you'd use your husband like your toy? Show me what you thought you'd do."

She melts back against me, sinking a tiny bit deeper. Rocking her hips back and forth until the wet sound of skin slapping makes the hair on the back of my neck prickle. I sink my teeth into her shoulder with a groan of ecstasy.

If this is what being her husband was like for the last sixteen years, it's no wonder why I never felt the need to be more adventurous. This is fucking sexy as hell.

"You told me to wake you up like this."

"Such a good wife," I pant against her skin.

Kate's ass bounces against my lap, picking up speed and jiggling in a way that makes me want to bite it. My fingers slap the side of her butt, then squeeze hard around her hip. The horny whine that follows tells me she likes that.

My fingers rap against her plump ass a little harder. Her back bows as she moans a raw, fervid, "Oh, God."

Oh, she loves *that.*

A hum of approval reverberates in my chest. "You're going to come, aren't you?"

Tightening around me like a vise, she nods frantically against the pillow. "Y-yes."

She quietly moans my name into her pillow. Begging for it harder. Begging to come.

Moaning, nails leaving crescent marks in my forearm, she's bucking her hips so I'm balls deep inside her tight cunt. My spine tingles. She's so slippery and warm, and I need her to come before I do. I need it *now.*

"Tease that pretty little clit for me," I rasp, losing myself in the feel of her riding me.

My teeth drag along the ridge of her shoulder, then turn to kisses on the nape of her neck. A few short bits of her hair are curled from sweat, and goosebumps speckle her salty skin. Within seconds of shoving her hand between her legs, she's pulsing around me and a tremor rattles through both of us.

"Kiss me, Kate."

My wife tips her head, and I finally catch a glimpse of her eyes. Full of desire. Need. Love. Pummeling into her with enough force she'll feel me between her legs for the rest of this trip, I grab her chin in my abrasive grasp and capture her mouth with mine. My balls slap back and forth between us, heavy and full of cum that I plan to pump into her. Lust let loose, it's fair to say we devour each other.

She falls apart in my arms with a convulsion that shakes the entire bed, and I hold tight around her torso to keep her against me while I fuck her into blissful oblivion. It's not enough for her to come; I want my wife to come so hard, there's a moment when we're both without any memory beyond each other now.

She sobs my name, hips ricocheting back into me as her climax keeps coming in unrelenting waves.

My heart thunders so hard, there's no way it's a safe rhythm. Heat coils in my spine, and I let myself have it as primal grunts rumble through the night air. White sparks blur my vision when I surge my cock in one final time, spilling inside my wife's beautiful pussy. With a stuttering breath, I give my hips a tiny writhe, emptying the last drops.

Our conversation about birth control earlier tonight was brief—she's not on it, neither of us want her to be. And maybe a few weeks ago, that thought would've left me feeling panicky and even more certain I'd end up letting her down. But that's exactly why I wasn't having sex with her then. Now I can't help but smile at the thought of getting to experience everything I forgot with Odessa and Rhett—not that I wouldn't kill to remember feeling them kick from inside Kate's belly or holding them tight to my chest as infants.

Kate pads slowly, wobbly, to the bathroom, returning seconds later and snuggling under the covers. I don't ask about sliding back inside her, because my dick's so sensitive the simple brush of soft sheets across it makes my entire body shudder.

So I hold her tight, smooth a rough hand over her wild hair, and dust kisses on her shoulder. She molds into me with an adorable little sigh. And as her breathing becomes slow and easy, I lie there wondering what on Earth I did to deserve this moment—to deserve her. Nothing made sense until I had her in my arms.

In the seconds before I drift to sleep, I whisper an "I love you" against her skin. And I mean it.

Steam curls off the water, blurring the edges of the world until it feels like we're the only two people left in it. My fingers drag languid loops across the surface of the pool, and I roll my neck to fight the lingering headache. Whether it was all the junk food we ate last night, the sex, the wine, or just shitty luck, I woke up feeling like I'd been hit by a freight train.

When Kate woke up, she found me sitting on the bathroom floor with my head between my knees, fighting like hell not to throw up. All I wanted was some one-on-one time with my wife. I wanted to reconnect and finally feel like husband and wife, rather than patient and care aide. But one night of bliss was all the higher powers bothered to afford me, I guess.

After a bit of bullying on Kate's part, I let her order me toast from the on-site restaurant. I ate it with minor irritated grumbling sounds and reluctantly let her waste the first few hours of our only full day here taking care of me. Water, medication, scalp massages . . .

Eventually, I got the idea that I needed to bully her right back. And I forced her to take an uninterrupted soak in the hot springs while I slept. The nap transformed my headache from a sledgehammer wailing against my skull to a child's plastic mallet.

By late afternoon, I'm *finally* getting to see my wife in a bikini.

Kate's across from me, legs stretched out under the water, arms propped on the pool's edge. Her hair's pulled up in that messy knot she always does when she doesn't want to fuss with it, a few damp tendrils curling down the back of her neck. Her skin, flushed from the heat, glows in the soft light, and a few droplets of water cling to her collarbone. And that bikini . . . *God help me.* I don't know who I used to be, but I know who I am right now, and I'd give anything to lean over and undo every knot holding it together.

"You're staring," she says.

I grin. "You're not wrong."

She flicks a little water my way. It hits my collarbone and neck, warm and teasing, sliding down over the branded scar I still forget is there sometimes—apparently my brothers, Dad, Red, and I all have the cattle ranch's brand permanently scarred on our chests. *Insane.*

Her gaze follows the trail it makes.

"You okay?" she asks after a beat.

"Better now." I sink a little deeper and reach up to wipe sweat from my brow. "Thank you for earlier. I . . . I hate that you have to keep stepping in to take care of me."

"I don't hate it at all. You know how many times you had to do the same for me when I was pregnant with Rhett and so sick I'd camp out on the bathroom floor for hours every day?" Her feet float to the surface, and cute painted toes poke out above the water for a second before she pushes them back down. "I love you on the good days, the bad days, and every single one in between. I wasn't lying when I said we can handle the rough moments—all I care about is having you here now."

"All I care about is being here now, too." Things have

been so heavy and emotional since I started really opening up about my feelings, and right now, I want a relaxing, flirty afternoon with my wife. So I clear my throat and steer the conversation another way. "Honestly kicking myself for not pushing through the pain and coming to the pool sooner. Pissed I missed valuable bikini time."

"But you got a lot of birthday suit time in."

"My favorite thing you've ever worn. You should rock that suit all the time."

She snorts at that. "In a house with cowboys traipsing in and out constantly? I don't think so."

"Maybe it's time we do some renovations—build a wing on the house with no cowboys allowed. Only me, you, and that sexy outfit," I tease in a low, husky tone, gliding through the water to sit closer.

"If you're going to lock me away, make sure there's a snack bar." She closes her eyes, pulling her arms from the edge and sinking up to her chin in the water. "And a real big bathtub."

Water gently laps around us, and our shoulders and knees brush. She's so tranquil as she soaks, arms suspended effortlessly in the hot water, dark curls of hair kissing the surface. Wired similarly to our high-energy, brazen daughter, Kate usually doesn't look this calm outside of sleep, but there's something different in her this weekend. She seems at peace with where things are—genuinely happy—like she's finally stopped waiting for me to be who I was, and started letting herself enjoy who I'm becoming. I feel it in the way she lets me come close without pulling away.

Her head falls to rest on my shoulder, and she lets go of a long exhale. "This is so nice."

"Thought I wasn't a bath guy, but if I'd known it was this relaxing, I would've found a way to get that soaker tub you wanted instead of sitting on the bathroom floor when you were in the bath." I squint above the rising steam, trying to recollect every detail.

A memory rumbles somewhere in the distance like thunder, edging closer until it vibrates through every cell in my body. Kate in the bath with bubbles from toes to collarbones, carefully holding a book above the suds, and a bottle of beer coated in tiny droplets of condensation resting on the wooden tub caddy I made for her for Christmas one year.

"You'd run the hottest bath a human could possibly survive, loaded with so many bubbles they'd tip over the edge and drip to the floor . . . and sometimes I'd just sit there while you read. Sometimes we'd talk."

Eyes still closed, she smiles. "I talked you into joining me once, and you acted like I was trying to scald you."

"I remember that," I whisper, feeling for her hand under the water and looping my pinky around hers. We rest them on her thighs, and she draws hearts on the back of my hand in the way she always does.

This memory feels different from the others, which have always come in bits and pieces, as if my brain's trying to retell me a story it heard from a friend of a friend. This one makes my heart pitter-patter and butterflies swirl in my stomach, like I'm right there again. I swear I can smell the lavender in her bubble bath and hear the quiet flipping of pages in her book.

"I hate that I forget all the big stuff. . . ." I sigh. "But I love that I'm remembering you."

Kate lifts her head, her hand slipping out of the water to stroke my cheek. And she kisses me. A teasing caress mixed with insatiable hunger. I lean into the feeling, grabbing her and kissing her back with such intensity, she couldn't take a breath even if she wanted to. Each time I kiss Kate it feels like our first and like we've been kissing for years, and I suppose both are true in their own right.

When we break apart, water runs in long strands down her cheeks from where I'd gripped her face to hold her close. And her kiss-swollen lips, red from the rough brush of my facial hair, curve upward into a satiated smile. Something in my chest soars at that.

"God," Kate mutters. "We should've come here years ago."

"If it's my fault we didn't, I apologize." I squeeze her thigh. "I was an idiot."

"Weird you're using past tense for that statement," she teases. "I think you turned it down because you were worried I'd get us thrown out when I had to kick some woman's ass for checking you out."

I raise an eyebrow. "My wife gets *jealous*? Oh, Kate, baby—that's hot. I like that."

"Don't get so smug about it." She pokes me in the cheek. "This little cutesy smile of yours is too damn risky. Wouldn't be the first time I've had to practically chase women away with a cattle prod, and that's while you were fully clothed."

"Well, I'd love to see that." I laugh under my breath, looking around at the few people soaking nearby and loitering on the pool deck. "Good thing all the women here are old enough to be our mothers or grandmothers."

Kate shakes a fist, creating small waves across the calm water. "I'll fight an old lady."

I press my lips to her temple with a loud kissing sound. "You have nothing to be jealous of. I'm all yours."

She narrows her eyes at me. God, she's adorable with that crease between her brows. "*Better be.*"

"You're cute when you're all mad and pruney."

"Not mad," she corrects. "Just sayin'—don't forget what I told you about the castration band being the only band you need to concern yourself with if you want to stay happily married to me."

I glance down at the empty space on my left ring finger. Despite months without a wedding ring, a noticeable indent in my flesh and a faint tan line remain.

"As if I could forget about that. Your car smelled like old

Cheerios and you were threatening to castrate me on the way to some remote ranch. I was a bit scared I'd accidentally left the hospital with a murderer posing as my wife."

"Yeah, I've been told I'm overly assertive . . . *unladylike*."

"That's what I love about you," I answer honestly. Without a second thought. It's exactly what I love about her. I love that she says whatever's on her mind, even when it's crude. I love that she's not intimidated by all the men around the ranch. I love that she wears my clothes and makes them look *good*. "Anybody who says you're unladylike has never seen you in your exquisite birthday suit. My wife's the hottest lady in Wells Canyon."

She grins, pulling me in for a soft kiss, slow and warm and familiar in all the best ways. When she pulls back, her eyes are shining with unshed tears. She must've picked up on the unspoken words my heart and brain shout every time I look at her.

"I can't tell if you constantly refer to me as your wife because you like the way it sounds or you need to remind yourself who I am."

"Maybe both?" I shrug impishly, then correct myself as she pulls her hand back, preparing to splash me. "*Kidding*. I like the way 'my wife' sounds, and even more than that, I like the way it feels—you being my wife. It feels right."

"We're going to be okay, aren't we?"

"Yeah, Kit. I think so."

KATE

A deafening sound shoves me headfirst out of a dream, and I splat onto our bed with a muffled groan. I reflexively grab either end of my pillow and press it against my ears, mumbling something incoherent about annoying alarms though my throat's so dry it comes out as a croak.

I clear my throat, licking my lips to wet them, and try again. "What the fuck is that?"

Jackson makes the racket stop and cuddles in next to me, rubbing his broad, warm palm over my bare back. "Time for our date."

How is it morning already?

With a groggy brain and bleary eyes, I pry myself from the pillow and come face-to-face with my enthusiastic husband grinning at me. The room's pitch-black, and the fire we fucked in front of before bed still has the orange glow of embers.

"What?" It's the first of a long list of questions I have for him, and the only one I'm awake enough to enunciate right now.

"Two a.m. date," he answers as if I'd previously agreed upon this date. I didn't even have a drink with dinner, so unless he asked while I was preoccupied with lava cake, this is a surprise.

I burrow myself deeper into the blankets in protest.

"Come on, Kit. I think you'll like this one." He gently brushes hair away from my face and kisses my forehead.

As a testament to my love for this man, I groan and peel back the sheets. I'd follow him anywhere, even into a surprise date in the middle of the night on my first child-free weekend ever.

From my reluctant perch on the edge of the bed, body swaying from exhaustion, I yawn loudly in protest. "I hope you know this is the first time I've been able to sleep without the threat of small children waking me up. And now I have you . . . and you're looking at me the same way Rhett does when he bursts into the room with a ridiculous dream he's itching to share."

"Promise when we go home, I'll leave you be for an entire night and stand guard outside the door in the morning to keep the kids away."

His arms stretch overhead, pulling the skin taut across his muscles. He's all abs and meaty ribs and broad shoulders. It makes me a little wet between my thighs. I quickly reach for my duffel bag, wanting to slip into some underwear before I leave a wet patch on the bed.

"Put on your bathing suit," Jackson says.

I spin to face him, confused. He's sliding a pair of black swim trunks over his powerful thighs, tucking his dick into the pouch sewn inside. He looks up at me as he ties the waistband string tight. His eyes locked on mine, he shakes his head. "Trust me, Kate."

Without a doubt, my cute floral bikini—high cut and cheeky—is still damp. And the only thing that'll make this middle-of-the-night wake-up call any more miserable is being forced to squeeze into a wet, cold bathing suit. So I pluck my spare bikini from the bag. I've had it for years and it does nothing flattering for my boobs, but the hot springs are closed and it's two a.m. so, realistically, nobody is going to see me.

I clothe my naked, tired body in that red bathing suit,

then try to massage out the weird patterns on my stomach from the rumpled sheets. Knowing it's likely to be brisk outside, given we're in the mountains on a spring night, I grab a sweatshirt and sweatpants to wear over it.

All the while, Jackson waits patiently with one hand on the door handle, two towels draped over his bare shoulder, eyes trailing up and down my body.

"You're going to be cold," I say, eyeing his torso.

He winks. "Not for long. Let's go."

I was right. The night air is frigid and the grass outside our cabin has sparkles of frost clinging to it. Pale moonlight brushes over the narrow pathway, and up ahead there's fog lying low over where the hot spring pools are.

I shiver immediately, freezing and silently wishing Jackson would change his mind and take me back to bed. But he grabs my hand, and between that firm touch and his coffee-brown eyes, he's the warmest thing in the world.

"Aren't the pools closed at night?" I ask quietly.

Wind rustles through the tree canopy overhead, and I step a little faster. It's eerily quiet around here. I'm used to being on a cattle ranch, where even in the dead of night, the animals are never entirely silent.

"They are." Jackson looks over his shoulder with a mischievous smile. "Which means we'll have it all to ourselves."

I whisper-yell, "We can't break into the hot springs."

Around the next bend in the path, we come face-to-face with a rustic metal gate. Jackson wiggles the latch in his fingers, bending down to get a better look at it, and it pops open a second later. The air's filled with the piercing sound of metal on metal, squealing so sharply I grit my teeth reflexively.

"If the gate's unlocked, does it really count as breaking in?"

Eyebrow raised, I jab a finger at the sign indicating they close at ten p.m. "Yes, it does."

"Okay, well then, guess we better make it quick. Come on, Kate. Don't make me soak in here all by myself."

Jackson swings the gate back and forth, wincing at the grating noise it makes as if he's not the one responsible for it. I swear, if that man ends up with a migraine in the morning, he can take care of himself while I treat myself to Belgian waffles in the restaurant.

"You keep fucking with that gate, somebody's going to hear you and come out." I roll my eyes and push past him, already pulling my sweater overhead.

If we're going to get caught, I'd like to have at least plunged into the hot water for a few minutes first. Make it worth my time.

Jackson's the first into the water, and he hisses at the feel of it hitting his cold, goosebump-covered skin. Then he sinks until there's nothing but his head showing above the water, obscured by a cloud of thick, billowing steam.

I set my clothes to the side and kick off my sandals, then gingerly walk across the stone pool deck and make an attempt at being graceful and ladylike when I hop in. The water prickles across my skin, stinging my frozen fingers and toes.

The warm steam rises in slow, drifting curls, immediately dampening my hair and coating my face in a thin layer of condensation. I push through the water toward my husband, smiling all the way into his big arms. He pulls me in, letting me cling to him like a koala, and carries me toward the deepest section of the pool.

The water swells around us and I smooth a wet hand over his hair—messed up and standing on end from sleep. Speaking of sleep, every muscle in my body is so relaxed, I could doze off right here.

We wade away from the singular light on the pool house, where during the open hours, one would shower off before and after being in the springs. In the dark, it's only me and him and the moon.

He calmly sets me down on a bench seat along the far edge of the pool and settles in beside me with a relaxed exhale.

"*There*," he says triumphantly, finding my thigh in the dark water and giving it a light tap. "An entirely uninterrupted soak for date night."

"I love this . . . even if I didn't love being woken up in the middle of a *great* sleep."

"I thought since we're going home tomorrow, and I screwed you over this morning, that I should try to make it up to you."

I pepper his jaw with soft kisses. "Thank you for this. All of it. We needed this trip."

"I needed to see you in a bikini." He fiddles with the long strings, flicking the small beads on the ends.

"You planned a romantic weekend away just to see me in a bikini?"

His touch moves upward, skimming my ribs before rolling the thin fabric of my top between his finger and thumb. "Money and time *very* well spent, if you ask me."

I laugh softly. "You could've asked me to wear one at home for you."

With a wet smack, his palm meets his forehead. "*Now* you tell me. . . . Still worth it, though. Getting out of the house, away from everyone—I like having you all to myself."

I like having him all to myself, too.

We've talked, we've cuddled, we've had plenty of loud, uninhibited sex. It feels a lot like when we snuck away to elope years ago.

"Plus, you've been dealing with all my shit. You deserve a break."

"First of all, I'm not 'dealing with' anything. I'm being a good wife—"

He leans in and nips my earlobe. "A very, *very* good wife."

That sets my entire body ablaze. Every part of me burns with the need to feel his touch.

"When did you become such a flirt?"

"It's that damn bikini," he says, eyes lifting to meet mine, heat blooming in the quiet space between us. "Distracting as hell."

"Oh yeah?" I adjust the triangles covering my tits, not because they need to be adjusted, but because I want to give the girls a little boost. Earn that stare of his. "Distracting from what?"

"Doesn't matter." He shakes his head, all the while fucking me with his eyes. "All I can think about is tearing it off and seeing if you're as wet as I am hard."

"Of course I'm wet, Jackson." Shooting him a flirtatious smile, I drag my fingers through the water, doing my best to appear entirely unperturbed by the thought of him being hard right now. "We're in a pool."

"You know exactly what I mean, Kit." His smirk makes my thighs clench.

"I'm not sure I do, handsome. Might need to show me how hard you are, so I can let you know if I'm equally as wet." My fingers curl around the back of his neck to twist the short, dark hair there.

His face looks pained, and that's how I know he's stiff as a board beneath his swim shorts long before he takes my hand and guides my touch there. My fingers skate up his thigh, gliding easily across the swimsuit fabric.

My heart flutters.

Oh, he's hard, all right. Sixteen years together, and I've still never gotten over how thick he is, nor the ache between my legs when I have to stretch to take him each time.

I palm his shaft through the thin fabric, eliciting a rugged groan from somewhere deep inside. And he tips his head back to rest on the pool edge, bucking his hips into my touch.

"Fuck, Kate," he grits out, rugged tenor making more heat swirl in my lower belly. "See what you do to me?"

"Oh, so this is my fault?" I kiss his ear. Nibble at the lobe.

"Bet you're really curious to know how wet my pussy is right now."

Hearing that, his hands shoot toward my lap, and I fend them off with a few swats of my free hand. All the while kneading the ridged head of his cock through his shorts. His thighs quake under my touch.

He stares at me, pupils blown out, desperation in every flick of his gaze down to my mouth.

"Is this what gets you off? Knowing I want you so bad it hurts?" His words come out mere shards of a wrecked voice. "I don't remember what this used to feel like with us, but I know what it feels like now. And I want you. *Right now.*"

He practically growls. A need. A demand. My pussy tightens around the emptiness, aching to feel him.

Jackson grabs my hips, tugging me onto his lap, and when I'm straddling him, the only thing I can feel is his cock pressing—*pulsing*—against my center. I drape my arms over his broad shoulders while his head falls back with a deep sigh.

Unable to help myself, I move my smiling mouth to meet his. And as soon as our mouths collide, the glowing ember turns into a roaring flame. An ardent kiss where we catch each other's groans and feed them back to one another in a clash of tangled tongues and love nips. My fingers clutch his hair, holding on for dear life, while he consumes every part of me.

His lips find their way to the column, then the crook, of my neck. Licking, sucking, biting his way around me.

The small red triangles provide a pathetic level of coverage, so a simple nudge of his knuckles exposes my right breast. He cups it, gliding his wet thumb over my hardened nipple. He curls into me, inhaling my skin and licking a trail through spots of water beaded on my chest, until he's swirling a tongue around my nipple in a way that sends silk strands slipping down my spine.

I moan into his hair—a last-ditch effort to muffle it. And he twists to grin up at me.

"Careful, Kit, or we might end up with an audience."

My eyes roll around the pool deck, checking for lurkers watching us. And before the surface tension on my anxiety breaks, Jackson brings me right back to him with a harsh suck on my nipple—bringing the entire thing into his mouth and letting go with a resounding *pop*.

My body leans into his and he cups my ass, holding me so each thrust of his hips sends pleasure rocketing through my core. Suddenly the thin bathing suit fabric is too much. My skin's too hot, too tight, too desperate to be touched.

"We should go."

Jackson's finger dips beneath the fabric of my swimsuit to swish across the trimmed hair over my pubic bone. "We should stay."

"What if somebody comes out here?" My mouth may be protesting, but my hips tilt to force his touch a little lower. Little lower. Until he's flirting with my clit and my entire body is tingling with anticipation. "We could get caught."

"That's what makes it so fun."

Who is this uninhibited man and what did he do with the man I've known for the last sixteen years?

"But you never used to . . ." An argument dies on my tongue when a finger presses my clit.

"My wife said she wants to be fucked in the hot springs. If I wouldn't have done anything about that before, I was a fucking idiot."

Holy shit. I know I said that, but . . . well, honestly, I didn't expect it to ever happen. It was said in the spirit of playing along with his questions. In the past, my husband was always gentle, soft, a rule follower to his core, and I loved him for it. But this? Oh, I love this, too.

He thrusts upward, cock rubbing the spot that makes me writhe and arch my back. "So tell me what you want, Kate. You want my fingers? Or maybe we'll sit you on the edge of the pool and I'll eat that sweet cunt of yours? Or should I shove you so full of my cock, you feel it in your throat?"

His words make my cheeks heat. I open my mouth, then close it hesitantly. *Is it crazy to say I want it all?*

I can't help but question if all of this is Jackson going through a bit of a crisis following his near-death experience and eventually he'll fall back into his cautious, rule-abiding personality. If that's the case, I don't want to let the moment slip away. I want to fuck my husband in the hot springs, with his filthy words bringing me to the brink of orgasm on their own.

And I know he's probably going to tell me to use my words, but they're gone. I'm stupefied by the hunger in his eyes and the insatiable need between my legs. So I nod. Frantically. It's the best I can give him.

He glides a finger inside me. There's no denying I'm wet in a way that has nothing to do with the pool water lapping over our bodies, and Jackson groans low in his throat at the discovery.

My chest rises and falls in a wild commotion. I swear I've never wanted anything the way I want his hands on me right now. I grip his forearms to keep his hands right where they are.

"You're so wet." His eager lips find mine. "Tight." *Kiss.* "Warm." *Kiss.* "Mine." *Kiss.*

I make quick work of undoing the tie at the top of his shorts and thrust my hand inside to grip him. Fist his shaft, circle my thumb over the smooth head.

"*Fuck,* you're amazing." He drops his head to my shoulder. The crook of his finger inside me nearly has me falling apart.

I pull myself together in the nick of time to twist around his cock and elicit a moan from him as guttural and loud as my own.

"Tell me I can be inside you," he whispers against the column of my neck before nipping the delicate skin there.

"Here?" I croak.

"Here, Kit. Let me fuck you in the hot springs like you wanted."

"Jackson, we don't have to just because I—"

He strokes my pussy, folding my entire body in on itself. And I rock my hips against him, desperate for friction.

"You're right, we don't have to." He's all flushed skin and dilated eyes, sweat beaded above his eyebrow. "But I really fucking want to. Haven't stopped thinking about it since you suggested it last night."

I chew the inside of my cheek, taking one last look around the pool deck, eyes narrowed.

"Okay," I whisper. "Fuck me right here."

Jackson pulls his finger from inside me, and in a frenzy that sends heavy waves rolling away from us, he tugs down the waistband of his shorts. Letting them hang low slung on his hips, he pulls out his cock and the slow pump of it cuts through the water.

I lift up, preparing to take my bottoms off, when Jackson pinches the fabric and pulls it to the side. The hem catches on my swollen clit, and the desperation of this moment—that we can't even bother getting undressed—makes heat pool in my core.

He notches himself at my entrance, and with a slow, steady push, he stretches me around him. I'm wet, but submerged in water, so there's a sharp pull initially. I gasp, widening my straddle, and sink a little farther. A little farther yet. Fed by the whimpers slipping from his lips and the tight grip he has on my ass.

"That's it. That's my girl," he moans against my skin. The rasp of his beard the perfect texture next to his soft kisses.

Once I'm fully seated on his cock, Jackson's free hand threads into my hair and he pummels his hips up into mine.

The water between us is electrified, zipping with energy as the buoyancy of the water makes each thrust more intense. His rough hands on my body pull me to meet him. I bounce up and down, splashing water across the stone slab behind his head.

What the fuck is my life?

Almost three months ago, I was cradling his injured body in the hospital. Then he was so depressed, I thought he might try to kill himself. I didn't know if we'd ever find our way back together. Now I'm kissing him within an inch of his life and riding him in a public hot spring. A star-filled night sky hanging above us, thick forest and the sounds of wildlife all around.

His cock hits all the right spots, and my frantic body becomes entirely loose in his arms. Each pulse of my pussy around his cock edging the both of us.

There's no way we aren't getting caught, with the volume of the moans. It's obscene, but I no longer care. Let them see. Let them watch the man I love make me come so fucking hard.

I rock my hips against his, finding my orgasm, feeling a wave of muscle tightness through my body.

"Jackson, I—*fuck*, I'm coming."

"Yeah, you are." He grunts on his next aggressive upward thrust. "Come on my cock, Kit."

He continues muttering absolute filth in my ear while his bruising grip controls my hips. Lifting me nearly off and slamming me back down. My heart beats out of my chest, and I ride my way through the orgasm, clenching and collapsing against him.

Without changing pace or letting up on pressure, Jackson presses his fingers into the flesh over my hips and keeps pumping into me. And my orgasm rolls through me in contractions of the most intense pleasure I've ever felt.

I come so hard, it's as if I'm the one who doesn't remember what it's like to be fucked and I'm experiencing it for the first time.

His eyes are dark with desire, face glistening with sweat. I wrap myself around his body, tipping my head back so he can lick his way up my neck. He buries his face there in the crook, and as the warmth of his cum fills my core, the sound of him murmuring "Kit" against my skin with nothing but adoration and love fills my heart.

We kiss and his hand gently strokes my back as we ease back down. And we stay there, with his cock fully seated inside me, flirting with the very real chance we'll be caught after being the furthest thing from quiet.

I roll my neck, glancing up at the stars, then back at him—*my sun*. Without him, I'm not sure how long I'd survive.

I whisper, "Over and over, you've stayed. Thank you."

He tilts his head, expression laced with confusion.

"I begged you to stay—on the floor of the barn and in the hospital and when you were talking about how it would be easier if . . . I'm just so happy you're here. You're with me and we're making memories again."

He rubs slow circles on my lower back. "This is the best type of memory to make. Let's do this a million more times. Where else do you want to have sex?"

I smile and kiss him. "Home. I want to have sex with you at home, in our bed."

"*Boo. Boring,*" he teases. Then, "Kidding. I can't wait to have sex with you in our bed—*and* everywhere else in our house."

"I can't wait, either."

I snuggle into his embrace, relishing the thickness of him inside me and the raw emotion as he holds me tight to his pounding chest.

"Also, I'm happy you gave me a reason to want to stay," he says softly.

My eyes close at his words, and I feel a familiar droplet of something—pool water or tear, I'm not quite sure—run down my face and drip from my chin.

He leans his cheek against my hair and adds, "I'd do anything for you, Kate."

KATE

Exhausted, heart brimming with love, and with a tender soreness between my legs, I reach across the car to run the backs of my knuckles over Jackson's short beard. He leans into the touch, twisting to give my fingers a quick kiss as they go by.

Rather than trying to squeeze in one last trip to the hot springs before leaving this morning, we opted to stay tangled up in bed, having languid sex bookended by more of Jackson's questions. He said his favorite color these days is the specific green shade in the center of my hazel irises, and insisted we need a trip to the beach before either of us can genuinely declare we prefer mountains. We kissed and touched and laughed, and I spent the entire time utterly in awe of him.

Reaching the end of the dirt road, we turn into the small town where Jackson bought the flowers. And I thought I couldn't love him any more than I did then, but it turns out I somehow love this man more and more each day.

"Looks like a market of some kind there," Jackson says, nodding toward a quaint park space crowded with vendors under pop-up tents. People are milling about in the midday sun, sipping giant plastic cups filled with what appears to be lemonade, and letting their kids run wild in an open field and on a massive colorful playground. "We should stop. See what they have."

"Well . . ." To be honest, I want to get home . . . but that damn excitement flickering on his face has me pulling into the parking lot before I can tell him no.

Jackson squints against the sun, and I hold out my sunglasses when we step out of the car. With a snort, he shakes his head and reaches for my hand. After so many years together, his touch was something I took for granted. The way our hands naturally slipped together when we were out in public, the loose hold around my waist he'd opt for sometimes.

I'll never take it for granted again.

I squeeze his fingers, bringing my other hand up to hold his firm bicep as we meander through the small crowd. The wafting scents of coffee and cut flowers and the earthiness of freshly picked produce dance around us, pulling my attention in a million different directions.

We stop for a taste test of local honey, followed by his incredibly sticky lips pressing to my forehead, then lips. And I want to *really* kiss him, but the damn smile on my mouth won't budge.

"Come on, handsome," I say, sticky and sweet, against his lips. "I smell espresso and it's calling my name."

"I was thinking the same about those lemonades everyone's walking around with."

Naturally, the two vendors are on opposite ends of the row of white and blue pop-up tents. I give him a gentle tap on the butt—one he reciprocates—and say, "Let's split up and meet back here?"

After a short peck, I watch him walk away. Fully checking out his ass as he goes. I'm allowed to do that again without feeling like a creep, and like I said, I'm not taking *anything* for granted.

The lineup at the espresso cart is long, which, though annoying, probably means it's some damn good coffee. And I need that after a night with little sleep. After the hot springs, we showered together, went to sleep with his dick inside me, and woke up for more sleepy sex as the sun rose.

I roll my neck, stretching and yawning, and tip my head to watch the slow movement of swirly, fluffy clouds across the light blue sky. The sun's hot on my head, even hotter when I smooth my hand down my dark hair. And by the time it's my turn to order, I'm nearly asleep where I stand.

Nothing a giant vanilla latte with an extra shot can't fix. Instead of sleeping, I'll be vibrating for the entire drive home. And probably needing to pee a hundred times. *It's fine.*

Cradling the cardboard cup like it's my most prized possession, I saunter through the market, and when Jackson's not at the agreed-upon meeting spot, I continue toward the distant, bright yellow lemonade stand.

"Hey, handsome." I sidle up next to him in line, slipping my hand into the back pocket of his jeans. "What's taking so long? It's lemon juice and water."

"My fault. I got distracted by something on the way here."

"Oh?" I lift an eyebrow.

His smile borders on smirking, smug and secretive. "I'll show you after I order."

"I do love a good surprise."

"Yeah? I think this is a damn good surprise."

I stay attached to his butt while he places his order, giving it a little squeeze that makes him jump. He laughs under his breath and shifts his weight, shooting me a look that's half scandalized, half delighted.

He taps his card and accepts the lemonade from the vendor. "You're lucky I'm still recovering, or I'd throw you over my shoulder and carry you out of here."

"I'd like to see you try," I say, bumping his hip.

"Come on," he says. "Let's go sit and enjoy the fresh air for a minute before we have to leave."

Jackson leads me off the path toward a quiet patch of grass under a wide old oak. He sits on the edge of a low stone wall and waits for me to settle beside him. Our knees brush, kicking my heart into overdrive the way it always does. He takes a long sip of lemonade, making a small noise of delight in the back of his throat.

"Oh, this is good." He lifts the cup in front of his eyes to inspect it with an impressed look. "Not too lemony. You should try it."

If I'm going to try what he's drinking, I only want to taste it from his lips. In a cool, refreshing, perfectly lemony kiss, I do exactly that. Sweeping my tongue across his, relishing the cold and the sweetness on his breath.

Pulling away, he looks at me—*really looks*. The sun picks up every freckle on his creamy skin. Normally by early June, he'd have a deep tan and overlapping freckles despite my insistence on wearing sunscreen every day. Free hand combing through his wavy hair, he's as gorgeous as ever backdropped by green gardens and a crisp blue sky.

"So, there's something I want to say." He glances down at the plastic cup in his hands.

I straighten a little, pulse skipping. "Okay . . ."

"I bought this while you were getting coffee." Reaching into the front pocket of his jeans, he pulls out a simple burnt-orange cloth bag. "From the silversmith booth—the one we saw with the fancy belt buckles you liked."

I nod, curious. The bag is nowhere near large enough to fit a buckle.

With shaky hands, he works to untie the knotted string holding the bag closed, and spills a simple silver ring into his palm—brushed, slightly uneven, clearly hand-forged. It gleams in the sunlight, not flashy, not perfect. But it looks solid. *Made to last*.

My heart sits in the back of my throat, watching him twist the ring around in his fingers.

"You've never made a big deal about me not having a wedding ring anymore, but I hated it." He hastily works down a swallow. "I'm not the same guy who put on the first one, but I'm still *yours*. I want to belong to each other, Kate. I want our family . . . and, even though you said it was unnecessary, I needed something on my hand to show that. Something to show you I'm staying forever."

The silver band glints in the sun as he slides it onto his left ring finger with quiet finality. It fits perfectly in place, sinking into the grooves in his flesh like it's meant to be there.

His rough hands move to caress my face, the cold metal of the ring pressed to my jaw, securing me in place. As if I had any intention of going anywhere. Watching his face is enthralling, and I could let myself get lost in his eyes forever.

"I love you."

It's everything I needed to hear, and everything I was terrified to admit I needed.

"Jackson . . ." The tears come fast, hot, and silent.

"It's been on the tip of my tongue for so long, but I wanted to make sure it wasn't muscle memory or obligation or . . . I'm not saying it because I'm trying to remember, Kit. I'm saying it because I *know*."

"You have no idea how badly I needed to hear that," I admit.

For the first time since the moment Red walked into my kitchen that morning, my lungs can expand to full capacity, and the world around us is in full Technicolor.

I add, "We're going to be okay."

"Yeah, we are, Kit. We love each other . . . and I think that's all it takes to be okay."

He tilts my head, seeking my lips, brushing kisses over them. Careful, reverent, and tinged with the faintest hint of lemon. Salt and sugar coalesce on my tongue, and the slight scratch of his beard sends arousal trickling down my spine to settle in my core. My husband's touch feels like a vow made all over again.

"I love you," I murmur, eyes flickering open to meet his.

His thumb sweeps across the plane of my cheek, chasing the trails of fallen tears and clearing them away.

"I know you do." His lips tug at the corners, stealing my heart and my soul entirely. "I love you, too."

JACKSON

The house is quiet in the way it only ever gets after bedtime as I tread cautiously down the stairs. My head's still buzzing from trying to string together something resembling a story for the kids.

I couldn't do it.

Lately Odessa's been the one handling bedtime stories, sharing funny moments and fond memories—often embellished with fart sound effects and obvious lies that elicit giggles from her brother. On the nights she doesn't feel up to it, I read the kids a book.

But tonight Rhett wasn't having it. He insisted I be the one to tell them a story, and when Odessa tried to tell him she was doing it, the two got into a scrap that made my eye twitch and my palms sweat as I fought the urge to tell the both of them to shut up.

So I agreed to a damn story.

Odessa tucked herself into bed with her arms around that ragged old horse she sleeps with. And Rhett smugly parked himself right next to me. I made up a memory from when Rhett would've been too young to remember and, truthfully, I think even Odessa was questioning whether it was real or not. It wasn't particularly funny and had some *serious* plot holes, but they stared up at me like I was their entire world.

And in that pretend memory—one I want so badly to be real—they were mine.

I step into the kitchen and consider turning around when I see Austin and Red are hanging out here tonight.

But Kate spots me first and gives me a smile. "Kids asleep?"

I sigh. "Yeah, finally."

Then I head straight for my empty spot at the table, letting my body go slack in the wooden chair. Austin and Red's conversation about moving cattle comes to a halt, both of them turning to look at me.

"Barely survive bedtime?" Red asks from across the table.

"They insisted I tell them a real story tonight." Shaking my head, I grunt. "Which is damn hard when you're reading from a book missing ninety percent of the pages."

"Kids don't even notice, man. I skip pages in Hazel's storybooks all the damn time." He cracks open a pistachio from the bowl in the center of the table and pops it in his mouth.

"I don't know. . . ." I force a breath out through my nose. "It feels like I'm failing them."

Austin clears his throat at the far end of the table, folding his arms. "You're not."

"But it *feels* that way."

I've found my way back to Kate and thank God for that. But the kids . . . It feels like they're drifting off to sea, and I'm still standing on the dock, promising I'll catch up when I don't even know how to swim.

Kate slides me a glass of water before taking the seat next to mine. Her cold hand falls to my lap to melt some of the anxiety burrowed in my chest.

"Odessa kept giving me this look tonight like she was trying *so hard* to be nice about the fact that my story was awful."

Austin chuckles. "Damn, she must've had to work hard at that."

Laughter ripples gently through Kate, culminating in a

tight squeeze of her hand above my knee. "She's trying to be patient with you. Give you the space to figure things out again."

"She shouldn't have to, though." I scrub my hand over my jaw. "She's only eight. And Rhett keeps asking if I'm all better yet. . . . *Fuck.* I'm trying, but I can't get there for some reason."

"It's only been a few months. They don't need perfection. They just need you," Kate says. Austin and Red hum an agreement.

"Yeah, but I feel like I'm not even giving them that. Most of the time, I'm faking my way through fatherhood. I smile, I listen, I say the things I think I'm supposed to say. But I . . . I don't *feel* like their dad."

Kate flinches. Barely. But I see it. She knew I was struggling with my connection to the kids, but I've been following my therapist's advice and sitting with them even when it's hard. Even when watching them color or cheering them on outside while they ride bikes is the last thing I want to be doing. So on the outside, it probably looks like I'm almost there with them.

I slipped a ring on my finger, promising her that I was ready for all of this. And I am. I *want* that connection with the kids. I love them, I think, but there's a gaping, aching hole in my chest whenever I think about Odessa and Rhett, and I have no idea how to mend it.

I run a hand over my face again, ashamed of saying it out loud. But it's the truth.

"You're still healing from a brain injury. It's gonna take time," Red says to cut the tense silence. "You think any of us know what the fuck we're doing as parents? Just wait, Aus. You'll be here freaking out about how to take care of a baby soon enough."

Austin lifts a brow, clearly not believing that. I'm not sure anything fazes him. Even when I remember the day our mom died, or the glimpses of the past I've gotten from the years when we were struggling with the ranch—Austin's always been the calm, collected, *get shit done* brother.

"Yeah, but you've got the cheat code," I say. "You remember loving them."

To my nonsurprise, that lands with a thud, and I regret saying it the moment the last word leaves my lips.

I quickly add, "I didn't mean it like that. That I don't love them . . . I do. I know I do."

Kate's hand falls away from my lap and one glance at her glassy eyes has my own burning. Austin and Red are staring wide-eyed, with mouths sewn in thin, straight lines. Nobody's so much as breathing. *Fuck.*

I exhale, pushing the heels of my hands against my stinging eyes. "God, I'm trying. Every damn day, I'm trying. But Odessa was *mine.* She was always by my side, right? That's what everyone keeps saying. And now . . . now I can't even tell a bedtime story without making her second-guess it." A little quieter, through teary eyes and a voice thick with emotion, I say, "I want them to feel like they're mine."

Kate's hand finds mine, pulling me from the dark thoughts swirling around the way the wind howls outside. When something falls over on the back porch with a loud *thunk,* we all turn to look at the window out of habit, but no one moves.

"I should get home before that storm gets too bad," Red says, standing. I'm sure he's really only leaving to escape the awkwardness of this conversation. Poor guy came over thinking he would be talking about cattle and feed prices with the boss and got saddled with hearing about my shit.

"Thanks for pulling extra weight around here lately, man." Austin stands, too, and claps Red on the back. "And offering to take on even more after the baby comes."

Red nods. "No problem. What brothers are for, right?"

I lick my lips and roll them together, mulling that over. An opportunity to feel like I'm useful would be great. "What are you guys doing tomorrow? I can help. . . . Be good to get out of the house for a bit."

Austin and Red exchange a glance, and Red shrugs. "Yeah, I mean . . . Aus barely even does any ranch work anymore. That's why he's getting so soft around the middle these days." He dodges the swing of Austin's arm and looks over to Kate—probably for reassurance that I'm *allowed* to do physical labor of any kind. "But you can come with me for the day. I'm sure we can find something for you to do."

Don't love that I'm going to be tagging along and likely given tasks Odessa's capable of doing. In fact, since tomorrow's Saturday, maybe we should bring her, too.

Kate leans over to kiss me on the cheek before she starts clearing glasses, and Red grabs one last handful of pistachios. "I'll be here before six. Think you're still capable of getting out of bed that early?"

I shake my head with a soft chuckle. "Yeah, yeah. I'll be ready, you ass."

The front door closes behind him with a thud, and it's just the three of us.

Kate hums softly as she rinses the last glass. I lean back in my chair, letting it take some of my weight. My head's heavy, painful fog creeping in like it does every night. Right now, it's a gentle reminder to take a heavier dose of medication so I stand a chance of sleeping tonight. Give it another few minutes, and I'll have no choice but to basically crawl my way to the bedroom.

With a long, slow sip of water, I let my eyes drift shut for a second. Long enough to see Odessa's face when she asked for a story tonight. That little hopeful smile she tried to hide. I couldn't give her what she wanted, not really—but she curled up beside me anyway, like she still believes I will, eventually.

Maybe tomorrow will be better. Maybe the work will help. Maybe bringing Odessa along will help spark something in me so I can squeeze my kids tight, kiss them on top of the head, and tell them I love them without feeling like a fraud. Maybe I'll be a dad again tomorrow. At the very least, I'm going to try.

The next morning I wake to the alarm set on my phone, and I understand Kate's disdain for the sound now—the loud beep cutting through the peace of sleep is nothing but obnoxious when I'm not waking up for a hot date with my wife. I shut the stupid sound off with a groan.

I move slowly down the hallway to the kitchen where Kate's dressed already, hair piled on top of her head, coffee mug in one hand while she stands at the island, staring out toward fields drenched from last night's rain.

Beryl's next to her, refilling the sugar canister from a bag that seems extraordinarily large for her spindly arms to manage, shooing my younger brother away when he tries to help. Denny rolls his eyes at her, squeezing past to grab a scone from the counter, and notices me.

"Morning, sunshine," Denny says, chomping down on the scone and quickly sliding his free hand under his chin to try and catch stray crumbs.

I yawn. "Mornin'."

Kate looks over at me then, and her smile's a little sleepy. I want to feel that curve of her lips against mine, so I close the short distance between us and kiss her, wrapping an arm around her waist.

"You're up early," she says once I've had my fill of her—*rather,* once I've had an appropriate amount of her, given the family members and ranch hands loitering in our kitchen.

"You think Red would let me live it down if I slept in?"

Red walks up and grips my shoulder in his massive palm. "Nope, I wouldn't. You ready?"

Kate tilts her head. "You should have some breakfast first."

"Nah, I'm okay." I shake my head. "Is Odessa up yet? I was gonna see if she wants to come with us."

Just as Kate starts to say she'll go upstairs to wake her up, Beryl cuts in with an insistence that I eat something before I go out with Red. The two women's sentences merge and somehow both of them end up giving me hell for skipping breakfast, so I make a show of grabbing one of the scones and taking a bite. Appeasing Kate enough that she heads off in search of Odessa, I lean against the counter to enjoy my breakfast.

Today's a jalapeño cheddar scone, which is a pleasant surprise. I'd say the upside to getting up early is securing one of Beryl's breakfast treats, since they always go so fast, but she's been secretly tucking one away for me every day for weeks. I could sleep until noon and still get one.

Kate's footsteps are slow and light as she saunters away.

A few minutes pass.

And her footsteps are fast and sharp when she comes back.

I straighten before she even speaks.

"She's not in her room."

JACKSON

Kate's voice is strung so tight, it's liable to snap, turn into a scream. "Has anybody seen her?"

A collective murmur of *no* vibrates through the kitchen, and Beryl calmly suggests, "Maybe she got up early and went to feed the barn cats?"

I think Kate and I are the only ones who know Odessa's been mostly avoiding the barn. She's willing to go down and see the barn cats in the middle of the day, when there are cowboys milling about, but it's pretty unlikely she'd be there by herself so early in the morning.

Even still, I say, "I'll walk down there and look."

Kate's eyes lock on mine, and she hastily works down a swallow. "Her bed doesn't even look slept in, and she's not in Rhett's room."

Austin pushes back from his spot at the table and tosses open the back door. "I'll head over to my place and see if she's there."

Kate nods, but her eyes are wide, glassy. There's a steady tick in her jaw as she glances around, clearly trying to think of where an eight-year-old might've gone.

"She's probably causing some trouble outside. We've got enough of us. . . . We'll find her quickly," Denny says, tossing back the rest of the coffee in his cup. His voice is casual, but there's an edge under it. I feel the same sharp squeeze in my own chest—something's off and none of us want to say it out loud.

"It rained last night—could be she's looking for tadpoles again," Beryl says.

"Yeah. I'll walk down to the cattle guard." Kate clings to that, wrapping her arms around herself, and looks at the other men in the room. "Can you guys . . . I don't know . . ."

"We'll scour the place," Red says, gesturing for the ranch hands to follow him outside.

Denny plunks his mug into the sink and gives Kate's shoulder a firm squeeze. "Five bucks says she's outside digging in your flower beds or some shit."

"Yeah, she'll be *so* grounded, if that's the case." Kate's voice breaks a little at the end, and it cracks something in my chest.

Kate and I follow behind the guys, silently and hurriedly slipping into big rubber boots and grabbing coats from a row of metal hooks by the front door. I wait, holding the door open, as her trembling fingers struggle with the zipper.

"She knows not to go outside without telling anyone," Kate says under her breath.

"Kids make silly mistakes all the time," I reply. "She's okay, Kate. *Promise.*"

"It's just . . ." She aggressively rubs a fist over her sternum, and I watch her try to breathe through it. "I'm trying not to panic, but this feels so much like that day."

"This isn't like that." I pull her in for a brief hug and a firm kiss planted on top of her head. "Let's go find our girl."

I head out toward the barn.

It's quiet. Too quiet. No off-key singing to her barn cats, no sound of disturbed animals. The door creaks when I slide it open, and light streams in from behind me to illuminate the dusty alley. I look around for a moment to find the light switch, and the overhead barn lights slowly hum to life, flooding the space with a warm glow. A horse blinks over at me.

Somewhere farther down, another scuffs its hooves across the concrete floor. But otherwise, silence.

Fuck.

While I assumed she wouldn't be here, it would've been a damn good surprise to find her casually sitting on a hay bale, playing with a kitten. All the worry in the kitchen would be for nothing, and we could carry on with our day.

I check a wood shed next, then an old tractor shed, and the chicken coop. Her name echoes through the valley, carried by the spring breeze across the tall grasses. Various tones and volumes from the dozen or more voices yelling out for her.

I lean against a wooden fence post, scrubbing my hand over my face, as the silence presses in, collapsing around my rib cage like a vise. It's not panic yet, but it's close. Because if she was anywhere on this ranch, she'd be easy to spot. Singing to the animals, lying stomach-down in a mud puddle playing with a toad, armpit deep in the garden soil, laughing hysterically as she splashes through water pooled in drainage ditches.

I've wanted to connect with my kids, and remember the kind of dad I was, since the day Kate showed me photo after photo of them in the hospital. Today there's utter desperation ransacking my entire body. I can't help but think Old Jackson would know *exactly* where to find Odessa.

Kate yells my name, grabbing my attention, and a shallow, hopeful breath inflates my lungs, only for her words to knock it out of me. "She's not by the cattle guard," she shouts.

Turning on her heel, she says something about going to check the river. I should follow. I should do *something*. But my feet feel heavy, rooted to the ground by the pressure building behind my ribs.

Kate's voice cuts through the air as she disappears around the side of our house, fraying more every time she calls Odessa's name. The early morning sun crests the hill, tossing a warm blanket of dense fog over the ranch the way one throws a blanket over a horse's back. That's what my brain feels like, too—airy thoughts swirling in my head, dissipating between my fingers anytime I reach for them.

I crane my neck to feel the heat of the sun on my face, and a memory floats in like dust glimmering in a sunbeam. I remember the sound of Odessa's small boots stomping through the quiet barn. She was mad, though I don't remember why, and I don't think she knew then that I was standing there.

No ladder. No fear. She'd climbed up into the rafters with ease.

And I remember craning my neck to look up there. Finding her dirt-smudged legs dangling down from one of the wooden beams, tear tracks down her cheeks, cat held close to her chest.

Without hesitation, I start walking.

I know my daughter.

The barn door rollers grate, the harsh sound of metal on metal, when I yank it open. My heart pounds, ricocheting everywhere inside, quickening with each step through the dimly lit barn. It's humid from the rainy night and, though there are no signs of her, I can't ignore the feeling deep in my bones. The protective fire in my veins where there's meant to be blood.

She's here.

"Odessa," I say softly, careful not to spook her.

It's silent, and that doesn't slow me down for even a second. I stride the length of the barn, to the stall where Kate said I got hurt. I don't know what happened that day, but being here makes the hairs on the back of my neck stand on end. Odessa was here then. She was here, saw everything, and that fucking guts me.

Stepping into the confined space, I tilt my head and squint up at the ceiling.

And there she is.

Perched on one of the thick crossbeams exactly like in my memory. One knee's hugged to her chest, the other leg dangling off the edge, pink cowboy boot swishing through the still air. Banana, that damn cat, is curled beside her like it's a regular Saturday morning.

Something wells up from the depths of my lungs.

"We've been looking all over for you," I say softly.

Her raspy, tear-filled voice topples down from the high ceiling. "I didn't think you'd look here."

"You told me this is your favorite hiding spot once." I pause. "You were mad at Mom that time. Remember?"

She sniffles. "You remember that?"

My ribs constrict at the way hope shapes her tone.

"I do. . . . So why are you up there this time, Princess?"

She's quiet for a moment. And it doesn't matter that I get a little dizzy standing here for so long with my head tilted back, I continue staring up at my daughter. The stubborn, brave-as-hell, spitfire girl with more heart than she knows what to do with.

"I heard you talking in the kitchen last night."

It's the Sahara desert in the back of my throat, and I swallow, swallow, swallow despite the burning sensation and gritty pain. A distorted version of every word I might've said plays on repeat. I'm not sure how much of it she heard, but anything is too much.

"I'm sorry. . . . Have you been up there since then?" I swallow hard. Thank God she didn't fall, especially if she climbed into the rafters in the dark.

"No," she says quietly. "I was too scared. I waited until the morning."

"Okay, good. Do you . . . would you like to come down? Talk about what you heard?" With held breath, I wait patiently for a response that doesn't come. In the distance, Denny's voice yells for Odessa, and I glance over at the open barn door briefly, then back to her. "I don't remember everything, Odessa. And I hate that, because I know we had a lot of fun together, didn't we? And . . . and I miss all those times I don't remember. But I know one thing for sure—I love you with my entire heart. You and your brother are the reason I keep fighting to get better."

More quiet.

Then, "I think I'm ready to come down now."

My guts twist as she swings her other leg down and shimmies along the beam. Then slowly lowers herself, long, skinny body outstretched until her toes brush the top of the fence rail. When they catch, she balances there like an expert gymnast. I close the space, arms open, poised to catch her. Though I'm not sure why I had doubts, because she only wobbles the tiniest bit as she lets go of the wooden beam and crouches down to grab the metal rail next to her feet.

When her cowboy boots hit the cement floor, I drop to my knees and let her collapse into me. I press kisses into her wild hair, holding her tight, rubbing a hand up and down her back.

"Wanna tell me what you overheard last night?" I ask once both of our heart rates have returned to normal.

She tips her head up to look at me with too much worry creased in her cute, freckled face. Her cheeks are streaked with tears and dust, and she looks so much older than eight. "You said . . . you don't feel like our dad. I thought maybe . . ."

"I'm so sorry. . . ." My voice cracks.

I squeeze her tighter, as if it'll somehow stop the pain in my chest from consuming me. My nose burns, my eyes burn, and no matter how aggressively I tell my tear ducts to get their shit together, I end up crying in front of my little girl.

My little girl.

For the first time, I hold her and it feels exactly like she's mine.

"I'm so sorry," I whisper. "I shouldn't have said that."

"I thought if I left . . . maybe you'd remember me."

Fuck. That lands like a punch to the gut. I squeeze my eyes shut for half a second, holding it in, then open them again and meet hers. "I don't need you to disappear to remember you, or to remember how to be your dad. I just need time. And you. And maybe a few more bedtime stories."

That earns a small smile.

"Can I tell you something?" I wait for her subtle nod. "I've been trying so hard to do all the things I used to do. I want to be your dad *so badly*, but I don't remember how . . . and I'm scared of getting it wrong, because you and Rhett deserve the best."

She gives me a side-eye. "You always say dads aren't scared of anything."

"Well, that was before I learned what it felt like to lose you guys. And that scared the hell out of me."

"Swear jar."

I crinkle my nose, sniffing back the tears with a hollow chuckle. "I'll pay up as soon as we get back to the house."

"Can we make a trade instead?" she hesitantly asks. "Like the five seconds of honesty your mommy used to do when you were a kid and did something naughty. You don't have to pay for the bad word if I can tell you a secret and not get in trouble."

Maybe a better parent would insist on consequences for whatever it is she's about to tell me, but every memory I have of my mom is filled with nothing but light, love, and acceptance. I think she knew what she was doing.

"Okay . . . deal."

Odessa taps the toes of her boots together a few times, stalling like this whole thing wasn't her idea.

"Well so . . . I'm not supposed to climb up to see Banana."

"*Right.*" I can assume the reason for that rule, based on how quickly my heart raced watching her gingerly climb down. One slip and . . . she could be like me, or worse. "Because you could fall."

"*I know-uh,*" she whines, rolling her eyes. "You always tell me that."

"If your secret is that you climbed up there today, I already know about that."

"It's my fault you broke your brain."

I blink at her, swallowing hard, and swipe the pads of my fingers over the dampness on my cheeks. "Odessa, that's not . . . it's not your fault."

Her eyes drop to the floor, where her boots are shuffling a piece of hay around. "It was. You always told me not to climb up there, but you didn't get mad at me . . . so I thought—you said the horse in here wasn't nice, but I wanted to say goodbye to Banana before we left, and I slipped."

"No." I grab either side of her face, squishing her cheeks between the heels of my hands, and pull her to look me in the eye. "It was an *accident*. Nobody is to blame, least of all you."

She shrugs, and her wet brown eyes are impossibly wide and so damn heartbreaking staring up at me. I wish I knew what to say to make her realize none of this is her fault.

"And it doesn't matter, anyway. We still have each other, and we have *plenty* of time to make new memories."

She looks up at me again, eyes searching, like she's trying to figure out if she can believe that. "I don't want you to forget me again."

Fuck. That does it. That's the sentence that splits my heart clean down the middle.

I wrap her up in my arms, resting my chin on her head, and smooth a rough hand over her curly, tangled hair.

Maybe if I hold her tight enough, love her hard enough, the world won't take anything else from us. Maybe my kids will turn out okay in spite of everything. Maybe I won't completely fail them, or Kate, or myself.

"Even if I forget everything else, I'll always come back to you, okay? That's what hearts do when they love someone—they remember."

She presses her cheek into my shoulder, small arms winding around my neck in a hug that nearly suffocates. But I'm loving every second of it too much to tell her to stop, even if my ability to breathe is severely limited.

We stay like that for a while, in the quiet hum of the barn, the only sound the soft exhale of horses and the occasional meow from Banana, still perched in the rafters.

Then I hear somebody yelling Odessa's name, and I'm reminded of the fact that everyone else on the ranch still thinks she's missing. Kate's probably worrying herself sick, while doing her best to keep a straight face and calm demeanor.

Before I can tell her we need to let the search party know she's okay, Odessa blurts, "Can we go tell Mom I'm not dead now?"

That pulls a laugh straight from my gut, rough and surprised and desperately needed. I stand and take her hand, holding it tight, not ready to let go quite yet.

"Yeah, Princess," I say. "Let's go give your mom her heart back."

KATE

Standing on the sidewalk outside the local florist, I check my phone for the second time since we left the ranch.

It's not that I don't trust Jackson, but this is his first time taking care of the kids since his accident. And sure, the other guys and his dad are all there, if he needs a hand with anything, but Odessa and Rhett are total agents of chaos at the best of times.

When the girls started planning Cecily's baby shower a couple months ago, I assumed I wouldn't be in attendance. I think they did, too. Jackson was in such rough shape, the only time I dared to leave the house was for Odessa's therapy sessions, and that was out of sheer maternal guilt because the last thing I want is for her to grow up blaming herself.

But today, I'm here. I'm here with my closest friends, about to spend the next two hours gossiping and creating bouquets. Everything feels so normal, it's almost as if the past three months were a dream.

Instead of the typical baby shower with silly games and pastel cupcakes, Cecily simply wanted us all to hang out somewhere other than my kitchen, for once. And when Blair mentioned that the florist down the street from her clinic was offering DIY floral arrangement parties, it was the obvious choice for our girls' day.

In single file, we weave through the maze of floral arrangements. White curtains dampen the sunlight, and in the center of the room is a massive oak table heaped with flowers to choose from.

I sink into a pink wooden chair next to Cecily at the table, then confirm the ringer on my phone is at full volume before tucking it into my purse on the floor beneath me. Around the table, Blair, Cassidy, Beryl, and Whit settle into their seats.

Looking at her phone, the corner of Blair's lip lifts. Then her eyes travel up to meet mine. "Apparently Odessa's making the guys eat mud pies."

"Sounds like something she'd do." With a breathy laugh, I relax in my seat. I knew the kids would be fine, but confirmation is always welcome.

The owner—a twenty-something woman with short, jagged black hair and arms filled with bangles—stands at the head of the table with pairs of shears in her hands and launches into her spiel about flower arranging. It should be straightforward, if you ask me. Pick flowers, cut stems to length, pop into vase. Apparently, that's not the case.

Once the obligatory tutorial's out of the way, the shop owner offers everyone lavender lemonade before leaving us to our own devices.

Whit takes a small sip of lemonade and plucks a spray of baby's breath from the pile. "This feels like the kind of thing women would be doing in a historical romance novel—all we need are Regency gowns and a scandal to discuss."

"We're severely lacking scandals," Blair says. "But since we're finally without kids and husbands hanging around, I'd love to hear all about Kate's trip to the hot springs."

Wide-eyed and excited, Cecily nods eagerly. I'm not the type of person to share intimate details about my marriage, but I needed to tell *someone* about our late-night pool break-in. And since Cecily and Beryl are in the kitchen with me for hours each day, they heard all about it.

"Oh, *yes*. Tell them, Kate." One hand resting on her large, perfectly round baby bump, she leans to grab a pink ranunculus.

"It was wonderful—two nights of kid-free relaxing, soaking in the hot water . . ." I shrug.

Blair looks up from where she's trimming some stems, eyes flitting between Cecily and me. "It was *nice*? That's all we get? Cecily's face right now says you're leaving things out."

Lifting her kitschy glass to her lips, Cecily murmurs, "Leaving a *lot* out."

I roll my eyes at her. "Okay, we did a lot of talking and sort of . . . getting to know each other again, which was lovely. And on the drive home, we stopped at a quaint farmer's market—Jackson surprised me by buying himself a new wedding band because the paramedics cut his off after the accident."

A chorus of *awwws* breaks out amid the sounds of snipping scissors and flower stems clinking on vases.

Cecily nudges me with her elbow, pushing for more. I swallow hard and pick up my lemonade. Between short sips of sweet liquid, I quietly spill the most salacious part of our weekend. "And he woke me up in the middle of the night to break into the hot pool and have sex."

Blair sits back with an impressed look on her face. "Damn. Go Jackson."

"*In the pool?*" Cassidy asks.

I confirm with a single nod. "In sixteen years, we've never done anything like that before."

"This is exactly the kind of scandal I like to hear about," Whit says. "There's really something in the water at that ranch, isn't there?"

Cass snips a stem. "Got that right."

"Whatever it is, it was nice to feel like Jackson and Kate again. We still have a ways to go, of course, but the trip was like a reset button."

Beryl's been so busy quietly putting together a variety of flowers, meticulous in her arrangement of them, I nearly forgot about her sitting on the other side of Cecily until she quietly says, "What I would give for a vacation away with a sexy man."

Laughter spills across the table from all sides.

"Don't start getting any ideas about snowbirding to somewhere tropical," I warn her with a teasing undertone. "We need you around here."

Beryl scoffs, placing a defensive palm on Cecily's stomach. "Oh, please. As if I could leave my grandbabies like that."

Blair slips a small bundle of light blue flowers into her vase and looks to Cecily. "Speaking of babies, are you and Austin still undecided on baby names?"

Cecily hesitates, her lips curving. "If the baby's a girl, we're going with Lucy. . . ."

We all nod solemnly. I remember discussing baby names with Jackson while I was pregnant—we went back and forth on naming our daughter after his mom, too. Even though it had been a few years since Lucy Wells passed, the collective family wound still felt too fresh when Odessa was born.

"And if it's a boy, I have no idea. You wouldn't believe the names Austin's vetoed."

I chuckle. "The man doesn't speak much, but when he does, his opinions are strong."

"I have a feeling she's a girl, anyway." Cecily smooths a hand over her stomach. "But we should probably agree on *something* for a boy. I've been having the weirdest dreams about names lately—like the other night, we named the baby Pickles."

Cassidy tilts her head. "Hey, I mean . . . we still call Hazel 'Little Spud' sometimes, so I'm on board."

My phone pings, and I race to pick it up, only to find Jackson's sent a picture of Odessa, Rhett, and Hazel—with muddy clothes and hands, disheveled hair, and the brightest smiles I've ever seen—standing next to a picnic table covered in plates with even more mud.

Jackson: The kids have been busy.
Hope you girls are hungry <3

My fingers lightly tap my lips, feeling the smile I can't hold back as it spreads across my face. I take a deep breath of floral air. Everything feels light and hopeful, and I gleefully show the photo to each of the girls.

"Speaking of little spuds, looks like Hazel has enough dirt in her hair to grow potatoes." Blair squints at the screen before passing the phone to Cass, who only shakes her head and laughs.

"Those are the happiest little kids I've ever seen," Whit says.

I settle back in my chair, the chatter swirling around me like the scent of peonies and lavender. And as talk settles into name suggestions, guesses on when the baby will arrive, and pregnancy cravings, our hands move as easily through the flowers as our conversation does. The vases fill like the hours, easy and unhurried, and for the first time in months, I'm not anxiously counting the minutes until I'm back home. I'm savoring them.

JACKSON

Odessa meticulously straightens a white-and-blue tea towel draped over her makeshift tree stump table, then slaps a paper plate covered in mud down on top of it. Stepping back to admire her work, she gives a little nod before spinning to face the row of lawn chairs me, my brothers, Red, and my dad are sitting in. When we set them up on the grass an hour ago, Denny said we looked like a bunch of suburban dads, just needed white New Balance sneakers and to cut our jeans into shorts.

With all the wives in Wells Canyon for Cecily's baby shower, us guys figured it might be more fun to sit in the sunshine and let the kids run feral for a few hours. Besides, Kate was hesitant about leaving me alone with the kids for the first time, so I hope she's able to relax and enjoy herself knowing there are multiple capable adults here.

"The restaurant is open," Odessa announces, brushing her dirty hands across the front of her pink T-shirt.

"What are you serving?" I ask hesitantly from my lawn chair.

"Anything you want." She beams at me. "We have pies and pizza and hamburgers and . . ."

Denny leans over in his chair to talk to me out of the side of his mouth. "And anything flat and patty shaped."

"Rhett and Hazel are my chefs." She gestures to where the

two younger kids are sitting in a pile of dirt, garden hose running between them to create a thick, goopy mud for their pies. "And Avery's my taste tester."

Denny's attention bounces between his niece and his infant daughter, who's content in her bouncer chair. He shakes his head. "No feeding mud to the baby, got it?"

"Fine, you can have her share."

"I'm actually on a no-mud diet right now," he replies. "But you go ahead and make your dad an extra-large pizza, he's still trying to make up for all that weight he lost eating hospital food."

"The mud pie's probably more appetizing." Austin stretches his denim-clad legs out in front of him.

"Nothing beats farm to table," Red says with a chuckle.

Dad adds, "Plus the chefs at this place are cute."

Rhett and Hazel sit shoulder-to-shoulder on the ground, mottled sunlight illuminating them through the branches of a nearby tree. Hazel's gleefully patting a pile of mud in an overturned Frisbee. Rhett rips up a handful of grass and sprinkles it over his own pie with a concentrated look on his face.

Odessa strides toward them and waits impatiently—hand on her hip and the ball of her left foot tapping the earth—as Rhett adds his final touches. Then she's headed in my direction with what I assume is meant to be an extra-large pizza. The hose has been running a little too much, so the mud's real sloppy, threatening to spill over with every step she takes. By the time she's crossed the lawn, the paper plate is nearly buckled in half.

I wince, prepared to be covered in slop when she hands it over to me. Thankfully, that doesn't happen, and I balance it on my lap while smiling up at her.

"Looks great, Princess. What's on it?"

"It's made with cheese"—she points to three sunken dandelions—"and peppers and love."

The last word slams into me, and I blink down at the plate of mud decorated with grass and dandelions because I refuse to cry right now. It's silly to be so affected by this.

For so long, I couldn't see any way to where we are right now, with me doing more than watching them play the way I have so many times before—disconnected and uncomfortable. Today I'm back in their world, and there's no place I love more.

So cleanliness be damned, I scoop a handful of mud and bring it to my face, pretending to take a massive bite. I munch and crunch on nothing for a few seconds, then with a dramatic swallow and a lick of my lips, I discreetly drop the mud to the ground and give the kids a dirty thumbs-up.

"Best pizza I've ever had." I grab another handful. "Compliments to the chef."

Hearing that, Rhett rushes to bring me even more mud. No need for a plate this time, he's carrying it in two widespread hands. When it splats on my plate, half of it sloshes over the side. Immediately I feel it oozing through my jeans and running down my leg, but I don't care.

"Great work, buddy. If becoming Spider-Man doesn't work out, I think you'll make an amazing chef."

Once Austin, Red, and Denny have their own specialty dishes, the kids wait eagerly for their reactions. And because I set the bar pretty high with my pretend eating, if I say so myself, they put on a show for the kids, too.

"Think the girls are having this much fun today?" Red asks, wiping mud from Hazel's lips and offering her a drink from his water bottle. Leave it to the toddler to miss the memo that we're all *pretending* to eat it.

"Not a chance," I say. "They're going to be so jealous they missed out on trying the best pizza in town."

At that, Odessa's eyes go wide, and she orders the littler kids back to their faux kitchen with a clap of her hands. "C'mon chefs, we've got more orders to make. The moms are gonna have a *feast*."

Once the kids are out of earshot, Denny leans back in his chair with a satisfied sigh. "Remember when we were the ones running around like that all summer?"

Austin grunts. "By the time we were Odessa's age, Grandpa and Dad had us doing chores all summer long."

Dad scoffs, shuffling forward in his chair to shake his head at Austin. "Now, now. You did a normal amount of chores and you had *plenty* of time for running around."

"Only because Mom made sure of it," Denny says. "She always came up with the most ridiculous games for us."

Dad laughs under his breath, and the relaxed summer air suddenly develops a rough edge. "That's the real reason why it felt like you were working all day—she'd keep you boys so busy doing silly shit, the chores took twice as long as they should've."

A smile erupts on Austin's face, and he tips his head toward the kids. "Guess we're keeping the tradition alive, making them do silly shit and calling it work."

I glance toward the kids, catching fleeting glimpses of the childhood memories they're referring to.

"Well, look at how good we all turned out," Denny says.

Red stops in the middle of picking grit from between his fingers to bark out a laugh. "That's not the sales pitch you think it is, man."

Dad clears his throat. "No, you should all be proud of the kind of men you are—I sure as hell am. That's why these kids are so incredible."

"Yeah, they're something else," I say hoarsely.

Then I pull myself from the chair without another word, focus homed in on my kids, and seconds later I'm plunking my ass down in the mud right next to Rhett.

"Mind if I be your sous chef?" I ask with a smile, then clarify when I remember he's not quite four. "Your helper?"

The way he lights up makes up for the fact that I can feel

the mud soaking straight through my pants and underwear, dampening my ass in the most uncomfortable way.

"You can put the cheese on." He fishes around in the pocket of his hoodie for a handful of smashed dandelions and sets them on my lap.

"I can handle that, I think." I pluck the thin yellow petals from one of the flowers, and when Rhett slides a mud pie my way, I get to work scattering them across the top of it.

"No, not like *that*." He huffs, then grabs a single flower and presses the entire thing into the mud, a little off center.

The way I was doing it looks a hell of a lot more like cheese, but then again, I'm not the head chef, so what do I know? Scratching my scalp with the less dirty of my two hands, I follow his lead and earn a pleased head nod from my son.

For the next little while, the kids and I work quietly in our supply chain, with the sounds of birds chirping and my brothers talking in the background. The moms better be real hungry when they get back, because soon we've not only covered Odessa's tree stump table in pies, we're close to filling a nearby picnic table with them, too.

"I need more *danbylions*," Rhett announces, standing up and leaping off the mud pile.

He takes off at a run, dropping bits of mud with every step. At this point, he's getting rinsed off with the garden hose and stripped on the front porch when we're done out here. I glance down at my own filthy pants. I'm getting the hose, too.

With my cheese duties paused until he comes back, I turn and watch Odessa finickily arrange the plates on the table. At some point, she picked some spring blossoms from the garden and stole my water bottle for a vase.

Then there's a shriek, followed by Rhett bursting into tears.

I'm instantly on my feet, racing over to him and falling to the ground next to where he's staring at his hand and wailing.

"Are you okay? What happened?" Saliva pools in my throat as I reach for his hand. The feel of his tiny touch floods me with intense sensations of love and protectiveness, similar to what I felt when Odessa went missing a couple weeks ago. "Let me see."

"I . . . I got . . ." He struggles to get the words out between sobs, shakily jutting his hurt hand toward me.

A bee sting.

"It's okay, buddy. Just a little ouchie." I try for a reassuring smile, but the pained looked in his eyes has moisture forming in mine.

Might be my eyes playing tricks on me, but I swear the bump on his palm is redder than it should be, then a thought rushes over me, making my chest tighten.

Without second thought, I scoop Rhett into my arms, letting him cover my shirt in his tears and snot, and I frantically head for the guys—still seated in their lawn chairs, unfazed by all of this. Rhett clings to me, and I press my cheek to the top of his head.

"All good, kiddo?" my dad asks. To Rhett or me, I'm not sure.

"I don't . . ." My throat clams up. "Bee sting. Is he allergic? Does anyone know? I don't—"

What kind of dad doesn't know that sort of thing?

Austin calmly states, "No, he's not."

I let out a relieved exhale.

Dad motions his head toward the house. "He'll be fine, son. Go get him cleaned up and slap some baking soda paste on the sting."

My eyes cut to Odessa, and Dad adds, "We'll make sure she doesn't get in too much trouble."

With that, I carry Rhett to the house, telepathically apologizing to Kate for the copious amount of mud I'm about to track inside, because a garden hose and stripping both of us naked on the porch isn't a priority when my son's in pain.

By the time I set Rhett down in the bathroom, his tears have mostly stopped, save for the few clinging to his soaked eyelashes. Salty tracks cut through the mud on his cheeks, and he has a snot bubble that inflates with every heaving breath.

I help him wash his hands in the sink, taking extra care around the angry-looking welt. Then he starts stripping out of his filthy clothes while I poke around in the medicine cabinet, exhaling some of my anxiety when I find children's Benadryl on one of the shelves.

"It hurts." He sniffs, making the boogers disappear altogether.

"I know, bud." I study the label, then him, trying to determine how much he weighs. "This medicine should help though."

"Bee stings fuckin' suck."

I bite my cheek to stop myself from laughing. There's something kind of adorable about a tiny boy in his Spider-Man underwear dropping an F-bomb. "Don't let your sister or mom hear you say that."

He winces as I study the red welt on his palm, confirming the stinger isn't embedded in his skin. I wish I could magically fix this for him. If there's one thing I want, it's for my kids to never know more pain after what they've been through with me in the last few months.

I dampen a washcloth and crouch in front of him to wipe the dried dirt and tears from his face. Then I brush a gentle kiss on the warm skin of his palm and pull him in for a really good hug.

"Spider-Man got his powers from a spider bite, right? I bet now you're going to be a superhero, too."

His arms tighten around my neck. "You think so?"

I cough, faking an inability to breathe. "You're already so strong, you're crushing my throat."

He steps back to look at me with fire dancing in his big, brown eyes. And though he relaxes his hold on my neck, the way he's still squeezing my heart is his real superpower.

KATE

The coffee's lukewarm because I don't stand a chance of consuming any drink at its preferred temperature, but the summer sun warms me right down to the bone anyway. I shift in place on the front porch steps, tapping the band of my wedding ring against the ceramic mug, and watch Rhett use Jackson as a human jungle gym on the lawn.

Jackson's stretched out on the grass, drenched in sunlight, trying his best to keep Rhett's flailing limbs from knocking him in the face. And Rhett—who's somehow ditched every article of clothing except his underwear in the hour we've been outside—is talking his ear off about the shapes of clouds overhead, and why Spider-Man is his favorite superhero, and his intricate plan to acquire his own superpowers.

Odessa zips by on her pedal bike, kicking up dust in the gravel driveway, and skids to a stop. She looks up to Colt's girlfriend's son, Jonas, like he's her big brother, and these skid-stops are his new favorite trick, so naturally Odessa's determined to learn.

She beams at me, and I give her a thumbs-up, smiling back over the rim of my coffee cup.

Placing his hands on Rhett's torso, Jackson presses his body up into the air with a grunt, holding Rhett above him like he's flying through the air. The silver of his wedding band glints in the sun.

"If Spider-Man's a superhero, why doesn't he fly?"

Rhett scoffs. "Because he's *Spider-Man*. He swings." He gives a wrist flick like he's expecting webbing to shoot out of his skin.

Jackson squints up at him. "Swinging sounds like a lot of work. I'd rather fly."

"Then you can be Superman because he's boring like you. When I grow up, I'm gonna be Spider-Man."

"Bold of you to call me boring when I could just"—he rapidly bends his elbows, making Rhett drop suddenly—"drop you." The two of them laugh as Jackson slowly lowers Rhett onto his chest.

My heart squeezes at the sight.

Something shifted with Jackson after Odessa's birthday, then shifted again the morning she ran away. Seeing him interact with the kids now, I don't know why I was so shocked by his kitchen table confession. He might've been present before, but now he's engaged. He's in love with his kids.

Odessa whips around the corner again, this time catching a particularly large rock on her attempted skid. The front tire wobbles, leading to a high-pitched shriek as the metal frame flops over, and she tumbles into the grass.

Jackson's head shoots up to look at her. I can't even tell where his craniotomy scar is hidden beneath the thick brown hair he's grown back in the months since the accident. "You okay?"

Odessa sits up, picking a rock from her knee, and quickly replies, "No blood!"

"So . . . that's a yes, you're okay?" Jackson's eyes bounce from our daughter over to me. "She's going to be the death of me, isn't she?"

I laugh. "Wait until you see her on a horse. You'll grind your teeth down to nubs."

I'm used to this—barely even flinched when she went over. Some days I long for when she was an immobile infant, because that was the last time I knew peace. The moment she learned to roll, we were in trouble.

"Speaking of which . . ." Jackson lifts Rhett off of him so he can prop himself up on his elbows and look over at Odessa. "I know it's a few months late, but I think it's time we get you that horse you were promised."

Odessa jumps to her feet, dead grass falling from her rumpled jeans and T-shirt. A wide smile splits her face, and she flicks her tangled brown hair away from her eyes. "You're serious?"

"So seri—" He doesn't have time to finish his sentence before Odessa's tackling him, arms wrapped around him in a hug, her entire body slamming him back down to the ground.

Rhett sees the opportunity to dogpile and doesn't hesitate. He flops his body on top of his sister's with a silly giggle. Jackson groans under the added weight, reaching up to tickle Rhett's side.

I sit there, smiling like a fool, reveling in all of this. The warmth of the sun, the laughter on the lawn, the total normalcy of this moment. And not the new normal I was worried about, where Jackson could barely bring himself to leave the bedroom and we all walked on eggshells. This is the old normal, but better.

Nothing screams total normalcy in this family like Odessa shrieking, "Ew, Rhett. You're naked—get off me."

"I'm not naked," he protests. "I've got undies on."

"Daddy, make him get off."

I remember the way Jackson flinched when the kids called him Daddy in the weeks following his accident, so clearly uncomfortable in his new-to-him role. But today, he wraps his arms tight around both of them, his booming laugh filling the air and settling into the few remaining fractures in all of our hearts.

When he finally loosens up his bear hug, both kids roll onto the grass, and the three of them lie in silence, staring up at drifting clouds. I'm tempted to go join them, but I can feel the importance of this moment radiating from Jackson's easy smile and easier laugh.

Hours later, when the kids are settled in with popcorn and a movie—*Spider-Man*, for the ten thousandth time—I find him in the kitchen and pin him to the counter's edge, one palm flattened over the brand imprinted on him, the other toying with the elastic waistband of his sweatpants.

Lifting to the balls of my feet, I drop kisses on the corners of his mouth. Coast my lips down the rough velvet of his beard to press them over his protruding Adam's apple. My fingers curl around the top of his pants, nudging them down slightly to expose the slight dip of an Adonis belt.

"What's this about?" he asks, palming my breast with a low growl.

"Watching you with the kids all day." I rub up against him. A flash of heat spreads down my belly. "Seeing you be a good dad—so fucking hot."

Hands splayed across either side of my ass, Jackson lashes me to his chest and kisses me hard. I feel the bulge between his legs growing harder against me, pressing so close to where I'm suddenly wet and clenching.

"That turned you on?" He licks into my mouth, fingers pressing into the soft flesh of my butt.

"Oh, you have no idea."

"Tell me." His right hand glides around to grab my hip, and the softest touch of his finger slipping beneath my pajama shorts reverberates through to my bones. His beard scrapes my cheek as he tilts his head to look down between us, dark lashes fanned across his cheeks.

I grab that hand of his, and together we watch our joined hands disappear beneath the cotton of my shorts. I trace my slit with his finger, and a sharp breath blows between his parted lips. In the silence of the kitchen, the glide of his fingers through my wetness is audible.

"Actions speak louder than words." I circle his finger around my clit with a whimper.

"Kate, *baby*." Somehow it comes out pained and patronizing at the same time. "You need me to take care of this, don't you?"

"Please."

He blows out a breath and surveys the room, then he yanks his hand away from my pussy, leaving me even more desperate for his touch. His other hand slaps my ass. Hard. And he nods to the opposite side of the room. "Pantry. Now."

I swallow hard, gathering my hands and looping them around his neck for one more kiss. "I love you."

"I love you," he replies, the solid ridge of him rocking against my core. "Let's go, before one of the kids comes looking for you."

His fingers, still wet from me, slip between mine and I let him guide me into the open pantry. Stepping inside, I reach for the light switch, but Jackson's hand flies up to stop me.

"If the light's on, they'll know we're in here."

The door closes with a soft click, and within seconds, Jackson has me backed up against the pantry shelves. His hands tangle in my hair, and I grip his biceps, holding on for dear life. His kiss is ardent, catching my lips and stealing my breath. My body shifts and angles in his arms, seeking relief I won't find with our clothes still on.

I push his sweatpants down over his hips, then let them fall the rest of the way. He pushes forward, and I feel the pressure of his cock on the throb of my clit. Then pressing into me, only thin cotton stopping him from sliding inside with ease.

I inhale the word *fuck,* and he laughs. Fucking laughs.

"You feel that, beautiful? How badly I want to be inside you?"

So I reach between us to encircle my hand over the crown of his cock, thumb gliding through slippery pre-cum and painting it down his shaft. A triumphant smile erupts on my face at the stuttered curse words slipping through his gritted teeth.

I thought this wild, adventurous side of him would disappear the moment we got home from the hot springs and fell back into some semblance of normal married life. But we've christened every room on the main floor in the weeks since, and it doesn't seem like he has any intention of slowing down yet.

This time, when I reach the base of his dick, I twist my wrist to knead his balls. He pitches forward with a throaty groan.

"Fuck, that's so good. You're going to kill me, Kit."

I hum my disagreement, tightening my grip around him so he groans and bites down on the back of his hand to quiet himself.

"Better take care of me first," I quip.

Jackson tugs my shirt up to expose my breasts, and bends to flick his tongue over my nipple. My back arches, giving him even more access to me, and he cups my breast to lick and suck my sensitive skin.

I hook a thumb under my loose shorts and shimmy out of them. On instinct, Jackson's hand moves to cup my pussy in a possessive way, pulling my pelvis toward him.

And when he drags up my wet heat, we shush each other with frantic, wide eyes and bitten lips. I hinge my leg to wrap around his waist, forcing him closer, notching the tip of his cock at my entrance.

When he pushes into me, my muscles ache and everything leaves my mind. The thick stretch of him inside me, the hushed moans between us, and the way he's watching me—all of it has the world falling to darkness as my blinks become longer with each inch of him inside me, until I can't open them at all. My head tips back, sending a row of cereal boxes falling like dominoes, and my lips part with a frantic gasp.

His hands find their way to my ass, lifting and pulling me so he can angle himself deeper. Hit my G-spot. Stuff me so full I can barely breathe. His whole body moves like a wave, with a slow, deliberate snap of his hips that fully tests my ability to remain quiet.

"*Fuck.* Your tight cunt's strangling my cock," he whispers between deep thrusts. "You want my cum, don't you, Kit?"

"*Please.*"

I grab his hand, bringing it to my neck with a whimper. And watch as his pupils—dilated from the dark—manage to fully overtake his irises. He carefully squeezes his fingers and thumb, putting pressure on either side of my throat, and finds a new pace for his hips. My need to come overshadows my need to breathe.

"Oh, my wife wants it rough, does she? You keep surprising me."

His willingness to try new things keeps surprising *me.*

Jackson pounds into me, his breath coming in ragged grunts. We don't stop, even as my roaming hands, seeking purchase on the shelving unit, knock over any number of things behind me. There are crashes and bangs and moans . . . and thank God *Spider-Man* is an incredibly loud movie.

My heel hits him in the ass, spurring him on. And through panting breaths, I warn, "Don't fucking stop."

I lick the pads of my fingers and slide my hand down to tease my clit, pushing me right to the edge of sated relief with only a few rough circles.

I alternate between muttering curse words and his name with such frequency, it becomes an accompaniment to the sound of his wet skin slapping mine. This is like nothing I've ever felt before—the black room, the rough pounding of his cock deep inside me, and the commanding way his hand's gripping my throat. I jerk into the release, every muscle becoming rigid, my skin so tight I feel like it'll rip wide open.

"That's my pretty girl." He kisses every inch of skin he can reach, not letting up on his punishing thrusts. "Be a good wife and come for me."

The orgasm washes over me like honey dripping from the tip of my head to my toes. Warm and relaxing, leaving me unable to do anything but gasp and stare up at my husband.

He grinds his hips into mine, hitting a new speed and intensity. It's overwhelming. Bordering on painful. I sob, clasping a clammy palm over my mouth to keep from screaming.

Aftershocks rock through me, then I feel the jolting of his orgasm. A deep moan rumbles through the small space, and my name is the last thing to leave his lips when he fills me with so much cum I feel it leaking out around the edges of his cock.

I pull him into me, crashing my lips to his and tasting the hotness of his breath. It's so humid in here, every inhale feels wet and the back of my T-shirt is disgustingly damp. And even still, I want him to hold me tight. Reeling from an orgasm that has my legs quivering, I need him. I've always been happiest in his arms, but since we started being intimate again, I find myself needing his touch more than ever.

He pulls out of me with an exhale, and I'm suddenly so empty, I could cry. I feel that emptiness deep in my core. A soft kiss to my lips, then a warning that he's turning on the light. I shield my eyes with a flattened hand, and still they burn as I blink rapidly to adjust to the vibrant, cool light overhead.

The place is a disaster. He's completely naked. I'm sporting a Winnie-the-Pooh situation. And there are pantry staples strewn all over the shelves and floor.

How did I not notice the container of almond flour spilling everywhere?

I giggle. A little bit at the absurdity, a little bit at the dread twisting in my guts at the thought of cleaning this up. The more I look around, the more that giggle turns into a laugh.

"Are you okay?" He lifts a brow, pulling his sweatpants up and letting the elastic snap around his hips. "Did I fuck you so hard I knocked something loose up there?"

"I mean . . . *probably.* I feel a bit drunk, to be honest. Sex drunk." I tip a box of Cheerios back upright just for it to topple over again. And that's where I give up. "Beryl's going to know we fucked in here."

"*Nah.* The damn raccoons got in here. I chased them out with a baseball bat. I'm a hero."

I smile, stepping into my shorts and letting Jackson slide them up my legs. A shiver races through me when he leans in to lovingly kiss my pussy before covering it.

"You were already a hero around here."

"Yeah. The *boring* kind." He straightens and brushes a strand of hair behind my ear. "Don't worry about the mess—I'll clean it in the morning. You take your time getting yourself together, gorgeous. I'm gonna check on the kids."

"Those are *by far* the sexiest things you've ever said to me."

"You're saying all that dirty talk was for nothing?"

"The dirty talk itself gets me halfway there. Don't ever stop."

"In that case, I want you to know that this"—a finger loops around in the air to gesture vaguely at the room—"was only the beginning of what I have in store for you tonight. I'm going to eat you until you're squirming, then fuck you bent over the edge of our bed. You're going to ride my face and then my cock while you hang on to the headboard. And I'm going to fill you with so much cum, you'll feel it leaking out of your sore pussy all day tomorrow."

I close my eyes, humming at the way his words send heat to my already-satiated core. "I can't wait to be a good wife and take it."

KATE

The scent of coffee and something sweet—probably the blueberry muffins Beryl made earlier—fills the air. Jackson softly closes the front door of Austin and Cecily's house shut behind us, and we kick off our shoes in the entryway. Jackson sets down the box of freshly laundered baby clothes I pulled out of the attic as soon as we heard they were being admitted to the hospital.

As we walk into the living room, my voice becomes so much softer and quieter than normal. "Hey, guys."

Austin's sitting on the couch, a yellow burp cloth draped over his shoulder. He looks half asleep, with a dopey smile tugging at the corners of his mouth. Fatherhood suits him in a way I never expected. If Cecily softened him, this baby has fully melted my grumpy brother-in-law.

Giving him a smile, I move straight on to Cecily. "How are you doing? You look so good."

Peaceful, radiant, tired. She's glowing in that post-birth haze of joy and sleep deprivation you usually only see in movies, and my heart tugs in a way I wasn't prepared for. Since letting out all my big feelings and sharing the miscarriage secret with Jackson, I honestly haven't really thought about how I should be pregnant right now. Maybe because my brain knows my body's not equipped for more pain anytime soon.

But this hurts a little.

"I feel good," she replies softly. "Exhausted, though. We both are."

I smooth a hand over Cecily's soft blond hair, pushing a few loose strands away from her eyes. "We won't stay for long—just wanted to come drop off those clothes and say hello to sweet baby Lucy."

"No, no." Cecily shakes her head. "You guys can stay as long as you want. Honestly, *please,* stay forever. I have no idea what I'm doing."

Oh, I remember that feeling all too well. Beryl was the only other woman around here when I had Odessa, and she spent many sleepless nights with me.

I laugh under my breath. "I'm literally right next door. You text me, or shine a flashlight at my windows, or anything, and I'll be right over."

"Careful what kind of promises you make. I'll do it." She gives me a look that devolves into tired giggles. "Do you want to hold her?"

"*Do I?*" I scoff. "Of course I want to hold my perfect little niece."

She's so small, yet chubbier than my own babies were. Her little mouth puckers in her sleep as I settle her against my chest, and I swear the world goes still. Her head's covered in dark fuzzy hair, and her tiny, wrinkled fingers curl instinctively around my finger.

"She smells like heaven," I whisper, completely taken.

"She *is* heaven," Cecily responds, smiling up at me through wet eyes.

I step back and sink into the empty spot next to Jackson on the couch. His arm falls around my shoulders, and I glance at him in my periphery, noticing the way he's watching with keen interest. The fingers on his free hand come up to delicately brush her smooth cheek, and I can't help but hope he remembers all the time he spent squishing Rhett's chubby, rosy cheeks when he was a baby.

I don't wait on him remembering things anymore, but when it comes to the kids, I wish he knew the joy of holding them for the first time as babies.

"Do you want to hold her?" I ask him quietly.

Jackson swallows hard. "I don't remember how."

"It's muscle memory." Getting one last good inhale of her baby scent, I pass her to him before he can say no.

He melts into the couch cushions, relearning the weight of a baby in his arms. And the look of wonder in his eyes is the exact reason why, once upon a time, I was willing to give this man as many babies as he wanted.

He stares down at her, quiet and reverent. His breath slows to match hers, and when she makes a small infant squawk, a cooing attempt to shush her comes naturally. I'm not sure I've ever loved my husband as much as I do here, now.

After we've accidentally overstayed our welcome—neither of us wanted to stop staring at her tiny button nose, big blue eyes, and long fingers—we say our goodbyes and promise to deliver dinner in a few hours.

I grip Jackson's hand for the short traipse across the lawn to our house, my flip-flops clacking with each step through thick grass.

"They looked good together," Jackson says, following with a long pause as he blinks up at an airborne robin. A muscle in his jaw ticks, and he opens his mouth for a long beat before words tumble out. "Would you want to do that again?"

The question catches me off guard. Not because I hadn't thought about it, but because I wasn't sure he had. After everything. After the hospital, the therapy, the slow crawl back to himself. After all the ways we've rebuilt the life we almost lost.

Sure, we agreed not to use birth control. And maybe to some people that would mean we'd agreed to have another baby, since we haven't exactly been trying *not to.* But this is different.

"Do . . . do what again?" I ask to be sure I'm not jumping to conclusions.

"Have another baby. I'd want that if . . . well, if you'd want to."

Jackson exhales like he's been holding back from asking for another baby for a long time, and a crooked smile tugs at the corner of his mouth. I glance over, and he's already looking at me without a hint of hesitation or fear or a need to fix things.

"I would," I say, my voice catching a little in my throat. "Yeah. I think I really would."

He squeezes my hand, then draws me into his arms.

I murmur against the fabric of his shirt, which smells faintly like a fresh newborn, "We've already done the impossible and started over from scratch. Who's to say we can't do it again?"

"This isn't starting over, it's growing." He kisses the top of my head, then lingers there.

He might not remember the beginning, but when his heart beats in time with mine, I know we're nowhere near the end.

Epilogue: Jackson

The ranch hands are drinking beer and cracking jokes around a low-burning campfire, and the kids are running amok, as they tend to do. Dusk settles over us and the skyline bruises purple along the edges. A cool breeze blows through the treetops, and Beryl has a Bluetooth speaker precariously placed on the tailgate of a pickup—classic country melodies back easy conversation.

After a long, hot summer, the cattle came back from their grazing lands for the winter, and one thing I've learned quickly about this family and ranch is that any big moment—be it branding, a big cattle sale, a great hay season, or taking the herd to and from grazing land—calls for a party.

My entire body aches in the best way, and I don't even care that I was merely helping operate gates as the guys sorted cattle, which is arguably significantly easier than being one of the ranch hands who just spent days gathering the herd up and driving them home.

But I don't care. I was doing *something*. For the first time since my accident, I feel useful here. And it's quieting the lingering, albeit irrational, fear that my brothers will get tired of financially supporting us while I do fuck all to pull my weight.

I stretch my arms above my head, then let my hands fall lazily. I cradle the spot on my skull where my hair is mostly grown back in—though it's quite a bit shorter than the rest—and run my thumb over the raised scar.

Maybe I'll never train another horse, but I didn't lose the ability to learn new skills. And I've got thirty-some years of manual labor ingrained in every fiber of my muscles. I'll figure out a place for myself.

Today was a good day. No sense ruining it with thoughts about a past I don't remember or a future I'm still trying to sort out. So I step away from the fire to check on the kids, squinting to make out where they're playing next to the tree line. Seems they're building a fort.

"Hey, handsome." Kate's voice sneaks up behind me.

She slips into my arms, the warmth of her back pressing on my chest. For a while, she rests in my arms in a comfortable silence, watching our kids play as the sun sets. When a song she likes comes on, our steady embrace becomes a gentle sway.

She twirls herself out of my arms as if we're on the dance floor of some country bar. Arms outstretched, fingers barely hanging on, a smile crinkling her eyes. Somewhere in the rubble of broken memories in my brain, there's a fragile flicker. I pull her back into me, wrapping my arms tight around her and nosing her hair to inhale the smell of everything good in the world.

Couldn't tell you the name of the song or who sings it, but when I shut my eyes, it's like I'm scuffing my boots across dusty wood planks. Spinning my bride around on the empty dance floor of a dive bar.

"This was our wedding song," I murmur into her hair with profound certainty.

Kate spins out, then in again so we're face-to-face. "We didn't have a wedding song. We didn't even have a reception."

For half a second, doubt washes over me. But . . . *but no.* My brain hasn't made up a single memory yet, and the feel of her tucked into my arms, her dress swishing around our legs, is too visceral to be imaginary.

I clear my throat, and though my voice shakes, I try to muster up some confidence in my memory. "We went to a bar after we got married and danced to this song."

Kate stills, ears perked to pick up the song amid the dinnertime chatter. Her eyes flutter shut, and a smile blows across her face. "Oh my God, you're right. I forgot about that. . . . I wanted to dance, and you tried to argue it because nobody else was on the floor, but I insisted you owed your wife a proper first dance."

The curated stories I was told after the accident painted Old Jackson as the *perfect* husband and father. And while I don't think I was *bad*, by any means, I'm pretty damn happy with the version of myself I'm discovering now. Because if Kate wanted to dance anywhere, anytime, I wouldn't argue it. I'd spin her around this patch of grass all damn night, not paying any mind to the audience we have or the music playing in the background.

"I think I owe you more than a proper first dance." I cup her chin in my hand, pulling her into a kiss. I linger above her lips, breathing her in as my insides swoop and soar. "Marry me again, Kate. You deserve a fancy wedding with dancing, cocktails, guests, and whatever else weddings entail."

She laughs and shakes her head. "I don't want a fancy wedding. We eloped because we wanted to promise each other forever—all that mattered was me and you, not the guests and cocktails."

We sway for another breath, another heartbeat, and then I press a kiss to her temple and say, "Okay . . . We'll skip the fancy party, but I still want to give you the most important part of a wedding."

She pulls back to look up at me, her brow lifted, curious and amused. "Oh yeah? What's that?"

"Vows," I say, the word catching a little in my throat. "Ones I remember."

She doesn't say anything, just searches my face with that quiet, unwavering strength that's carried the entire family through the last seven months.

"I might not remember every version of us . . . but I know this one. The one where you stayed, even though I wouldn't have blamed you for leaving. You stayed when I didn't know your name . . . didn't know my own kids." I pause, pangs of old guilt pressing sharp behind my ribs. "I love you, Kit. I promise I'm not going anywhere. Not now, not ever. I want to stay happily married to you forever."

Her eyes fill with tears, and she clutches the front of my shirt, so clearly searching for words. And Kate pulls me in for a kiss unlike any that have come before or will come after. That's all the promise I need.

When she pulls back, she's flushed and teary and radiant. I don't need memories to know or love this woman. My heart was always going to remember her.

"I stayed—*and I'll always stay*—because it's always been you. You're my person."

The gentle rocking of our bodies dancing on the grass, the air filled with campfire smoke and laughter, is interrupted by Rhett crashing into my legs. My knees nearly buckle.

"What on Earth?" I grab him by the shoulders to stop him from toppling over backward.

"Dessie's being mean," he immediately tattles. "She's not letting me play with her."

Looking toward the tree line, I see Odessa storming toward us. She has that no-nonsense look Kate gets when she's focused on something.

"I'm building a fort with Jonas, and Rhett keeps wrecking it."

I look down at the preschooler, who beams back at me. "I'm playing Spider-Man."

"He's trying to climb the walls, and they keep falling over," Odessa protests.

"Okay, okay, okay." I scratch my head, trying to make sense of all of this. "Um . . . can we hug it out?"

Odessa's face twists with utter disgust. "*No.*"

Damn, you'd think I'd suggested we make s'mores with cow patties instead of chocolate.

One hand still on Rhett's shoulder, I snare Odessa's wrist with the other and keep her from running away. In one fell swoop, I crouch down and yank both of them into my chest, shifting my weight on my heels so we don't all fall over.

They smell like dirt and, for some unknown reason, a bit like wet dog. Odessa has leaves in her wild hair, and Rhett has a smear of something red—hopefully not blood—across his forehead. And none of that stops me from planting kisses on their heads.

"I can't breathe," Rhett wheezes, very clearly still able to breathe, given how hard he's laughing.

"You're squishing me," Odessa whines.

"I'm squishing your attitude," I reply.

Somewhere behind us, Kate laughs, honey-sweet. I hold my kids tight, until the wiggling struggle to escape stops and their groans turn to giggles. The tension between them is broken then.

When I let them go, it's reluctantly.

"Rhett, let's keep the Spider-Man game *off* Odessa's walls, okay? Go climb a fence or tree or somethin' instead."

He turns and eyes up a particularly good climbing tree. "Okay, Daddy."

As they take off toward the trees again, Kate slides back into my arms like she never left, her head pressing against my chest. The pure joy in her eyes is unmistakable. "You're a pretty great daddy, you know?"

"You think?"

"The best." She balls my shirt up in her fist and cranes her neck to kiss me softly, pumping sunshine into my veins. "I think we'll keep you."

"I'm the luckiest man alive for that."

I look down at her, then out at my kids. My family. This ranch. And even without memory of the way things used to be, it feels like my life is exactly as it should be. There are no rough edges between then and now. Old and new are smudged by the soft brush of my wife's fingers on my torso, and I kiss her coconut-scented hair, because she deserves to be kissed as many times as I can fit into a day.

Somewhere in the distance, Beryl yells something to the group about dinner being ready. My stomach growls in response.

"Let's go eat. You must be starving after working so hard all day." She tugs me toward the fire.

Once Beryl's filled two bowls with steaming chili for us, and I've stuffed my pockets with Kate's cheesy buns, I follow my wife to a pair of camping chairs with a perfect view of the crackling embers and my family gathered all around.

Directly across from me, Denny huffs through a too-hot bite while simultaneously loading a spoon to shovel more into his mouth. Behind him, Blair's walking in slow circles, bouncing the fussy baby to get her to fall asleep.

"You good, bud?" Colt slaps Denny on the back mid–coughing fit.

Once he gets the molten-lava bite down, Denny blinks over at Colt with glassy eyes. He tries to talk without the use of his tongue, before giving up and gesturing something at Blair.

She laughs softly. "He's trying to eat fast so he can rock Avery while I eat . . . but given how hot the chili seems to be, I think I'm okay with waiting awhile."

"Yeah, that." Denny sucks air through his teeth. "Damn, Beryl. You set this on fire right before handing it to me?"

She laughs, scooping a ladle of chili into a bowl for my dad.

He walks around the outer edge of the circle, stopping behind me to lay his broad hand over my shoulder. He left a few weeks after Cecily had the baby, but since then he's made a conscious effort to spend more time at the ranch. He might not be living here full time, but he's so attached to his grandkids he can't seem to stay away for more than a few weeks at a time.

"Wanted to let you know I'm proud of you, kid," he says quietly. He's not one for public speeches or having all the attention on him, and neither am I, so I'm glad Kate's the only other person hearing this. "I didn't . . . I didn't know if you'd be able to turn things around. But you bucked up. And . . ." He hastily works down a swallow. "And your mom would be incredibly proud of you, too."

"Thanks, Dad." I give him a half smile. "I'm doing my best."

"You're doing better than that, son." With a quick pat on the shoulder, he carries on to his seat. Never one for talking, whether in my memories of him or in the time I've spent with him post-accident.

I focus back on the banter filling the circle of family and friends with more warmth than the fire. The teasing has shifted to Colt now, instead of Denny. Maybe because Denny's managed to inhale his extra-hot chili and is standing on the outskirts of the chair circle with his baby girl held tight to his chest.

The only thing that's been harder for me to accept than my own kids is seeing my brothers as dads. Austin's a brand-new dad, who's fumbling as often as I am when it comes to caring for his daughter, but he looks at her with the same soft, protective look he previously only gave to Cecily. And Denny's carting around his kid like he was born to hold a baby in his arms. Then there's Red—the unofficial brother who's in almost as many of my childhood memories as Denver and Austin—who worked half the day today with his toddler sitting in front of him in the saddle.

It's probably going to take a long time before I fully understand how to be a dad again, but I've got some damn good examples around me.

Based on the way he's fanning his panting tongue with both hands, I'm gathering the chili is either too hot or too spicy for Colt. His face is flushed, so red it borders on purple.

"If Beryl had stuck with macaroni and cheese, like I requested, I wouldn't be dying right now," he defends himself, giving Cassidy a thankful smile when she offers him up a sippy cup of milk she brought for Hazel.

"Oh, ignore him," Red shouts at Beryl over his shoulder. "Colt's idea of seasoning is touching his food while he has ketchup chip dust on his fingers."

All Colt can muster up for a defense is, "Hey, man. Ketchup chips are the bomb."

The queen of being prepared for anything the cowboys could need, Beryl perks up at that. "I have some in one of the tote bins in the back of the truck. Help yourself, honey."

"Well, hot damn. This dinner is saved after all." Colt practically leaps out of his seat, giving a kick of each leg to straighten out his jeans. He hands off his bowl of chili to Red, who shrugs and carefully adds it to his own half-eaten bowl.

For a moment, it's quiet. Everyone's eating good food, slinging back bottles of cold beer, and relishing the calm after a long, hard day's work. Kate sets her empty bowl on the ground and leans into me, resting her hand on my thigh.

And after some time, Austin clears his throat loud enough to grab everyone's attention.

"So, uh . . . good work today." He nudges his Stetson back on his head, glancing over at Cecily, who's sitting next to him with their baby cradled in her arms. "Wanted to thank Dad, in particular. You've been busting your ass around here a lot since Jackson got hurt and . . . it's meant a lot."

Dad winks at him, saying nothing and everything.

Denny holds a hand over his daughter's exposed ear like a muff before shouting, "Beers on Austin."

Raucous cheers from all the ranch hands.

"Whoa, whoa, *whoa*." Austin holds his hands up to stop them. "Let's not get ahead of ourselves here. I have more to say."

"For the first time in his life, Aus has *more* to say?" The words slip from my lips before I realize what's happening. Bizarre younger brother muscle memory, I guess.

Kate snickers, rapping her fingertips against my denim-clad thigh.

"Cute. You're bickering like when you guys were kids," Blair muses between bites of cheesy bun.

Everyone—*even Austin*—laughs at that.

"Okay, if you'll all let me finish." Austin raises an annoyed eyebrow.

Kate puts a quick halt to the waning laughter with a bold, threatening, "*Enough.*"

"Thanks, Kate," Austin says. "Anyway, I also wanted to thank Red."

Slowly lowering the bowl of chili he's slurping up, Red cocks his head at him.

"You already know you're like a brother to me."

Red's mouth drops and he whisper-yells loud enough we all hear him. "He *finally* admits it."

"Don't make me regret what I'm about to say." Austin shakes his head. He's so damn amused by all of this. Night and day from the interactions I had with him when he came to the hospital after the accident—he was so stoic and gruff, and I hated seeing a grown man who was hardened by life, because my older brother was quiet and determined as a kid, but he wasn't a grump. *This* version of Austin in front of me today is who I remember.

"So get on with it, then," Denny chirps, grinning at our brother.

"Red—you've always been so much more than a friend or a ranch hand. You're one of my brothers. And this year, you've single-handedly kept this place running. You took so much weight off all of our shoulders, and . . . I just really wanted to thank you, man."

Red's lips press into a thin smile, and he nods along with what Austin's saying. "That's what brothers are for."

"Denver, Jackson, and I were talking a while back . . . before the accident, but it feels even more merited now. This place is as much yours as it is ours, and we want to make it official. Give you a piece of the ranch—the business and the land."

I don't remember this conversation, naturally, but it feels right. Even with limited memories of the last thirty-some years, I know he's one of us. This day should've come years ago.

"I don't . . . I don't know what to say." Red sniffs back his emotion, giving Cassidy's hand a squeeze before standing. He steps into Austin with a firm, back-smacking hug. "Thanks, man. Love you."

Denny shimmies between two chairs to join them. "Love you guys."

Thanks to a gentle shove from Kate, I'm reminded that I'm technically part of this conversation, too. So I stand up and a few seconds later, my arms are wrapped around my brothers.

The hug turns into an awkward group pile-on, which gets even worse when Colt joins in, grinning like an idiot and throwing an arm over all of us. "Is this a brother-hug or a cult initiation? 'Cause I'm down either way."

The entire group of us shift, nearly imploding or toppling over, and Cassidy shouts, "Sit your sentimental asses down before one of you falls into the fire."

"Please," Cecily adds. "Can we not have any more hospital visits this year?"

So we break it up, and I sink back into my seat with a sigh.

"You good?" Kate quietly asks.

"Yeah, I feel . . . lucky." It feels like a weird admission, given everything that's happened. But it's true.

"Because you are. We all are." Her thumb begins its usual routine. Hearts on my skin. I'm so damn lucky.

Across the fire, Colt raises his beer. "To Red!"

Everyone joins in, with an echo that has the kids stopping mid-play to stare at us.

Red lifts his chili in a mock salute. "And to Austin. For pretending to hate us all but secretly being a giant softie."

Austin groans. "Wasn't pretending."

"And to Jackson," Kate says suddenly. The spotlight feels unearned and uncomfortable, but the way she says it—soft and sure—pulls everyone's eyes to her. "For being here. For fighting his way back to us."

My dad tips his hat toward me with a quiet, "Damn right."

"Fuck it, let's cheers to everything. It's making the beer go down quick." Denny laughs, holding up his nearly empty bottle. "To Wells Ranch."

The best damn home, family, life anyone could ever ask for. No memories required—this feeling is enough.

"To Wells Ranch."

ACKNOWLEDGMENTS

Thank *you* for being here. Thank you for reading my books, screaming about them from the rooftops, and loving my characters as much as I do. I'm forever in awe of how many people are excited to read a story I made up in my brain.

If you're wondering where we go from here, I promise it won't be as far as you'd expect. And thanks to my daughter's insistence that I hurry up and write the next book (only because we buy a Dairy Queen ice cream cake every time I finish), you won't have to wait too long for it, either.

As heavy as this book likely was to read, it was just as emotionally draining to write. So thank you to my friends and family for supporting me, checking in on me during the extra-devastating chapters, and reminding me to eat something more nutritious than Nerds Gummy Clusters.

Abby, Ceilidh, and Danie, thank you for being the first to read this, and for crying along with me for this entire journey. Thank you for loving these characters and world (and me!) with your entire hearts. I'm so lucky to have my queens in my corner.

Speaking of people in my corner, Kayla and Elliott, I'm forever grateful to call two of the most badass, brilliant, beautiful women my friends. I wouldn't be here if it weren't for your support, advice, and the NSFW art you're constantly sending me.

Sarah and Tarah, the *ah's*. Thank you for talking me down from far too many spirals, and for being the reassurance I needed every time I questioned whether this book might be a little *too* sad (even if your opinions are slightly biased). I'm so blessed to have such sad and horny friends.

Thank you to Blair, for giving this one the final read-through I needed to feel confident in Jackson and Kate's story. I would say I'm sorry for all the trauma you endured reading this, but I'm really not.

From the moment I decided to write this story, I knew I didn't want to shy away from the hard realities of traumatic brain injuries. A few years back, my mom underwent two brain surgeries, including a craniotomy, and I saw firsthand how hard the recovery process was for her. It feels weird to say "thanks for having to get your skull cut open" but . . . thank you. Without realizing it, you shaped this story.

Speaking of which, I owe so much of Jackson's point of view to the people who have publicly shared their stories on r/TBI. I spent hours reading, empathizing, and learning from them. While amnesia in books is often portrayed as a condition that disappears overnight, memory deficits following a traumatic brain injury can last a lifetime, which is why Jackson never fully regains his memory. Though it's likely none of the r/TBI users will see this, it feels necessary to give them credit for this book.

And thank you so much to Emily for your invaluable feedback and insight into traumatic brain injuries from a medical professional's point of view.

Despite how hard this book was emotionally, Jackson and Kate's story was also so vivid, it made it one of the easiest books I've written. And because of my amazing editors, Alicia and Bhavna, it was also one of the easiest to edit. Massive thanks to both of you for always making my stories as strong and deep and emotionally fulfilling as they can possibly be. It's been such a pleasure to work with you on this series.

To the rest of the teams at Dell and Doubleday, thank you for all you do. Whether you've had a direct hand in publishing this series or not, I appreciate you so much. Extra thanks and forehead kisses to Megan, Katie, Caro, Chalista, and Kaitlin for working incredibly hard to get my books in the hands of readers.

Sanah and the entire team at Orion: I'm forever grateful to have such dedicated people working on my books across the pond.

To my agent, Carly, thank you for your wisdom, guidance, and hand-holding throughout this series. I can't wait to see what we accomplish next!

I have so much gratitude for all the booksellers and librarians out there. As a library kid, and a reader who didn't own a Kindle until the pandemic, seeing my books on shelves is an experience I don't think will ever get old. Thank you for helping share my stories.

Speaking of sharing, I truly would not be here if it weren't for so many incredible people in the BookTok and Bookstagram communities. Thank you for being my biggest hype people. Thank you for begging to have Jackson and Kate's story, and I'm sorry it wasn't the cutesy prequel you were hoping for.

Wow. Five stories finished. I can't believe it's over. It only seems right for my final thank you to be dedicated to Wells Ranch. These stories changed my life. So thank you to the characters who feel like real people for letting me share their stories with the world. This isn't goodbye, it's see you later.

He's worried she won't stay.
She's worried she will.

The last place city girl Cecily Kennedy expected to end up was a cattle ranch. But she needs a job-and refuge from her abusive soon-to-be-ex-husband.

If only her new boss, Austin Wells, would make it clear whether he hates her or wants her. His gaze makes her feel things she hasn't in years. Though getting over her ex by getting under her grumpy boss isn't worth the potential fallout.

Austin's a gruff, no-nonsense rancher who's seriously regretting letting his head cook hire her own help. As far as he's concerned, Cecily won't be sticking around for long. Nobody ever stays. And the wedding ring indent still on her finger makes her more trouble than she's worth.

When Cecily's past catches up with her, Austin discovers that she's already placed a branding iron on his heart. *He wants her to stay. But first he needs to keep her safe . . .*

She lives by the rules.
He lives to break them.

Cassidy Bowman has strict rules to uphold her good-girl reputation: she doesn't date the Wells Ranch locals, and she definitely doesn't sleep with men she isn't dating. But after a run-in with her ex-boyfriend-and a few too many drinks-she's ready to buck those rules and allow herself one night of recklessness.

On the other hand, local cowboy Chase "Red" Thompson has never met a rule he didn't love breaking. With a long-time crush on Cassidy, he's more than willing to accept her offer of a one-night stand and her one condition: he must agree to never speak of it again.

That is until two pink lines render Cassidy's entire rule book null and void. Cassidy isn't looking for a relationship with the rough-and-tumble cowboy, and Red doesn't need anyone to tell him he's not good enough for the sweetheart of Wells Canyon.

So the two make another agreement-they'll be friends and co-parents, nothing more. But as their carefully designed boundaries begin to blur, Cassidy might just realise that perhaps some rules are worth breaking . . .

He broke her heart once before.
Can she risk him doing it again?

Five seconds of honesty: Wells Canyon is the last place Blair Hart wants to be.

But her mother's illness leaves her no choice except to return to the hometown-and the traumatic past-she's spent thirteen years hiding from. A run-in with the boy who tore her life to pieces is inevitable in a town like Wells Canyon, but that doesn't mean she's prepared for the way Denver Wells can turn back time with a single smile.

Thirteen years ago Denver's world crashed around him. Since then, he's done everything he can to outrun his demons, until a flash of brown hair knocks him from his saddle. But if he wants her back, he'll need to prove he can be the man Blair needs-the same one she used to love.

With a thousand sticky notes worth of responsibilities, Blair doesn't have the time to sift through their messy history and resolve things with the man who's determined to be in her life. And Denver's going to need more than cowboy charm and five seconds of honesty to convince Blair he's worth a change of heart.

She's afraid she's not enough.
He'll make damn sure she knows she is.

Single mom Whitney Hart is, quite simply, overwhelmed. She's struggling to raise her ten-year-old son, Jonas. Her ex-boyfriend only seems to come around and help take care of his son when he's single and hoping to get back together. With Jonas acting out more than ever, Whitney enlists the help of her sister Blair to keep an eye on Jonas over summer vacation.

Enter Colt, a fun-loving Wells Ranch cowboy who is tasked with giving Jonas work to do around Wells Ranch to keep him busy. In Colt, Jonas finds a mentor and male role model for the first time in his life. And in Jonas, Colt discovers a friendship that brings a new kind of joy into his life.

Colt and Whit slowly develop a friendship of their own through a shared concern for Jonas, and over the course of the summer, it begins to spark into something more. The attraction and chemistry between them are hard to ignore, but Whit's insecurities and hesitancy to trust men causes her to pull away.

As miscommunications give way to understanding, the two will discover that sometimes you have to first be broken before you can become whole, and that there's no one way to create a family . . .